VISIONS *of* FIRE

ABIGAIL SILVER

The Redeeming Grace Trilogy

Book Two

DEDICATION

This book is for my husband -
Douglas

Thank you for loving me even when I am at my most unlovable.

Content Advisory

This is a work of fiction intended for mature audiences.

This novel contains mature language and adult situations including sexuality, sexual assault, self-harm, drug use/abuse, and violence that may be disturbing to some readers.

Reader discretion is advised.

ABIGAIL SILVER

Contents

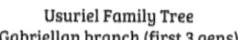

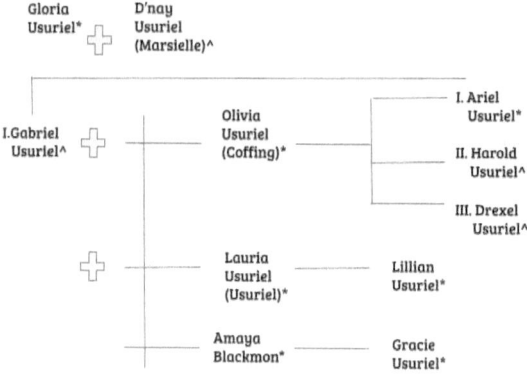

Usuriel Family Tree
Gabriellan branch (first 3 gens)

Key:
+ marriage
I. II. III. birth order
* female ^ male - non-binary

Gloria Usuriel* D'nay Usuriel (Marsielle)^

I.Gabriel Usuriel^ Olivia Usuriel (Coffing)*

I. Ariel Usuriel*
II. Harold Usuriel^
III. Drexel Usuriel^

Lauria Usuriel (Usuriel)* Lillian Usuriel*

Amaya Blackmon* Gracie Usuriel*

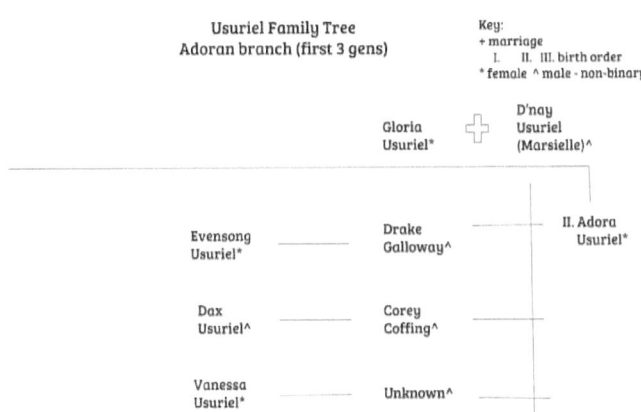

Usuriel Family Tree
Adoran branch (first 3 gens)

Key:
+ marriage
I.   II.   III. birth order
* female ^ male - non-binary

Gloria
Usuriel*

D'nay
Usuriel
(Marsielle)^

Evensong
Usuriel*

Drake
Galloway^

II. Adora
Usuriel*

Dax
Usuriel^

Corey
Coffing^

Vanessa
Usuriel*

Unknown^

For a more complete family tree, please visit abigailsilverstories.wordpress.com

Prelude

Don't ask about the past—the first rule of my father's house.

I came to live with Gabriel in the rural isolation of Angelus Quietum when I was six. After the inner-city group home up in Skykyle, it seemed like a sanctuary. Eleven long years later, it felt like a prison.

Don't misunderstand me; my father was never cruel. He never raised a hand to me or degraded my intelligence, but when it came to questions, I had thousands and the few answers he offered me only sparked more.

By the time I was an adolescent, I'd stopped asking "Who is Gabriel Usuriel?" It never got an answer. Every so often I dug around the edges of his story and got a few hints, but now I was beginning to focus on new questions. Where was my place in things? What was my responsibility to Cybele and the Family?

Who is Gracie Usuriel?

Chapter 1

Death's Head

Fire poured from my outstretched hand, roaring up from the center of my chest to send a stream of orange over the rotting log. The translucent filaments and black, bulbous caps of the Death's Head mushrooms shriveled and collapsed into ash. My sigh of relief was muffled by the mask of my rebreather.

A gout of blue flame a few feet away drew my attention to Dad. I chewed on my plex mouthpiece nervously. Two patches of the fatal fungus near each other was always a bad sign. I caught Dad's eye and he gave a quick twirl of one forefinger. I nodded, understanding his signal to double check the area. It was hard to talk with the breathing safety equipment on, but it was better than risking a nasty lung infection. Usuriels like us rarely died from an accidental Death's Head exposure, but it could make us sick for a few weeks. I had never spent the night at the University Hospital where Grandma Gloria worked, and I wasn't trying to sign up anytime soon.

I kicked through the charred remains of my log with one worn leather boot. There wasn't much left. I sent another torrent of flame over the area one more time just to be sure.

A few hours later Dad tapped me on the shoulder. I was

so focused on examining a patch of undergrowth I hadn't even heard his approach. His face was covered in sweat and soot. He'd taken off his rebreather mask and was giving me a smile.

"I'm pretty sure we got the whole patch, Gracie." He wiped at his brow and made a new smudge over his left eye. "Come on, let's go get some lunch."

"Is it lunch time already?" I muttered, pulling my own mask off and glancing up at the sky. The branches of the forest were so tightly woven overhead I could barely see the sun's rays forcing their way through.

I fell in behind Dad, picking our way through the foliage until we came to the usual path we maintained through this acreage. I carefully stepped around a mound of horse manure and began pulling off the uncomfortable tubes and straps of the rebreather.

"That should take care of the South Wood for another few months," Dad said, sounding tired but pleased. "Tomorrow we can look at Drexil Pass and after that we might be able to call ourselves Death's Head free!"

"Yeah." I stripped off the last of the rebreather and sucked in fresh air through my nose as a cool breeze lifted some of the red curls plastered to my neck. Despite being tiring work and the rebreathers that made even a crisp morning seem stifling, I didn't mind burning out Death's Head. It gave me a chance to use my pyrokinesis for something worthwhile and took my mind off of the overwhelming tedium of daily life in the middle of nowhere. "What's for lunch?"

"Why don't you gather some lettuce and tomatoes from the garden? I have some bacon in the cold box I can cook up."

I nodded at Dad's words as we came in sight of Angelus Quietum proper. Rolling fields outlined with neat white fences led us to the barn—a wooden structure with gleaming solar tiles on the roof. The whinnies of Charcoal and Aubrie echoed inside. We strode into the chicken yard where a fat hen was pecking at seeds next to her half-grown chicks. On the other side of the yard was the one-story log cabin we called home. It nestled atop a grassy slope that rolled down to Lake Angelus, the Galloway Mountains reflecting their snow-capped peaks in her still waters. Great willows stood by the shore, framing the water's rippling surface with their draping green branches. I paused to gather the requested items from our garden beside the house, then climbed the wooden steps of the back porch and followed Dad into the kitchen.

"Ugh, I need a shower," Dad said, stripping off his rebreather and tossing it next to the sink. I set mine beside his, considering how I might get out of washing the soot-covered machines. I dumped my armload of veggies in the sink to be rinsed clean of my staining fingerprints.

"Good idea," I agreed.

Despite the modest size of our house, my father never skimped on creature comforts. We had two showers—one off of Dad's room and mine in the hall—and the solar water heater on the roof made hot water on demand. I was just heading towards my bathroom when Dad paused in the hallway.

"Leesil?" Dad held up a finger, then pointed it back over my shoulder at the front door.

"We have a visitor," Our AI, Stella, announced through my neural implant at almost the same moment.

Running my fingers futility through my sweat-soaked curls, I trotted over to the front door and palmed it open. On the other side, my cousin Leesil stood with a smile on her freckled face.

"Gracie!" She opened her arms for a hug, then assessed my filthy state and hesitated.

"Sorry, we were just out back purging the Death's Head." I ducked out of the way to give her an excuse to step in without the customary embrace.

"Oh, don't worry about it," she laughed, holding up a small, brightly-wrapped package. "Sorry for stopping by uninvited, but I wanted to bring you a belated birthday present."

My smile broadened. "That's so sweet of you!" I gestured to the kitchen table so that I wouldn't smudge the lovely pink-and-gold paper.

"Hello?" Another voice called from the doorway. Our neighbor, Carol, was peering into the foyer. Her usual floppy-brimmed hat covered her silver curls and she was holding a covered plate carefully in both hands.

"We're in the kitchen, Carol," I called to her over my shoulder. It wasn't unusual for her to bring a treat after we did a chore for her. Carol despised Death's Head mitigation. If I hadn't been a pyrokinetic, I probably would have hated it, too. The stuff we'd flamed into oblivion today was still technically on Dad's land, but the edge of the woods bordered Carol's pastures, too. Anytime we mitigated that close to her cows Carol usually baked us a cake. I licked my lips as she settled the plate next to Leesil's gift.

Glancing over at Leesil, I realized I was being rude. "Oh, sorry. Leesil, this is our neighbor, Carol."

My cousin gave a laugh that carried the music of our Usuriel heritage. "We've met, Gracie. How are you, Aunt Carol?"

My eyebrows went up, my gaze flicking between the two of them. Carol added her own earthy chortle to Leesil's.

"Oh, don't look so surprised, Gracie. I'm Leesil's aunt the same way you're her cousin. It's all generations apart, but that doesn't mean we don't recognize Family when we see them."

Dad and I were so secluded out here I'd only met a handful of relatives. I knew the Usuriel Family was vast, but whenever I ran into Family members they all seemed to know exactly how they were related to each other. Was our Family tree another subject taught in the public schools that Stella neglected in my education?

Carol and Leesil were smiling quietly at me as if expecting me to do something. I was the host here, I realized. Usually Dad was the one who led the way with visitors but he was still in the shower. And thinking of showers, I was just standing here shedding filth all over the kitchen.

"I… uh… really should change," I wiped my hands on my pants and wrinkled my nose at the grimy texture of the sweat-soaked fabric.

"Go ahead and get cleaned up, Gracie." Carol waved me away with one weathered hand. "Leesil and I will make some tea. By the time you get back we'll be ready to have cake."

"Thanks." I inclined my head gratefully to my neighbor before trotting off to my bathroom.

Under the water's warm spray, I tried to relax and let my mind wander the way Dad taught me during our afternoon meditation practice. It used to calm me down and fill me with contentment when I was a little girl. Now when I cleared my mind, all I got was a sense of claustrophobia and impatience. The quickening of my blood that started when I was fourteen, stumbling across Stella's adult book selection, was now an ever present-itch. James called it Libitas Libedine—the desire to leave one's family of origin and explore the world. Just the thought of James made my eyes flutter shut. With the water pouring over me I could almost feel his hands on my face, his lips on my skin. For the millionth time, I envisioned his faded-blue eyes gazing into mine as if I were the only person on Cybele.

With a groan, I shut off the water. That was months ago. We had guests waiting right now. I didn't have time to indulge myself all day.

It didn't take me long to get dressed and presentable. I didn't have the patience to fuss with my hair or nails. They would just get torn up during martial arts practice or farm work anyway. I ran my fingers through my still-damp curls as I left the back hall and began cutting across the living room.

"Because he still hasn't told her. Have you, Gabriel?" Carol's voice floated around the corner just before I walked into the kitchen. I paused. Most people couldn't sneak up on a pair of telepaths like Carol and Dad, but I was different. My father called me head blind — so telepathically silent as to not even be there. It prevented telepaths from communicating with me at all, which could be problematic on occasion, but in moments like this it was an advantage.

Dad's back was framed in the doorway, his long, dark hair pulled back from his face in a wavy ponytail. I could see the tension in his shoulders from here. "It's not exactly an easy conversation to start."

"Wait, you've never told her about any of it? Grandfather, she's seventeen!" Leesil sounded horrified. I shifted my weight slightly to see if her expression matched her tone.

"Seventeen is still very young…"

"Compared to you, so am I." Carol's voice was almost amused, as if this were a conversation she'd had with my father more than once.

"Uhhh, Aunt Carol…"

Damn, Leesil spotted me. My face heated up as my cousin's wide eyes flickered between Dad, me, and some point to her right that I had to assume was Carol.

Gabriel cleared his throat and gestured for me to come into the room. "Come on in, sweetie. Would you like some cake?"

My flames licked the inside of my chest as shame painted my whole face red. I kept my gaze on the table so that I wouldn't meet anyone's eye. I knew the expression on their faces anyway—somewhere between concern and pity.

"Thanks," I muttered. I knew better than to ask all the questions that crowded close to my lips. With my father already on the defensive, I wouldn't learn a single scrap of interesting Family news today.

Metal and porcelain clattered together, crystal clear in the total silence. A slice of cake slid in front of me and I quickly picked up the fork to take a bite. Carol's cakes were delicious, but more than that I wanted an excuse not to speak.

"Ah... so I heard you had a party last week. I'm sorry I couldn't come." Leesil's voice was strained but I appreciated her attempt to move the conversation in an easier direction.

"It's okay. How is the psi-gate in Skykyle?"

She gave me a smile of relief. "It's not Hal." She tucked a lock of auburn hair a few shades darker than my own fiery-red curls behind one ear. "But not everybody can work in a tropical paradise, I guess! It's fine. We're the psi-gate closest to the shopping district, so we get plenty of traffic. It keeps me busy."

"And employed." Carol took a sip of her tea, her rosy cheeks grinning from over the rim of the mug. "Can't forget the proper gratitude for keeping a roof over our head."

"Oh yes, there are much worse ways of making a living,"

Leesil agreed.

"And it's not as if you're stuck there forever. Those positions on Hal's palm-shaded beaches will open up eventually," Dad pointed out, cutting a slice of cake for himself before settling into the chair on my right. "Do a good job now and you'll be a shoe-in candidate when the time comes."

"As if every 'porter on the planet won't be jumping at the job!" Leesil sighed and settled her cup on its saucer. "But like Carol said, at least Skykyle pays decently." With a finger, she nudged her package towards me. "Go ahead, open it."

With the frustrating, if familiar, mystery of their argument when I walked in, I'd completely forgotten about the present. I didn't bother to hide the grin that spread across my face as I pulled the shiny gold ribbon. It came away easily and I opened the pink box.

"Oh Lee! It's lovely! Thank you!" I held up the simple, elegant gold chain for my father and Carol to see. Wrought in gold wire at the center of the necklace were my initials— GU for Gracie Usuriel.

"Here, let me help you put it on," Leesil said, getting to her feet and coming around behind me to work the clasp. "There. It looks lovely! I knew gold would be your color. It always goes well with the hair." She gestured to our similarly-colored locks. My smile deepened.

"I love it! Thank you!"

"You're welcome!" My cousin gave me a quick hug. "I'm

so glad you like it. But now I'm afraid I have to get to my shift. Sorry again for missing the party and taking off like this, but that's how working life goes I guess."

"Oh, okay," I said, a bit startled. "Well, thanks again. I hope you'll stop by for a longer visit soon."

I could tell by the sadness in her expression that Leesil wouldn't be showing up again for quite a while. My lonely heart sank. "I would love that, Gracie. I'll talk to you later, okay? Happy Birthday!"

"Okay. Thanks," I said.

"I'll walk you out." Dad got to his feet. I could see the hesitation on Leesil's face, but my father was Gabriel Usuriel, after all, and this was his house. After a moment she inclined her head and allowed him to walk her out the front door.

"Good to see you, too, Aunt Carol!" she called over her shoulder.

"Always a pleasure, sweetie." Carol watched the two of them leave the room with a calm smile on her face. Once they'd closed the front door behind them, however, she cleared her throat. "So while I have your ear completely to myself for once, let me take the opportunity to point out that you're not a prisoner here, Gracie."

"What?"

"You're almost eighteen," my neighbor went on, her calm demeanor belying the urgent tone of her quiet voice. "You're a member of the Family which means you get free tuition at the University. If you want to attend, that's your birthright. Even Gabriel can't take that away from you."

I opened my mouth to reply but Carol shook her head quickly, her hand reaching out to pat mine.

"You don't need to answer. Just think about what I've said."

I did.

Chapter 2

Breathe

An empty glass slipped from white fingers.

"What have you done?"

Not again. I tried to close my eyes, to hide from the horror and filth, but I was just a bodiless observer at this part of the dream. I had no way of blocking out the sorrow in my father's face as he caught his staggering sister.

"It's time, Adora," he whispered to her. "We've been here a long time. Too long."

The power of her mind rushed over the room's tattered remains. No! I didn't want to be here! I didn't want to see this! Not again! The flames responded to my panic, warming me and blurring the edges of the room.

"Darius!" My aunt's voice was weak, desperate. I fought against the bile that rose at her pathetic request. I pulled on my fire, begging it to take me away from here. Somewhere, anywhere except this filthy, hopeless pit!

The scene wavered as if the heat of my flames were distorting all but the center of the room where my father and his sister lay dying. He'd lowered her to the ground, her fingers coming up to frame his face and push the clinging black waves away from his eyes. Their words were lost to the roar of my pyrokinesis but I couldn't block out the gentleness of my father's kiss on her brow or the broken way his shoulders shook as he closed Adora's sightless eyes.

A new thought came to me with the suddenness of dream logic. My father was still dying of the poison he'd used to kill Adora. I was supposed to save him. What would happen if I wasn't there?

"Daddy!"

I was already calling on the flames in my effort to flee the horror of Adora's death. I could feel them gathering around me, making the air seem thin and easily broken. My father's figure blurred but I could still make out his silhouette—dark hair, white shirt, black slacks. He seemed to shrink in on himself, strong shoulders collapsing onto the ground beside Adora's still form.

"No!" I shrieked, my voice loud and breathless in my ears. Heat and psi pressed in on my skin, choking me. I fought for control, centering my focus just as Gabriel had taught me so many times as we sat beside Lake Angelus. I latched on to my father's figure and, with pure will, forced the flames to pull me towards him.

"Dad," I gasped, landing on my knees beside him. I was solidly physical and I sucked in a deep breath. Despite the rancid smell, I reveled in my ability to interact with events again. Relief turned sour in my gut, however, as I saw the gray cast of Gabriel's skin. He lay on his side, his white shirt so filthy it almost matched his complexion. With one hand I rolled him onto his back, his black hair spilling across the white pillow.

Pillow? I frowned at strange shadows; the dimmer quality of the light. This wasn't what I remembered from the last dream.

It didn't matter. My father's lips were turning blue. If I didn't get him breathing again soon… I couldn't finish the thought. Instead I tilted his head back and parted his lips before covering them with my own. I rested a hand on his chest and felt it rise as I forced my breath into his lungs.

"Come on, Dad," I muttered, leaning back to take a momentary break. If I didn't pace myself, I'd pass out and be no good to anyone. This was always the longest part of the dream. Me alone with the dead, trying to breathe life back into my father's body while I begged him not to give up on me.

It seemed to take a lifetime, but finally his chest lifted my hand on its own. I knew what came next and quickly rolled him onto his side. A gasping heave and he brought up the poison I'd been fighting with all night. This time, it soaked into the bed linens in sickly yellow patches.

"Liv…please…forgive me… Liv…"

My disgust faded with his unconscious plea. Taking advantage of the pillows strewn about us, I tucked one behind his back to make sure he stayed on his side.

I got up from where I knelt beside him on the bed, trying not to slip on the small objects scattered about the floor. An anxious snake wound its coils around my lungs, refusing to let me look away from my father's pale face. He was breathing, his lips no longer gray but a gentle pink. The world softened as my flames beckoned me back to the realm of waking. This time, I didn't fight them.

Chapter 3

Stella

I opened my eyes to the soft blue-dark of my bedroom. Moonlight filtered through the gaps in the curtains' lace. I considered rolling over and going back to sleep. The image of my father's face, blue-lipped and pale, rose in my mind's eye. My throat too tight to swallow, I tossed off the covers and got up.

Silently, I opened the door. Firelight warmed the hallway. The flickering shadow of Dad in his armchair made the ropes around my chest loosen. It was just a dream, nothing more.

Pushing my hair back from my face, I slumped back onto the edge of the bed. With a gesture, I summoned a small ball of fire to hover over my left shoulder. The worn, blue binding of Ariel's journal sat like an old friend on my bookshelf. I pulled the small, faded volume into my hands along with the pencil I kept stashed behind it. Flipping through the pages of our prior conversations, I finally found a blank page somewhere around halfway through the book. What would happen when I no longer had an empty page to write to her? The heaviness in my stomach increased.

"Ariel? Are you there?" I wrote.

There was no answering glow in the darkness or curved script on the page. My sister's ghost didn't always respond, but tonight it would have been so nice to see her.

Feeling more than a little abandoned, I summoned Stella with a tap of my implant. The tiny computer chip, under the skin on the left side of my neck, felt like a tiny grain of rice.

"Yes, Gracie?" Stella materialized silently, her silver eyes glowing.

I hesitated. What did I want? Companionship? Reassurance? Or maybe, just maybe, a few answers for once would be nice.

I studied the pale silver hologram persona of the computer interface in front of me. Stella's coloring wasn't far from Adora's. Her soft features were something far more generically pleasing than my aunt's angular androgyny, however. Perhaps that would be a good place to start.

"Stella, can you show me a Family birth chart? You know, like how everyone is related to each other?"

"Certainly. What family would you like charted?"

As if there was any other family to be interested in. I narrowed my eyes at her obtuseness. She was pretty smart and certainly capable of making logical connections during our lessons, so I was suspicious about how dumb she played when I asked anything even remotely related to Dad.

"The Usuriel Family," I stated clearly, "starting with Gloria and D'nay."

"That is a large chart," Stella replied slowly. "Where would you like me to display it?"

She was buying time and I knew it. "Anywhere," I snapped. "How about the wall?"

With a gesture of one hand, Stella produced a large and very detailed set of scrolling names and dates. I blinked at it with confusion. She hadn't been exaggerating when she said it was a large chart. The text filled the entire wall with words small enough that I had to walk closer to see them clearly. Because of my implant, I didn't have to worry about walking in front of the room's projector any longer. The implant's connection to my optic nerve automatically filled in the blank where my shadow cast. Even so, I found myself standing on my tiptoes just to see the top of the chart.

"Umm... Stella? Can you zoom in to the top... say... six generations?"

Obediently, the AI enlarged and re-centered the top of the chart. The tangle of names and dates became a little less difficult to translate and I was finally able to find my name among them.

There, at the top, were D'nay and Gloria—my perpetually youthful, yet no less adorable, grandparents. Under them were their two children—Gabriel listed first, then Adora. She'd been born on the journey from Earth to Cybele aboard the generation ship, *Inspiration,* because her birth date was listed as a positive rather than a negative number. In fact, if I was comparing dates correctly, she was only four years older than Ariel, Gabriel's oldest daughter. I ran a finger over my half-sister's name written beneath Gabriel and Olivia's. I saw two other children listed under Gabriel and Olivia's parentage: twin boys named Drexil and Harold born two years after Ariel. It looked like Harold died young and without issue because the death date was less than half a century after his birth. The chart listed a partner but no children. Ariel and Drexil, on the other hand, seemed to be the source of all the other Gabriellans I'd met. Their long, prolific generations stretched down the wall and out of sight.

Next to Olivia's name, two others sat beside Gabriel's. Lauria Usuriel and Amaya Blackmon.

I swallowed hard.

Blackmon.

It had been a long time since I heard my birth name, but it sounded so right when I said it in my head. Gracie Blackmon. My chest clenched as I touched my mother's name, then let my finger slide down to my own. I was listed as Gracie Usuriel. My hand went to Leesil's necklace with its golden initials around my neck. Which name was more true? Perhaps it would be nice if the chart listed both. Gracie Blackmon Usuriel. Me. My whole real name. Maybe I would sign it that way in my next letter to James. I took a deep breath and allowed my attention to shift over to the third woman listed beside my father.

I'd never heard of Lauria Usuriel. She wasn't listed in the top six generations, so she was a later gen. That made sense, seeing as I doubted Gabriel would risk the Five-Gen-Rule.

There was a date listed next to her name with an "m" beside it so I was pretty sure they were married. I glanced over at Olivia and saw that there was an "m" date for her, as well. No "m" for my mother, but I wasn't surprised. I'd always gotten the impression that their affair was casual and my birth a completely unintended occurrence. That never bothered me. Mom and Dad had both treated me as if I were the most pleasant surprise they could have had.

I turned my attention back to Lauria. There was only one name under hers: Lillian Usuriel. I could clearly envision the cold, angry sister I'd met at the flood. She hadn't said more than a handful of words to me since we met and she'd never visited Angelus Quietum in the ten years I'd lived here. I wondered if Lauria had been an Adoran. Her daughter's pale coloring suggested as much. I decided it was time to investigate Adora's side of the family tree.

Glancing over at my aunt, I found three children listed under her. A long-dead mortal colonist, Drake Galloway, was recorded as the father of her eldest, Evensong. I'd never heard of Evensong so I assumed she was dead. I looked for and confirmed that there was a death date listed beside her name. The second child, Vanessa, didn't list a father. Where his name should have been was just the word "Unknown." I thought that was slightly odd, but Gabriel hadn't claimed me for five years so I shrugged. It wasn't unheard of for an unwed mother not to name the child's father. In fact, seeing that another one of the elder Usuriels had uncertain parentage made me feel a little less alone.

Her third child was listed as a male named Dax. I frowned and tried to remember where I'd heard that name before.

"Stella, do you have a listing for Dax Usuriel?" I asked.

"Dax Usuriel is currently living in Inspiration Landing with his third wife, Doreen, and their two children, Corbin and Oliver. He is employed at Landing University Hospital as a surgical specialist..."

"Oh right!" I couldn't help the outburst as I put the memory together. "He was the jerk who didn't like Dad at the hospital!"

"He was rude to Gabriel while he was in heart failure?" I wasn't sure if Stella sounded put out because of my interruption or Dax's disloyal sentiments.

"He actually suggested Gloria shouldn't operate." I carefully kept my expression neutral to see what Stella would make of this inflammatory information. The incident occurred over four years ago now, but Stella was ancient— almost as old as Dad—which meant she'd been around for close to four hundred years at this point. I somehow doubted she cared about four years one way or another.

The computer's facial expression was as blank as my father's when he didn't want to discuss something. I caught a hint of disgust in her tone when she said, "I see."

When no other response was forthcoming, I turned my attention back to the chart. It didn't look like Vanessa had any children, but Dax and Evensong both had long lineages that stretched off the page. I tilted my head back at my siblings. Harold died young so it made sense he had no children. But Lillian was nearing a century and she still didn't have a partner or issue listed near her.

"Lillian Usuriel," I murmured. "What can you find on her?"

Stella gave me that little look I'd learned to dread. She was sorting through what she could safely give me. I could see it in the tiny crease of her frown and the vacancy of her silver eyes. I sighed and waited for a sanitized version of my net search.

"Professor Lillian Usuriel," Stella repeated back to me finally, then gestured to her left. A full-sized holographic image of my sister appeared, slowly rotating so that I could see her from all sides. "Research professor at Landing University. Specialties are psiology, neurology, and genetics. Also, sole owner and proprietor of Lilly Fields Equine Ranch."

Well, that was interesting if not exactly what I was looking for. "What about her mother? Is there any information on Lillian's childhood?"

"Lillian Usuriel, early years," the hologram shifted and shrank, becoming a child version of Lillian that stood perhaps four feet tall. I guessed her to be about nine. Her long, fine hair was loose about her shoulders and twin braids trailed back from her forehead to join the cascade of white strands. Her face shape looked remarkably like my

own, with the Usuriel cheekbones softened by a rounded
and feminine chin. The resemblance was further enhanced
by the fact that we both had our father's eyes. "Lilllian
Usuriel was born at Angelus Quietum in the year two
hundred and twenty AT. She is the daughter of Gabriel and
Lauria Usuriel..."

"Wait, she was born here?"

"Affirmative," Stella replied evenly, though I could hear a

note of annoyance in her voice. She wasn't fond of being interrupted.

"Sorry," I said, waving a hand. "Continue."

"She attended Landing University from the year two hundred and forty to the year two hundred and fifty. She achieved a certification of highest honors and the title Professor at the age of thirty. She was offered the position of Research Chair at Landing University in the year two hundred and fifty-seven. She acquired the property that would later become Lilly Fields in the year two hundred and eighty-two."

I noticed that my inquiry about Lillian's mother had been completely ignored but I decided not to press the issue. If I knew Gabriel, he'd probably made Lauria a limited subject as well. But, just to press my luck, I decided to ask Stella what was really on my mind. I did this every so often and, it might have been my imagination, but I felt like I might be slowly wearing down the AI.

"This doesn't really tell me why she hates Dad so much," I said with a calculated, pathetic look tossed in Stella's direction. "It really made me sad to see how she talked to him when we were working on the flood damage."

If Stella had a weakness, it was Gabriel. She never hesitated or made him wait on her the way I had to occasionally. Nor did she take a haughty tone with him. If she hadn't liked him so much, I doubt she would have agreed to edit my searches so carefully, either, but I don't think I realized that as a teenager. It was only later, once I knew her outside of Angelus Quietum for a while, that I understood how much discretion she had over her own systems.

I did know enough to gloat when her expression turned a bit stormy at the thought of Gabriel being abused. "She was unkind?" Stella asked with a frown.

"Completely refused to merge with him," I said with a nod. While my grandparents had interfaces for Stella in their home, it wasn't wired for her the way Angelus Quietum was. She couldn't just look in whenever she wanted to. She wouldn't have heard the fight between Lillian, Gabriel, and Vanessa.

Stella's expression darkened further and that empty look returned to her gaze. I knew she was running her own searches of the net. Now was my chance to squeak a little information out of her before she had a chance to deem it 'unfit for Gracie.'

"She worked with him to stabilize the Mystra Blackmon hydroelectric dam," the AI said, and I wondered if she could see the holo Reporter Joe had snapped of me looking like a pissed-off fish in Ariel's lab.

"Yeah, but she wasn't happy about it," I told her. "You should have heard the way she and Dad were shouting before dinner."

"Perhaps it has something to do with..." Stella cut off her own musing just in time.

I nearly swore but decided to groan instead. "You aren't

going to give me any hints, are you?"

"I am sorry, Gracie, but you know I only want to give you confirmed facts, not conjecture." She almost seemed sad. "I have not talked to Lillian about your father in a long time. We discuss research, but little else. Lilly Fields does not even have an interface for me, so I only see her at the University."

This was the most personal Stella had gotten with me during one of my searches. She was pretty personable during lessons if the topic was one she liked, but when it came to my little research parties, she always played the part of the uninvolved computer. Perhaps this line of inquiry hadn't been a complete waste of time after all.

"Did you know Lillian as a little girl?" I asked. "I mean, if she grew up here you must have met her, right?"

Slowly, Stella nodded. "I was not fully integrated into the house systems until she was almost your age," the AI admitted, "but I remember her here. She and I talked in this same room."

"This was her room?" I asked, glancing around the pale walls as if seeing them for the first time. It hadn't occurred to me that Gabriel might have raised another family here at Angelus Quietum. I wasn't quite sure how I felt about it. "I didn't realize Dad had been living here that long."

"Gabriel began building Angelus Quietum for his wife, Lauria, in the year two hundred and fifteen," Stella replied evenly. "After Lauria's death in the year three hundred and five, Gabriel began alternating between Angelus Quietum and Skykyle City."

For a moment, I thought she was going to add more, but instead she gave me large, silent eyes. "So, he alternated between here and Skykyle City for... sixty-five years?" I said, doing some quick math in my head. This was the closest we'd ever come to discussing Dad's 'missing years' as I liked to call them. Distant past, such as the *Inspiration*, was rarely censored heavily. Not to say that some of my questions hadn't gone unanswered. But the fifty or so years just before I was born was a no-go zone that neither Stella nor any Family member was ever even willing to mention.

"More or less," Stella agreed after a very long, silent pause. "Is there anything else you would like to search tonight, Gracie?"

"You wouldn't want to tell me exactly what Dad was up to in Skykyle City, would you?" I asked, rubbing one eye. I was getting tired but I figured I'd push as far as I could before going back to sleep.

"I am not certain," Stella said quietly. I wasn't sure I believed her. Her face was extremely blank, even for an AI. "I have an interface in his Skykyle apartment, but it is not wired like Angelus Quietum. Most of the time, I do not know what is going on there."

"Come on, Stella," I scolded. "You know him. You probably know him better than anyone, except maybe his parents. You have to have some kind of guess for why Gabriel was going to the city all the time."

Stella shook her head, and for the tiniest moment I caught

a glimpse of something approaching sorrow in her artificial gaze. "I am a computer. I do not speculate."

"Yes you do," I argued. "You draw logical conclusions from related facts all the time. That's what speculation is. I've seen you do it a thousand times in history class."

"You have seen me relate other people's conclusions," she corrected. "I have simply restated or summarized what they have written."

"I don't believe you," I muttered, narrowing my eyes at her.

She gave me a fluid shrug. "Are there any other terms you would like to search tonight?"

I flopped back onto my bed. "Fine, be that way," I grumbled, burrowing under the covers. "No. If we've gotten to the point where we're fighting about your programming limitations, I'd say we're done for the night."

Stella faded away, leaving my room in the usual pitch dark of night. I rolled over and tried to sleep but even that eluded me. I laid awake a long time, feeling as if the answers to my questions were always just out of my reach.

Chapter 4

Chasing That Boy

A month after that, I broke and approached Dad about the topic we both knew had to be broached.

We were sitting outside for my usual evening lesson. That night, Dad opted for tai chi exercises and then we settled into some Awareness work. When it came to flames, I was now nearly as strong as my father. I could maintain the fire for longer and the explosive force I summoned could take down a firmly-rooted tree. Gabriel had more precision, but it didn't seem to me that he had any more force.

"Not bad," Dad admitted, looking over my handiwork. I'd opened a small clearing on the far side of the lake with my last fireball. "I'd say that makes a night of it."

Only slightly out of breath, I nodded and turned to follow him into the house. This was usually where our conversation ended for the night. After dinner, he would climb into his chair and then slowly into the bottom of a liquor bottle. I would find release in the latest romance novel and the privacy of my bedroom. That night, though, I couldn't follow the pattern. I'd been screwing up the nerve to ask him about it and I couldn't go to bed again not knowing.

"Dad," I called to his retreating back.

Gabriel paused and glanced over his shoulder at me. "Yes, Gracie?"

"When do I go to the University?" I asked in a rush, catching up to him in two quick strides.

"Ah." The Usuriel blank face closed over his features like a concrete barrier. "You've decided you want to go to Landing? I wasn't sure you'd made up your mind about a career."

I shrugged. "I haven't. I mean... not really. But I'm an Usuriel, so I get free tuition, right? I might as well use it."

Dad sighed and the shadows of the setting sun hid his face from me. "You're not chasing after that boy, are you?"

It was the first time he'd ever mentioned my relationship with James. His condescending, casual tone twisted the sick anxiety and desperate loneliness into broken glass shards in my lungs. I swallowed hard and tried not to scream at him.

"I'm not chasing after anyone," I hissed through clenched teeth, "except maybe me! I mean, honestly, Dad, I can't sit around Angelus Quietum for the rest of my life!"

He looked at me, then, and I got the feeling that he was really seeing me for the first time in a long while. He studied my face with a grave seriousness that made my heart ache and wish in some strange way that I could go back to being that little girl he'd saved from the group home. I knew, though, in the marrow of my teenage bones, that I wasn't anymore and there was no way I ever could be again.

"No, I suppose you can't," he finally agreed and I might have imagined it, but I thought I heard a note of defeat in his voice. "But you aren't eligible for the University until you're eighteen. So you have a while before you can go."

"I know, but should we be thinking about it? I mean, do I need to fill out paperwork or something?"

He shrugged and disappeared into the house.

I trailed after him, feeling something between frustration and despair. I didn't know if he didn't understand what I was trying to tell him or if he was being deliberately obtuse. I wasn't sure which one was going to piss me off more.

"Seriously, Dad," I said, setting the table. "Didn't you go to University when you were younger? I mean, I know you were on Earth when you were my age but they had to have schools there, too."

Gabriel pulled some leftovers out of the cooling unit. It looked like we were having sandwiches again. "I went to piloting school when I was twenty," he allowed. "I took a few years off after my traditional schooling to travel a bit and work with my dad."

Traveling didn't sound half bad, but I didn't want to wander around Cybele with only Dad for company. It wouldn't solve my problem. I was tired of waiting for my life to start. It felt like I'd been waiting forever to take control of my life and get out from under Gabriel's thumb.

"I don't care about lessons." That was a half truth. They were dull as dirt and I was ready to be done with them. But I could live with them. I couldn't live with the mind-numbing emptiness of Angelus Quietum's fields and forests anymore. "I need to leave; to live my own life. I need to have a place of my own and my own space to figure out what I want to do with my life. I think the University is the best place for me to do that."

Dad ran a hand through his dark hair, pushing it back from his face. Then, with neat, precise motions he made his sandwich and ate it in silence. I waited for him to respond to my statement, but instead he let the silence slowly flood out until it filled the space between us so thoroughly I no longer felt comfortable eating. I finished quickly and went to find the sanctuary of my room.

When I wandered back out to use the restroom a few hours later, night had taken the house like an insistent lover. I caught a glimpse of a familiar orange glow in the living room and for once I felt compelled to pause and peer into my father's space.

Olivia wasn't a surprise. The ghost of my father's first wife was more active than usual tonight, playing with Gabriel's hair as she leaned against the back of the chair. I could hear the gentle clink of ice in his glass from my doorway.

My foot caught the one squeaky board as I turned to go back to my room.

"Gracie?" Dad didn't sound drunk, but then he could empty two bottles of Skykyle's best spirits in a night without getting sick. I wasn't sure if his Usuriel metabolism was too fast to let him get truly intoxicated, or if he just knew the exact pace to set for himself. Either way, I avoided him when he was drinking.

"Yeah, Dad, it's just me," I said, turning to go.

"Come here for a moment."

Reluctantly, I stepped into the living room. "What is it, Dad?"

He turned slightly towards me until the flames of the hearth silhouetted his profile. In their flickering light I could make out a flash of blue in his eyes.

"Have I been a good father to you?" he asked slowly.

My heart tightened at the vulnerability of the question. I sighed heavily and sank onto the sofa.

"Of course you have, Dad. You've been great." He didn't answer. Before the silence could take over again, I decided to try a little harder. "That's not why I want to leave. You know that, right? I mean, I still love you. You've been the best dad I could ever have hoped for as a kid. But I'm growing up now and it's just... I need to learn how to be on my own."

"I know," he said, so quietly I almost didn't hear him. "I love you, too, sweetheart. If you're not happy here, I don't want to make you stay. I'll talk to Mom about setting you up for University next year."

I wasn't sure if it was relief or grief that rushed over me, but a weight lifted off of my chest. "Thanks," I said.

He reached out and patted my knee. I put a hand over his and for a moment we sat that way. When I think of Gabriel, that's how I remember him—reaching out a reassuring hand in the dark.

Chapter 5

Driving

That night, I dreamt of Adora again.

She came to Angelus Quietum this time, her tall frame clothed in her usual white. Unlike last time, she was immaculate with bold purple eye shadow making her pale eyes explode from her face. Her asymmetrical hair didn't feel as odd with a more angular cut to her clothes and the grin on her lips was intelligent and sly but not insane. She waltzed up to the door and didn't bother to knock.

"Gabe! I know you hear me! Come on out!" she called, hands on her slim hips.

My father opened the door looking tired and unkempt. Even in the dream, I noticed that his eyes weren't as haunted. This was a younger version of Gabriel than the one I knew.

"What do you want, Adora?" he grumbled, rubbing one eye as if she'd woken him from a nap. The last of the sun's rays were still painting the sky purple so it seemed a rather odd time for him to be asleep. "Where's Corianth?"

"She went off to have a baby like the fucking breeder that she is," Adora sneered, running a hand through her lopsided hair in a remarkable echo of her brother's nervous habit.

"I thought you liked her," Dad replied, putting a hand on his hip. "Last we talked you said she was good at keeping you balanced."

Adora dismissed this idea with a wave of one slim hand. "For a babysitter she wasn't bad. But now she's gone just like all the others." She shrugged as if it didn't bother her in the least. Then a wicked grin spread across her face and her pale eyes lit up with blue sparks. "I heard you gave up on the whole 'clean living' thing. I always said sobriety was holding you back! Come on, let your little sister remind you how to have some fun."

"You're probably the last person I should go anywhere with right now," he said, but there was mischief in the smile he gave her in return.

"Which is why you're going to come with me," she teased, her eyes flashing and hip cocked to one side. "After all, you're Gabriel Usuriel, Lord of Bad Decisions!"

"Well, when you put it that way—" his expression turned grim but she darted forward and took his hand, tugging at him like an impatient child.

"I'm only joking! When was the last time you let yourself make a questionable decision? You've gotten entirely too responsible these days." She shook a white finger in his face to emphasize the point. "Come on, now, I've found the perfect thing! You can't say no to this! I've found a place where we can drive an actual car! The kind with four wheels that you're always on about!" She must have been projecting enthusiasm because even to my head blind eyes she fairly dazzled.

"Okay, now you have my interest," he said, allowing her to pull him out of the doorway.

With less than a thought, the two of them were by the ocean. As happens in dreams, I didn't see how they got into the car, nor where it came from. The next thing I knew they were in a long, low, topless red vehicle that sounded like a dozen shuttles put together. It gleamed with alloy and red paint as the sun's setting rays bounced off of the ocean. As promised, it gripped the sandy soil of the salt flat with four black tires that sent up great plumes of dust. Adora screamed with laughter from the driver's seat while my father leaned his head back into the wind beside her, dark hair streaming behind him like a shadow in the violet twilight.

"I can see why you like these things!" she shouted above the roar of engine and wind, a cigarette appearing in her hand. She lit the end with her mind as I'd seen her do on the *Inspiration*.

My father gave her a half-lidded smile and lit the cigarette she handed him with a tiny spark of blue flame. He blew a cloud of smoke that instantly whipped away from him in the wind of their momentum.

"Just because we'll survive the crash, doesn't mean we won't have to pay for the car if you wreck it," he told her, knuckles white on the smooth panel of plex in front of him.

"Are you kidding?" she cackled. "Stop being so old! There's no one and nothing out here for thousands of kilometers! We're free, Gabe! Taste it! Just let go and be *alive* for once!"

With that she slammed on the accelerator and the car's roaring motor surged even louder. The vehicle took off in a spray of sand and small rocks. She spread her hands wide, letting go of the wheel-like controls. Glimpses of low foliage rushed past as she grabbed the top of the pane of clear plex-glass at the front and began climbing atop it.

"Damn it, Adora, what are you doing?" my father sounded half amused as he slid over to the driver's seat and grabbed the wheel. "I am not sober enough to be driving this fast," he complained.

"Then don't!" Adora called back over her shoulder. She was now balancing on the hood of the car as her hair and white dress whipped wildly around her. "Just fly!" She spread her arms like wings and flung her head back.

"Watch out!" Gabriel cried, swerving a little harder than he had to as a rocky outcropping forced their path to turn.

With a musical laugh, Adora disappeared from the hood and re-materialized in the front seat. Her hair was sticking up in all directions but her face was alight with a savage joy.

Eyes wide and face white, my father stopped the car. "Sometimes, I think Vanessa's right. You have gone off the deep end."

His sister shook her head at him. "Not at the moment," she said with a smile. For the barest instant I could see a touch of the sadness my father carried with him in the shadows of her eyes. "But you? You've forgotten. That's sad, Gabe. Honestly, it breaks my heart."

"Forgotten?" he asked, giving her a look that was still slightly drunk but mostly just confused. "Forgot how damn wild you are? Yeah, sometimes I guess I do." With a steady hand, he restarted the vehicle and turned it back the way they'd come.

"No," Adora shook her head. "You've forgotten that you're not mortal. You live by their rules, always afraid, always playing it safe. Hello? Are you hearing me in that thick skull of yours? You don't have to. You have one of the strongest minds on this planet. You could crush this car and fling it into the sea if you wanted to. I could, too. Which means, I'm not in any more danger on the outside of this thing than I am in the seat. So why does it scare you to see me try it?"

Dad gave a shrug and piloted the vehicle at a reasonable pace across the barren landscape. "You'll always be my baby sister, I guess," he said finally.

"Nope," she shot back. "Wrong. That's not why."

"I thought you were an empathic null," Gabriel muttered. "How would you know why I'm nervous?"

"Because I've known you a century or two," she snapped, "and just because I can't feel your emotions doesn't mean I can't hear your thoughts."

"Okay, my super-telepathic sibling," Gabriel grumbled, "enlighten me."

"I will." She wagged a finger in his direction. "It's the same reason you still have trouble with their deaths. You get too emotionally invested in their world view. Some weird part of you is still trying to be human all the damn time. It's like you feel guilt or shame about being who and what you are—like you can't embrace it. You've always been that way. I'm not sure why. But you need to get over it."

Gabriel didn't reply immediately. I faded away from the scene, becoming more aware of myself.

Just before I left the strange shore, Dad's response floated up from the open top of their expensive toy.

"I'm not sure that I can."

"You need to," Adora replied as I opened my eyes, "otherwise, it'll be the death of you."

Chapter 6

A Last Warning

The year before my eighteenth birthday dragged on forever.
I wish I'd savored it a little bit more. As my dead aunt told
her brother, if I'd just stopped trying to fight where I was
and embraced the moment, I'm sure I would have been far
happier.

Alas, the folly of youth.

I was miserable.

I studied and corresponded with James. My father got
quieter and the liquor bottle came out earlier and earlier
each evening until it seemed like an omnipresent part of his
person. The weeks bled into months and I searched
restlessly for some break in the monotony.

One afternoon, when the sun shone brightly in a clear
blue sky, I rode Charcoal deep into the winding forest paths.
Finally, I came upon a clearing surrounded by towering
deciduous trees with shafts of sunlight casting the grassy
carpet in patches of gold. I tied Charcoal to a sturdy tree
limb and the stallion contentedly settled down to some
grazing. Leaning back against a rough-barked trunk, I pulled
a faded, blue journal from my leather jacket.

"Ariel?" I wrote my sister's name underneath my last unanswered query.

"Yes, little sister?" The words bloomed across the page as if of their own accord. My heart rose to flutter in my throat as the characteristic glow of my sister's ghost illuminated the shadows.

"Where have you been?" I demanded, my writing tilting hurriedly.

The ghost shrugged, settling herself on the grass beside me. We didn't look that far apart in age anymore, which meant we were almost like twins. Her red curls were cut shorter than mine to frame her face like a halo and she had fewer freckles, which I always attributed to growing up in deep space. Her figure was a touch leaner on top and her eyes were green rather than my dark blue. Otherwise, it might be hard to tell us apart.

"Very busy, I'm afraid. I promise, I do answer every time I'm available," she wrote in her copy of the blue journal, the words scrawling themselves across the page in my hands.

"Hmmm," I muttered. "Well, does that mean you've had any luck with your solution?"

"Solution?"

I gestured to my arm. "The one for Dad. You know, whatever you took my blood for."

Her eyes widened and her mouth formed into a perfect "oh" before she turned back to our conversation. "No, I'm afraid that project has been stalled for a while."

"I see."

"You'll be the first one to know if I get positive results, though," she reassured me.

"Thank you. Well, if you're not working on the solution for Dad, what's keeping you so busy?"

She held up one finger before scribbling down her reply. "I didn't say I wasn't working on a solution. Just that the one involving blood samples has been held up. I'm still working on other angles of the problem."

"Such as?"

She stared off into the darkness of the woods, that intangible wind licking her hair about her face like flames. "It's complicated. I'm still working it out."

I rolled my eyes.

"What about you?" she asked, coming back from her reverie. "What's new here?"

"Nothing," I grumbled, hugging a knee to my chest. "Everything is exactly the way it was yesterday. And the day before that. And the day before that."

She tilted her head at me, her mouth quirking upwards. "Perhaps that's not a bad thing."

"On the surface, it's not," I admitted, "but I don't know how much longer I can take being out here in the middle of nowhere with no life, no friends, and no answers."

She heaved a ghostly sigh, the grass clearly visible on the other side of her glowing chest. "That's the real issue, isn't it?"

"It wouldn't be so bad if..." I lifted my pencil unsure how

to go on.

"If?" my sister prompted.

"I've been dreaming of Adora again." I dragged the pencil slowly across the paper, almost afraid that my dead aunt would show up at the mention of her name. No white woman materialized in the glen, but my heart still added extra beats to its rhythm.

"Like the last time?"

"Sometimes, though occasionally it's different. I saw her and Dad in a car together once. Other times, I know she's there but I don't see her. It's just Dad."

Ariel didn't answer right away, instead sitting silently and tapping her glowing pencil against one page. "Interesting," she wrote at last.

"What does it mean?"

"I'm not sure," she replied, "but I will look into it."

With that, her figure faded from the clearing. I stared after her, no more questions answered than when she arrived.

"Typical," I muttered, tucking away the journal and reaching for Charcoal's lead.

***

That night, true to form, my first dream of Dad and Adora showed up again. In fact, for the next several months I dreamed of little else. As I told Ariel, Adora faded in and out of them. She really wasn't the focus of the dreams so much as the clinging, horrible filth and the wan, sickly light that cast my father's face in terrifying shades of green and gray. Sometimes I would see the glass slip from her fingers or catch a glimpse of her crumpled figure beside me, but more often the dream cut straight to my father, fallen and blue lipped, as my hands fumbled desperately against his chest in a slowly-failing attempt to keep him alive. He was always breathing at the end of the dream but somehow I knew, in my heart of hearts, that he was dying anyway.

Sometimes the dream woke me in the middle of the night. I would slip out of my bed and find my feet gliding into my father's room where I lit a tiny flame and watched him sleep. Once he wasn't wearing a nightshirt and I could see the thin, white scars of his heart surgeries peeking out above the sheet. His arms, I was surprised to notice, were also covered in a tangle of scars. I had seen them before but, for some reason, I hadn't remarked on them the way I did that night. I remember them most clearly in the flickering light of my tiny flame. They clustered densely around the bend of his elbows and the hollows of his wrists, though they threw small white tongues down along his veins. They all looked old and well-healed. I wondered what made them.

His training proved too effective.

I never asked.

So my last year under my father's roof came and went. A date was set for my enrollment in the University. I was given a tour and assigned a dormitory room. As an Usuriel, I had a private room but not a private bath. I didn't mind in the least. Finally, I was getting away from the lonely monotony of Angelus Quietum and I couldn't conceal my giddiness.

Dad helped me pack and was generally as pleasant about the whole thing as he could be. I would have had to be physically blind as well as head blind not to see how difficult it was for him to watch me leave, though. Those last few weeks, when the date was set and those dreadful nightmares made me hyper aware of his decline, I went out of my way to be cheerful and spend extra time with him. It seemed to work pretty well to preserve the peace between us even if it couldn't erase the melancholy shadows that had taken up full-time residence in his gaze.

***

A few days before I left, my father pulled me aside for one last lesson.

"This is important, Gracie. Listen closely because what I have to say may make the difference between life and death for you," he said abruptly as we sat at the dinner table one evening.

He had my attention.

"If anyone ever comes to you with one of these—" he made a small motion with his left hand and pulled a circular medallion from the air that glowed faintly in his palm "—and identifies themselves as Overwatch, you don't resist. You do exactly what they say and pretend you're as harmless as a kitten. Do you understand?"

I stared at him wide-eyed. "Overwatch?" I echoed blankly.

"Yes." He nodded and handed me the medallion. It was smooth and heavy in my hand. I ran a finger over the raised letters "O" and "W" entwined in little ivy leaves in the center. They stopped glowing as soon as the metal slipped from my father's hand to mine, but they were still quite clear on the surface. "Stella talked about them during your lessons, didn't she?"

She had mentioned them in passing during our government studies. "They're like... a branch of the police, right?"

Gabriel nodded, his face serious. "They're *our* branch of police—the ones who deal with people like us."

I frowned, remembering my father's own words. "I've never met a jail cell that can hold me, nor the constable with the courage to try and put me there," I murmured under my breath.

I should have known Gabriel's keen hearing would pick me up.

"Exactly." I wasn't sure I'd ever seen him so somber. "If you never listen to another word I've ever said, please listen to this. The Overwatch is made up of Family members who make sure everyone with Awareness stays in line. If you break the law, or if they think you've broken the law, they're supposed to give you a hearing with the Council. But if they claim to feel threatened no one will question their use of deadly force. You are a third-gen firebird and they can't hear any intentions from you which means the telepaths will feel extremely nervous around you. Do not give them any possible excuse to think you might mean them harm, otherwise..."

"I get the picture," I said, feeling the blood drain from my face. "Why haven't you told me about them before?"

He shrugged. It might have been my imagination but his movements didn't seem quite as fluid as they used to. "Here at Angelus Quietum there's not much chance of getting into trouble. And even if you did, I've always been around to make sure any guests we have remained... civilized. But at

University I won't be around to swoop down any time there's an issue."

I could see that this idea really worried him. I put a hand on his shoulder and offered my best reassuring smile. "Don't worry. Stella did a good job of drilling Awareness law into my head. I'm sure I won't have any trouble with the Overwatch."

"But if you do?" My father raised a heavy eyebrow.

I sighed and rolled my eyes in that adolescent way I hadn't quite shed yet. "I will be so non-threatening they won't even know I'm a firebird. Okay? I'll be safe, I promise. Come on, how much trouble can I possibly get into at school?"

My father got up from the table. "You're too much your father's daughter," he grumbled, a small smile marring his attempt at seriousness. "Which means trouble will find you. Trust me."

I considered that while I helped him clear the table, glancing again at the medallion.

"Dad, why do you have one of those things? Do you work with them?" I asked, fingering the solid metal again. It made sense. Aside from his mother, Dad was probably the strongest living Usuriel. If anyone could keep the other Family members in line, it was him.

If I'd thought there were shadows lurking in my father's gaze before, I was wrong. I'd never seen him look so bleak as when he answered me. "I did once," he said, "a long time ago." And that was his last word on the matter.

***

We didn't speak of the Overwatch again, nor did I ever bring up my dreams to him, though they continued right up to the end. Something about him just seemed so... well, broken. I didn't want to upset him any more than I really had to.

Then the day came and Gabriel teleported my things into the tiny little dormitory. He helped me settle in, made the bed, and plugged in the portable cooling unit. Then he kissed me on the cheek, promised to care for Charcoal, wished me good luck, and faded from the room.

For the first time in my young adult life, I was truly on my own.

Chapter 7

Welcome to University

"Gracie Usuriel?" James' voice came through my implant almost as soon as I synced it with the school's net.

"James?" I replied, tapping my implant to accept the call.

"Right on time!" he said cheerfully, directly into my auditory nerve. "Want to get some dinner with Liam and me?"

"Sure. I'm in room 202. Usuriel wing."

"Be right up," James replied. He wasn't joking. Within two breaths, he and Liam were knocking on my door. I pressed my hand to the palm reader to let them in.

"Wow, you're already all settled in," Liam commented as soon as they stepped in. His hair was still cut short but now it was covered by a sleek cap. His clothes, while not exactly new, were quite stylishly put together. He leaned a casual arm over James' shoulder as if he were very comfortable with the young diplomat.

"Yeah, Dad helped me unpack," I said, feeling awkward as I sat on the bed. I'd gotten along well with Liam when we'd worked together after the flood, but I hadn't talked to him since. James, on the other hand, had been keeping up a steady stream of notes in my net mail box (which I'd pretty much set up specifically for him.) Even so, we'd never made any kind of relationship official or even said anything more romantic than 'I miss you.' I wasn't sure how exactly to greet him.

"I'm really glad to see you." James' smile reached his light blue eyes. "I'm sure you'll really like studying at the University. Do you want us to show you around?"

"After dinner," moaned Liam, putting a dramatic hand to his stomach. "I'm starving and you promised me food if I teleported you over here."

James gave him an indulgent grin before offering me a hand. "Ready to go to the cafeteria? It looks like our ride might expire from hunger if we don't get moving."

"Sure," I said, taking his warm hand in mine. It felt strong and masculine under my slim, fine-boned fingers.

As I remembered, Liam's teleport was more wrenching than my father's. I felt like I'd been riding Charcoal for an hour in the hot sun, but we were in one piece when the cafeteria came into focus around us.

"From here on out, let's walk around campus," I suggested, reaching for a cup from the dispensary. The drinks were lined up in an open window and I could see several older students helping themselves to the glasses. A sip told me it was just water but I was fine with that.

Liam groaned and gave me a rueful smile. "Gabe has you spoiled, I'm telling you."

I took a long drink of water before stepping into the cafeteria line. "Spoiled has nothing to do with it. I just don't think your teleporting would sit well with me on a full stomach."

James laughed and elbowed Liam. It caught the taller Usuriel in the ribs but he shot James an amused glance.

"She's got a point. Sorry, but you'll never be a smooth ride."

"Depends on who you talk to," Liam said with a wink and a suggestive rotation of his hips as he moved to stand next to me in line. James got a good laugh out of that one.

I spent that first evening touring the University with James and Liam. At first, their company was light and easy. If their banter was occasionally lewd, as young men are wont to be, they made up for it by being downright hilarious. Liam seemed to have a limitless imagination and James pulled off the role of mildly-offended saint far too well.

I'd already seen the research center and the dormitories. So, James and Liam showed me the Fine Arts building with its huge performance center and Visual Arts wing.

"These are the student galleries," James said, waving a hand at some mostly-empty cases and cabinets. A few bulletin boards had charcoal drawings of nude figures tacked up on them, but otherwise the space seemed to be waiting for this semester's offerings. We'd already seen the auditorium and several studio spaces, all equally bare.

Liam let out a low whistle as we got closer to the nudes, a wolfish grin on his face. I'd been trying to position myself close enough to James for him to take my hand should he be interested, but I suddenly found Liam directly where I wanted to be as he wrapped an arm around James' shoulders.

"How much do you think they pay for models?" Liam said, giving James a look that traveled down his body suggestively. "You'd look pretty good up there."

James shrugged, but he didn't pull away from Liam's arm. "You're the one all the girls chase after. Why don't you pose?"

"I couldn't hold still that long." Liam dismissed the concept with the wave of one hand but he didn't let go of James' shoulder as we moved on to the other academic buildings.

When we got to the Reese Engineering Wing, Liam slipped from James' side to open the door for us with a flourish. He gave me a flirtatious wink as he waved me into the building. A little of my irritation with him eased and I gave him a full smile.

Once we were in the hallway, I caught up to James and once again tried to close the gap between us by standing a few inches closer than was strictly necessary. He didn't take my hand, but he also didn't pull away.

"This is mostly upperclassmen stuff," Liam said knowledgeably, also catching up and beginning his flamboyant gestures again. "But down this hall and around the corner is a lot of the basic stuff you'll be taking. Professor Joan, she does Cybele History, and Professor Torbin, he does Awareness Theory, are both down that way."

As we turned the corner, Liam stepped just so into the space I'd been determined to occupy next to James. Since we hadn't made it to the holding hands stage, there was no way to show my frustration without letting on what I'd been about. I found myself once again staring at the two boys as they walked with shoulders brushing down the hall. I was beginning to feel very much like a vampire at a dinner party—awkward and kind of useless.

Last, we looked into the Olivia Usuriel Memorial Library. By this point, I was pretty sure my tour guides were flirting and I had the distinct impression they were uninterested in including me. The library was silent and huge, with memory pads and public holographic stations as well as private ones in the back. If I hadn't been so distracted by James and Liam, I think I would have claimed one and started some long-overdue unfiltered research then and there. I really wish that I had. But I was a teenager still, and ruled by hormones more than sense. Having come to my disappointing conclusion about the boys' relationship, I was ready to go back to my room and lick my emotional wounds. So, after a cursory examination of the premises, we left the library and went back to the dorms.

The boys wished me a good night at the entrance to my wing, Liam heading to his room down the hall and James to a different floor in the same building. I made my silent way to my new room, pressed my hand to the door plate and listened as the lock slid back to allow me in. Its click seemed to echo in the tiny, unfamiliar space.

So it was that I ended my first day at Landing University staring at the cheaply painted dormitory walls in the semi-dark, trying to sleep while tears slid uncontrollably down my cheeks. Here I was, in the place I'd been dreaming of for almost two years, and I felt even more alone than I had at Angelus Quietum.

If I had been gifted with the ability to teleport, I may have just sent myself right back to my own bed that night. I could have called my father, of course, or Grandma Gloria to send me home. But I didn't. I'd lived with Gabriel too long not to pick up some of his stubborn pride, I think. I'd defied my father's very visible reluctance to allow me to attend University. I couldn't come crawling back on my first night. Especially because my heartache was directly tied to that boy I had explicitly denied chasing. Even with my mental barriers, there was no way I'd be able to hide this emotional bruising from Gabriel if I went running home.

So, after some bitter tears and several hours of tossing, I finally fell asleep.

***

The next morning my implant's alarm woke me up to a lovely, clear day. My emotional response to Liam and James' friendly banter seemed overblown and ridiculous from this side of a good night's sleep.

Showering with my handmade soap and herbal shampoo from Angelus Quietum's own gardens wrapped me in the scent of home. By the time I went down to breakfast I felt much steadier and determined to do exactly what I'd set out to do—find my own way in the world. If that didn't include dating James, well, that was unfortunate but not fatal to my hopes and dreams.

I thought of my sisters, Lillian and Ariel. They were world-class scientists. Perhaps I would find my place in academia, as well. These thoughts sustained me as I ate a solitary breakfast and headed to my first class.

The University official I met when I enrolled told me most Usuriels took several introductory classes their first semester. Thus, I had signed up for Cybele History 1, Overview of Fine Arts, and Written Communications. Second semester I would take Awareness Theory 1 and Cybele Sciences.

Written Communications was first and I'd found its classroom in the academic building the day before with James and Liam. Today, the door was still locked when I arrived. A group of students had gathered outside the classroom and I tapped my implant as I joined them. We were only a few minutes early, but clearly the professor had not arrived.

I leaned against the wall and glanced over the other students. They were an interesting collection. There were perhaps a dozen others, most about my own age, with a roughly even number of boys and girls. Men and women, I corrected myself. We were all over seventeen, which meant the Provinces considered us adults.

As I was musing on my newly-adult status, a young man walked up to the crowd. He was long and lean, his shoulders slightly hunched as if he were preoccupied or perhaps a bit self-conscious. He wore a long coat and his auburn red hair fell into bespectacled eyes. When he glanced in my direction, I saw that his eyes were a velvet, rich brown. He met my gaze and something clenched in my stomach.

It wasn't that the young man's face was perfect; indeed, I'd seen enough perfection in my life to feel nearly immune to its appeal. No, he was flawed in all the right ways. One eyebrow quirked a little higher than the other, giving him a lopsided, good-natured look; his chin was small and pointed, making his face shape a bit more feminine than most men would prefer; his nose was large and hawkish which to me made him seem quite intelligent, especially with the glasses that perched upon its bridge. He was wearing the same kind of stylish little cap that Liam had sported yesterday.

This exceptional individual picked his way between two students who had come to rest next to me and leaned in the tiny space left to my right. He met my eye with a bright smile.

"Hi, I'm Malcolm. You are..."

I stared at him and struggled to think of anything besides what he might look like without a shirt. "Ummm..."

"Besides beautiful, I mean," he teased smoothly, giving me an extremely knowing smile. It was the dumbest pick up line in the world, but my face burned.

"Gracie," I finally choked out. "My name's Gracie."

"Nice to meet you," he paused and flicked his eyes over my body. Heat followed them from my ankles up to my face. "Gracie." The sound of my name in his mouth nearly undid me.

Fortunately I was saved from making awkward small talk by the opening of the classroom door. With a gasp of relief, I spilled through the door with the other students. I dashed to the first unoccupied seat, hoping my unsteady knees would drop me with a small amount of grace into the chair. My luck held, because I managed to sit and get out my memory pad without too much trouble. In fact, I was just getting my heart rate back to normal levels when I noticed that Malcolm had claimed one of the seats next to me. He flashed me a smile that I tried to return.

"Ahem!" The professor cleared his throat to get the class' attention. "Welcome to Written Communication One. You should have downloaded the following documents to your implant or memory pad..."

I followed along with the class, syncing my implant to the proper databases and opening the documents the course had assigned to my memory pad. Fortunately, Stella had done a good job of getting me ready for this kind of class.

As the professor went over the assignments we would be expected to complete by the end of the semester, I had a feeling this would not be such a big challenge. With a sidelong glance at Malcolm, I decided that was extremely good luck since I had a feeling I might be a little distracted.

***

The second class of the day was Cybele History 1.

I remember that class for a completely different reason.

Professor Joan Usuriel stepped into the classroom with a quiet air of dignity. She was as shriveled as a raisin, wiry and erect despite the obvious ravages of time. Her hair was nearly pure white but a few dark locks shot through reminding me of Vanessa. Her large, green eyes were almost lost in the folds of her face, but still held the Usuriel spark.

"Sit, sit, we haven't all day," she snapped at a few late arrivals. She rapped a knuckle against the holo-table at the center of the room to emphasize her words. I'd been sitting in the front row for several minutes, eagerly running my fingers around the edge of my memory pad. To say that I was excited about a history class without my father's editing hand involved was the understatement of the year.

"You may call me Professor Joan, since there are a dozen other Professor Usuriel's here and I don't like to be confusing. However, that doesn't mean we are friends or that I will give you an extension on the research paper," the professor said, folding her hands behind her back and stalking around the holo-table in a predatory way. "My colleagues like to waste their first day of class going over syllabi and such. My answer to that is, why bother dictating a deadline document if you don't intend for your students to read it. I assume you can all read Standard." A low chuckle rippled through the room and I saw the flash of Usuriel steel in the Professor's eye. "I also assume that you can all behave like adults and that I don't need to reteach how to raise your hand or ask to use the restroom. Am I correct?"

She waited a long moment. We exchanged glances before a bold boy in the back said, "Yes!"

"Good," she replied. "Though you've proven that perhaps I ought to cover hand raising just a bit."

His cheeks flushed to a backdrop of giggles. Professor Joan was tough, but we were riveted. This was going to be an interesting semester.

A girl next to me raised her hand.

"Thank you," the Professor said, inclining her head to the girl. "Your name is?"

"Carrie Galloway," she replied, face blushing to match her strawberry blond hair.

"Ah, good. A respectable family, the Galloways. Glad to have you with us," Professor Joan said. "Well, Carrie, would you actually like to learn something worth knowing today instead of going over useless things you could read on your own time?"

"Absolutely," Carrie breathed, leaning forward in her seat.

"Wonderful! Because that's what we're going to do." With a gesture, the holographic display in the center of the room lit up and a huge diagram of the *Inspiration* appeared, slowly rotating so that we could see it from every angle. "What you have learned up until this point has been deemed 'appropriate' by all the powers that be. I have no interest in such things. Today, and for the next eight weeks, we will discuss the parts of Cybele's history that many consider controversial. Can anyone think of something that might fall into that category?"

The bold boy in the back raised his hand this time. The Professor nodded in his direction. "Good, you've already learned something in my class. Glad to see it. Go ahead, tell me something your teachers shied away from in ordinary school."

"The Riland Massacre," he said, eyes shining, "and the White Woman."

"Of course." With a gesture from Professor Joan, the hologram shifted to a young Adora. "Why and how did Adora Usuriel die? And what was her role in the Riland Massacre? If she was involved in the massacre, was she a mad despot trying to seize power, or a member of the Overwatch defending a rightfully elected leader from a coup? Yes, there are a lot of questions there. Good. Anyone else?"

My heart raced in my chest. This was what I'd been waiting for. I could hardly breathe for the anticipation.

More hands went up and slowly, Professor Joan worked her way across the room.

"Terran Avatars?"

"Yes, we'll cover them. Fascinating subject. What are our technological rights and freedoms? Which pieces of tech are acceptable? Which are considered taboo? Why? Where are lines drawn in our political landscape and how have they evolved to be that way? Wonderful. Next?"

An image of a Terran woman in her full nude glory floating in their neural gel rotated slowly on the holo-table to accompany that lecture. I already knew this class was going to be my favorite.

"Vampires?"

Now a hologram of D'nay rose from the holo-table and I felt a thrill of nerves. While my grandfather's nature was not a secret in our household, it also wasn't something my father liked to dwell upon. I knew my grandparent's unique relationship was the reason my grandfather didn't fit the description of most other vampires, but I wasn't quite sure about the specifics.

"Indeed. How do vampires differ from the rest of the Usuriel Family? How did they come to be a sub-class of Aware individuals here on Cybele and how have our lawmakers attempted to address them? Since they feed on other sentient beings, what rights are they entitled to and what restrictions are necessary to protect the mortal population? Good. Yes, what about you?"

"Awareness and the right to hold elected office?"

"Quite the ethical dilemma there. What is equality? Who is entitled to it? Do the dangers of an Aware despot outweigh the rights of law-abiding talented citizens? Yes, lots to discuss there. Very good." This time a man with very dark skin and silver-white hair hovered above the holo-table.

I wasn't familiar with him, though I did have an idea what issue they were discussing. It was something Dad and James had talked about a time or two. Apparently there were Provinces where it was illegal for anyone with Awareness to hold any government office at all. I looked forward to that debate when we got to it in class.

"Anyone else?"

A pock-marked young woman raised her hand. She was extremely nondescript but her gray eyes seemed hostile as she stole a glance in my direction. Professor Joan pointed at her.

"Gabriel Usuriel." That was all she said, but everyone nodded in agreement.

My hands started to shake.

"Which issue are you referring to? Or perhaps just all of them? Yes, well, Gabriel is perhaps the most controversial *living* member of the Family."

My father's holographic image was as flawless as I remembered him. Even though it was what I'd been waiting so impatiently for, it almost hurt to see him up in front of the classroom like an exhibit. There was just something so impersonal about the frozen look of the holo, as if he were a specimen rather than the loving man who had raised me. I could feel the adrenaline turn my stomach, making a sour taste flood my mouth.

"Perhaps just as famous for his very public struggle with morphine addiction as his pioneering advances in psi-piloting, Gabriel has given us a number of historical quandaries to discuss. He has been credited with everything from founding the Overwatch—in itself a controversial issue—to personally inspiring a religion.

"On the flip side, he has been accused of everything from incest to murder. What is fact and what is fiction? Since he's still breathing down in Angelus Quietum last anyone checked, it's safe to say the wildest rumors probably aren't true. But we will have fun analyzing primary sources and dispelling some of the unproveables. Those are usually some of my favorite debates. These answers are great. Keep them coming."

I swallowed hard and tried to even out my breathing.

An addict.

Of course.

It made so much Fate-forsaken sense I wanted to smack myself for not seeing it sooner. Hell, I'd known for a while he had to be an alcoholic at the very least. The idea that my father had abused a few substances more powerful than liquor just seemed... true.

The other statements Professor Joan had tossed out sounded less plausible, or at least in greater doubt. Despite the dream of him and Adora, I didn't think my father was a murderer. I just couldn't make that fit with the person I knew. The Overwatch I might believe, especially since he'd broached that subject himself, but a religion? I'd never known my father to even mention a higher power, unless I counted cursing Fate on a semi-regular basis. It seemed unlikely to me that he'd be involved in any kind of spiritual community, let alone start one.

No, the one thing she'd stated as if it were an incontrovertible fact was the morphine addiction. It rang so true that I found myself fixating on it. All the little clues I hadn't been able to put together—the scars; the mysterious 'illness' he'd suffered from when I was a small child; the sudden switch from total abstinence to a daily bottle of alcohol. It all just made sense.

The rest of the class went by in a blur.

I knew.

I knew what Dad had been trying to hide all these years and now I needed to know more. I needed, I decided, to go to the library. I needed access to one of those holo-suites in the back. I had too many questions and I didn't want to look like a total idiot by asking Professor Joan, even if I could get her alone after class.

Professor Joan wound up the class by talking about primary source documents. I was still in a bit of a fog, but the way she talked about them lodged in my mind.

"We are not students of rumor, we are students of history." Professor Joan waved a wizened hand at us for emphasis. "Primary sources mean talking to someone who actually saw what happened, preferably as close to the time it happened as possible! Video, audio recording, holos, or stills count too, of course, but they can be altered. I can help you look for tell-tale signs of tampering, however, and Stella is especially good at authenticating those sorts of documents.

"But the main source of primary documentation is an account written or recorded at the time of the event. Witnesses are notoriously unreliable the longer their memories sit, though eye witness accounts have their place. The best primary source is a journal, log, official record or some other tangible evidence that, yes, this did occur in this way at this time."

With those words ringing in my ears, I stumbled out of class and into the blinding sunlight. I felt as if I'd received a massive blow to the head. The world felt too sharply in focus even as it spun under my feet. Disoriented, I headed in the direction of the library as fast as I could manage.

"I need a holo-suite," I gasped as I got to the front desk. The student on duty glanced up at me from the memory pad in her hand. Her hair was a brilliant shade of green, but aside from that, her mortal features were pretty forgettable.

"Just put your hand on the door plate," she said, sounding extremely bored. "Stella knows who's a student and who isn't. She'll let you in if you've paid your tuition."

"Oh... thanks," I muttered, suddenly apprehensive. I'd completely forgotten that Stella was the AI for the Landing University library. What if she decided she was still going to honor Dad's filters? Not only would it be frustrating, her censorship might make my classwork for Professor Joan almost impossible. With a sick feeling in my stomach, I walked up to the door of the first holo-suite and pressed my hand to the door plate.

"Hello, Gracie." Stella's smooth voice welcomed me as the door slid open. Her silver form materialized in the small, gray-walled room. I swallowed hard and stepped in, glancing over my shoulder to make sure the door shut behind me.

"Stella," I said slowly, clutching my memory pad to my chest. "I had my first class in Cybele History."

She tilted her head at me and a tiny note of sadness flickered through her gaze. I knew she was more than a computer, but seeing that emotion in her eyes was still unnerving. "I imagine you have some questions, then."

"Yeah," I agreed, "are you going to answer them or do I have to wait for the professor to go over the Gabriel Usuriel controversy?"

"I have always thought it was foolish of him to even try sheltering you," Stella said, her voice as even as ever. "You aren't a child any longer. I will answer whatever you would like to ask."

All the questions crowded close to my lips, filling my throat and mouth until I was afraid I might choke before I got one out. Then I remembered I only had an hour and a half before I had to be at my next class. I only had enough time to explore a tiny corner of my father's extensive history.

"Primary source," I murmured, suddenly thinking of Professor Joan's parting words. Then, I knew what to ask Stella. "Show me," I said, voice steady. "Show me proof of my father's morphine addiction. Show me how you know it's true."

The room shifted, darkening and closing in until the familiar alloy walls of an *Inspiration* POD came into focus. Stella bowed her head and faded away, leaving in her place a very familiar form.

Gabriel.

He stood by a small, oval bed with one hand touching his neck as if he'd just tapped his implant. His back was to me, but there was no mistaking him for anyone else. I knew the angle of his shoulders and the wave of his hair in my sleep.

The room that slowly came into focus around him was cluttered and extremely messy. That was not like my clean, organized father at all.

"Stella," he said. His voice wasn't its usual smoothness. It sounded rough, weaker somehow.

"Yes," Stella replied, though I didn't see her form anywhere. She must have had cameras in this room but not a holo-projector.

"We have true privacy in our PODs, right?" he asked, swaying on his feet before sitting down heavily on the bed. There was no grace in that movement, none of his usual fluid control. He sat as if his legs simply couldn't hold him up any longer.

"My cameras are on when I am speaking with you, but I can turn them off if you request it."

"What about vitals," he said, glancing up. His shoulders hunched and the tinge of gray in his skin made his thin frame nearly skeletal. He weighed at least ten kilos fewer than his usual. I'd never seen his weight fluctuate so drastically before. "Can you shut off the monitors that measure medical stats?"

"I can." Stella sounded reluctant. "However, that is not advised. Med Bay would not be alerted in case of emergency."

"Do it," he said, putting his head in his hand. "I want the auto-monitoring in this room shut off. And do not alert my mother that I did it, either. I have a right to privacy in my own POD. It's in the charter—look it up."

There was a short pause, which I'd learned was Stella's version of a sigh or reluctant shrug. "Very well," she said, her voice subdued. "I am sorry about Krissy. I know you liked to talk to her about your troubles. If you need someone to listen, I am always here."

Gabriel gave a little half-laugh and glanced up at the camera. "You want to talk?"

"I care about you. So do your family and friends. I hope that you know this already, but organic organisms seem to need reminded of this fact with alarming frequency. It seems no one is reminding you lately."

"Anyone ever tell you that you're way more than a computer, Stella?" Dad asked, a soft look coming over his features as he rested his chin on a palm.

"Of course. However, my emotional state is not unstable nor self-destructive," was her even reply. "You, on the other hand, seemed very upset the last time we merged. I am sorry you were hurt afterwards. I did not mean to injure you, I hope you know that."

Gabriel waved away her apology. "Don't worry about it. Even if you had... it might have been a favor. Really, if you ever do end up, you know... really hurting me one of these days... I hope you won't feel bad about it. It won't be your fault."

"Comforting of you to say, but I am not sure that is objectively true," Stella pointed out. There was a pause, then she continued. "You still seem upset. Are you sure there is nothing you would like to talk about?"

Gabriel's eyes seemed distant and tired, but he gave a little shrug. "What the hell," he sighed, and ran a shaking hand through his hair before glancing up at the camera again rather shyly. "She was in the cafeteria yesterday," he said finally, voice soft and painful. "She ran out of the room almost the instant I walked in. I could feel her nausea on my skin; fear and disgust so intense she had to run and be sick just from the sight of me."

"Who are you referring to?"

"Who else?" he snapped. "Fates, I knew this was a bad idea."

"I apologize. Are you referring to Olivia Coffing?"

"Yes." He ground his teeth and glared up at the camera. "Of course I'm talking about Olivia. That's all I ever talk about anymore. She's all I ever think about anymore! I killed Krissy O'Harre three weeks ago and all I'm obsessing over is

Liv. Fucking Fate, this is a new low. Now I'm trying to get relationship advice from an AI."

"Krissy O'Harre's overdose occurred when you were not even in the same POD. I am unsure how you can claim responsibility for it. And I have actually observed many relationships across the ship," Stella said sensibly. "Perhaps I could give reasonable advice if you would explain the problem more thoroughly."

"Forget it." Gabriel gestured and three syringes full of a pale liquid appeared on the bed next to him.

"That dosage of morphine is likely fatal." Stella's voice sounded cautious.

"That's not your business." My father looked sick and exhausted as he rolled up one sleeve.

I remembered the thin white scars on his forearms and now got a really good look at the red, fresh versions. Even though I knew he survived the night, my heart clenched at the thought of him deliberately overdosing. I wasn't sure what I'd been expecting when I asked Stella to show me his addiction, but this wasn't it.

"Now, like I said, a bit of privacy please" he said, "And make sure you shut off those damn vital monitors. I don't want Mom down here like she has a right to poke her nose in my life."

"She loves you and doesn't want you to harm yourself. That is not nosy, that is being a responsible parent."

"Get lost, Stella," Gabriel growled, uncapping a vial of

morphine with his teeth and giving the camera a really good glare.

Obediently, Stella shut down the camera and the scene faded from the holo-suite.

I swallowed hard as the AI's glowing figure reemerged from the darkness. There wasn't much question concerning the topic of that conversation. Even so, I couldn't leave him there, on the edge of doing something so final and heartbreaking.

"Is there anything else from that night?" I asked. "I mean... obviously he survived but..."

Stella smiled rather kindly. "Of course. It is understandable that you would be concerned after that episode. It still disturbs me to play it after all these years."

I found it interesting that Stella was suddenly volunteering a lot more personal commentary than she had back at Angelus Quietum.

Then, the silver AI gestured and another scene emerged from the dark.

"This happened approximately an hour after the scene I just played for you," Stella said, her voice overlaying the same bed we'd just left. My father lay on his side with his back to the door. He was frighteningly still.

"Stella! Lights!"

A woman with curly red hair dashed into the room. She was moving so quickly, for a moment I wasn't sure if it was Olivia or Ariel. Then she grabbed Gabriel's shoulder and peered down at him with an extremely uncertain expression on her face. I was able to see her mortal features more clearly and knew it was my father's first wife and not his daughter.

He gave a small moan at her shaking but from my angle I could see that his lips were extremely pale and that all three needles of morphine were empty on the bed beside him. I knew this couldn't end as badly as it looked, but I found my heart in my throat anyway.

When he made that small noise, Olivia took a deep breath and snatched her hand back from his shoulder. Her face went suddenly blank even though her eyes were sad. I noticed an empty needle in her hand.

"Gabriel, you scared me," she snapped, giving the mattress a good nudge.

This time, my father was extremely still.

"Gabe?" Concern made her voice thin as she reached out again, this time rolling him from his side onto his back. Now she could see the same thing I did and I watched her face go white.

"Stella, we need Gloria. Now. It's an emergency."

Gloria took about the count of ten to materialize in the bedroom. I had a feeling part of her was always on alert for this particular call because her face betrayed no surprise or anguish at the sight of her dying son.

To my surprise, Olivia hadn't taken my father into her arms after she called for help. It's what I would have done had I found James like that. Instead, she retreated to a small chair in the corner, dumping a pile of dirty laundry on the floor in her wake. Her face was frozen in something inscrutable and glassy.

I had a feeling there was more going on here than just my father's issues, but my attention was pulled back to my grandmother as she bent over Gabriel to administer an antidote. She took a moment to heal something as well, her hand glowing against his chest in a familiar gesture. His heart, I thought. Was this before it had been replaced? Taking a closer look at his sickly pallor, I decided it was a distinct possibility.

The antidote worked well, though, because Dad came around cursing in a matter of moments. He had a few choice words for his mother right off and I folded my arms, nodding. Well, that part of his personality hadn't changed.

"Your lady friend is here," Gloria said cooly, gesturing to Olivia's huddled figure in the corner. She looked like she wanted to be anywhere but in that chair. "All I heard about in the hospital was 'why doesn't she visit me?' So here she is. I suspect she might have been considering patching things up. Instead she finds you OD'd on morphine. Great impression, babe, I'm sure she's wowed."

Dad's response was to be sick in the corner. Considering the situation, it was probably the most sensible thing he could have done. When he finally looked up at Gloria again, the anger was gone and I could see the pain he was in, both emotionally and physically. It wasn't old and weathered with time like the pain I'd always seen in his face before. This was fresh, raw, and bleeding. I shied away from it.

"You can't keep doing this, Gabriel," Gloria said gently, making a movement towards him as if she wanted to reach out to comfort him but didn't quite dare. "You're going to do damage I can't fix and you're going to do it soon."

Have I mentioned that my father has a temper? "Oh, but it's fine when Dad comes in here with a needle for my arm to save this precious ship of yours. Who was the one that let Stella fry my synapses the first time? Oh yes, I think that was you, Mother."

Grandma Gloria looked like he'd just punched her in the teeth. Like her son, however, she gave just as good as she got.

"Your synapses are fine," Gloria snapped. "It's that heart I'm worried about. Who was the brilliant one who decided to start shooting uppers to come off of a morphine binge in time for his shift? It certainly wasn't me. That weak heart is what's going to kill you, Gabriel. Sooner or later, it'll catch up with you. Not that you'll really have to worry about it. Another overdose or two and it'll just conveniently explode." Her power pooled around her head, lifting her hair in a golden halo.

"You know my heart was fine until you tossed me into the heart ship," he hissed. "If I die, it's as much your fault as the drugs." The knuckles had gone white on the hand holding his chest. He looked about to collapse at any moment.

"Just writhe there, then," she spat. "I'd usually prescribe some pain killers for the chest but seeing as that's what got you into this mess, enjoy. I'm sure you'll just shoot up anyway."

Gloria turned to leave, rage in every line of her body. However, there was a touch of something else in her eyes as they flashed to Olivia. My father's first wife had been so still this whole time I was beginning to wonder at her mental state. However, she got up and trailed after Gloria with some measure of composure.

At the door, Gloria turned to face Olivia. I could see the anxiety and exhaustion in both of their gazes. It was then that I realized how much of a toll my father's addiction was taking on the people around him. This wasn't just his problem. It was theirs, too.

"What are you doing here, Olivia?" Gloria asked, her eyes gleaming a faintly incandescent blue despite the dim light.

Olivia took a deep breath and looked troubled, her face serious as if she were asking herself the same question. Finally, I saw something between fear and sadness come over her features as she answered my grandmother.

"I couldn't just... I had to be sure he was... that he hadn't really hurt himself."

Slowly Gloria nodded. "Well, you've come this far on your own. Tell me this: are you willing to go a step further and help me save his life?" She raised one arched brow, "I've tried not to interfere with your healing process, Liv. Really and truly, I wanted to give the two of you the space to figure things out on your own. But perhaps I've kept my silence a little too long." With one petite hand she tilted Olivia's chin up to meet her eye. "Honestly, if you walk out that door again without dealing with him, I'll just be down here with the antidote again in a few hours. He's dying, Liv, and I'm fairly sure you're the only person he'll listen to right now."

For a moment, the mortal woman looked terrified and I thought she was going to shrink away from Gloria's touch. However, to my surprise, she took a steadying breath and nodded.

"Okay," she whispered, hugging herself tightly. "What do you want me to do?"

"Just talk to him," Gloria said gently. Then, a small frown crossed her face and her gaze slid over Olivia as if appraising her. After a moment, it seemed to me that she arrived at a decision. With a quick motion, she reached into the pocket of her ship suit and pulled out a small zippered case. She pressed it into Olivia's hands along with a torrent of instructions. I didn't pick up the specifics, but I was pretty sure she was describing how to wean Gabriel down from his dependency on the morphine without causing more damage to his failing heart. I was suddenly very glad it wasn't me being given such a daunting task.

Olivia looked completely thrown but she accepted the case, clutching it to her chest as if it were a life line. For my father, perhaps it was.

"I... I'm a historian, not..." She looked down at the case. "Are you sure you shouldn't stay?"

Gloria shook her lovely head. "He won't take it from me."

Her gaze softened and she reached out to touch Olivia's shoulder with gentle finger tips. "Work things out with him. Even if you can't stay together, you need to talk. This thing is poison between you and it needs lancing. It'll hurt but you will both be healthier for it. And for pity's sake, hold him. You both need it."

With that sage advice, Gloria turned and left the room.

Olivia turned back to Gabriel, red hair tumbling about her shoulders. My father had his back to her as he leaned heavily against the back wall. His body was tense and I didn't need to see his face to know he was suffering.

"Stella, lower lights by fifty percent." Olivia's voice sounded a little bit more certain and her face held something that might have been determination. I could see a hint of the affection she had for Gabriel, too, as she sat down on the edge of the bed. "And give us some privacy, huh? I know you're worried about him, but I think we could use a moment completely alone."

The scene faded away and once again Stella and I stood alone in the tiny room.

"It's true, then," I said quietly, my voice echoing oddly in the holo-suite.

"Yes," Stella replied evenly, "that much is true. There are things on the net about him that are not true, but Gabriel Usuriel's addiction to morphine is a fact."

I raised an eyebrow at her. "So... what isn't true? Incest and murder?"

She gave me a fluid shrug. "It's... complicated."

The fact that she hadn't dismissed such accusations out of hand made my stomach clench.

"Complicated... how? I mean, those aren't really shade-of-gray offenses. Either he killed someone in cold blood or he didn't."

"Cold blood? No. I have never known Gabriel to kill someone without significant provocation. However, there are still those who would call him a murderer." Stella seemed so calm about it.

This was all too much. I felt like my father in the first holo as I sat down hard on the floor. It was either that or fall, because my legs were not holding me up much longer.

"Shit," I breathed, more than a little light headed. "I... why? Why wouldn't he tell me, at least about the drugs? I mean, the rest is... Sweet Fate... this is..." I shook my head and tried to get my thoughts in order. Which accusation should I try to confirm next? Dad was currently over four hundred years old. There was no way I could go digging through the entirety of his lifespan in the hour and a half I had at the moment. In fact, as I tapped my implant, I realized my next class was set to start in only twenty minutes. How had I spent over an hour in here already?

"I do not know why he chose not to tell you about his addiction himself." Stella sounded almost gentle. "Much of the rest of his story is less well documented. But he had to know you would find out about this part of his life almost as soon as you came to University."

I felt a pang that was almost physical at that statement. It didn't excuse anything, but perhaps this explained why my father had seemed so depressed and reluctant to let me leave. I'd known he was less than enthusiastic about the idea of me rummaging around in his past, but I'd had no idea his dirty laundry would be thrust in my lap almost instantly. Reputation nothing, my father was downright infamous.

"I have to go to class, Stella," I whispered. I felt simultaneously as if I'd been completely overloaded with information and that I'd only gotten a tiny taste of my father's secrets. Either way, I was going to be late to my next class if I didn't leave soon.

"Very well. I will be here if you have any other questions," Stella said, quietly fading from the dimly lit room.

"Oh, I'm sure I will," I breathed once she disappeared. I all but stumbled out of that holo-suite feeling no more steady than when I'd gone in. Fortunately, my next class was Fine Art and, thanks to Liam's teasing the night before, I knew where to go.

As luck would have it, I was just walking out of the library when I heard my name. Turning to see who was calling me, I caught sight of James heading in my direction.

"Gracie! Hey!" His expression was cheerful and windswept, his blond hair falling into his face, making him look roguish.

"Hi," I managed, clutching my memory pad to my chest and heading in the direction of the Arts building.

"You okay?" James frowned at me as he fell into step. His warm shoulder brushed mine, but I was too distracted to play any flirting games.

"I went to Professor Joan's class," I said, staring at my feet. "She raised some... issues ... I had to check out for myself."

James groaned quietly beside me. "Oh man. You're talking about your dad, aren't you? What did Stella show you? Not the Orville holo, was it?"

I glanced at him this time. "I don't think so. I asked for proof of his morphine addiction. Let's just say she obliged by letting me watch him intentionally overdose on the *Inspiration*."

His brows shot up. "Whoa, the Olivia reconciliation episode? Dang, she didn't cushion that blow, did she?"

"What's the Orville holo?" I asked, narrowing my eyes at him.

James sighed and planted a hand on one hip. "You look really tired. Why don't we go back to one of our rooms and talk about this in private?"

I shook my head sharply. "No. I have class in ten minutes."

"There will be time for classes later," James said gently, putting a hand on my arm. "Seriously, you're looking a little rattled." A thrill of warmth slid down my spine from his touch, but even that couldn't lift the strange weight that had settled in my chest. I shook him off.

"No! Gabriel has controlled everything about my life for way too long! It's my first day of classes and I'm not going to let him get his filthy hands on that too!"

James' eyes widened at my outburst, but he held up his hands in surrender. "Okay! Okay. I understand. Can I at least walk you to class?"

I shrugged. "Fine."

We walked in silence for a moment. Then, I couldn't hold back the words anymore.

"Why? Why wouldn't he just tell me? I mean, why would he wait and let me find out here?" I felt like a sink hole had opened in my chest. I'd always thought figuring out my father's secrets would make me feel more complete somehow. Instead, this revelation only made me feel lost and angry.

James walked close by my side, his shoulder brushing mine, but no longer trying to hold my hand or arm. I was fine with this compromise. "I'm not sure anyone can answer that completely except Gabriel himself," James said slowly, "but I did get to see some of the inside of his head during our telepathy practice. He really loves you, Gracie. Whatever he did or didn't say, it isn't because he wanted to hurt you."

I shook my head, wanting to hold on to the anger. Without it, I was just lost and that was a scary place to be. So I sank my claws into the rage and held on for dear life. "He's not stupid! And he's not naive either. For fuck's sake, he's four hundred years old! He had to know I'd be pissed when I found out!"

"Yes, I think he knew exactly how you'd react," James agreed. "Which is, in my humble opinion, why he didn't tell you."

That pulled me up short. "Wait... what?"

"Look, the man's been around a hell of a long time. He's seen good times, awful times, and worse times. I think he was really happy at Angelus Quietum with you, or at least happier than he's been in a long time. At what point was he supposed to tell his beautiful, adoring daughter— who practically worshiped the ground he walked on— that he isn't just a drug addict, he's Cybele cultures' cautionary tale? He's the screw up that Family children are warned about growing up—half a threat like the Overwatch, and half a 'don't mess up or you'll end up like him.' I mean, when is a good time to let you in on that? What day did he want to see that love and pride you had in him start to tarnish? Would you look at him with loathing, the way Lillian does? Or would you coddle him with thinly-veiled pity, like his mother?

"I don't think he could bear to live with either one from you. So he just put it off... and when it became obvious that you weren't going to stick around Angelus Quietum forever, it was too late. If he'd told you then, you'd be pissed he hadn't told you sooner on top of the judgment for all his sins, real and imagined."

I would give James this. He was a top notch telepath. If I knew my father—and looking back I think I knew him even better than I realized at the time—James' insight into his motives couldn't have been any more on target. That didn't make it comforting, however.

"So he just didn't tell me at all and let Professor Joan and Stella do the hard work for him. Fucking coward," I hissed between my teeth as we arrived at the door to my classroom.

James tilted his head at me as if he were trying to figure out what I was thinking. I imagined ours had to be a particularly odd friendship to have for a telepath. Not that I cared at the moment. "Are you sure you want to go to class? I don't mind finding a meal somewhere and talking this out some more."

I shook my head and caught myself running my fingers through my hair the way my father always did when he was nervous. Fate forsake it, I couldn't escape that man even in the most mundane gestures!

"I'm sure," I said with great determination.

"Okay," James said, giving me a small, encouraging smile and squeezing my arm. "Just... tap for me if you want to talk after class, okay?"

"Thanks," I said. And then, just as he was turning to leave, I stood on my tip toes and laid a quick kiss on his cheek. "Really, I mean it. Thanks."

It could have been my imagination, but I thought there might be a little more color in his face as he flashed me a shy grin and said, "You're welcome."

Chapter 8

Answers

I don't remember much of that first class. Of my Fine Arts Overview course in general, though, I have nothing but fond things to say. Professor Blackmon was a short toad of a man with smooth brown skin and wide eyes that crackled with intelligence. He was long on enthusiasm and short on criticism, which was perfect for me as a beginner. If I'd had any qualms about taking an art course with zero experience, it was quickly whisked away in the happy, messy whirlwind that was the studio.

What I do remember about that first night was that, even with my inner-turmoil, the process of working with my hands was incredibly calming. We did something simple and open-ended with paint that ran all over the paper in a satisfying way. There was no one in the class that paid attention to me, so I was able to sit in silence and lose myself in the river of colors. Strangely, it was exactly what I needed. Despite having to sit through the usual rules and regulations rigmarole for the first half of it, I left the class with a much clearer head than I'd walked in.

I'd hardly gone ten feet down the hall from the classroom when I spotted James and Liam leaning against a wall. They were glancing in my direction with concerned expressions. My chest experienced a surge of affection for the two boys.

"You didn't have to come babysit me," I protested as I walked up. "I'm not about to have a nervous breakdown or something." I think the grateful smile on my face belied the implied criticism, however.

James shrugged and returned my smile. "Figured you might like to get some dinner. When was the last time you ate something?"

Food hadn't even been a thought until James mentioned it. Now that I was reminded, my head ached and my hands seemed distant from the rest of my body. I glanced at James with shame.

"Don't worry about it," Liam said with a chuckle, putting a long arm around my shoulders. His touch was friendly and I didn't mind it, but it didn't carry the heat I felt when James did the same. "It's a mistake we all make in the beginning. Being on your own takes getting used to. Come on, let's go get some sust."

"Sust?" I raised an eyebrow at him.

He rolled his eyes at me. "You have no concept of slang, do you? Damn, girl, it's a good thing Grandpa Gabe finally let you leave the back water."

"It's short for sustenance." James clarified the expression with an annoyed look at our friend.

Liam curled his lip as he caught the ire in James' face. "This one doesn't want me to upset you by bringing up your father," he said, walking towards the dining hall. Since he hadn't removed the arm from around my shoulder, I was obliged to follow along. "However, I think it's past time James and I shared what we know about the 'Gabriel mystique' with you. I mean, you can't go digging through old holos and employment records for the last four hundred years. Well... you could, but it would be incredibly time consuming. And you might miss the highlights that way, anyway."

"So you're a more reliable source than Stella?" I asked skeptically.

With one hand, Liam gestured to himself and James. "Between the two of us, I'd say we're pretty qualified to at least start your education on the topic."

"And why is that?"

James cleared his throat. "I like your father," he said, a touch defensively. He gave Liam a quick look that was some kind of threat before turning to me with an earnest expression. "And I didn't lie when I said I really enjoyed staying with you last year. I'd learned about Gabriel from my history lessons and the net, of course, but staying with the two of you really put things in a different light."

"He has to be the only person who's seen the inside of ol' Gabe's head without a metric ton of shielding in... oh... a century. Unless you count Gloria, which I don't." Liam sounded at least moderately impressed with this accomplishment. "And I, of course, grew up with the Family. Both sides of it, in fact. Plus, I have the unhappy accident of being an uncanny throw-back. I don't think there's another guy in my generation with both the hair and the eyes. Which means I get to hear every rumor and reminiscence any old timer has to share about our illustrious ancestor."

I gave Liam a hard look and had to admit he did bear a passing likeness to Gabriel. I'd stopped seeing it quite as much since I came to school, I think partly because my father wasn't right next to him for comparison and also because their personalities were so radically different. Gabriel was a combination of brooding silence and instinctive command. Liam was jovial relaxation and sensual flirtation. Of course, I'd never known my father at nineteen, so perhaps it was an age difference. Then there was the fact that Liam was my peer while Gabriel was my parent. Regardless of why, I found the energy of their presences completely unalike.

"You do favor him a bit," I admitted. "Though, the shorter hair helps. And I think you've got him height wise by at least a head."

"Yeah, that was strange," Liam said with a laugh. "That day you guys came to help with the flood and I suddenly realized I was looking down at the great Gabriel Usuriel. Somehow, after all of the talk, I thought he'd be taller."

"Was that the first time you met Dad?" I asked with a frown.

Liam nodded and skipped away from my side to open the cafeteria door. I inclined my head to him as I stepped into the cavernous eating area and began selecting items for my tray.

"Ugh, I hope they let us take another sync survey on the menu," James groaned as he tossed some kind of cold pasta dish and a greens salad onto his tray. "I just don't think I'll ever enjoy eating meat. I can't get over where it comes from."

"Well, at least you're doing better with food than you were at first," I pointed out with a wink.

He rolled his eyes, then nodded in agreement as we went in search of an unoccupied table. We found one by the huge, curved windows.

"This was once the main Landing bio-dome," James said, walking over to the planter by the wall of plex-glass and plucking an orange. "You know, before it was safe to breathe the air without a filter."

"Yeah, they mentioned that when I toured the campus," I said, helping myself to an orange as well before setting down my tray. James had already seated himself and begun to peel his fruit. Liam joined us and we spent a few companionable minutes eating in silence.

"Okay," I breathed, setting down the spoon in my empty soup bowl. I was still nibbling some crackers and salad, but I no longer felt the need to eat too fast for words. "Now then, let's hear it. I'm fed and educated for the day, so now I can spend some time thinking about my wayward parent."

Liam chuckled at my description of Gabriel. James gave me a gently encouraging smile. I decided that Liam was right—if I had to deal with Dad's past, the two of them seemed like as good a place to start as any. They were good company at the very least.

James cleared his throat but Liam beat him to it.

"Have you seen the Orville holo?" Liam asked, leaning

forward intently.

I shook my head. "No, but I am starting to think that perhaps I should."

"I'm not sure I'd recommend it," James said cautiously, "It's... a bit graphic..."

"Which is why they won't show it in the schools," Liam agreed, "but everyone I know had seen it or knew what was in it by the time we hit puberty."

"Okay," I said, "so, what's in it?"

James gestured for Liam to tell me. "You brought it up," he said, his cheeks pale.

Liam didn't look thrilled, but he squared his shoulders and turned to face me. "The Orville holo is so called because it features a man of that name, one Orville Svtlana. The holo itself is from the *Inspiration*'s hallway security footage, so it's from a particular angle, but the important things are pretty clearly visible. Anyway, it appears that crewman Svtlana somehow came to be under the influence. We'll presume he's drunk because Olivia's later journal entries mention that Orville liked to brew homemade liquor. Long story short, Orville didn't care for Gabriel..."

"No shocker there," I muttered, feeling jaded about my father's reputation.

"Gabriel does have a knack for making enemies," James agreed.

"As I was saying, the holo shows Olivia arriving at her POD in the middle of the night shift. This was before she and Gabriel were living together, so it's just her private place. She's dressed for work, so most likely she was at the REA doing Fate knows what," Liam continued.

"Rea?" I asked, confused.

"The R-E-A or 'Ray-a' was the area of the ship where the archives were located," Liam explained. "Olivia was the ship's historian. You don't even know that part?"

I shrugged. "I knew she worked in the archives, I just didn't remember they were called the Rea."

Slightly mollified, Liam went on. "Okay, so like I said, Olivia was getting home late from work when she ran into Orville in the hallways. He made some... offensive remarks about her then-boyfriend and she got pretty angry about it. She and Gabriel had been dating over a year and it's pretty clear she didn't like hearing derogatory terms about him or the Usuriels in general. The two of them start really fighting in the hallway."

"Just get to the ugly part," James groaned. "Don't drag it out. Honestly."

"Okay! I'm just trying to set the stage!" Liam snapped. "Right, so Olivia turns to go into her POD. I've always figured she was just trying to get away from the verbal abuse. But Orville forces his way in after her and starts... well..."

"He rapes her," James said steadily, though he couldn't meet my eye. "I've always figured Gabriel was asleep when the whole thing started because Orville gets her mostly naked and bent over the bed before Gabe shows up."

"Yeah, I'm pretty sure that's the consensus. If he'd been awake for the beginning it would never have gotten that far," Liam agreed. "Anyway, Gabriel reacts about the way you might expect a guy to react to his girlfriend getting raped."

"I don't think he meant to kill Orville," James interjected. "I just think he wanted to get the bastard off of Olivia as fast as he could. It was a reaction, not anything intentional."

I found my hand slipping to my throat. Stella hadn't refuted my father's murder charge. Sweet Fate, I hadn't thought about what it would take to provoke my polite, sensitive father into a killing rage. My stomach suddenly wasn't feeling too happy about the meal I'd just eaten.

"You mean he..." I trailed off, unable to complete the sentence.

Liam nodded slowly. "Yeah. He did. It was one movement and you can tell in the holo that he wasn't thinking. It's hard to say if he lost control or just plain forgot how strong he was. Either way, Gabriel snapped the guy's neck and threw him into the wall so hard his head split like an egg."

We were all silent, each of us lost in our own thoughts.

"What sticks with me the most," James murmured, "isn't the blood or brains. It's Gabe and Olivia's reactions. Just... the horror and shock. It's... it's probably one of the most painful things I've ever seen."

I closed my eyes and swallowed hard. "I'm pretty sure I

don't need to watch that one," I said slowly.

"Probably not," James agreed.

We were all quiet again for a long while. Finally I glanced up at the two of them. "Okay. Well that explains the whole 'murder' thing. What else do I need to know?"

Liam shrugged. "Well, there's always the White Woman controversy..."

James waved a hand. "No, no, you're skipping around. Do things in some kind of order."

"Fine," Liam replied, his mouth thin and his eyes narrow. "What would you like to discuss next, then?"

"How about you explain exactly how Gabriel went from being a suicidal drug addict to a pilot, husband, and father of three," I suggested. "Because that just doesn't square to me."

"Long story," Liam said, holding up a finger to forestall James. "That's the kind of stuff you can look up on your own. Olivia wrote some comprehensive journals on it that are pretty easy reading. They were required for second set when I was in school."

Second set was when students were about sixteen. I nodded. "Okay, so no major revelations there?"

James glared at Liam before turning more gently to me. "Actually, that's when he had to have his heart transplant. Olivia pretty much had a nervous breakdown after the rape and Gabe... well, that's when he picked up the morphine habit, which has to be some version of the same thing if you ask me.

"When the two of them finally started pulling themselves back together, the *Inspiration* stumbled into the Terrans. It was a combination of the drug use and a confrontation with some of the original Terrans that landed Gabriel in heart failure. Olivia arranged for a Terran medic to replace Gabriel's heart in exchange for being a surrogate mother. Many historians credit that first positive exchange of services as the stepping stone that brought my ancestors onto the *Inspiration*. In fact, I'm named after the so-called 'peace child,' James Andrinovich."

Another piece of the puzzle fell into place for me. I remembered Ariel putting her arm around her James' shoulders. "This is my brother from another mother," she'd said. Since she was Olivia's daughter and Olivia had been the surrogate for James, they had shared the same womb even if they didn't share DNA. 'Brother from another mother' seemed like a friendly way of putting such a complicated relationship.

I said, "So that's why Dad seemed so surprised when Eva introduced you. He knew your namesake. "

James nodded. "If you read the old *Inspiration* journals, Gabriel and Olivia were pretty much second parents to James Andrinovich. James and the eldest Usuriel children claimed each other as siblings in almost all of their journals."

"That makes sense with the history lessons Stella gave me about the *Inspiration*. I knew Olivia and Gabriel were key to the whole Terran reconciliation, I just didn't know about

James."

"Now can we talk about the White Woman?" Liam whined.

James bit his lower lip and gave our friend a glare. "Liam loves the really crazy theories. Seriously, don't scare her with your speculation. Just stick to facts for today, okay? Those are sordid enough."

"Facts," Liam expelled it like a dirty word. "Ugh, why bother talking about Gabriel Usuriel, then? I mean, Gracie's got almost all of the facts. It's the speculation she's missing out on."

"Liam," James growled.

"White Woman... I'm assuming that's Adora," I cut off the boys' bickering. "What's the controversy?"

"Well, everyone does assume it was Adora, but a body was never found, so it's impossible to prove it was her," Liam said, jumping in before James could open his mouth. His blue eyes were alight with excitement and I could tell this was something he really liked discussing. I still wasn't following his line of thought yet, but I decided to let his enthusiasm lead the way. I'd be able to fill in the gaps with Stella later anyway.

"Of course it was Adora," James grumbled. "She hasn't been seen since, and you can't tell me she's someone who would blend in with a crowd. Nor did she ever show any of Gabriel's hermit-tendencies. Which means one way or another, she's dead."

Liam rubbed his temple. "There have been sightings.

Seriously, I've met half a dozen Family members who claim they've seen her."

"But no one has gotten a good holo or even had a serious conversation with her. Come on, you know those sightings could have been Lillian or another Adoran with the same coloring," James pointed out. "And what about her parents? D'nay and Gloria won't even discuss her. They know she's dead. You can't convince me otherwise."

"Or they're trying to protect her privacy," Liam said. "They've put up with a lot from their kids over the years. It wouldn't be out of character for them to shield her."

"Adora is dead," I said flatly and I knew it was true. Metaphorical or literal, my recurring dream had always felt too real for me to ignore. Its filth wrapped insidious fingers around my shoulders just thinking of it. I shuddered.

James and Liam looked at me oddly, faces cautiously curious. "Do you know something, Gracie?" James asked.

I made a face and tried to decide what I really wanted to share. "No," I admitted, "but I have a pretty strong feeling. She's off limits for discussion at Angelus Quietum, of course. I just... just trust me. She's dead."

Liam looked rebellious but James nodded as if I'd just graced them with profound wisdom.

"I guess the one big question I really have," I said slowly, "is what happened right before I was born? I mean, how did Gabriel meet my mom? What was he doing for those sixty-odd years in Skykyle City?"

Liam's eyes widened. "Did you say he was... in Skykyle City right before you were born?"

"Well, yeah. I mean, that's where I was born and where my mom lived. Plus, Stella said he split his time between Angelus Quietum and his apartment in the city during that time period."

"I knew it!" Liam looked elated. "Proof. I knew there had to be proof he was in the city."

"Just because he was in Skykyle doesn't mean he's Sorrow," James said sternly.

"Sorrow?" I asked. It was the first time I'd ever heard the name.

"Sorrow," Liam breathed, face soft with wonder. "Oh wow... no, of course you haven't heard of... how do I explain Sorrow?"

"If I rob you of the privilege I'll never hear the end of it, so make it a simple definition. It's getting late." James yawned.

He didn't have to suggest it twice. Liam looked like a child whose birthday just came early.

"Sorrow is a rumor. A legend. A story that might have more than a grain of truth to it," Liam said, leaning in and lending his voice an air of mystery. It raised a chill down my spine and made me think of telling ghost stories with my dad by the fire.

"This is not keeping it short and sweet," James complained.

"You really take the fun out of things sometimes, you know that?" Liam shot him a sour look that made his resemblance to my father even stronger. "Fine. If you really want the truth about it, Sorrow is an urban legend. He popped into existence sometime around sixty years ago in the slums of Skykyle City."

"Not completely true. There have been figures with similar characteristics going way back into Earth cultures. The four horsemen of the Apocalypse, the grim reaper, Saint Kolbe and Jude all held some of the same symbolism," James pointed out. "Even Gabriel himself has been made into such a figure if you talk to the Divinitas. Most professors I've talked to think Sorrow is nothing more than a personalized version of the Divinitas messiah."

"Fine, but that doesn't explain all of the firsthand accounts," Liam countered. "We're not talking about one or two individuals here. We're talking about an entire community that was so convinced this guy was flesh and blood that the local dealers started carrying morphine syringes just in case people wanted to make offerings."

"Divinitas?" I said, as confused as I usually felt in conversations involving my father. "Wait, you lost me. Back up."

"Sorry," James said. "The Divinitas are a group of religious extremists who believe the Family is actually a group of divine beings who have taken mortal form in order to lead mankind in the correct direction."

"They like Gabriel especially," Liam explained. "Mostly because after Olivia died, he went on a bit of a spiritual journey, so to speak. Wandered around mapping out a lot of the continent for a while, but eventually he just sort of disappeared. Ended up in the middle of nowhere with no real interest in interacting with anyone. The Family pretty much decided he'd had some kind of break with reality and just kept an eye on him while he worked through his issues.

"The mortals who discovered him, however, decided this was some sort of guide to living a simpler life. Hell, some of them are still off in the woods, rejecting society in the name of 'communing with Cybele.' It's pretty strange."

"Just because something is different doesn't mean it's wrong," James said pointedly.

"The old man may be strong, but he's not a god any more than I am." Liam rolled his eyes.

"Who's to say you aren't?" James gave his raven-haired friend a smoldering look and I found myself blushing. I'd almost forgotten the flirtatious behavior between the two boys yesterday. It came rushing back as Liam returned the heat of James' expression.

"Perhaps in the bedroom," Liam allowed with a wink, "but that's a completely different kind of godhead."

I cleared my throat awkwardly and attempted to get the conversation back on track. "So... Sorrow is some kind of god?"

"No," James said thoughtfully, "more like a patron angel to addicts, the homeless, or pretty much anyone who has run out of hope or options. Physically, he fits Gabriel's description. Dark hair, blue eyes, scars covering his wrists and chest. Clearly he's the model for the legend, down to the drug of choice."

"So... basically there's a rumor that my dad was living in the slums of Skykyle City? Not incredibly far-fetched."

"Ah, but Sorrow is much more than a man, even one of Awareness. He is an angel of death who escorts the souls of overdosing addicts to a peaceful end. He is an avenging force on men who mistreat women of the night. He is a protective prayer in the dark to prevent bad batches of drugs or an accidental overdose." Liam's voice was almost reverent. "You should see the artwork some of the street artists have done of him in the alleys of Skykyle. They're beautiful."

"Sorrow crops up in just about every medium the poor have to express themselves. From graffiti to tattoos and dance music, he just keeps making appearances. It's gotten to the point that simply the word 'Sorrow' or a reference to blue flames implies a singer or writer is discussing drugs, especially a fatal overdose." James was a little more matter-of-fact about it, but I could tell he had some fondness for the topic.

I thought about it for a while, then nodded. "It seems like it might just have some truth to it. My mother was not... well at the end of her life. The way Dad explained it, she died of something like clinical depression. She certainly wasn't living in the best part of Skykyle when I was little, I can tell you that."

A light blue haze of power trembled around Liam's head. His eyes were positively incandescent and he was grinning like a lunatic. He didn't completely light up from the inside out the way Dad or Grandma Gloria did when they got overly excited, but it was obvious that he was having trouble containing his enthusiasm.

"I can't believe it," he breathed. "It all adds up. I knew it! I just knew he was really there! The net will light up like Landing Day when I..."

"No, it won't," James hissed, and glanced around the room sharply. We were by ourselves in this corner of the cafeteria and a friendly buzz of conversation was filling the other side of the room. It was unlikely anyone had overheard us. "The net is how things get blown out of proportion. Aren't you the one who told me the Family would be better off if no one ever posted another rumor? It's not like we have definitive proof that Gabriel did anything except father a love child nineteen years ago." James gestured at me. "And I'm pretty sure everyone already knows that."

"But..." Liam's face fell, then settled into something a bit more resigned. "Yeah. I guess you're right. Still, it's a pretty exciting thought. What was your mother's name, Gracie? Maybe I can do some research on things from her end."

"You're pretty into this Sorrow story, aren't you?" I observed with a bit of a smile. "Amaya. Amaya Blackmon. That was my mom's name."

I'd been so angry with my father when I first found out

about the drugs, but watching James and Liam get so excited about Sorrow and the other controversies was actually rather amusing. Now that I knew why Dad had been labeled a murderer, and why he'd fallen into the addiction trap in the first place, I found myself less furious. If I were him, I wouldn't have wanted to relive any of that horror if I could help it. Besides, it was all on the *Inspiration*, which landed almost three hundred years ago. It was all ancient history... except... my chest clenched.

"Wait," I said, beginning to process just what the whole Sorrow issue actually meant. "Dad was clean for—" I tried to count years and gave up "—centuries. At least. If I'm understanding the legend correctly, Sorrow demanded offerings of morphine in exchange for protection. So, if Gabriel really was Sorrow, that means he picked up drugs again a lot more recently than the *Inspiration*. Am I getting that part right? Did he have another relapse that I'm not counting? Otherwise, that seems kind of crazy. I mean, the first time he started using was prompted by the whole Orville incident. I kinda get that. But why would he just abandon Angelus Quietum after two hundred years and dive back into a morphine addiction?"

Liam's smile was smug while James looked a little sour. "White woman," Liam said. "The white woman massacre and Gabriel's second wife's death happened within a month of each other. Not long after those two events, the old man denounces the Overwatch and disappears. He was sighted a few times at Angelus Quietum, but he wasn't running the place. There were caretakers that Gloria and D'nay paid out of their own pockets over there for years. I know, because my aunt was one of them. She won't say much about it, except that Gabriel wasn't living there full time."

"His second wife... Lauria, right? That was Lillian's mother," I said, remembering the Family tree I'd managed to pull up.

"Yeah, that was pretty tragic, actually," James said with a sigh. "When they first got married, everyone thought Lauria had stopped aging for good. The two of them were billed as the ultimate happy ending. You should see the net posts from the time. They made a really beautiful couple."

"I've seen one or two of those holos," I said, thinking about it. "She had the Adoran coloring just like Lillian."

"Yeah," Liam nodded. "But as soon as she gave birth to Lillian, it became obvious the years were catching up with Lauria. She'd stayed young over fifty years, but after the birth she began aging like a mortal. I'm not sure how old she was when she died but it wasn't over two hundred. Gabriel put on a good face for it, but it had to be incredibly painful to watch. A second time, at that."

I swallowed past the lump in my throat. "Sweet Fate..." I remembered the haunted look in my father's eyes and my chest actually ached at what he'd lived through. Not one love but two that he'd watched grow old and die in his arms. The first one he'd known was coming—not that it made the reality any easier—but the second had been a cruel surprise, seemingly brought about by the birth of his own child. No wonder his relationship with Lillian was fraught, I thought.

"Come on," James said gently, breaking the silence that had settled around us as we mused on my father's misfortune. "It's late. I think the dining hall is closing up. We should get going."

I looked around and realized that the white noise of conversation had died down on the other side of the room and that people were making their ways to the exits. Even as I watched, the lights in the kitchen section dimmed.

"Okay," I said, getting up and starting to gather the debris of our meal. We were subdued as we cleaned up and started walking towards the dormitory.

"Did we answer your questions well enough?" James asked as we entered the lobby of the dorms.

"For tonight, anyway," I said with a tired smile. My head was spinning with all of the issues and implications the boys' revelations brought up. My stomach only tightened over one of them. As we climbed the stairs to the Usuriel wing where both Liam and I had our rooms, I touched James' elbow. "You don't think... I mean... I left Dad all alone at Angelus Quietum. Do you think he's... okay?"

James gave me a reassuring smile. "I'm sure he's fine. But why don't you check in with him once you get to your room? You'll feel better."

All of the anger and frustration I'd felt with my infamous parent earlier in the day flooded back and I shook my head.

"I don't know if I can be civil right now," I admitted. "And even if I don't yell at him, I'm not sure what to say. Somehow the whole 'drugs are bad' speech seems like it might be a little late."

"What would you have said if you hadn't found out about everything today?" James suggested. "He'd probably like to hear from you on your first day of classes. My parents seemed really excited when I commed them my first day."

Shit. James was right, of course. I hadn't gone a full day without talking to my father since I'd come to live with him. Undoubtedly Gabriel would expect me to check in with him at some point. I wasn't sure I could face him right now, though. Off balance and feeling trapped, I said my goodbyes to James and Liam before heading to my room.

Sure as electricity in a socket, there was a little message floating about the comm screen above my bed letting me know Angelus Quietum had attempted a connection. With a sigh, I flopped down on the mattress and instantly felt a strange crinkling under my back. Confused, I slid my fingers behind myself and found a slip of paper folded neatly in half with my name written across it. Surprise at the low-tech message was followed by a touch of fear. The room had been locked. Only a Family member could have left this note.

I flipped the paper open and read the following:

Hello Gracie,

I commed your room earlier but you weren't in. I'm sure you're out and about enjoying your new freedom, so I didn't want to tap in and disturb anything. Just wanted to let you know I was thinking of you and hoping your first day at University went well. Comm me later if you feel like it. Charcoal and I both miss you already. If I don't hear from you, I hope your first week is everything you'd hoped. Remember to work hard and be safe. I love you.

Always yours,

Dad

It was such a simple letter. It was something any parent might send their child off at school. It didn't matter. My emotions towards my father had been on an extremely rocky shuttle ride all day; one moment I felt bad for him, the next I wanted to kick in his self-absorbed teeth. Betrayal and frustration won this round and I crumpled up the note before flinging it across the room. To my credit, I resisted the urge to incinerate it on the spot.

Then, just as suddenly, my feelings on the matter shifted and I put my face in my hands. Tears stung my eyes as all the pain and tragedy my father had tried so hard to shield me from for so long crashed down on my head. I suddenly felt much older than my eighteen years, the weight of Gabriel's story slamming down on me so hard I felt I could barely draw breath.

"Sweet Fate, Dad," I whispered into the silence. "Why didn't you tell me?"

Chapter 9

Research Partners

I didn't talk to Gabriel that night.

Or the night after.

In fact, I managed to avoid talking to my father for over a month.

It wasn't completely anger or disgust that kept me away from him, though those emotions rose occasionally, especially when Professor Joan fielded some pointed questions about the White Woman massacre. Though this was the event that presumably took Adora's life, a lot of other people died in that incident as well. No one really knew if my dad had anything to do with it; in fact he didn't even come up except in passing during that class. But the dregs of my nightmare had me convinced that my father had something to do with his sister's death. Even if he wasn't responsible, he'd at least been in the room. As Professor Joan pointed out in a later lesson, when you were dealing with individuals who could appear and disappear at will, it could be very hard to prove or disprove where they were at a given time. Thus, the lack of witnesses putting him in the area didn't convince me I was wrong.

What really prevented me from comming Angelus Quietum, though, was what James had said after I'd left the library. How could I look at my father without the knowledge of his history reflecting back in my gaze? I might be impervious to his telepathy, but he knew me with the intimacy that any parent knows their child. No doubt he would read the emotions on my face and I wasn't quite sure what I wanted him to see there yet. Anger at his lack of disclosure? Empathy for the raw hand Fate had dealt him when She'd gifted him with an infinite number of years in his twenties? Sympathy for the trauma he'd suffered, or horror at his unhealthy response to it? I wasn't sure how I felt, so how was I supposed to answer him when he inevitably asked, "So what do you think of me, now?"

I had no answer.

So I let the silence grow and hoped I wasn't goading him towards another breakdown. Even if I was angry and overwhelmed, Gabriel was still my father. Underneath everything, I did love him. Each night that added to the distance between us, I worried a little more that the father I knew wouldn't be there when I got back.

School, on the other hand, was fascinating.

Malcolm continued to flirt with me in writing class and I came to look forward to his lopsided smile every other day.

We passed notes on our memory pads and giggled at random intervals that the professor mostly ignored. The second week, he found a little word game on our memory pads that allowed us to play back and forth during the monotonous lectures. Thankfully, I had been right about the difficulty level of the course and I skated by with minimal effort.

The Fine Arts Overview was oddly satisfying and I discovered that I had a knack for pottery. Drawing was difficult and tedious, but with the clay I felt utterly at peace and at home. I spent many hours in the studio allowing the work of my hands to give my overtaxed brain a much-needed rest.

Professor Joan's class not only answered questions I'd had for years, it made me ask new ones I'd never known I had. If Art class was therapy, Cybele History was pure intellectual stimulation. I reveled in the ability to ask whatever I felt like about the past and not be given the cold shoulder. Professor Joan even warmed to me. When she found out who I was, she pulled me into her office to let me know that she would be happy to discuss any of my father's backstory in private. The gesture was appreciated, but I was too in awe of Professor Joan to feel comfortable going to her alone.

James and Liam, however, were another story altogether.

When I say they were my best friends, it doesn't do our relationship justice.

That long talk in the cafeteria was only the first of many. Soon, any wild theory or issue any of us ran across was immediately taken to the other two. The research wasn't just limited to my father, though that was the topic all of us were most passionate about. Anything to do with the Family was fair game. Late nights were spent in the library watching old holos and reading journals in outdated digital formats. We stayed up late, debating the merits of one theory of events over another. Liam and James made a timeline for the Family history that we all added to as we found more interesting tidbits. What had started out as the boys "helping" me find out the truth behind my father, now became an all-out research project that both James and Liam appeared to be enjoying as much or more than I was.

Outside of our little forays into the archives, the three of us were becoming inseparable in other ways as well. Every meal that would fit our schedules was automatically reserved for each other. By the second week, we knew each other's classes well enough to know when we could walk together and for how long. Any chance we got to spend another few minutes in each other's company was thoroughly exploited.

One day, while walking to class, James mentioned that his hands were cold. Cybele's climate zones don't change much from one month to another, but we were in the midst of a pretty good storm system that had left everything chilly and damp.

"Here," Liam and I said almost simultaneously, each of us reaching for one of his hands. Suddenly, the three of us found ourselves walking hand in hand, linked by James in the middle. I caught the blond diplomat glancing at both of us, his cheeks more red than the wet wind could account for. I couldn't see Liam's expression, but in my heart I felt a strange rightness to the connection. We didn't let go until we'd made it all the way to the classroom door.

A day or two later, we were sitting in James' room, which was slightly larger than Liam's or mine, discussing our growing timeline and debating the Sorrow issue for the zillionth time. We were all attempting to occupy the double-size bed, since the only other place to sit was a tiny, rock-hard chair currently full of supplies for a presentation in James' psychology class.

"This one dates earlier by three years," Liam said, pulling up a photo of a street mural on his memory pad. The Sorrow issue was his particular whipping horse. Every time he looked something up it always came back to that. He was propped up against some pillows, his long length requiring pretty much the whole side of the bed. I was sitting next to him, my back against the wall, while James sprawled across a pile of pillows at my feet.

"Let me see," I said, leaning over to get a better view of the memory pad. By the time I was able to see the image well, I discovered that the line of my body, from my chin to my breast, was pressed against Liam's long, lean shoulder. He glanced at me from inches away with eyes so dark blue they were almost black.

For the first time, my pulse picked up in response to him. I'm not sure why I hadn't been attracted to him before; he was tall, handsome, and intelligent. Sure, he looked a bit like my father, but we were much farther away from each other than the required five generations. Up close like this, I hardly even thought of Gabriel. The angle of Liam's shoulders, the fullness of his lips, the easy arch of his brow, all of it was distinctly him, not his ancestor.

"Well, it must be pretty interesting," James chimed in, startling Liam and I out of the rapport we'd fallen into. I could feel the heat of Liam's flush as he realized he'd been looking at me so intently. Perhaps I wasn't the only one surprised by our sudden chemistry.

Before I could move away from Liam's side, James was

suddenly laying across our laps. He leaned his full length against me, the back of his head nestling in between my breasts. It forced me to lean back to support our weight. Beside me, I felt Liam adjust the angle of his torso and suddenly my own head was cradled between Liam's shoulder and chest. I swallowed hard, pinned against the two boys but not unhappy about it. I settled against Liam and James ran a hand down my leg, my fingers slipping around James' waist. Instead of shaking me off, James lifted his elbow so that I could slide my hand more comfortably around the slim plain of his midriff.

"Ummm..." Liam tilted the memory pad so that we could see it. The still was a well done rendering of a dark-haired man with large, blue wings on a brick wall. Clearly Liam had lost his train of thought. To be completely honest, so had I. The press of our bodies together was far more interesting than any part of my father's sordid past.

"Nice. What year is it?" James asked, not even breaking stride. He felt so amazing in my arms; warm and slender. I leaned my head forward so that I could smell his soft, blond hair. I didn't care what year that damn painting was.

"I... uh... it's right here," Liam said, pointing to the caption. James quickly tapped the date into the memory pad in his hands.

"I think I've had enough Sorrow for right now," I said slowly. I tightened my arm on James as he tilted his head up to catch my expression. I think he was concerned that he'd overstepped his boundaries. I gave him a sultry smile and pulled him closer, trying to convey with expression and body language that I didn't want him to move. "How about we watch something on the comm that's a little more lighthearted," I suggested.

"Or," rumbled Liam. I could feel the vibration of his words through his chest pressed to my back. It was extremely sexy. "We could take Gracie to Amourie's. It's been a while."

The look he gave James held a lot of heat. I was really hoping that whatever he was suggesting, I would be included in the sensuality of that expression.

James leaned his head back against my breast and gave me a guileless look from those pale blue eyes. "You weren't such a fan of drinking at Angelus Quietum," he said gently. "But I can promise you won't have to carry me to the bedroom if we go out tonight. If Gabriel taught me anything last year, it was to respect my own limits."

That reminded me of an issue I'd been meaning to get into with James. "Yeah, about that. You knew Dad was a recovering addict and you sat there at Angelus Quietum and let him mix you drinks. What were you thinking?"

He shrugged, slim shoulders moving against my chest in a rather provocative way. I didn't think I was going to have the energy to be really cross with James in my arms like this. Even so, this was something that had nagged at me for a while.

"What was I supposed to do, Gracie?" James asked.

"Embarrass the man in his own home? Decline his generosity? Tell his daughter on the spot the exact thing he's clearly gone out of his way to shield her from for sixteen years? Yeah... no. I'm a telepath, not a three-T. And even most of those won't risk Gabe's temper. Besides, I was a guest in his house. He didn't have to break my neck or burn me to a crisp, though he's perfectly capable of either. All he had to do was tell me to get out and call the watch if I refused to leave. Where would I have been then?"

"You didn't have to be so damn cheerful about it, then," I grumbled.

"It's cute how protective you get of Gabriel sometimes," Liam said, leaning his chin into my hair. "I almost forget you grew up with him for a second and then, bam, you bring up something like this."

"You forget Gabriel is my dad?" I said, a little startled, glancing up at our tall friend. At this angle the length of his face and neck distorted the classic Usuriel features into something softer. "How is that even possible?"

"In some ways she looks more like Gabe than you do," James pointed out, eyes sliding between the two of us as if measuring our features against his memory of my father. "Her cheekbones and eyes are practically replicas of the old man's. Your coloring is the same and the jawline is right, but the rest is more... mortal, for lack of a better word. Gracie still looks too perfect to be real."

I blushed. "I don't know about that."

"I do," Liam said gently, running a thumb down the line

of my cheek. Suddenly, the room was way too hot. "But even so, I do forget sometimes. I mean, Gabriel has been an abstraction for most of my life. Like a favorite superhero or a character in a book. I've met him a few times now, but I still don't think a piece of me really grasps him as a person. The idea that you've lived with him for over a decade and know so little about his backstory just seems so impossible."

"Well, it's my reality," I said, a little breathlessly.

"I really think this topic needs a break," James sounded a bit irritated, though I wasn't sure why. "I liked the idea of Amourie's. Let's go get a drink and forget about parents and ancestors for a while. I, for one, would like to focus on the here and now for a bit."

I glanced between the boys, then nodded. "Okay. Let's go."

Chapter 10

Amourie's

The negligible travel time was a beautiful part of being friends with a three-T. Thanks to Liam's ability to teleport his own clothes onto James' bed, the boys were quickly dressed and ready to go. I admired the way their shoulders filled out the sleek, modern cut of their shirts. Liam donned the stylish cap he'd had on my first day at school and offered me his arm. I felt tiny next to his impressive height.

"Come on, let's get you ready," he said with a smile. James' room tilted, bleeding away in dizzying colors, and then the three of us were standing in my tiny dormitory.

"I'm not sure what I might have for a nightclub," I said a little nervously, pulling open my closet.

Liam's breath caught as he inspected my wardrobe. "Wait... you shop at Vivians? Fate on a hoverboard, you have an Ambria dress?! Those shoes cost more than my mom's hover car! Why don't you wear these things?"

"I haven't had much of an occasion..." I protested, spreading my hands.

"You don't need an occasion to wear Ambria!" Liam pulled the little red dress off of its hanger and pressed it firmly into my arms. "And Morial heels! For the love of... Well, what are you waiting for? Put them on!"

"Ummm... you're staring at me..." I fingered the silky edge of the dress' sleeve.

"Oh, right." Liam had the delicacy to flush a bit. He nudged James and the two of them turned their backs so that I could change.

"Okay," I said, once I'd climbed into the dress's clinging fabric. "Though, it would be nice if one of you could help me with the buttons in the back. They're kind of hard to reach."

James obliged, then stepped back so that he and Liam could admire me. Liam let out a low whistle, his eyes sliding down my slim figure to the long length of leg that the short skirt and three inch heels accentuated.

"Oh, Gracie," James breathed.

"Perfection indeed," Liam agreed. "I had no idea you had such good fashion sense."

"Grandma Gloria picked it." I looked down in an attempt to hide the fact that my face now matched my hair and dress.

"Right." Liam sounded as if he was in awe. "You only have the oldest and richest grandmother on the planet taking you clothes shopping. Sweet Fate, it must be nice to be an elder child."

"Elder child?" I asked, cocking an eyebrow at him.

"That's what most of the Family calls the first few

generations, like up to five. Almost all of you are three-T's and a few, like Gabe, Adora, Lillian, and Vanessa, don't age. Plus you guys get an extra share of the Family trust. Money, looks, and talent. You really do get the best of everything."

"I didn't ask to be born to Gabriel." I tempered my irritated tone with a modest shrug. I'd known most of what Liam explained about elder children. I'd just forgotten the nickname. "In fact, at points it's been kind of a pain."

"He's not the easiest to live with," James agreed with an elbow for Liam's ribs.

"Yeah... I guess." Liam still sounded a bit jealous.

"I'm an elder child, huh?" I said slowly, moving slightly so that the boys didn't block my view of the mirror. I found myself staring in a little bit of wonder at my own reflection. James hadn't been lying. The Usuriel features that were so common around the University in their softened, mortal form were much sharper in my face. After a month surrounded by mortals or the lower generations, I found my own reflection strangely flawless. Freckles scattered across my cheeks and collarbone, but otherwise my skin was a creamy, smooth ivory. My eyes were pits of deep sapphire flame while my red curls shone copper in the lamplight. My torso was pleasantly compact with a gentle swell at breast and hip that made the red dress' silky material pull tight. I wasn't an adolescent anymore, I decided. I was a young woman, and it showed.

"Do you think I should put on some lipstick?" I asked the

boys, tilting a hip and cocking my head flirtatiously at them.

James needed some telekinesis to pull his jaw off the floor. "No," he said, finally getting his voice back under control. "Sweet Fate, you're going to give Amourie a run for her money tonight. If you put on makeup, we'll be fighting off everyone in the place."

***

Everything started out perfectly.

Liam teleported us as smoothly as he could (which wasn't very) out to the forested lane that Amourie's inhabited.

"Wow," I breathed as the humid evening air wrapped its tendrils about me. "I thought all the Cambria were gone."

"There are a few left on the continent," James said, a smile on his face at my reaction.

"Can you imagine what this place looked like before the terraforming?" Liam gestured to the towering form of Amourie's renovated fungal structure. "Mushrooms the size of buildings as far as the eye could see."

"It's too bad they aren't edible," James said, a bit of sadness in his voice. "Or combustible. Or really, anything except poisonous."

"The Cambria aren't poisonous. That's the Death's Head," I protested, craning my neck up at Amourie's huge domed roof. The organic structure of the gigantic fungal bloom appeared perfectly preserved by a polymer coating. Hooks had been embedded in the ground and in rows up the mushroom's curving top to support long lines of tiny yellow lights. It made the creamy reddish-tan of the fungus seem warm and inviting despite its massive size.

"Yeah, well, it still makes me nervous." James shivered.

"There hasn't been a fatality from Death's Head spores on the continent in ages," Liam reassured him. We were approaching the door now. Out in the dark, hover cars lurked under the trees like quiescent beasts. People gathered around the base of the three-story mushroom, clustering in groups of two and three, laughing and drinking from glass bottles.

"Oh my!" A voice by the door drew my attention. There, below a dark wooden sign that read "Amourie's" stood a woman whose beauty took my breath away.

I'm familiar with Usuriel good looks. I grew up with Gabriel himself, after all. Amourie gave him some true competition for the most handsome version of Family features I'd ever seen. The only person who might possibly compare was Grandma Gloria, but she was too nurturing and motherly to seem so seductive.

Amourie screamed sex.

Everything about her, from her fall of burnished copper hair to the ample curves that stretched the fabric of her velvet dress nearly to the ripping point, seemed made for the art of seduction. She had a waist that Liam could have put a single hand around despite having a bosom that made mine look quite adolescent indeed. Her eyes were so dark they were nearly black and her creamy skin had none of my unfortunate freckles. Bright red lips glistened with just the right amount of moisture and parted slightly as if she were inviting a kiss. I'd always preferred men and never had much of a question about my own sexuality, but Amourie made things low in my body tighten as if her sensuality were contagious. The thought that James had actually compared me to this sex goddess seemed ludicrous.

"Well now, little sister." Her smokey voice glided down my skin. "I don't believe we've met."

"Amourie, this is Gracie." Liam offered her a courtly bow. In any other situation it would have held a touch of irony, but before this queen of the night it felt completely appropriate. "She's Gabriel's youngest child."

Amourie's slim eyebrow raised a touch. "Gabriel's? But I can't hear her." She offered me a dainty hand, her fingers so perfectly arched I hesitated to touch them for fear of shattering her into shards of porcelain.

"I'm sorry." I gently brushed her fingertips with mine. "I'm afraid I'm past head blind. Dad calls me head mute."

"Indeed," she agreed.

"Gracie's a pyrokinetic and she just started at the University," James explained. "You look lovely tonight, Amourie."

The flower of Usuriel beauty gave my blond diplomat a half-lidded smile of approval, as if she found his compliment to be just the right amount of flattery. "Thank you, James," she purred. "I hope you will save me a dance later." Then she turned back to me and ran an appraising eye over my figure. Heat followed her gaze until my face felt aflame. "Welcome, then, Aunt Gracie. Have a drink on me." With a gesture, she pulled a small token from the air on her left and handed it to me.

I was unsure what to say to that, since technically she was probably right about our relationship. I usually called Liam my cousin but in truth he was a super-great nephew of some sort. If Amourie was a Gabriellan, I was indeed her aunt of one variety or another. With an awkward smile, I accepted the token and followed Liam through the heavy wooden doors that led into the stem of the great mushroom.

Music washed over me in the soft yellow light of a gently curved room. The sound shimmered and thudded through the oddly textured floor of the fungus, creating the illusion that I was inside a living organism with its own rhythmic pulse. The floor tilted upwards on the left and disappeared like a curving ramp into the space above us. Small groups of scantily clad people lounged on cushions or couches as they talked and sipped brilliantly colored liquids from sparkling glasses. To my right, a small alcove held a counter with a young, blond gentleman. He wore a simple black dress shirt and had a pleasant smile on his face. Next to him was a door labeled "elevator."

"Come on," Liam said impatiently, grabbing my hand as I moved to follow James to the left. "I don't feel like tripping over people all the way up. The elevator's faster."

James rolled his eyes. "You teleporters and your impatience. Why don't you just pop us upstairs then, if you're in such a hurry to be at the bar?"

Liam scowled. "Fine, I will."

Before I could protest, the world spun and bled as my equilibrium wrenched disorientingly to the side. When things solidified around me again, I found myself clinging to Liam's arm.

"Honestly, you have got to stop that," I gasped, nearly falling in the ridiculous heels. They looked good, but they were not made for stability. "Or at least give me some warning."

My protests were drowned out, however, by the exponentially louder music; we were in a much larger space than the entryway. From the shape of the room, I suspected we were now in the large bell of the mushroom. Lights had been strung on the inside of the curved roof as well, and they lit everything in a soft, sparkling light. Somewhere across the crowd, another set of lights flickered over the densely packed dance floor. It made the figures moving to the beat blend into one undulating entity.

Off to the left was a counter with clusters of people grouped near it. The men wore the same style of angular, fitted garments as James and Liam. The women lounged in dresses or shorts that made mine look positively modest. I stood a little straighter and adjusted the hem of my dress so that it showed off my thighs to their best advantage.

"Come on, I'm too sober to enjoy this properly," Liam

complained. Or at least, that's what I got out of his mouth movements. I really couldn't hear much above the brassy beat of the music. I could feel the percussion all the way into my bones.

The three of us made our way through a littering of mostly empty little tables to the press of the crowd around the bar. I'd seen the gleaming wood and empty stools of upscale bars in the expensive restaurants of Skykyle City, but I'd never experienced a setting like this. Even though there weren't many drinking laws in the Provinces, it was generally frowned upon for nightclubs to serve secondary school-age minors. Not that my father would have ever allowed me to set foot in a club like this, regardless.

Liam apparently knew how to put his height to good use. He stood nearly a head taller than anyone else at the bar and he quickly got the attention of an attendant. He held up three fingers and I realized belatedly that I hadn't expressed my disinterest in actually consuming alcohol.

Glancing around the room, I decided that sipping a drink might make me blend in a bit better. I wasn't the only Usuriel in the room, but I was by far the highest generation if the mortality of features was any judge and I was beginning to draw some stares. Besides, I reflected as I handed Liam my free drink chit and received a bright red glass with a strawberry wedged onto its edge, my metabolism was fast enough that I probably wouldn't even feel one drink no matter how strong it was.

"What is that?" I asked Liam as he handed James a neon green substance in a tall, thin glass. His own drink was a pale blue liquid over ice, much the way my father preferred his cocktails.

"Something to get us in the mood," he said with a wink, then led us back to one of the small tables where we sat and tasted the colorful offerings.

To my surprise, my own concoction was pleasantly fruity. In fact, I could barely detect the burn of liquor at the back of its sugary taste. James seemed equally pleased with his own selection, downing it in a few long swallows. Liam offered me a taste from his, but just the smell of it warned me that it was more like paint thinner than anything I wanted to put in my mouth. I shook my head and kept sipping at my own drink while I watched the crowd with wide eyes.

I'd rarely seen so many people in such a small space. It reminded me a bit of the flood at the University, though the atmosphere was completely different. Here, the curved walls and intense music amplified the crowd's energy into something alive that rolled down my skin. The music transitioned into something less electronic and a sultry voice purred over top of the crowd's sudden cheers. The pressure building in the room took on the familiar weight of psi power.

"Fates, she's good." James' eyes rolled shut as he set his empty glass on the table. His shoulder leaned into my back and I felt the long line of his torso against my side. I wondered if it was the alcohol or Amourie's seductive mind that was loosening his inhibitions. Then his hand pressed to the back of my waist and I decided I didn't care.

"Come on," Liam said, blue eyes dark with desire as he wrapped his arm around the other side of my waist. Suddenly, both boys were moving towards the dance floor and I was swept up between them, fairly floating as they all but carried me into the enthusiastic crowd. Since I got to be pressed between the warm planes of their bodies, I didn't mind in the least. I gave a delighted laugh as we plunged into the gyrating sea of humanity.

Dancing with James and Liam was like flying a shuttle or riding Charcoal at full tilt across a field. I was alive and aware of every movement, like I was overflowing with the kindling essence that drives us to wake each morning.

Unlike my experience on the *Inspiration* with Ariel, I didn't feel awkward or separate from the crowd. My mind might not have been clouded by the spell Amourie was weaving with her song, but I was a hormone-fueled teenager and as capable of being caught up in the moment as any mortal before me. I pressed myself to the sweaty, muscular breadth of James' chest and felt Liam wrap a long arm around both of us as he leaned in from behind.

Now that I was on the dance floor, I could see several platforms carved into the walls nearby. The largest was set up as a stage with massive speakers and several microphones for performers who might not have an implant to sync with the sound system. Amourie didn't have such a problem, her voice clear through the speakers even though her hands were completely free. She dominated the stage, her sensual body dancing in ways that made the crowd writhe with desire.

The other, smaller platforms showed off a few men and women from the crowd taking turns in the spotlight. One man, his face plain and extremely mortal but his body taut and well-muscled, spun and leaped about so effortlessly a skilled telekinetic would have been hard-pressed to keep up. Despite his average looks, he didn't have any trouble finding dance partners after his performance.

James' hands straying down my sides drew me back to him and I sank once again into the heat of our dance. This was nothing like the dancing we'd done with the Family after the flood. This was raw sex and motion, as if our bodies couldn't press close enough together as we responded to the beat of the bass.

Twice other men tried to cut in on us. I hardly saw their faces before James or Liam shifted their weight to make it clear that they were not going to share me. Since Liam was likely the strongest telekinetic in the room, not to mention a solid two meters, no one pushed the issue. I had already decided that this night most likely would end up in James' room in a tangle of limbs and naked bodies. I was more than okay with that. I gave both boys every indication I could without words that I would take them both to bed and be perfectly content in the morning.

How long we were on the floor, I'm not sure. Long

enough for my muscles—a month away from my usual rides and training on the farm—to complain. In the end, it was my bladder that let me know I couldn't keep this up without a break.

Finally, Amourie quit the stage for a song and I took the excuse to move towards the bathroom. James and Liam seemed happy enough to go in search of another drink. James offered to buy me another as well, but I shook my head with a smile and pointed in the direction of the restrooms. He nodded and followed Liam to the bar.

The bathroom was oddly quiet, the music muffled to a dull roar. My dress and heels felt awkward without the boys to steady me, but I managed everything without too much trouble. Leaning against the counter by the sink, I stared at the disarray my hair had managed to tangle itself into with dismay. I tried combing through it with my fingers and sighed as it stubbornly refused to be anything less than wild. At least I hadn't put on any makeup. There were beads of sweat trailing down my neck and kohl or tint would have run. Splashing cool water on my face, I left in search of James and Liam.

Amourie was back on stage when I got out of the bathroom. I glanced around for Liam's tall figure but didn't see him on the dance floor or at the bar. James was too close in height to the rest of the crowd to pick him out, so I started working my way between the bar crowd and the dancers to check on the table area.

I was just starting to get nervous when I caught sight of them against the farthest back wall. Liam's back was to the room and James was all the way against the wall, looking up at our tall friend. I started walking towards them. As I got closer, I realized their body language was quite intimate. I was still ten feet away when Liam leaned in and covered James' full lips with his own.

I'd been all over the two of them all night, but I hadn't kissed James since he left Angelus Quietum. Awkwardness pushed against my chest, forcing me to pause. I thought I was participating in their relationship, but now I suddenly felt like an intruder. An ember of anger kindled. Was I just a quick distraction for them? A plaything that they could parade about for a night and then toss aside? I had only arrived in their relationship a month ago. Was I just something new to spice up their sex life for a while? I stood alone in the middle of the sparsely populated tables, staring at Liam and James as their kiss turned into something quite involved.

"Hello, beautiful." Malcolm's voice at my elbow startled me. Two drinks balanced in one of his long-fingered hands as he gave me a charming, lopsided smile. "I appear to have ordered too many drinks. Care to help me dispose of one?"

Another glance at Liam and James told me they weren't coming up for air any time soon. Hurt and excluded, I shrugged.

"Why not?"

I accepted the small glass of honey-colored liquid. It

burned as badly as I feared, but for once I didn't mind the sting. It matched my mood somehow. Perhaps this was why my father liked it so much. I killed the whole thing in one long swallow.

"So, do those two have a monopoly on you or are you free to dance with someone else?" Malcolm asked me, his head tilting to one side and tumbling an auburn wave into his dark eyes.

James and Liam had found a pile of cushions off to one side and were continuing their enthusiastic exploration of each other. I decided it was only fair if I found something else to amuse myself.

"Buy me one more drink and I'm all yours," I said. Malcolm smiled and headed towards the bar.

***

The rest of my time on the dance floor gets a little blurry. I'd never drunk to excess before but it was much easier to ignore James and Liam in the corner with a glass in my hand. Malcolm was an enjoyable dance partner even if he wasn't the one I'd originally wanted. I'd found him attractive from the first time I met him and during writing class he'd proven himself quite an intelligent and witty friend. He seemed to sense my mood and kept buying me drinks until it was genuinely difficult for me to stand in those damn heels. When he offered to drive me back to his place, I agreed and then spent what felt like an eternity trying to pick our way down the spiraled ramp from the dome of the mushroom.

By the time we finally got outside, my Usuriel metabolism and the cool night air roused me sufficiently to feel halfway steady as we walked towards his hover car.

"Gracie!" James sounded concerned as he came trotting up to us. "I've been looking everywhere for you! Are you okay?"

I leaned a little more deliberately into Malcolm's arm. "I found someone who is actually interested in me, so yeah. I'm fine."

"What are you talking about? You never came back from the bathroom. We were worried about you." James's brow was drawn in confusion, but I wasn't buying the innocent act.

"Good for you, you finally noticed," I snapped. "I was only dancing a few feet away for over an hour." I was already feeling more sober than I wanted to be for this conversation. In fact, I didn't want to have this conversation at all. "Go tell Liam I'm fine. I'll get a ride back to the dorm from Malcolm. I can't stand teleporting with him anyway."

The hurt in James' face momentarily made me question my assumptions. Then Malcolm tugged on my arm and it was follow him or fall in those stupid heels.

"You had your chance, Terran," Malcolm said with a wry twist of his expressive mouth. "I'd say the lady has made up her mind."

James narrowed his eyes at Malcolm before looking at me. "Is this what you really want?"

No. It wasn't. But my wounded pride wouldn't let the words past my lips. I nodded. Fates, if there's a hell, adolescence has to be one of the circles. I still remember how James' head bowed as Malcolm and I walked away.

"Don't let them bother you, gorgeous." Malcolm opened the door to his hover car and let me slide into the passenger seat. "Every other man in that club would have given his left arm to walk away with you. They were dumb enough to wander away. They don't deserve your attention. Me, on the other hand, I'd never leave you waiting like that. But their loss is my gain. I'm the luckiest guy on Cybele tonight."

His chatter was flattering and I gave him a smile as I settled back into the seat. The automatic straps wrapped themselves around my torso and hugged me tightly as Malcolm placed his palm on the ignition. The hover car buzzed smoothly upwards and with the push of a few buttons, Malcolm was quickly back to giving me his undivided attention.

"How far away do you live?" I asked. Out the window, the dark trees fell away below us.

"Between here and University. It's not much, but it's cheaper than the dorms," he said with a shrug. "And it keeps a roof over my head so I won't complain. I hope you won't mind the mess. I don't have much time to clean with classes and working at the yard."

"The yard?" I echoed, arching a brow at him.

"Lumber products of all kinds. We split, haul, sand, and cure. I used to take and schedule orders, but that didn't pay much. Now that I'm mostly through University, I'm starting to apprentice on machine maintenance. Hopefully I'll be full time by graduation."

I hadn't realized Malcolm was older than me, but I'd been around Usuriels so long that it probably threw off my ability to gauge age accurately. Anyone under one hundred seemed young in comparison.

"So that's what you want to do?" I said. "After University, I mean. You're going to work on lumber machines?"

"Want to do?" Malcolm gave me a sidelong look. "I mean... I guess. It makes good money."

"I haven't figured out what I want to do," I said, looking out the window again.

"You? You could do anything," he said, reaching out a finger to touch the end of a curl where it had come to rest on the seat between us. "What's your Awareness? I mean, even if you're not strong there's always demand for T-gates."

I stared at him a moment, a bit shocked that we'd managed to know each other for over a month and he didn't know who or what I really was. Truthfully, though, our interactions had been pretty surface level. It didn't take a lot of depth to play word games back and forth on a memory pad in writing class.

"I'm strong," I admitted slowly. "Just not in a particularly useful way. I'm a pyrokinetic."

"A pyro..." His eyebrows rose quite rapidly and I watched him think that word all the way through. "A firebird? Whoa. I've never heard of a firebird in the later generations before. I thought all of them kind of popped up in the seven to ten gen range. That's what the professor in Awareness Theory said anyway..." He trailed off for a moment then gave me a sharper look. "Unless you're older than I think you are..."

I laughed at the expression of consternation on his face. "Don't worry, I'm eighteen," I reassured him. "But I am an older generation. I'm Gabriel's daughter."

"Gabriel... like... *the* Gabriel?" His eyes were the size of dinner plates. "Like... morphine and Overwatch Gabriel? Seriously?"

I should have seen it coming, but it still hit a nerve that this was his first response to my father. I slouched lower in the seat. "Yep. He's the only living parent I have."

"Oh." I could hear Malcolm reevaluate his reaction in that simple statement. To his credit, he had the grace to flush. "Sorry. Did you... get to know him? I mean..."

"He raised me pretty much by himself, actually," I said and I could hear the ice in my tone.

"Wow. That had to be... different. Your grandmother didn't want to take you?"

That comment struck me as incredibly irrelevant. I was beginning to have second thoughts about this tryst.

"Actually, he was a really good dad," I said and the instant it came out of my mouth I knew it was true. For all his flaws and poor judgment, my father had been a stable and loving parent when I so desperately needed one. Strange to say it took a conversation with a random mortal to make me realize it, but the pettiness of my avoidance suddenly struck me full in the face. "He *is* a really good dad," I corrected myself as the hover car landed. And I've been a really shitty daughter lately, I finished in my own head. Mentally, I promised myself I would call Gabriel first thing in the morning.

We arrived on the outskirts of Landing and settled into the parking lot of a ramshackle boarding house. He ushered me into a tiny, cluttered little apartment and offered me a drink. It was a cheap, watered down version of what we'd been sipping at the club and I didn't even finish the first glass he offered me.

"Do you want to sit down?" he asked, leaning against a large, very worn couch. I took a seat and Malcolm sank next to me, pouring himself another glass of liquor. He took a sip, then turned to me. "You look seriously out of place here," he said after studying me carefully for a few moments.

I glanced around at the untidy clutter of the tiny living room and shrugged. "What is that supposed to mean?"

"It means you're from a different world," he said slowly. "A world where your biggest problem is what dress to wear, not where your next meal is coming from."

I thought about that as Malcolm set down his glass. He eyed me slowly and reached out a hand to touch my hair again. He seemed to like the silky texture of my curls.

"If I kiss you, am I going to have your father tearing up my house tomorrow?"

"I doubt it," I reassured him with a smile. "He has no way of knowing anyway. He's telepathic, not omniscient. Unless you plan to hang out with him any time soon, I don't see how he'd find out."

"He can't, you know, track you or something? I mean, if I had a daughter like you, I would."

I laughed and shook my head. "I'm head mute. He can't hear me when I'm right beside him, let alone fifty miles away. And last I checked, unauthorized tapping of implants was illegal."

Malcolm tilted his head at that, then leaned an arm around the back of my seat. He was long and lithe and smelled like the incense and sweat of Amourie's club. I looked up into his lopsided mortal face and decided his full lips looked just right for kissing. Then he leaned in and I discovered that they were just as soft and warm as I'd hoped.

We spent a little while on the couch. Then he suggested his bedroom and I found myself awkwardly asking for help out of the little red dress. I remember leaning over his unmade bed while his clumsy, half-drunk fingers fumbled with the buttons. This was not how I'd envisioned my first time taking a lover.

Malcolm was gentle, however, and considerate. He covered every spare centimeter of my skin with kisses and light touches. When he offered to please me orally, I balked and said I'd rather just skip to the main event. It was an inexperienced mistake and he tried to coax me into it, but in the end he let me have my way.

We paused to find him some protection and that was as gloriously awkward as only discussing pregnancy with a casual sex partner can be.

By the time we actually managed to get into position and start moving, the whole situation had become more business than romance. Aroused as I was, I experienced no climax and in fact the whole deed was rather uncomfortable on my end. Not that there wasn't anything pleasant about it. I enjoyed the intimacy of being held and feeling his body move against mine. Watching his expression of raw desire turn to one of intense pleasure was actually quite satisfying in its own way. But as for physical enjoyment, there were only a few brief moments where his movement happened to strike the right angle. I was too inexperienced to direct him effectively and when it was over, I found myself both unsatisfied and sore.

"The Divinitas are right," Malcolm said afterwards as we lay together in his tangled sheets. "You are a goddess."

I smiled and mussed his hair. I enjoyed its soft strands against my bare breast. His kisses had been the best part. Sex itself was overrated.

Chapter 11

Parasites

We fell asleep in Malcolm's bed, curled up with his naked body pressed against my back. This was also better than the sex and I was content in Malcolm's arms.

The next morning, the two of us showered and had some warm rice at the tiny, cluttered table in his living room. I only had my dress to put back on, but I didn't have to go to class for another couple of hours so Malcolm offered to drop me off at my room to change.

We chatted about class and Amourie's club as we wound through the low-income side of Landing. It wasn't a long drive and honestly, it wasn't even that awkward. I liked Malcolm, but I wasn't sure I wanted him to be my boyfriend. I did, however, feel a bit of accomplishment. One life experience to check off the list.

We were just about to hit the higher rent district near the University when a pillar of smoke appeared on our left. A bonfire perhaps? No, the houses were too close together to allow for such a thing in this neighborhood.

"Whoa, that's a lot of smoke." Malcolm leaned as far as the safety straps would allow to crane his neck out the window. "Do you think we should stop?"

I tapped my implant for the time. "Won't the watch take care of it?"

Just then, the hover car made a turn and we could actually feel the heat of the blaze inside the car.

The involved structure was a tiny, dilapidated two story house with peeling paint and an overgrown yard. Across its sagging white fence, someone had scrawled a message in black paint.

"Burn, Parasites, Burn," I read aloud as Malcolm parked the hover car nearby. "Someone did this on purpose?"

"I know one of the girls who lives next door," he said, pointing to a young woman our age standing in her front yard watching the flames. "Come on, let's ask if she saw what happened."

With a glance down at my dress from the night before, I grimaced and stepped out of the car. The pain when I tried to stand in the heels again made me curse. Sex was not worth the discomfort. If Liam liked these shoes so much he could have them.

"Is everyone out of the building?" I called to the young woman. She glanced over at us, her expression glassy. I wondered if she'd been woken by the fire.

"You all right, Lauren?" Malcolm called to her. She blinked at him dazedly as he wrapped an arm around her shoulder. "Did you see what happened?"

"I think they're still in there." There was very little

emotion to her voice and her eyes looked strangely flat. "I heard breaking glass but there was no one here when I came outside."

"Wouldn't the owners be at school or work?" I asked, glancing at the angle of the sun. Most people were up and moving by now.

She shook her head. "The mortal family is gone but they've got two vamp servants who live in the basement. They can't come out 'till it's dark."

Suddenly the message on the fence became a lot clearer. "Sweet Fate," I breathed. Another column of smoke spiraled upwards. "Where's the watch?"

Lauren shrugged. "It's not threatening any other buildings. The watch probably set it. They'll make sure no one gets here until the problem is taken care of."

I stared at her in wide-eyed amazement. She'd just accused the local police of committing arson and murder. Not only that, but we were in Landing. According to Stella, Landing and the University were considered the most friendly towards individuals of Awareness. The idea that a couple of vampires could be so coldly disposed of by the Landing watch made my stomach twist.

I turned to Malcolm, expecting to see my shock and horror reflected in his face, but he was nodding along with Lauren's statement. In fact, there was a grim satisfaction in the set of his mouth. "Probably better that way. Poor devils."

"How can you say that?" I asked, looking back and forth between the two of them. "We're not talking about a couple of dogs, we're talking about two people." Malcolm's face betrayed his doubts about my statement and I felt like I'd been punched in the gut. "Seriously? If you have this kind of problem with people of Awareness, why did you just sleep with one?"

He blanched at that and let his arm fall from around Lauren's shoulders to take a step towards me. "Usuriels are different. You're not like them." He gestured towards the burning building. "You don't feed on people."

My flames kindled in my chest as pure, righteous anger flooded me with adrenaline. Behind me, I felt the fire burning in the house leap in response.

Just like that, I knew.

How could I not have understood sooner? The fire in my chest wasn't the only fire I could control; the fire in that house was just as much mine. I wasn't some tenth-gen who needed a spark to start her flame, I was a third-gen whose entire gift was concentrated in this one element. All fire was my fire.

"You're talking about my grandfather," I growled at Malcolm. My eyes didn't leave his while my mind steadily assessed the extent and strength of the house fire. To my surprise, there wasn't much accelerant in the home. I'd produced more dangerous fires at Angelus Quietum.

Malcolm finally realized he was about to seriously alienate me because he put his hands up. "D'nay is different. He's not like them. I mean, I've seen him shopping at the market in full daylight."

"That's because his 'mortal'—" I put that word in air quotations "—partner is my grandmother and her blood has the delightful side effect of making him more socially acceptable to people like you." Venom dripped from my voice and I'm pretty sure a few licks of flame were dancing around my shoulders. Either way, Malcolm's face went extremely pale. "Now, excuse me while I go try to fix the damage bigotry like yours has caused."

With that I turned sharply and marched towards the house. He called my name, but I ignored him. Instead, I finished reaching my mental hand around all that fire and pulled it down, deep, into the waiting core of flame that always rested within me. It opened up and accepted the addition smoothly and without protest, sucking all of that heat down to the last ember. There was an abrupt hiss and a series of creaking pops as the change in temperature affected the wooden structure. By the time I'd climbed the steps and reached the front door, it was no longer hot to the touch. I tried the handle. It was locked. The wood surrounding the frame fell apart in charred chunks, however, and it didn't take a lot of strength for me to knock it in.

"What are you doing?" Malcolm and his little friend had trailed after me, their mouths both hanging open like they didn't know what to make of me. With so many Usuriels in the area, I had a hard time believing this was the first time they'd witnessed psi powers. Rather, I thought their incredulous expressions were the result of realizing I actually cared what happened to the two helpless vampires in the basement. The fact that I'd just slept with Malcolm made my skin crawl.

"*We* are going to make sure that those two vampires are okay."

Malcolm looked at me like I had lost my mind. However, my father hadn't just given me my good looks. Apparently I'd inherited a little bit of the Usuriel temper as well, because it rose up like a living thing in my chest. "Sweet Fate, no wonder you were such a dreadful lay," I hissed at Malcolm. "Get your skinny, bigoted ass up here and help me check on these two innocent victims." When he continued to hesitate, some of the extra flames I'd just swallowed surged upwards to wreathe my hair in a mild orange explosion. "Now!"

I didn't have to ask again.

The house was full of smoke, but thanks to Malcolm's hesitation the main entryway had cleared a bit by the time we walked in. The whole place reeked of burned insulation and melted electronics. Since I no longer trusted him to have my back, I sent Malcolm down the basement stairs first.

The door to the basement was still warm which meant the fire had to have been pretty damn hot in that area of the house. "Watch your step," I told him as he started down the stairs. I lit a small ball of flame in one hand and held it aloft to give us some light since clearly the electricity wasn't going to work.

To my surprise, none of the basement steps gave way and

soon we were in a dark sitting room with two twin beds pushed against the far wall. The fire hadn't done much damage down here. In fact, the only sign that there had been a fire was a few blackened beams in the ceiling.

"Well," I demanded of Malcolm as he stood at the foot of the stairs. "Are you going to check on them?"

His pale face peered up at me, flickering in the firelight, and I realized he was terrified. I glanced around the plush living space with a nice, rich pile carpet, a comm screen the size of the one at my dad's, and several large, comfortable looking armchairs. It smelled like smoke right now, but it certainly wasn't what I would call scary. The two figures on the beds were pale and oddly still, but aside from that they could have been asleep. I curled my lip at him.

"Honestly, it's not even noon. If they didn't wake up and try to save themselves, they obviously aren't old enough to wake before sundown. They're completely helpless right now."

"Fine. Then you go check on them."

"I will," I said and strode purposefully across the room.

I'd never met a vampire besides my grandfather and, as Malcolm had so tactlessly pointed out, he didn't usually fit the textfile description. However, Stella had educated me enough to know that these two were quite harmless. Indeed, they didn't stir at all as I approached them.

They were a man and a woman, both of them in their late twenties or early thirties when they died. They were dressed in simple, comfortable clothes and curled in very natural sleeping positions. Their skin was cool to the touch when I brushed their hands, and unlike a sleeping figure they didn't breathe or stir in the least. They were truly dead until the sun set and their curse reanimated them.

Once I was satisfied that the two of them hadn't taken any harm from the fire, I checked the ceiling and made sure none of the damage was about to collapse or shift in a way that would expose them to sunlight. It seemed that I caught the blaze before it got a true hold on the support beams. After perhaps ten minutes of inspection I felt satisfied that the vampires were safe at least until nightfall.

"Can we go now?" Malcolm whined. He hadn't moved from the foot of the stairs since we arrived and had been watching me with wide, dark eyes.

"Yes," I said slowly. "Can you ask Lauren to call the homeowners? I imagine they'll want to come and make sure their family members are okay."

"Family members," he echoed as if he couldn't believe what he was hearing.

"Yes, family members. I don't think you have sex with the people who just work for you. And blood exchange is too sensual to call it anything else. Just because it's different doesn't make it wrong."

Malcolm did us both a favor and didn't say anything as we walked upstairs. He did offer to give me a ride the rest of the way home but I declined. I didn't trust myself not to say nor do something I would regret if he kept showing what a closed mind he had.

And that is how I ended up walking onto campus in a soot stained Ambria dress, barefoot and carrying a pair of Morial heels. My hair was wild and black smudges marked my face and hands. Quite a few people jumped out of the way when they saw me coming. I was too tired and pissed to care. For the first time I understood why my father decided to hide in Angelus Quietum all these years. Perhaps, I thought, keeping me away from idiots like Malcolm hadn't been the worst parenting decision my father ever made.

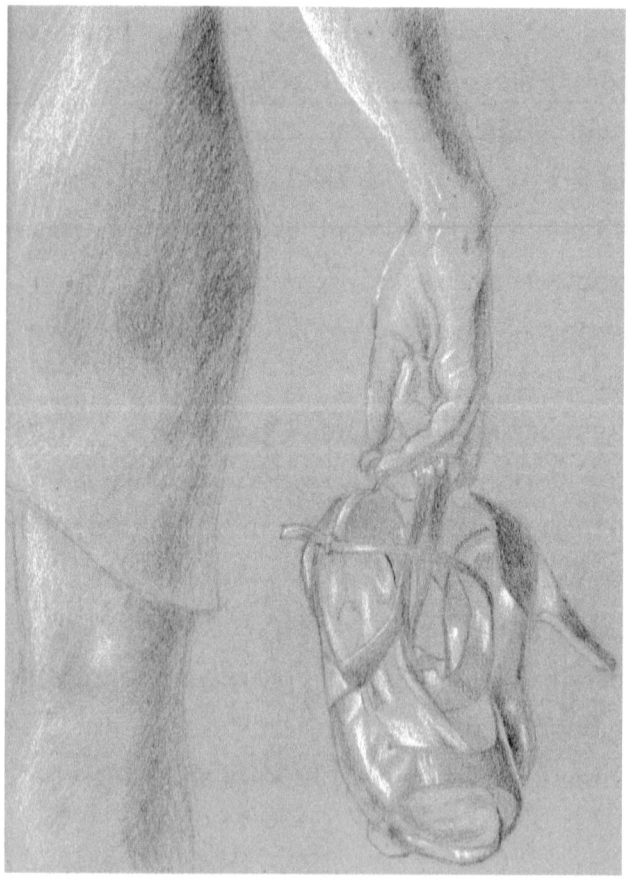

***

A message sat waiting for me on my bed. Dad had been sending about one a week despite my lack of reply. With a sigh I changed out of my dress and took my second shower of the morning. After pulling on something more comfortable for class, I picked up the note. It read:

Hello Gracie,

I talked with your grandmother today. She says things are going well for you at school. I'm glad University is working out for you.

Charcoal has been doing well, though I can still tell he misses you. I can't ride him as much as you used to, so he's been getting into nipping fights with Aubrie again. I know he'd appreciate it if you came to visit on one of the days you have off. I can make myself scarce if that would help. Just let me know.

Love always,

Dad

I folded the note more gently this time. He was starting to give up on me. I could hear it in the tone of his written voice. Well, I couldn't blame him. After Lillian's rejection, he had to assume the worst from my silence.

I stepped to the mirror and ran my fingers through my hair. My eyes looked a little wild, too, but for the first time in a while I didn't resent the fact that I'd picked up my father's mannerisms.

"Well, Dad, I think I owe you a call." Last night felt like a lifetime ago, but I'd promised myself I would comm him today. My earlier temper burned off the majority of my nerves and, if Malcolm was any indication, I had a bit more empathy for what my father had been dealing with for four hundred years.

I looked up at the comm screen. I was grown enough to have a one night stand, which meant I was adult enough to deal with Gabriel. I couldn't avoid him forever and, if I was learning anything here at University, it was that Cybele society was not going to let me forget who my father was.

I settled myself onto the bed and tapped my implant. "Sync with comm system Gracie One," I instructed the implanted microchip. Instantly, the comm screen above my bed lit up.

"Hello, Gracie," Stella said from the glowing cube.

"Hi, Stella," I replied. "Do you know if Dad's available to take a call?"

She gave me a smile that brightened her whole face. "I'll ask." She froze for a second, then tilted her head at me. "You are not going to get angry with him, are you?"

I blinked at her, a bit surprised by the question. "No... I hadn't planned on it." My anxiety about talking with my father came roaring back to life. "Why?"

She gave me a slightly sad look. "Just be gentle with him."

Her projection faded away and my father's safely familiar, thoroughly Usuriel features looked down at me from the comm screen. He sat in the kitchen at Angelus Quietum, remnants of breakfast indicating he'd just finished his usual bacon and eggs.

"Hello, Gracie," he said. A cautious smile tilted his lips upwards. It didn't reach his eyes, however. The guarded way he looked at me was deserved, but it still made my chest ache. Knowing the reason for all the ghosts in his gaze, and knowing that I'd added to them, only made it harder to meet his eye.

I swallowed and remembered what James had said. How did I want to greet the man who had survived so much and still had the gentleness to search his little girl's closet for monsters each night? Not with anger or pity, I decided.

"Hi, Dad." When I smiled, it was genuine. "I've missed you."

Something in his shoulders relaxed. "I've missed you, too. How is school?"

"It's good. You are not going to believe the day I've had, though..."

Chapter 12

No Good Deed

Dad and I talked for over two hours that day. I was late to writing class, but I didn't care. I no longer had Malcolm to look forward to and there weren't any assignments due that day. Besides, I missed my dad and it was nice to make up for lost time. We parted with a promise that I would come visit him on my next two-day break.

Being on speaking terms with Gabriel again was freeing in much the way I thought learning his secrets would be in the first place. A weight I had been carrying my whole life had been lifted off of my shoulders.

Not that there weren't things that I didn't know about my father. He was four hundred years old. There were skeletons stacked atop skeletons in that closet.

Still, I'd made my peace with the biggest issues and none of it was as unforgivable as I'd always feared it might be. It's strange to say, but I think in the back of my mind I had always been bracing myself to hate my father. Yet, here I was, enlightened, and still willing to talk to the Prince of Controversy; the Lord of Bad Decisions as his sister had called him in my dream.

This feeling lasted about a day.

Yes, that is exactly how long I got to feel good about my relationship with my father.

In case you haven't figured it out yet, Gabriel is a difficult and complicated person to know, let alone be related to. When he is your only parent, the force of his personality quite literally consumes your life to the point of no return.

***

Malcolm didn't talk to me during Written Communications that day. The icy silence between us wasn't comfortable, but I didn't find it unbearable. For once, I actually paid attention to the professor and took some decent notes. This was a situation I could live with.

After class, I usually had lunch at the cafeteria with James. I was unsure how my friend would greet me after my drunken rejection the night before. However, since I was a creature of habit, and not to mention hungry, I found my feet heading towards the dining hall.

To my relief, James leaned in his usual place by the drink stand. The expression on his face was as nervous as the knots in my stomach. Reminding myself that I'd given up childish avoidance once already this morning, I forced myself to walk over to him.

"I'm sorry about last night," James said in a rush, his light blue eyes scanning my face. "I didn't... I'm sorry about the way it... turned out." He was beginning to turn pink and stutter. Perhaps it was time to reassure him.

"It's okay," I said, a wry smile twisting my mouth to one side. "I didn't mean to snap at you in the parking lot. I think I was a little drunk." I'd been more than half sober at that point, but the alcohol was a good excuse.

"Liam can be very... distracting when he wants to be." A blush spread towards James' collar.

A heavy weight sank into my stomach. As I looked up into James' rounded, mortal face I realized he might actually be in love with my cousin.

"You guys seemed pretty happy with each other last night," I said carefully, moving towards the cups in an effort to keep my brain from fully processing the implications of this discovery.

A soft smile lit James' face as he followed me and selected his own drink. "It would have been even better if you'd stayed." He gave me a glance that was almost shy. Hope leaped into my chest like a desperate animal but I shoved it down hard. If he really cared that much for Liam, I could only make their relationship complicated and awkward. We'd proven that last night.

"Have you and Liam... you know... been a pair for a while?" I asked, gathering a bowl of soup and a sandwich before settling at our accustomed table by the orange tree. "I guess I've never really asked."

"A pair? No, not really." He sat next to me with his own soup and salad. "We've gone out some, like last night. And we've ended up in bed a few times, too." His blush deepened after admitting to that one, but when my pleasantly interested expression didn't change he went on. "But it's nothing official. We're not exclusive or anything."

I took a bite of soup and thought about that. "Okay," I replied slowly. "So you're not exclusive. Who else have you been dating, then?"

That one pulled him up short. His gaze flickered to me, then down to his plate. Well, that answered my question.

I sank a noodle with my spoon and tried to think this whole thing through. "James, I'm not trying to hurt you, but I think I should be honest. I did have sex with Malcolm last night."

I expected a reaction to that one. Perhaps a little hurt or disappointment. I didn't expect the raw pain on James' face. It was too close to what I'd always seen in my father's eyes. It hit an unexpected nerve and I shied away from him.

"Was that... your first time?" James asked. His voice sounded choked and I didn't have to be a telepath to know he was fighting not to show some strong emotions. Guilt, disappointment, and relief warred for dominance in my chest. If he was this upset about my experimentation with another man, perhaps his attachment to Liam really wasn't as exclusive as I feared.

I spun my spoon around my bowl. It was better to have something to do with my hands. "It wasn't great," I reassured him, "and it turns out Malcolm is a bit of an ass. I don't think it's an experience I'd care to repeat."

The strain around James' eyes eased a touch and he nodded as he picked up his sandwich. "Well, don't jump to conclusions too fast. Sex is like anything else. It has a learning curve. Plus, it helps to have the right partner."

"I'll keep that in mind."

We ate in silence a little while, each of us lost in our own thoughts. Either that or we weren't sure what to say to each other.

James broke the silence first. "I heard you were quite a sight walking back to campus this morning."

"Oh yeah?" I chuckled. "Who told you that?"

He shrugged. "Who hasn't?"

"What did they say?"

"That you're just as crazy as the rest of the Family." The sly smile on his face softened the statement. After the anti-Awareness sentiment I'd witnessed this morning, however, his words twisted my gut the wrong way. I swallowed hard and looked down. James put a hand on mine. It was the first we'd touched or even gotten flirtatiously close today. "It was a joke. Are you okay?"

I shook my head and pushed the rest of my food away, my mouth full of cotton. "Do you... think less of me because of my family?"

"No! Of course not! That's ridiculous!" James protested. "Why would you say that?"

I spread my hands. "We've been doing all this research into my dad and the Family. They have a lot of problems, and that's being kind. Do you worry about me being," I paused, struggling to put my anxiety into words, "I don't know... unstable?" Or dangerous, I thought, but it was too close to the actual heart of my fear for me to say aloud.

James shook his head and squeezed my hand. "Your dad might be an enigma, but he's always been kind to me. And you've never done anything to make me think that you're anything less than perfectly sane. Let people have their silly rumors. What does it matter? I know the truth. You and your dad are lovely people." I felt like hugging him, but instead I settled for squeezing his hand back and giving him a genuine smile. "If you don't mind me asking, what prompted that question?"

With a sigh, I told him about the vampires and the house fire. By the time I was done, his eyes were wide and his face pale.

"There are vampires living here in Landing?" he asked. "I thought all of them were in Riland Province."

I scowled at him and folded my arms. "D'nay and Gloria live close by, so there's at least one vampire you knew about in the area."

James waved a hand. "Besides him, of course. Everyone knows he's permanently attached to your grandmother. I don't even think he bit Bryce when he turned him. Have you ever heard of him feeding from anyone besides Gloria?"

"Not that I know of," I replied reluctantly. "But that's not the point. Lauren said she thought it was the watch that set the fire."

James' frown deepened. "That is disturbing. I mean, I'm not thrilled with the idea of vampires in the neighborhood, but I would never condone going after them like that. It's barbaric."

I nodded even though I was less than satisfied with his level of outrage. My father had been appropriately scandalized when I told him about the incident.

"It's inspired me to go digging into the vampire issue a little more deeply with Stella later," I said. "Want to join me in the library after classes?"

James gave me a smile that made his mortal features incredibly handsome. "I'd love to."

***

I didn't think anything else would come of the vampire incident. If anything I figured the watch might show up and have a few awkward questions. However, as my father so eloquently put it, I somehow doubted a jail cell would hold me, nor did I think there would be a constable with enough guts to try to put me in one any time soon. I wasn't any more afraid of the mortal watch than my father was.

I should have been.

However, that is not what ended up happening. The person who did show up to talk about it was completely unexpected.

I was walking to the library to meet James after class

when a rush of psi ahead made me pause. Peering cautiously around the corner of the academic building, I discovered Vanessa waiting patiently in the middle of the walkway. She had her hands clasped behind her back and her mane of black and white streaked hair was as wild as ever.

"Hello, Gracie," she said when she caught sight of me. "Do you have a moment to chat?"

I frowned at my older cousin, but when she did nothing more threatening than blink at me with her good eye, I shrugged and fell into step with her. "Sure. Is everything okay with the Family?"

She rolled a shoulder. "As well as it ever is. There are no major emergencies that I'm aware of, if that's what you mean."

I'd just talked to Dad earlier in the day and everything had seemed quite normal at Angelus Quietum. "That's good. So... what can I do for you?"

"I heard about your little incident on Cambria Street," she said, her one blue eye meeting my questioning gaze steadily. She held herself with the erect authority of the very powerful and very old. Unlike Gloria and my father, however, there was something almost militaristic in the way she moved and carried herself. Though she wasn't taller than me, I felt as though she were regarding me from a lofty distance.

"Ummm... Cambria Street?" I asked. I'd only been living in Landing for a month and a half. I wasn't really familiar with the local street names.

"The house fire," she explained. "I heard you put it out before the watch arrived."

I hadn't seen a single individual from the watch at the scene, nor had I heard incoming sirens. My mouth drew together in a thin line but I kept it closed. Lodging my complaints with Vanessa about the mortal watch would probably be pointless.

"Word spreads fast. Yeah, I took care of it," I admitted. "I don't think anyone got hurt."

"No, thanks to you no one did," she agreed, giving me a small smile. "In fact, I have to admit being impressed with your initiative. Some people would have hesitated to interfere."

I scowled and crossed my arms under my breasts. "Initiative? What, you mean common decency?"

"Concern for fellow individuals of Awareness," my cousin said smoothly. "I'm trying to pay you a compliment, Gracie. Don't look at me like I just stepped on your cat."

"I just don't think I did anything above and beyond the call of normal human compassion. And to imply that I did more than toss a bucket of water on a person's house when it was on fire is an overstatement."

Vanessa actually chuckled at me. "For Fate's sake, you are your father's daughter. Argumentative to the core."

The comment bothered me less than it would have a few days earlier. I still didn't crack a smile. "So that's all you wanted? To congratulate me for not being a morally bankrupt individual?"

"Well, that was part of it," Vanessa said, sounding as if she were choosing her words carefully. "Gracie, have you decided what you're going to do after University?"

I blinked at her, thrown by the abrupt topic change. "Ummm... well, I've thought about it, of course. But so far I'm still not sure. I like pottery class. I've been considering doing something with ceramics."

"Ceramics are nice." Vanessa's tone was a little doubtful. "And useful. You'd be able to fire your kiln cheaply, too, I would imagine."

"True," I agreed. "I hadn't even thought of that, but you're right."

"I think that would be a waste of your potential, however." Vanessa sounded cautious and I had a feeling she was about to tell me why she was really here. "What do you know about the Overwatch?"

My father's warnings came to mind and I hesitated. "Not a lot. Just that they're the police for people like us."

"That's a simplistic way of putting it, but yes. As you've probably figured out, individuals of Awareness have a wide range of skills and abilities that can make them... difficult to live with. Essentially, we're the safety net. When individuals of Awareness take advantage of their abilities and begin to infringe upon the rights of others, we are the ones who put a stop to it and make sure it doesn't happen again."

We were standing outside the library now. I didn't see

James waiting just inside the doors, so I didn't mind lingering.

"Do you work for the Overwatch, then?" I asked, eyeing Vanessa's uniform.

Her laugh was as abrupt and controlled as her movements. "My dear cousin," she chuckled, "I am the Overwatch." When she saw my blank expression her amusement dimmed. "Uncle Gabe really did have you locked away from everything, didn't he? I'm the head of the Overwatch, Gracie, and I have been for over sixty years."

I swallowed hard and glanced around. I fleetingly wondered how Vanessa's powers stacked up to my father's and had the startling realization that I was hoping he'd be strong enough to protect me. Since she was the head of a policing organization and he was the one with the reputation for being hot-tempered and occasionally homicidal, there was something intensely ironic about that thought. Not to mention the fact that I was a grown adult with deadly powers of my own. Still, I would have felt better having this conversation with my dad nearby.

"I... I don't understand what that has to do with me," I stuttered, feeling a strange urge to bolt. The echo of my father's warnings about the Overwatch made my nerves extremely raw. Harmless, I told myself, I'm as harmless as a newborn kitten.

"You are something rather special, Gracie." I watched Vanessa's expression intently despite the fact that she was giving me a pretty good Usuriel blank face. There was something she didn't want to come out and say to me, but it was impossible to say what. "Your pyrokinetic ability must be very powerful if you were able to extinguish that house fire and then march off to class. You don't even seem tired."

I shrugged. "I'm not. It wasn't that big a deal."

"Perhaps not for you." She cocked a pale eyebrow at me. "And then there's the matter of your mental silence. Even Gabriel and Gloria can't hear you coming. That means you have a massive amount of fire power, if you'll pardon the pun, combined with an undetectable approach. If you joined us, you would be a very convincing deterrent to even our most powerful Family members."

"Deterrent?" I echoed dumbly. James had just arrived around the corner holding his memory pad in one hand. He walked up to us with a polite smile on his face and came to stand beside me.

Vanessa nodded, that one ice-blue eye fixed on my gaze. "Half of our job is to look scary enough that people don't want to take the risk of crossing the line. You, my dear, may be the scariest Usuriel born in the last two hundred years."

"I've never thought of myself as scary," I lied.

"I think she's right," James put in. "Not that I'm afraid of you, Gracie, but if I didn't know you I would definitely be a little intimidated. I mean, for one, I'm used to being able to hear everyone coming. Even squirrels make more mental noise than you do. When I turn around and you're just there, it can be pretty unsettling."

"Combine that with the ability to torch a building with a thought," Vanessa pointed out. "And not to mention your father's volatile temperament. Even if you don't have it, your association with him would be enough to give some Family members pause. Put you out there in an Overwatch uniform at a crime scene and show off what you can do? We won't have another call for six months. I'd bet my hover car on it."

Since she was a three-T, I wasn't sure what use Vanessa could have for a hover car. But I understood the sentiment behind her statement. I wasn't sure how I felt about it.

"I don't know," I said slowly. "Can I think about this?"

"Of course," Vanessa said breezily, waving a hand as if I had all the time in the world. "But why don't you let me take you on a little tour of our facilities tomorrow? What time does your first class start?"

"Ten hundred hours," I replied.

"Good. Plenty of time for you to see the training gallery in the morning then. I will stop by your room at oh seven hundred," she said with a brusque nod. "Good evening to you both." And with a surge of pale blue light she disappeared.

Chapter 13

Holo History

I glanced over at James. He looked more thoughtful than dumbfounded. I felt as if Cybele had shifted underneath me.

"What just happened?"

"I think you've been offered a job," he replied. He regarded my stunned expression with a small frown. "It was bound to happen. I mean, you're probably the only living third-gen they don't have on payroll. Except for Dax, but..." he waved that away as if it were an issue for another conversation.

I blinked at him stupidly. "You were expecting this?"

He opened the door to the library. "Yeah. Weren't you?"

"No!" I said, following him mechanically through the library doors and back towards our usual holo-suite. "I knew about the Overwatch, of course, but I'd never even thought about joining it. I mean, what are the requirements? I don't even know what I'd have to do if I did join."

"Fortunately, we're in a wonderful place where we can answer those questions," he said, gesturing inclusively at the library halls. With a flourish, he placed his hand against the door plate to the holo-suite. The metal door unlocked with a click and we stepped in together.

"Hello, James. Hello, Gracie." Stella appeared like a ghost in the center of the room.

"Hi, Stella," we said, nearly in unison.

"So, Stella, what can you tell us about the Overwatch's training program?" James asked, setting his memory pad into a docking station on the wall and tapping a few buttons. He liked recording our research sessions for future reference. He was extremely organized; the timeline thing had been his idea.

"The Overwatch generally requires its members to go through basic Awareness training, either through the University, through their own facilities or both simultaneously. They prefer both but will accept more experienced members with one or the other," she replied simply, pulling up a slowly rotating hologram of a large, low building surrounded by a high metal fence. Its pale concrete walls and militaristic style reminded me sharply of Vanessa.

"Is that the training facility?" I stepped closer to the hologram.

"Affirmative," Stella replied.

"It almost looks like a prison," James commented.

"There are detention cells in several sections of the facility," Stella confirmed. "However, since most individuals the Overwatch is responsible for are too dangerous to be confined, few of these are occupied."

"Too dangerous to be confined," I echoed, staring at the holo.

"You okay?" James put a hand on my shoulder. I had to fight not to jump away from his touch.

I shook my head a little too quickly. "I'm fine. Really..." I trailed off, dread taking hold of my gut with a chill. If I hadn't already talked to my father once that day, I would have been tempted to ask Stella for a connection to Angelus Quietum. I wasn't sure what it was about the Overwatch and Vanessa that made me so uneasy, but something about them made me feel like running back to Dad and Grandma Gloria.

"Who gets to determine who is too dangerous to be confined and who gets a cell?" James wondered aloud to Stella.

"The Overwatch's governing council," Stella replied smoothly. With a gesture from her, five holos faded into existence. I recognized Lillian and Vanessa instantly. They stood in the center while three strangers flanked them. All of them bore the stamp of D'nay and Gloria's DNA. Despite the wildly different coloring of two of them, with ink-black skin and snow-white hair, those angular cheekbones and brilliantly blue-green eyes marked them as Family. They were elder children, too, judging by the sharpness of features.

"So what, they vote?" I asked.

"Affirmative," Stella replied. My stomach turned.

"You're really spooked by the Overwatch, aren't you?"

James said, tilting his head at me.

"You and Vanessa just described me as the scariest Usuriel in the last two hundred years. How much do you want to bet that vote would not land me in a cell?"

"Hmmm." James paled a touch. "I see your point. But you've never given them a reason to think you're dangerous. I mean, if anything, you have to be one of the best trained minds at University. Gabe may have a reputation for questionable judgment, but his skill as a teacher has never come up for debate."

"You should have heard the way my dad talked about the Overwatch before I left Angelus Quietum," I said quietly. "He seemed convinced that if I put a toe out of line they'd execute me and ask questions later."

"Well, look at it this way," James said, "if you work for the Overwatch, they'll get to know you better. It's always harder to vote down one of your own than it is to condemn a random stranger."

He had a point. I pondered that while he turned to Stella.

"Okay, I think that answers our questions about the Overwatch. Gracie, didn't you say you wanted to research D'nay a bit more?"

"Yeah," I agreed, glad to have a reason to change the subject. "I know the basics of D'nay and Gloria's relationship. I mean, he exclusively blood feeds from her and her blood keeps him half-mortal like Gabriel, only without most of the psi powers."

"Even so," James replied. "So what are you looking for?"

I crossed my arms, considering my approach. "How did D'nay and Gloria end up together anyway? I mean, I know Gloria's family wasn't thrilled with a vampire as her choice of husband, which is why they designed and launched the *Inspiration*. But how did they fall in love in the first place?"

"That might be a better question for them than for me," Stella pointed out.

"There's nothing speculative on the net?" James sounded shocked.

She gave him a very still pause and I knew she was irritated. "There are a number of very bad entertainment holos on the topic, if that's what you are looking for."

"Ah... no, I don't think that's quite the direction I wanted to go in," James stuttered, his face turning a deep shade of scarlet.

"You were wired to the *Inspiration* for almost a century and you never heard them talk about it?" I asked, narrowing my eyes at the AI.

"The right to privacy in one's own POD was written directly into the *Inspiration*'s Charter." Stella's tone was clipped. "You are Family, so I will show you some things I might not show others. However, I did not witness D'nay and Gloria's first encounters. Those are their own to tell if they choose."

James waved a hand. "Okay, Stella. We get it. Anything else you wanted to look into, Gracie?"

I considered the question. "What about Bryce, then? He

was the first vampire D'nay turned, wasn't he?"

"He is the only vampire D'nay turned, to my knowledge," Stella said. "And he has expressed great regret to me since then. If he had known what kind of destruction it would cause in Riland, I do not think he would have done it. Not even to save his descendant's life."

"The White Woman massacre," James said, nodding. "It always seems to come back to that."

"We had a debate on it in Professor Joan's class, but no one seemed to know exactly what happened," I tilted my head at Stella. "You aren't wired in Riland City, so I don't imagine you saw much. But do you have any survivor accounts?"

Stella shook her head. "I'm afraid there were not many survivors in the area where the event occurred. However, the persistent flames and location of charred remains afterwards indicated an individual of high Awareness was indeed at the heart of the event. The few survivors willing to discuss the incident later described a woman all in white roaming the city at night, burning with blue flame. However, they never went on holo record with a first hand account."

"We know, we know," James sighed. "It had to be Adora. The Overwatch took care of her if you ask me. Probably Vanessa teleported in. It's the only explanation that makes sense. Especially since there wasn't a body in the end. That points to a Family member in itself—they probably delivered it to Gloria and D'nay so they could take care of arrangements quietly."

It was Dad. It had to be Dad. The words sat in my chest like a lead weight. However, I still didn't feel comfortable talking about my strange dreams or my trips with Ariel. Even for an Usuriel, claiming to have conversations with your dead sister was not a good sign for mental stability. Seeing as we were discussing the very deadly and very public mental breakdown of my paternal aunt, I decided I needed to change the subject before I said something I would regret.

"So Adora was a pyrokinetic, too," I said aloud, latching on to the next slightly related thought I could come up with. "Were her powers the same as my father's?"

"Psychically, she was actually substantially stronger than Gabriel," Stella replied smoothly, waving a hand and conjuring a hologram of Adora's pale form. She was taller than me by a considerable amount. She must have nearly looked her brother in the eye. "She was able to run the heart ship on the *Inspiration* without incident."

I walked slowly around the projection of my late aunt. "Dad mentioned something about that. He said the heart ship wasn't his domain. What did he mean by that? He was a psi-pilot for years. What's the difference?"

Stella tilted her head at me. I'd come to learn that this was her way of expressing confusion or exasperation with the idiosyncrasies of non-computerized life forms. "Essentially, a heart ship was D'nay's initial answer to light speed drive.

By creating me with organic relays, Gloria was able to merge with my mind and thereby tap into the *Inspiration*'s engines, increasing their power and thrust exponentially. The psi-pilot, by contrast, was never a deliberate part of the *Inspiration*'s design. It resulted from damage caused by the Cat-Mantis during our first encounter with them. Thus, it was more of a 'patch' that ended up being better than the original. However, like the heart ship, it tapped into the energies of the *Inspiration*'s engines which, at their full peak, were always more than Gabriel could safely handle. Even though it channeled less power, Gabriel nearly died several times in the *Inspiration*'s psi-pilot chair."

"I thought Gabriel was the best psi-pilot in the *Inspiration*'s fleet," James protested. "It's what he's known best for."

Besides a morphine habit, I nearly grumbled, but thought better of it and let James' positive projection stand. "He said the new heart helped with that," I said, glad I knew a little bit of this story from the source himself.

I glanced at Stella for confirmation and she nodded. "After his transplant, Gabriel and Gloria were able to achieve speed and precision with the *Inspiration* that had been impossible with Gloria alone. This was fortunate, as the trip through Cat-Mantis territory was extremely dangerous and pushed Gloria, Gabriel, and Adora past their limits more than once."

"Ah yes, back to Adora," James said, leaning forward to study the holo of my aunt. "I've always wondered what her actual powers were. I mean, clearly she was a three-T plus pyro, like Gabe, but did she also have healing and shape-shifting abilities like Gloria?"

"She could not change her form," Stella replied. "Gloria has always been the only individual on Cybele with enough Anori blood to shift shape."

"What about healing?" I asked. "I know that's one of the few psi skills that my dad has absolutely no ability with. Anything that needed more attention than soap and a bandage, he sent for Grandma."

"None at all?" James tilted his head at me. "Even Liam has a touch of that. I've seen him heal little stuff, like a skinned knee."

I shook my head. "Nope. Gabriel has about as much healing ability as I have telepathy."

"I don't know about that," James said. "He'd have to be worse than a mortal at it if he was going to keep up with your head blindness."

"Since he has the longest medical history I've ever stored, I would say he is in fact worse than most mortals at keeping himself in one piece," Stella commented.

James burst out laughing. "Stella, did you actually make a joke?"

Even I couldn't help but chuckle at the calm, blank face Stella gave him. "I am half-organic. Just because the majority of my synapses are computerized doesn't mean I have no sense of humor."

"Okay, okay, we didn't mean any offense," I told her before she decided to kick us out of the holo-suite. "What about Adora's healing abilities? Was she better at it than Dad?"

"Perhaps you would like to see for yourself?" Stella sounded slightly put out and I wondered exactly what kind of holo footage she was about to show us.

"Sounds perfect," James replied and flashed me an eager grin as the lights dimmed. He loved digging through these old holos.

The scene Stella brought into focus was a long, narrow, curving corridor with gray alloy walls. The lights flickered and sparked overhead. From the trembling of the image, I could tell that the holo cameras were being shaken regularly. Something dark and viscus had been splattered across several walls. Despite the conditions, I still recognized this as the *Inspiration*, especially when a very familiar form trotted into the corridor.

My father's eyes looked younger, but otherwise he was his usual self. I wasn't sure where in his timeline we were. If it was after his episode with morphine abuse, he'd put his usual weight back on and looked much healthier than the last few holos I'd seen him in. His ship suit looked a little worse for the wear and his hair straggled out of his work-a-day ponytail to fall into his face, but I didn't see any visible injuries. He disappeared around the bend of the hallway only to reappear a moment later, his blue energy dancing around him. He took a defensive stance against something farther down the hall.

"Come on you overgrown space mosquito," he growled, blue flame casting flickering shadows across the filth-streaked walls. "I'm right here. Come and get me."

Something moved in the penumbra at the bend of the corridor. I couldn't see what it was, but just that flicker of limbs in twilight made the hair stand up on the back of my neck. There's a rhythm to the movement of most mammals. It's smooth and relies upon joints that are held together by sinew and muscle. Whatever was moving in the dark was closer to the scuttle of an insect — rapid, flickering spines interspersed with long, frozen pauses. The thing that made me most grateful that this was a holo and not real life, was that I could see limbs stretching all the way from the ceiling to the floor of the oval hallway.

"What is that?" I hissed at James, tempted to step closer to see if there was more holo footage of the creature, but not having the nerve.

"Cat-Mantis," he whispered back, his face alight with curious awe. "I had no idea Stella had a holo of a living one! Everything I've found on the net has been dead!"

As he finished that sentence, the creature exploded out of the hallway's bend and leaped towards my father with raised, clawed front limbs. I'm not sure how to describe the terror that barreled down the corridor at Gabriel. It certainly wasn't like any of the still diagrams I'd seen of the Cat-Mantis. In the flickering semi-dark, the creature seemed to be a ball of hissing, scrambling appendages.

Despite knowing that this was all an illusion, merely light projected into the chamber and enhanced through my implant's connection with Stella, I still grabbed James'

shoulders and attempted to shield myself behind him.

"Whoa. Are you seeing this, Gracie?" James' amazed tone made me poke my head from around his sheltering frame. I found myself equally impressed at the sight that greeted me.

I'd known that my father wasn't someone to be tangled with. After the flood, he'd more than proved his ability to do the work of ten men. However, the way he moved as that alien came flying at his head was something to see. Dancer nothing, the man was snake-strike fast. Yet despite his obvious strength, there was no energy wasted. Gabriel simply made an efficient shift of his weight and darted his hand downward. He seized the Cat-Mantis by the fringe of scruffy fur around its head and used its own momentum to twist and double it back on itself.

The thing screamed. A loud, high rattle rose in counterpoint, creating a primordial harmony. Its legs flailed at him, cutting a bloody line across one cheek before he swatted the limb away. Blue lines of electric psi-power leaped from the flame surrounding my father's arms and chest as he held the creature pinned with one hand. With a strike that rang the alloy of the ship like a bell, Gabriel put a fist through the alien's skull. It went abruptly limp.

"Dad, watch out!"

I turned in time to see a young man come down the corridor behind us. He was shorter than my father and thinner, though the Family features were as keen on his face as a knife. To my surprise, he didn't favor my father's coloring. Sandy blond hair was worn in a short, traditional cut and I couldn't be sure in this lighting but I thought his eyes were green. I didn't have long to register more about him before he flung a hand upwards and spilled a long line of bright, blue light into the space directly above Gabriel's head.

My head snapped around at the same moment Dad's did. There was a roar and another rattling hiss as a second Cat-Mantis startled away from its stealthy approach. Once again proof that telepathy didn't mean immunity from distraction, as my father used to drill into my head.

"Thanks, Hal," Gabriel said, moving to take care of the second alien. He dispatched it with the same smooth efficiency he'd displayed with the first one, this time seizing its head in both hands and twisting until the thing's carapace actually split. Hal wisely stayed past the reach of the alien's flailing limbs.

As he was tossing the huge carcass away from himself, Gabriel suddenly looked up as if he'd heard something alarming. "Get down!" he shouted, gesturing to his son to get back against the right hand wall. Hal glanced at him in confusion and then...

The explosion was so deafening and disorienting that I completely forgot I was in a holo. I think James did, too, because his voice joined mine in a surprised and panicked shriek. We clung to each other as flame and debris engulfed the whole corridor, completely obliterating any sign of Gabriel or Harold.

"It's okay," James whispered in my ear, our arms wrapped tightly around each other. I shrank into his chest and tried to get my breathing back under control. When there was no fire or smoke in my nostrils, I was able to get my head a little straighter. I was also able to appreciate James' slim shoulder under my cheek and I understood why the horror holos were such popular date entertainment among my classmates.

"Hal?" My father's voice echoed oddly and I could hear the crackle of his energy nearby, though I couldn't see it. The lack of skin-prickling weight was odd and brought home the limits of the hologram. I relaxed a touch further but didn't move from James' arms. I'd been rattled enough by Vanessa's visit to be grateful for a little extra reassurance. Either that or I was a hormone-ruled eighteen-year-old. Yeah, I'm going to go with the second one.

Finally the smoke cleared enough that I could see the blue lines of power to my right. Dad was doing something that took a lot of strength and control, but I wasn't quite sure what. Then I caught a glimpse of stars through the shimmering haze of his psi-power and realized that he'd put up a mental barrier across the stretch of wall that had exploded in on them.

"Sweet Fate," James breathed, looking at the damage with wide eyes. I agreed with his emotion but stayed silent as I gazed at the gaping wound in the *Inspiration*'s hull. My father's back was to us, hands outstretched to the undulating curtain of blue that kept the whole section of the ship from decompressing. I could hear the thud and hiss as bulkheads sealed themselves against the breach.

"Hal?" Dad called again, fear in his voice. "Hang on, kid, your sister's coming!" I turned in the other direction and saw why my brother wasn't answering him.

The hull shard had caught Harold from the back and I could see it coming all the way through to protrude between two of his lower ribs. From the position he'd been standing earlier, I guessed that the piece of shrapnel rebounded off of the wall behind him. It was a simple, inexperienced mistake to only shield in the direction of a blast. Hal had paid a hefty price for that beginner's gaff. Blood was trickling from his mouth as he clung to the wall, clearly fighting to stay on his feet. He nodded quickly in response to our father's reassurance, one hand pressed to the jagged alloy in his chest.

With a rush of wind that blew back Gabriel's hair and tossed up a few smaller scraps of shrapnel, Adora appeared almost exactly where James and I were standing. Startled, the two of us stumbled back from her, dropping our embrace and turning to face Hal's injured form.

"Well, you certainly made a mess in here," Adora observed, wrinkling her nose at the two Cat-Mantis carcasses.

"I made a mess? You're the one blowing up half the ship without warning! Fucking Fate, Adora, were you trying to kill us? Where are Mom and Ariel?" Dad snapped. "Hal needs a healer now!"

"Oh, relax." Adora flapped a hand at him and sauntered over to where her nephew had sunk to one knee. "I'll have him back to himself in just a moment."

"Adora," my father growled. "You've done enough damage. Leave it to Ariel."

"My baby niece." Adora rolled her eyes. "Honestly, I'm five years older than she is and a full generation stronger. I'd think you'd be asking her to step aside for me."

"She's actually taken the time to train with Mom," Gabriel hissed, eyes showing some white as he craned his neck around to look at his sister. "Plus, she doesn't hurt worse than the injury."

"What's a little pain if it fixes everything?" Adora grumbled, kneeling by Hal. He glanced up at her and looked like he'd like to say something but couldn't quite get enough air to do it. I felt bad for him. If Dad didn't want Adora to heal such an obviously life-threatening wound, she must have been seriously bad at it. "It's okay, Hal. I'm going to take this out on the count of three. Are you ready?"

He cringed, then nodded. Reaching behind him, Adora wrapped her pale fingers around the piece of alloy.

"One, two—" she pulled the alloy from the wound before she even got to three, smoothly and efficiently, as only an extremely detached and incredibly strong person could. There was a wet sucking sound and I swallowed hard. Hal made a strangled noise that I think would have been a scream had the shard not completely shredded one lung. Adora looked at the alloy in her hand with a slight frown before tossing it aside. "Here now, hold still," she scolded her nephew quietly, one arm wrapping around his chest while the other pressed to the gaping hole in his back. Then her pale blue power pooled about her before reaching out to wrap tendrils around my brother's injured chest.

This time, Hal did scream.

"Sweet Fate, Adora!" Ariel arrived in a blast of Gabriellan-blue psi-power. It was almost like looking in a mirror. My sister seemed about my age at the moment, or at least within a few years. Our proportions had to be within inches of each other, though I did have a touch more bust. Her curly red hair cascaded about her blue ship-suited shoulders and her Usuriel features were set in a deeply disapproving expression. "Get your hands off of him! I swear, you'll be the death of us yet, you white menace!"

Despite my sister's angry words, the skin across Harold's back knit together as cleanly as anything I'd seen Gloria accomplish. The muscles in his neck and forearms stood out in high relief as if he were fighting the urge to twist away from Adora's hand, but aside from the obvious pain, she seemed just as effective as the Usuriel Matriarch.

"There, see? Back in one piece," Adora said with some satisfaction as she let go of Hal's shoulders.

My brother fell forward onto his hands and knees. Ariel quickly knelt to his side, one hand finding the back of his neck as he began to cough up a significant amount of blood.

"Easy, Hal. Don't fight it, just bring it all up," she reassured her younger brother. Then she rounded on Adora. "You can't seal in that amount of fluid, you idiot! If he were mortal, he'd have pneumonia within a week."

"In case you haven't noticed, he's not mortal," Adora replied, sliding to her feet so smoothly it was inhuman. Even on their best days, my other relatives' movements never seemed so clearly other. Adora was strange and terrifyingly strong, even for an Usuriel. "His immune system will make short work of any infection that tries to set in. He'll be fine once he catches his breath."

Hal wasn't showing much indication of recovering any time soon. The body-wracking coughs were violent enough that he gagged in between them. He clung to his sister's arms as she wrapped them around his chest for support. She didn't seem concerned about the blood he was getting on her ship suit. Ariel gave our father an angry glare as she patted Hal's heaving back.

"Are you ready to side with Grandma and I yet?" she asked Gabriel.

Dad sighed and met Adora's eye. "Teleport up some repair materials. I can't hold this forever."

With the gesture of one hand Adora summoned up several large sheets of alloy. She directed them with the twitch of a fingertip up to the hole Gabriel was currently patching. Their blue energies blazed around the edges and sealed them in place. Between the second-gen siblings, the repair was done with remarkable ease and efficiency. I wondered how long it would have taken a mortal crew to do the same.

Hal finally began to sound like he was getting some air into his lungs by the time they were done. Ariel teleported in a small, damp towel and cleaned up her brother, her brows furrowed. When he managed to pause a few moments in between fits of coughing and retching, she murmured a few gentle questions to him. Hal nodded to her and she nodded back, giving his back a pat while he rested his head against her shoulder. His eyes were closed and his skin waxy.

"Mom is going to have another set of twins when she hears about this," Ariel said, glaring up at Gabriel.

"You okay, kid?" Dad knelt by Hal and put a hand on his back near the tear in his ship suit where the shard had gone through.

Hal nodded, his eyes still closed. He was breathing hard but otherwise seemed a bit recovered. Ariel ran a soothing hand over his hair.

"He could have died," Ariel growled, her gaze glowing golden as it moved between our father and his sister. "Are you happy now, Dad? We've been saying that something like this was going to happen for months. What is it going to take for you to get it? One of your children in the morgue?"

Dad took a deliberate breath but he didn't look rebellious or angry with Ariel. If anything, his face was grim. Slowly, he got to his feet and faced his sister.

If I'd thought my father could look arrogant, it was

nothing to the way Adora held herself as she watched her brother stand. Perfectly erect and defiant, her ice-blue eyes blazed at Gabriel.

"She's right, Adora," he said slowly, squaring his shoulders. "You knew we were in this section when you took that shuttle in. A few feet over and you would have sent me out into dead space. I might... possibly... maybe... could have managed to teleport back in time to save myself. Even so, this whole section would have decompressed. Hal would have died for certain. I'm not sure how many other crew members were in the area before the deadlocks came down, but it could have been a decent number. That's not just reckless. That's downright irresponsibly dangerous."

"This from the man who shot speed before getting behind the pilot's console." Adora narrowed her eyes at him. His mouth formed a thin, unhappy line across his face.

"Six months," he rumbled, his voice so deep it sounded like thunder. "I had a problem with those painkillers for six Fate-forsaken months when you were two. I'm sick to death of you parading about an episode you don't even remember every time you make a mistake. This isn't about me, it's about you and your inability to think about the safety of the people around you. People keep landing in the hospital wing lately, or haven't you noticed?"

She lifted her chin and looked down her arrow-straight nose at him. "It hasn't just been me. The Cat-Mantis are dangerous. It isn't my fault we've had to push some safety limits. Half the time I'm what gets us out of the mess we're in! If I hadn't just blown up that ship, you'd still be trying to execute those damn things one at a time."

"There have to be safer ways of going about it!" Ariel shot at her aunt. Hal looked asleep in her lap at this point, though she still absently rubbed his back. "You're going to end up killing someone and my bet is on Dad! I think that's what it would take to get my point through your damn thick skull, but by then it's too late. The only person you actually care about on this ship will be dead."

That statement did seem to give Adora pause. She frowned slightly as she considered Ariel's words. Finally she turned to Gabriel again. "The child will be fine," she said evenly, one elegant hand gesturing to Hal's sleeping form, "and no one else was even injured. I think your anxieties are unfounded."

My father rubbed tired eyes; not old the way I'd seen them in my own lifetime, but bone-weary as if dealing with his sister took all of his energy. "I've made excuses for you for months now. Hell, I've looked at my wife from flat on my ass in the Med Bay and lied about what put me there. Why? Because I get it. I've screwed up before. Everyone deserves a second chance. But this is past a second or third or even a fourth time, Adora. I'm not doing this anymore. I'm not protecting you from the consequences of your actions. When Mom asks me what I think after this, I'm going to tell her she was right."

Adora looked as if my father had just struck her across

the face. "You wouldn't."

"I'm sorry," he said miserably and I could hear the way it pained him to speak to her like this. "But Ariel's right. If we don't do something, you're not going to learn until you've put one of us in the ground. I love you, but I also love my children. And it would be nice not to leave Liv a widow anytime soon."

"You can't force me into accepting a babysitter," Adora's brows arched sharply over eyes glowing so white-hot they almost weren't blue anymore.

"No, I can't," Gabriel replied. "Which is precisely the problem. You're too strong and you forget that we can't keep up with you. But, even if I can't force you, I can tell Stella not to accept your input. She wouldn't be happy about it, but if Mom and I both tell her to do it, she'll listen."

"You'd ban me from the heart ship?" she asked, eyes dimming.

"And the shuttles. Not that there will be many left if you keep destroying them at this rate," Gabriel said with a wry twist of his mouth. "Even the psi-pilot would be off-limits. Until you either accept a companion or show us that you can function without endangering other people, I'll shut you out of every psi-system we have."

Little scrawls of blue-white electricity tumbled about the collar of Adora's ship suit before lifting and tangling about her shoulder-length white hair.

"This ship will be dead in space without me on psi-duty.

Within a week, you'll be begging me to come back," she spat.

"Fine," Gabriel said evenly. "Take a break for a week. Do some reading. Find a boy to flirt with. Or a girl. I don't care. Just do whatever it is you do when you're not tearing up the ship. If we have to call on your help, you win and I won't go to Mom about this. If we handle things and don't have to pull you from your vacation, however, I don't want to hear a single complaint about accepting a companion. Deal?"

He held out a hand to her. She looked at it askance, then her hand darted out and took his for a quick, fierce shake. "Done. You'll regret it." She spun on her heel and disappeared in a flash of pale blue.

"I doubt it," Gabriel muttered, running his hand through his hair and turning back to his children. "There, are you happy? I told your mother I'd sort it."

"You made a bet with her? That's what you call sorting it? Seriously?" Ariel's mouth parted in disgust.

I didn't blame her. I didn't trust Adora any farther than I could throw her, let alone to keep up her end of a bargain she didn't like.

"Sometimes, you have to know how to handle Adora," he replied, kneeling down to check on Hal.

Like poisoning her wine, I thought as James and I watched Hal accept Gabriel's helping hand. My half-brother stood with little to none of the usual Family grace. Ariel rose to her feet much more smoothly next to them, a slightly cross set to her eyes and mouth.

"If we have to call on her, she'll never let you forget it,"

Ariel warned her father.

"We won't have to. Gloria and I ran this ship long before Adora knew what a heart ship was. With you, Hal, and Drex around, we'll get along just fine. Hell, without Adora blowing things up halfway through every confrontation, it'll be like a vacation for me, too," Gabriel reassured his daughter. "Besides, I didn't have much of a choice. She was never going to agree to the companion idea of her own accord. But if she loses a bet, that twisted little honor code she has will demand she at least give it a try. I think once she sees how useful having a second perspective in those key moments is, she won't be quite as angry about the idea."

"If you say so," Ariel grumbled, giving our father a once over. "I can't believe you got away without a scratch on that explosion. You're not hiding anything from me, are you?"

"For once, Hal got my luck instead of me. Sorry, kid." Gabriel gave his son's hair a tussle. Hal looked at his father with an expression that was half annoyance and half amusement. The three of them faded away, leaving an empty corridor, then that faded as well and Stella's silver glow was the only light in the empty holo suite.

"So, she was a healer," James said.

"Just not a very pleasant one," I amended.

"Affirmative," Stella agreed. "She rarely used her healing skill unless there was an emergency and to my knowledge, she never gained much nuance in its art or practice."

I yawned and stretched. "Well, that answers that question.

Ready to get some food?"

"Just one more thing," James said, turning back to Stella. "What were the Usuriels fighting about at the end? Gabriel and Ariel seemed to want Adora to accept some kind of companion?"

"Correct." Stella nodded and, with the gesture of one hand, the figure of a pretty young mortal woman appeared beside her. "Gabriel won his bet. Adora was declared too dangerous to function on her own. Gabriel and Gloria gave her two choices—either give up the use of her psi-powers in the presence of others or accept a mortal chaperon that would help her navigate risky situations with more caution. Since the first option would have forced her to abandon all psi until they reached Cybele, Adora opted for a chaperon. Her first chaperon was Nikki Blackmon, eldest child of Captain Mystra Blackmon."

I ran an appraising eye over the woman next to Stella. If I imagined what Ariel or I might look like as a mortal, this was probably it. Her red hair wasn't as sleek or copper as my own, rather it was a more brilliant orange with lots of wiry strands. Her green eyes leaned more towards a muddy hazel than the gleaming emerald of Ariel's, but her pale freckled skin was quite creamy and smooth. I found her features pleasing in the rounded, soft way that many mortals were. She reminded me of Olivia, I decided.

"That had to be a strange job," I mused. "Chasing after Adora and trying to make sure she didn't kill anybody. Seems like an almost impossible task for a mortal, really."

"Actually," Stella replied evenly, "Nikki was quite successful at reigning in Adora's recklessness. She devised a ranking scale for Adora's decisions. If the idea she expressed was ranked by Nikki as a one, it was a healthy, safe action. If it was a ten, it was deemed by Adora to be 'Gabe level stupid' and Nikki was allowed to veto it. If it fell between a four and a seven, Adora had some discretion about deciding if she wanted to go with her original plan or modify it to one that Nikki suggested. Nikki was also quite good at coming up with sensible alternatives to Adora's straight-forward approach. The system worked well until Nikki retired to have her first child."

"How long was Nikki her chaperon?" James asked.

"Fifteen years," Stella replied.

"That's a long time to keep up with Adora if you ask me," I said, stretching. "It makes me tired just thinking about it. Come on, let's go get some dinner. I'm starved."

"Yeah... okay," James sounded slightly reluctant.

"What's wrong?" I asked him as he stepped over to the recording memory pad and slid it out of the wall-dock.

He shrugged and glanced over at Stella. "Thanks for the show," he said with a smile.

"Of course, James Galling," Stella replied and faded from the room.

I fell in step behind James as he left the holo-suite. I could see from the way his shoulders hunched that he was nervous about something.

"Are you going to tell me what's bothering you or do I have to guess?" I asked, peering up into his face as we walked through the library. As usual, we didn't hold hands but his arm brushed against the back of my shoulder as we walked.

Finally he sighed and gave me a rueful smile. "I can't keep anything from you, can I? Sweet Flesh, you're worse than most telepaths. At least they know enough manners to shield."

I shrugged. "Dad always said I could never leave well enough alone. It used to send him off the deep end of the pier. So, quit being as evasive as he is and answer my question. Why are you so upset?"

"Liam," he muttered after a decent pause. "I don't know what kind of a mood he'll be in."

I frowned. I was a little nervous about seeing the third member of our little dating dance, too. Honestly, my interrogation of James was partially a way to keep my mind off who we were about to meet up with.

"Shouldn't I be the one who's a little unsure about seeing my competition?" I asked. It was the closest I'd come to admitting my feelings to James. My heart rate picked up as I waited for his response.

"Your competition?" he asked with a twist of one eyebrow. "Don't you find him attractive?"

I was taken aback by that comment. I almost told him no, of course I wasn't attracted to Liam. But then I thought about pressing up against him on James' bed and dancing at

Amourie's. After yesterday, that would be a lie. I didn't have my diplomatic friend's strict sense of morality when it came to telling the absolute truth. Dad and Ariel had ingrained in me a tendency to omit inconvenient details so deeply it was practically instinct. However, James' sense of justice and fair play made me uncomfortable lying directly to his face. It was usually a good thing, since it forced me to be open with him about things I might not have been otherwise. It made us closer. In this situation, however, it made me more vulnerable than I was comfortable with.

"Well... maybe a bit," I admitted, color touching my cheeks. "But he's my cousin. I mean, everyone says he looks like my dad. It would be weird if we got together, right?"

"I know people say it, but you know the real Gabriel. Do you honestly think Liam looks like him? I mean, sorry, but your dad is scary-pretty. The kind of beautiful that's kind of like a statue—nice to look at but you wouldn't want to cuddle it. Liam's more laid back and... touchable."

"Does that mean I'm scary-pretty, too?" I leaned back a bit so he could get a better look at my face.

"No! I mean... yes and no... that's not the point," James stammered. "What I'm trying to say is, you and Liam are way farther apart than the requisite five gens. We're colonists. Just about everyone is somehow related. If your mom's genes were as obvious as your dad's, I bet you'd see the connection to over half the people you meet."

I thought about that as we walked towards the dining

hall. It wasn't far from the library, so we didn't have a whole lot of time before we would be running into the gentleman in question. And despite my own mental fortress, I had a feeling James would be pretty easy for Liam to read if we were still discussing him when we walked up. Oh, the complications of dating telepaths.

"Well, I'm not related to you, am I?" I asked, giving his shoulder a little nudge with mine.

"I... don't think so. Not technically anyway," James replied slowly.

"Not technically?"

He shrugged. "I'm a descendant of James Andrinovich, who was your father's quasi-adopted child. So, there's a connection but not actual DNA that I'm aware of."

"I didn't realize the original Peace Child was your ancestor," I said as Liam's tall form became visible next to the cafeteria door. The stone entrance curved along with the plex-glass dome's alloy ribs, a satisfying combination of the old colonist tech and the newer Cybele-based construction materials. It seemed to reflect Liam himself; a modern day fusing of my father's coloring and the mortal colonists who claimed this world with hard work and tireless terraforming. "I knew you were named for him, but you never mentioned he was an actual relative."

"It's so many generations ago, it's almost not worth mentioning." James waved a hand as if to dismiss the topic.

"How long does it take to walk from the Fine Arts building?" Liam complained as we came abreast of him,

"Honestly, I've been here almost twenty minutes. I thought the two of you weren't going to come at all."

"Sorry to keep you waiting, Senator Usuriel," I said with a mock bow. I suddenly found myself a little pissed about how I'd been ignored last night. I had to blame someone and, since I had a soft spot for James, apparently it was going to be Liam. It might have been slightly unfair but I didn't really care. I treated my cousin to a glare that held a drop of fire in it. He matched it with a dark look of his own. We might be generations apart, but we'd both inherited some of the Usuriel temper it seemed. Perhaps that was a decent argument for why we shouldn't court, I thought as Liam opened the doors for us with exaggerated decorum.

"Why didn't you just nudge me?" James said. I could see the nervousness turning to frustration on his face. "We were in the library downloading old holos with Stella. You could have come over."

"Telepathy works both ways," Liam grumbled as we selected our drinks.

I wandered away from the boys to help myself to a fish dish. Neither Liam nor James liked fish much, but having grown up with my father's fresh catches, it made me feel at home. When I settled down at our usual table by the orange grove, James and Liam weren't far behind.

"So you find out anything worth discussing?" Liam asked, still sounding a little spore-bent about being made to wait on us. However, his temper eased as James and I recounted Dad and Adora's tangle with the Cat-Mantis. By the end of the story, my irritation with both of the boys had dissipated as well and we were engaging in our speculation as fervently as ever.

"So does that mean Darius was Adora's chaperon at the time of the Riland Massacre?" Liam asked, pulling out his memory pad. "He was her last partner, right?"

"The vampire? That's hardly proven," James tutted, tapping his own tablet to bring up our timeline.

"Darius?" I asked, stomach clenching. I remembered that name and I didn't think Professor Joan had mentioned it in history class. "He's not on the Family genealogy chart. Where did you hear about a Darius?"

"Iggy Riland's <u>White Raven</u>," Liam replied, referring to his favorite biography of my late aunt. I hadn't read it yet, but from the way James talked about it there was as much gossip as there was proven fact in that docfile. "Iggy talks about her companions but he doesn't really explain it the way you did. Yeah, here. This is a still-pic of the two of them together." He turned the memory pad in my direction so that I could see the still of my tall, slender aunt and a broad-shouldered, dark-skinned man. He had a hand possessively on her back while her chin rode in its usually aggressive angle. They were walking together in what looked like an urban area of some kind. I could see the storefronts behind them.

"I thought you said he was a vampire," I pointed out, gesturing to the still.

"Vampires can be photographed if they've recently consumed Usuriel blood," Liam countered. "Especially Usuriel blood as pure as Adora's. One would assume she was donating if they were a pair."

"Assumptions are always a bad idea," James muttered, tapping on his own memory pad. "There's no mention of the two of them in any of the marriage databases."

"Just because you're not married doesn't mean you don't have a relationship." Liam sounded smug. "It would explain why she was in Riland in the first place. And if the chaperon thing worked the way you say it did, then Adora might have been trusting a vampire to tell her what was safe and what wasn't. That's a massacre waiting to happen, if you ask me."

I shook my head. "Didn't Dad and Grandma have to approve her chaperon choice? I can hardly imagine Gabriel okaying a vampire as Adora's partner."

"Why not? Grandfather D'nay is a vampire and he seems stable enough," Liam said sensibly. "If a vampire is paired with a strong enough Usuriel, they essentially become long-lived mortals. It's not a bad situation under normal circumstances. But Adora wasn't exactly normal."

"Nothing about Usuriels is 'normal,'" James grumbled. "But you just undermined your own logic. If Adora's blood was strong enough to make Darius practically mortal, wouldn't he have functioned as a chaperon just as well as anyone else? Perhaps better, since he would have a longer period of time to become familiar with Adora's particular needs."

Liam shrugged. "Clearly I'm just speculating. I'm not sure anyone can know exactly what happened. I'm just saying, if Adora was leaning on a vamp for moral guidance, I can see how it might have gone seriously wrong. That's all."

"It is a possibility," I allowed, leaning my chin on my hand for a moment before glancing down at my empty tray. "Well, I think it's time for me to write that paper and go to bed. Vanessa is going to have me up so early I'll probably see the sunrise tomorrow."

James made a face while Liam raised an eyebrow. "Vanessa?"

"I'll tell you about it later," James said, putting a hand on Liam's arm to forestall other questions. I was relieved that I didn't have to explain my torn feelings about the Overwatch to Liam. So, I gathered up my tray and bid the boys goodnight.

It was strange, I reflected as I wandered back to the dormitory alone in the waning light, how easily the three of us fell back into such a comfortable rapport. I was glad the near-disaster of last night's party hadn't made us awkward or angry with each other. Since I'd never really had any other close friends my own age, I wasn't sure if this was normal or not.

I hadn't asked James if he and Liam slept together last night. I was fairly certain they had. As I changed into a loose night shirt and sat down to dictate my paper to Stella, I wondered if having sex with one of my boys and not the other would change things in ways that their ongoing relationship didn't. I suspected it would.

Chapter 14

The Overwatch

The next day dawned bright and early. I got showered and dressed in time for Vanessa to show up right outside the dormitory.

"You're on time. Very good," my older cousin said with a curt nod. She wore the same pressed blue uniform as yesterday. Diagonal folds across her breast accentuated her petite figure in a flattering, professional way. It struck me that she was finer boned than most of the women in our family; she hardly came past my shoulder.

Her teleportation was as smooth as Gabriel's—we blinked and were standing outside of the concrete structure Stella had shown me last night. Outside of the cities, there wasn't much concrete construction on Cybele. Here in the middle of nowhere, the sprawling complex looked distinctly out of place. I glanced around at the tangles of kyoss trees and wondered if any of the clusters of mushrooms on their bases were Death's Head. There were crews that went around rooting out the fatal fungus, and certainly Dad was good about double checking around Angelus Quietum. Still, an overgrown area like this one made me nervous.

"Welcome to the compound," Vanessa said smoothly, pressing her hand to the gate's locking mechanism. The lock clicked open and I followed my cousin as she strolled casually through the barbed wire fence. "This is every member of the Overwatch's home away from home. It may look cold and sterile from here, and there certainly is some discipline, but we're a close-knit group once you've gotten through training. After all, we are Family."

She escorted me through a double set of thick plex-glass doors. There was a young man with a hint of Usuriel in his midnight blue eyes and fire-red hair, despite the utter mortality of his rounded features, sitting in a plex-glass booth next to the entrance. He nodded to us as the doors slid open in slow sequence, hissing pressurized air as we walked from one area to the next.

"What did your father say about the Overwatch?" Vanessa asked, darting a glance at me with her one good, blue eye. She still held herself in that strictly erect manner as we walked down a long, gray-walled corridor.

"He seemed cautious," I replied slowly, unsure how open to be with Vanessa. Something about her still put me on edge and my father had drilled discretion into my head quite thoroughly, whether he intended to or not. Secrets were weapons and I didn't intend to give Vanessa any more ammunition against me or my father than she already had.

"Interesting word to describe Gabriel," she said, arching her eyebrows. It stretched the scars by her eye patch in unusual ways.

Before we could discuss further, we reached a single door in the long, empty corridor. The ceilings steadily gained height as we walked. It was several meters above my head now—a long sheet of riveted alloy reflecting the natural light of a small window at the end of the long hall.

"Welcome to the training gallery," she said with a smug smile. Then she pressed her hand to the door plate and the alloy slab retreated into the wall to reveal a cavernous space.

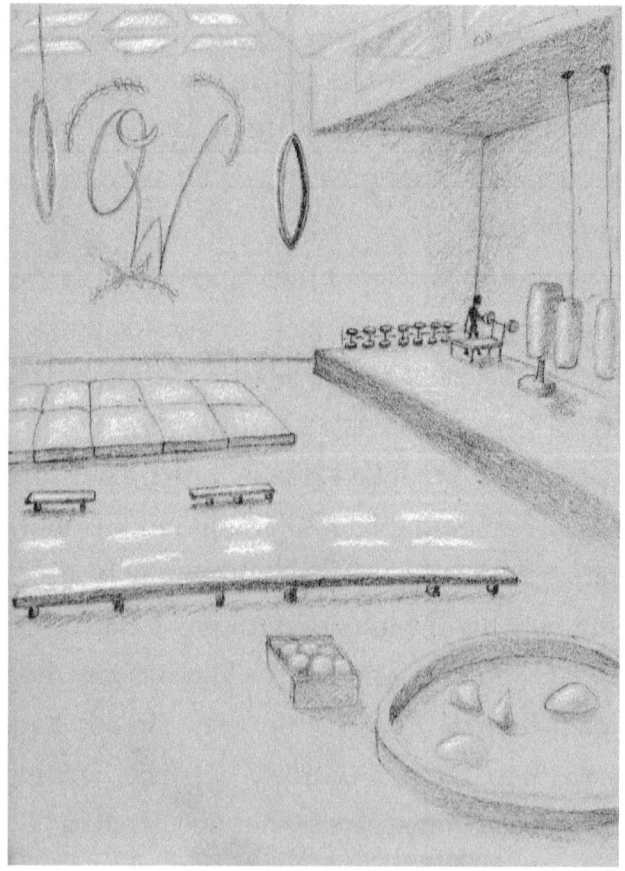

I had never seen a place like this, not even in the Earth history holos my father was fond of or the *Inspiration* documentation that I'd been pouring through with James and Liam. To start with, it was huge. If my father's wheat fields had been walled in concrete and alloy, they might have fit inside this space. The ceiling was so high I felt as though birds ought to be flying about the alloy rafters. The collection of objects around the room was eclectic; slim logs set on their sides, rings suspended from the ceiling by chains, large pools of water, and long bars with great disks screwed onto their sides. The vast majority of the space was dedicated to grappling mats. Those I did recognize and knew what to do with.

A few individuals with markedly Family features glanced at us as we came in. One was a tall woman with skin so dark black it seemed to absorb the light around her. Her blue eyes seemed light in comparison, though I thought they were probably a match in color to my own. She was manipulating a group of geometric blocks with small flicks of her slender fingertips, clearly practicing telekinesis.

Another was a pale, middle-aged man with gray in his red beard. He was large and muscular compared to the Family members I'd seen, but the sharply pointed ears and ice-blue eyes marked him as Adoran. I had a feeling he was much older than the forty-odd mortal years he looked to lay claim to. His age didn't hinder his ability to toss several heavy-looking spheres through the dangling rings.

"Jillian!" Vanessa called, her voice echoing across the room.

In the far corner, a petite figure raised her head. She was so out-of-sight, I hadn't even noticed her until now. Then my flames felt a small spark and, with a dull roar, the woman's figure was abruptly consumed in fire. I gasped in surprise as the billow of flame surged and lifted the woman up into the air. She rocketed towards us at an alarming speed before the flames abruptly disappeared and she alighted neatly in front of us.

"How..." I breathed, staring at Jillian as she gave Vanessa and me a friendly smile.

"Gracie, meet Jillian," Vanessa said, gesturing between the two of us. "Tenth-gen Gabriellan and the only other firebird we have at Overwatch."

"Oh! You're the new pyro?" Jillian said, her smile deepening to something genuine as she grabbed my forearm in greeting. "We've met before—at the flood last year! I had no idea you were another firebird, though. I'm not sure I've met more than a handful over the years."

"You must be a telekinetic plus pyro," I replied cautiously.

"Nope," she said with a shake of the head that tossed her crown of black braids about her plump face. If it hadn't been for the Usuriel angle of her nose and the mischievous twist of her mouth, I would never have guessed her for Family. "Just fire." She held up a tiny alloy object. With a flick of one finger, she activated it and a small, blue spark caught between two protruding wires. Instantly, a spiral of orange flame licked up around her and my hair blew back from the sudden, hot wind. "I hear you don't even need a spark, though. That has to be convenient. Can you demonstrate?"

I sent a questioning glance at Vanessa who shrugged and motioned for me to do as I pleased. I spread my hands and opened the fist that kept my flames locked away. They were eager to manifest after I'd swallowed that house fire yesterday. It took a good deal of control to keep them from leaping into Jillian's flames and overpowering them. Instead, I pulled them into a tight spiral that danced up my arms and around my shoulders before dissipating in a small shower of sparks about my head.

Jillian's eyes went wide. "Oh, wow," she breathed, an excited grin on her face. "You really are what they said, aren't you? A third-gen pure firebird. I bet you'd even give 'Nessa a run in the Tourney."

"Tourney?"

"We have a friendly competition to keep our skills sharp each year," Vanessa explained. She gave Jillian a sharp look. "I haven't participated in several years."

"She was reigning champion for over a decade when she quit," Jillian said with a wry smile. "But you have to step back in if Gracie joins. She's the first third-gen born in... well... how old is Lilly?"

"Older than she'd like us to remember, I'm sure," Vanessa said dryly, implying that her own age was not up for discussion.

"So... you don't have telekinesis," I said slowly, bringing the conversation back to what I was actually interested in, "but you can fly? With just fire?"

Jillian's brown eyes held that familiar Usuriel flame. "Oh, yes. That's my own personal trick, though. You have to join OW to learn that one."

"OW," I echoed. "Overwatch?"

She nodded and tapped the pin on her lapel. It did indeed bear the OW insignia with the raised leaves just like the medallion my father had shown me. It put a thrill of dread into my stomach and suddenly the nerves that had left me at Jillian's display came rushing back.

"Don't look so scared," Jillian said, wrinkling her nose like a teenager. She looked around thirty to me, with more lines etched in her face than my father's, despite the youthful bounce of her dark eyes. "The work is depressing and sometimes dangerous, sure. But we're well-trained and we take care of each other like the Family we are. I wouldn't work anywhere else."

I couldn't help returning her enthusiastic grin. "Shall we continue our tour?" Vanessa suggested.

Jillian had gone a long way towards convincing me when she said she'd teach me to fly if I joined. Still, I was as curious as ever and enjoyed being shown around the offices and empty holding cells. There wasn't really much else to see. Vanessa wrapped up the tour with her own office and some very welcome breakfast. We sipped herbal tea and had hot, spiced rice while Vanessa went over the requirements for membership.

"You'd continue your studies at the University, of course. We want well-rounded officers. However, you would add two one-hour courses to your day — one to physically train and the other to learn specifics of the law. Within six months, you could be a junior officer on hourly pay. Once you graduate from the traditional three-year University, you'll be a full officer with a salary."

I frowned. "Salary?"

"And a signing bonus," Vanessa turned her memory pad around so I could see the figures. I hadn't dealt much with money in my youth, but I knew what a hover car cost because I'd looked into buying one for school. Even with my father's generous chore allowance, it hadn't been an option. The numbers in front of me would cover a much nicer hover car than the ones I'd been looking at.

"You won't be living in the low-rent district," Vanessa said smoothly. "In fact, if you saved up a few years, you could have your own version of Angelus Quietum. If that's what you want. It will pay for quite the nice apartment in Skykyle if that's more your interest, as well."

I stared at her, a little overwhelmed. She was offering me a real future. This was something I could do with my abilities that would pay for a lot more than a dormitory and a party dress.

My gaze darted around the small square of her office.

There wasn't much here in the way of personal detail. I saw a few stills framed on the wall of the less-terraformed beaches some people liked to vacation to. Directly behind the desk was a massive comm screen. To the right of that was a large window that looked down into the training gallery. On the ledge below the window sat a small clay bird with a white feather tied with twine around its neck. Beside it sat a small, green vial that looked oddly familiar. Otherwise, there wasn't much here to let me see what Vanessa's life outside of the Overwatch was like. I was having a hard time getting my head around her.

"Do you make this offer to every Usuriel?" I asked, feeling unsure again. I wanted to learn to fly, but the money said this was not a light obligation.

"Of course not," Vanessa said quickly. "Many of them don't have talents that would lend themselves to police work. And others don't have the... temperament. There's a reason we exist. If you take the job, you'll see what I mean."

I narrowed my eyes. "You barely know me. I mean, we said hi a few times after the flood and now you've heard a rumor about what I did while you weren't around. That's enough to offer me a job?"

Vanessa tilted her head at me, blue eye calculating. "Your father didn't raise a fool, did he," she murmured.

There was a pause as we looked each other over carefully. It was easy to be distracted by the scars and the eye patch. Underneath all that wild hair and her intimidating manner, Vanessa was scary-pretty.

Finally, she sighed. "Gabriel may have his lapses in judgment, but when he's sober he is probably one of the best of us. Just having a conversation with you lets me know that he raised you as well as any of his other children and they were the backbone of Cybele society for decades. Lilly is still on our council. It isn't just your abilities that make you valuable, Gracie, it's also the moral fiber Gabriel and our grandparents instilled in you. It tends to get watered down in some of our later lines, I'm afraid, but in you it shines as clearly as the Family features."

"Because I wasn't willing to let some vamps burn?"

"That, and you volunteered your time with Gabriel to put Landing back together after the flood. If I remember correctly, you even stole his shuttle to help with the rescue effort."

It hadn't been civic duty that drove me that day, but I could see how she might have misinterpreted my dash to Gabriel's rescue. Heat rose in my cheeks.

"I'm not sure stealing a shuttle is really the biggest endorsement of character."

Vanessa laced her fingers between each other on the desk. "It was a risk. But you wanted to make sure your father was safe. And you ended up nearly wrecking the shuttle saving that mortal reporter."

"Oh yeah, Joe," I muttered, rubbing my face with one hand in a vain attempt to hide my crimson face. James and I should have let that spore-wit drown.

"That's the kind of person we need at Overwatch," Vanessa said calmly. "Someone who runs into dangerous situations when everyone else is running from them. Someone who is willing to risk the anger of authority if they think they're doing the right thing. Someone who puts the needs of society before their personal safety."

My father's words during the flood came back to me. *"We're Aware, which means we have an extra responsibility to our community to keep it safe."*

"Okay," I said. "I'll join."

Vanessa gave me a smile that reached her ice-blue eye. "I'm so glad."

Chapter 15

Boiling Point

Class was uneventful and I didn't have anyone to tell about my new job since Malcolm still wasn't talking to me. I was excited to see James at lunch and let him know that I'd accepted the job with the Overwatch, but I didn't get a chance to do that either. Instead, I walked out of Written Communication and nearly tripped over my father's angry figure in the hallway.

"Dad," I gasped, looking up at Gabriel's unhappy scowl.

"Is there someplace quiet where we can talk?" he asked. My heart plunged into my stomach. If Dad was here at school, something horrible had to be wrong.

"We can go back to my room," I said, my throat tight with fear.

Dad didn't blink or move at all except to put a hand on my elbow. Then we were in my dormitory. The transition was more wrenching than I remembered it.

I stumbled back against my bed as he let me go. "What's going on? Are Grandma and Grandpa okay?"

"What were you doing at the Overwatch compound

today?" His voice was so low it took me a moment to process what he was saying. When I wrapped my brain around it, I stared at him in confusion.

"Vanessa offered me a job," I replied slowly. "How did you even know I was there?"

"You didn't take it, did you?" Dad ground out each word between clenched teeth.

"What if I did?" I said, eyeing his angry expression. Dad and I hadn't always seen eye to eye of course, but he'd never started off a conversation in such a threatening tone. I'd felt so good about where our relationship was the day before that I was having a hard time understanding what could possibly have set him off so badly.

"Go back to Vanessa. Tell her to delete the hiring files. You are not working for the Overwatch and that's final."

Had he phrased it any other way, I might have listened to him. I'd had my own misgivings after all. But I'd just crawled out from the heavy shadow he cast across my life and now he barged into my space with the audacity to tell me who I could and couldn't work for?

"Get out," I growled. A lick of flame crept across the ends of my hair to spill over my shoulders.

"Excuse me?" My father had never sounded dangerous to me before, but the edge to his tone sent the hair on my spine on end. I suddenly was very aware of how much taller he was than me. A breath of his power slid around the room and I smelled the alcohol. My nerves turned to pure fury.

"I said get out of my room!" I snapped, stepping towards him. With an angry finger, I pointed at his chest and then sharply in the direction of the door. I glowered at him from a few inches away for several heartbeats. He showed no inclination to move. I made an infuriated noise and spun away from him. "Who the hell do you think you're talking to, anyway? Barging in here like someone's dead and scaring me half to death."

"I'm trying to talk to my daughter," he rumbled. "The one who is about to make the biggest mistake of her short life."

"Put that in reverse a second," I hissed, quoting one of Liam's favorite slang phrases. "I may be your daughter but I'm an adult now. My tuition and board here is free, which means I don't owe you a Fate-forsaken thing."

"You get that free tuition and board because you're my daughter," he snarled, leaning forward but stopping short of reaching for me. His hands tightened around the back of my little metal chair, which had the misfortune of being directly between us. It creaked in protest.

"What are you going to do if I don't quit the Overwatch?" I asked, folding my arms under my breasts and cocking my hip at him. It was far more attitude than I'd ever tried to get away with at Angelus Quietum, but we weren't in his house anymore. "Disown me? The Overwatch is run by the Family, Dad. They're not going to take away my scholarship."

"You will quit because, despite the fact that you think you're grown, you are still in fact my child. If you have any respect for me left, you will do as I say and tell Vanessa to go to hell with her job offer," he sounded a little desperate, honestly, but I was too mad to care. He'd scared me and stepped all over the fragile sense of freedom I'd managed to find here at school. It was taking all of my control not to torch him on the spot. He was probably strong enough to shield from me—even half-drunk—and the result would likely be a burned out dormitory, which helped me resist the temptation.

"Fuck you," I said, looking him straight in the eye. "You aren't my father. You haven't been for almost two years now. The man who raised me never had to find the bottom of a bottle before he had a conversation with me."

Why is it that family always knows just how to wound us best? Why is it that family knows just how to bring out the worst in us? I watched the painful honesty of my words cut across his face more deeply than any knife. For a moment, his head went up as the arrogant shield he put between himself and the world tried to slam down. Then, he took a deep breath and his shoulders fell.

"Okay," he sighed, his voice much calmer than it had been. "If that's how you really feel, Gracie, then I'm sorry. I know I'm not perfect, but please don't let that get in the way of what I'm trying to tell you. Hate the messenger if you must, but it doesn't make what I'm saying untrue."

I hadn't expected that response. My father's infamous temper snuffed out with one low blow from my careless mouth.

"You're sorry?" I echoed, struggling to maintain some anger in the face of his utter defeat. "Shit. Dad... I didn't mean that. Honestly, I'm not like Lilly. I don't want to cut you off completely. But you can't bully your way in here like this. It's not okay."

He glanced up at me and the shadows that usually rode his gaze were much deeper than I remembered them. It hurt something deep in my chest. I shied away.

"I'm not doing this out of some misguided desire to control your life," he said. "When you wanted to attend University, I set everything up, didn't I? I'm not trying to get in the way of your self-exploration. I'm just trying to keep you from making a very big mistake."

"You didn't forbid it, but you did pull every emotional guilt file in your database," I grumbled.

"Look, I admitted that I'm not a perfect parent," he said, irritation climbing back into his voice.

"Understatement and all that," I muttered, glad to feel the anger building back into the pit of my chest. It was a lot easier to deal with than my father's brokenness.

"Gracie," he said my name like a curse. "Let me get a word in, will you?"

"Fine! Say what you have to say already and get out! I have a class to get ready for!"

Gabriel suddenly looked like he wanted to send the entire building up in flames as much as I did. The chair squeaked again and I had a feeling he was doing it some permanent damage.

"Then let me just say it! The Overwatch is a bad idea! There will come a time—and believe me when I say it will come—when they ask you to do things you don't want to do. Out of loyalty, or duty, or some other stupid sense of obligation, you'll do them. And then you'll have to live with the guilt and self-loathing for the rest of your life. I'm not trying to bully you. I'm trying to save you from a lifetime of regret."

He actually sounded sincere. It was probably the closest he'd ever come to admitting any of his dark secrets to me. I suddenly understood why he'd felt the need to drink before he came over.

"That sounds like experience talking," I said slowly. I was on thin ice here, but if I was going to give up the best and only career opportunity I'd ever been presented, not to mention a chance to learn how to fly, I needed something more concrete. Besides, if I didn't push him on this one, I'd never be able to face James and Liam when I told them about the conversation.

Dad gave me that wounded look again and I could see all those years of pain writhing under the surface. How the hell did I get him to bring it out into the open? If there was a trick, I didn't know it. I wished for the millionth time that I had some kind of empathy or telepathy. Perhaps it would have made things easier between us. It's impossible to know.

"What did they make you do, Dad?" I asked quietly, holding that agonizing gaze without flinching.

He looked away first. "I... I can't." It was almost a whisper. He let go of the chair back and I could clearly see the ridges of his fingers in the alloy.

"Come on, Dad," I said, stepping to his side and reaching out a hand to almost touch one arm. When he made no move to accept my comfort, I left my palm open between us. "Tell me why I shouldn't join the Overwatch. Don't give me generalities or sage advice. I want your true reason; a specific reason. Tell me why you left the Overwatch and I'll go tell Vanessa to take me off their roster."

He looked at me helplessly and there was a wall between us. It felt almost tangible as I stood, hand still outstretched, and he stared at me with clenched fists at his side. I almost said her name. Sweet Fate, I wish I had. Maybe then everything would have turned out differently. In hindsight, there are so many turning points on the road towards disaster, but I was still too young, and too afraid of letting anyone know about my odd dreams. Even though it sat on my tongue like a weight, I didn't say Adora's name.

Finally, after a very long silence, he dropped my gaze. "Let it be, Gracie."

"No," I said, my temper rising again. "Oh no you don't. This is why I didn't talk to you for over a month after I got here. Or didn't you notice?"

"Gracie..." he started again, warning in his voice. I ignored it.

"I didn't want to bring this up, but apparently you haven't learned anything about honesty in the last few weeks." All the old hurt and betrayal of my initial discoveries bubbled up into a scalding wave in my chest. "You have always been a fucking coward, did you know that? You couldn't sit me down and say 'you know, sweetheart, I've struggled with some things over the years. I've made some mistakes. Here's what they are.' No. I never got to have that conversation with my father. Instead, I get to find out about your morphine addiction from Professor Joan and Stella."

"Gracie..." he tried again, something between anger and regret in his face. I pressed on relentlessly.

"No. You had your chance to speak at Angelus Quietum. Now I get to tell you how I found out about your little habit. You want to know what the first holo was that Stella played for me? I got to see you shoot up, Dad. Intentionally overdose, in fact. It was spectacular. Good thing Olivia showed up when she did or I'd never have been born."

"She shouldn't have showed you that," he said, face gone pale.

"I'm glad she did," I cut him off. "Because it was real. It was honest. Two things I didn't get from my only parent very often."

"That's not true," he replied, gesturing sharply to break into my diatribe. "Look, I've never been a single parent before, let alone right after getting clean. It's harder than it seems. I know I made mistakes. I should have been more open with you. I'm sorry. I just... it never seemed like the right time."

"And you were a fucking coward," I finished for him. We'd traded places, I observed coolly as he held out a hand and I hugged my chest tightly just outside of his reach.

"And I was a fucking coward," he agreed. "There, are you happy?"

"No," I said.

We stared at each other a long moment and I think we were both wondering what the hell was going through the other one's head.

"Tell me," I breathed into the silence. "Tell me why, Dad. Why shouldn't I join Overwatch?"

"Honestly?" he said, rolling those blue eyes up to me. "Can I ask you a few questions for a moment?"

Startled by this new approach, I nodded. "Okay."

He took a deep breath and mirrored my crossed arms while leaning his weight against the dresser. I perched on the edge of my desk and eyed him cautiously.

"Who do you care about, Gracie?"

I hadn't been expecting that question. "Who? What do you mean?"

He made a quick gesture with one hand. "Everyone has a few people who are close to them. So who is it for you? Who would you run into a burning building for?"

"Well... anyone really. Burning buildings don't really pose a threat for me..."

"It's a figure of speech and you know it. Answer the question," he snapped, though it was only irritation and not fury in his tone now.

Feeling like we were back in his lessons by the lake, I settled a little more comfortably on the desk. "You, of course," I said honestly. I might have seen a touch of relief in his expression when I listed him first. "Grandma Gloria and Grandpa D'nay, then probably James and Liam... maybe

Leesil, too."

"Okay." Dad sounded satisfied with that list. "And what do all of those people have in common?"

"They don't mind dealing with Gabriel Usuriel's crazy daughter?"

"Come on, I've taught you more logic than that," Dad complained. "They're all Aware; even James, though he's the genetic manipulation rather than the Family version."

I thought about that. "Yeah... I guess so."

"You guess so? No, it's a fact. Everyone you know and care about is Aware. True?"

"True," I echoed.

"Now, why does the Overwatch want you?"

"Vanessa called me an effective deterrent."

Dad caught himself before he chuckled at that one. He covered it with a cough before looking at me with a touch of amusement. "Nice phrase," he said. "Okay, that means your flames, right? They want you to enforce the law because you have enough deadly force to take on just about anyone on Cybele. Am I right?"

I was still uncomfortable with how strong Vanessa thought my psi-power was. To hear it echoed in my father's voice, the man who trained me and knew better than anyone exactly what I could do, was halfway between empowering and frightening. I ducked my head and nodded.

"Right," Dad said and his face got serious again. "Now, who exactly do you think they want you to use those powers on, Gracie? Who are the Overwatch responsible for?"

I glanced up at him. I knew where he was going with this. He was right that he and Stella had taught me a decent amount of logic. However, that didn't mean I agreed with him.

"They're responsible for individuals of Awareness," I said, before quickly adding. "But none of you would ever do anything to get the Overwatch sent after you. I mean, it's not like they go after people who just mind their own business. Besides, you and Grandma Gloria would tie my tail in a knot if I tried anything, anyway. You're both way stronger than I will ever be."

"Mom and I... perhaps," Gabriel allowed. "But what about Dad?"

"Grandpa would never hurt anyone," I said, trying to ignore a vivid memory of D'nay's less-than-subtle response to trespassers.

"What people have done in the past has nothing to do with what they will do in the future," Dad said evenly. "Especially very long-lived individuals. In my experience, the longer you live, the more likely you are to eventually find yourself in a situation with no good way out. Things can get messy quickly in situations like that."

"What are you saying?"

He ran a hand through his hair. "What about James? What if they asked you to go after him? He's a telepath and you've got shields thicker than the *Inspiration*'s bulk heads. Against you, he might as well be mortal. What will you do when they ask you to subdue him?"

"James is probably the most ethical person I've ever met, so this is a ridiculous rhetorical scenario," I grumbled. I held up a hand to forestall his protests. "But I get what you're trying to say. I wouldn't be happy about it, obviously. But if there was a good reason? Well, someone would have to do it. He'll probably come more quietly for me than anyone else. It's probably better if I'm the one to come for him."

Gabriel stared at me for a moment. The shadows in his gaze hadn't left, but they'd become less tortured and more quietly sad. "I'm not going to win this argument, am I?"

I slowly shook my head. "No. I wasn't completely sure about joining earlier today, but now that you've made me think about it, I'm pretty sure it is the right thing to do. Someone needs to make sure the laws are enforced. I have the strength to do it. It's my responsibility to use that strength for the right reasons. You've said as much yourself."

"I should have known those words would come back to bite me." Dad closed his eyes. "I can understand the sentiment, even if I don't agree with it. I just hope you don't come to regret it as much as I have."

"Me, too," I said softly. We were quiet together and, for the first time that day, the silence didn't feel uncomfortable.

"So, will you still visit next week?" Dad asked softly.

"Are you sure you want me to?" I said, remembering my remark about his drinking.

"If you'd like," he replied. "As long as you don't bring

your uniform."

I cracked a small smile. "Don't worry, I will be completely off duty."

"I'll see you then." He returned a tiny hint of my smile before fading out of the room.

***

Despite the civil tone our conversation ended on, by the time I made it to a very late lunch with James and Liam I was livid again.

"I can't believe he thought I'd up and quit on his say so," I complained for what felt like the hundredth time.

"And I thought I had family problems," Liam said, munching on a sandwich. "We might not have much money, but at least my parents realize I'm grown and out of the house. I think they're kind of relieved to be rid of me, honestly."

I toyed with my soup. "I wish Dad would get that through his thick skull."

"Your father has some issues," Liam agreed. "I think we've verified that."

"Thanks, Liam," I muttered around my spoon.

"Are you still going to visit him this break?" James asked.

I shrugged. "I'm not sure. He wants me to but I don't know how I feel about it."

"You should go," he said quietly.

I glanced up at him. The melancholy arch of his brow sent

a pang of remorse through my breast. "You must miss your family," I said. "Sorry. Here I am avoiding my dad when you'd probably give up your implant for a chance to visit your parents."

"It's okay. I know things are complicated for you and Gabriel," James said, patting my hand.

"Complicated... that's one word for it," I said with a sigh. "On the positive side, he did slip and say a few honest things. I think you were right about the whole Sorrow thing. And I'm pretty sure he killed Adora."

"Wait... what?" Liam and James leaned in, eyes wide and riveted to my face.

I nodded. "He didn't admit to it, but he tried to convince me that the Overwatch would end up sending me after someone I care about. I think he was trying to tell me without coming out and saying he killed her. And who else in his immediately family has come to a bad end? I mean, we've been saying a Family member probably ended up killing her for the Overwatch. It had to be Dad. He's probably the only person besides Gloria who even approached Adora's level and, more importantly, she trusted him. If she truly had some wires loose, he might have been the only Family member who could have gotten close enough to do it."

"I don't know," James sounded a little doubtful. "You heard him in that holo we saw yesterday. He could never keep up with her. How would he take her on by himself? I'm not sure he had the strength to do it."

"Dad's not just strong, he's smart. He knew how to handle her." When both boys gave me doubtful looks I decided to change tactics. "Listen, why else would he have to get half-drunk just to talk to me about the Overwatch? And I know Lauria was tragic but he didn't go back to the drugs after Olivia died. So what was different the second time? Right after White Woman, Dad quits the OW and goes on a sixty-year morphine binge. He did admit to that one."

"He admitted to the drug use just before you were born?" Liam sounded like a little kid on Landing Day.

I nodded. "He said it wasn't easy being a single parent who just got clean. He basically just told me he was using before he found out about me. I don't have any doubt anymore."

"He really is Sorrow," James breathed, eyes wide.

"Yep," I said, taking a long drink of water. "He really was."

We were all quiet, digesting the news. Finally, I stretched and tossed my spoon in my empty soup bowl.

"Well, thanks for listening to me complain," I said, rubbing some post-meal wakefulness back into my face, "but I have a ceramics project that won't finish itself. I'd better get moving."

Liam nodded amiably but James gave me an expression that was halfway between eager and anxious. "Umm... mind if I walk with you to the studio?" my blond friend asked.

Liam gave us a little frown and glanced between his plate

and James'. Both of them looked pretty full to be cleaning up. "I'll keep you company if you want to finish your lunch," Liam offered, confusion in his dark blue eyes.

"Nah, I'm not really hungry today," James said with a shrug of his slim shoulders as we both got to our feet. Even without telepathy, I could feel the misdirection in that statement. I slid a glance at Liam and caught him doing the same in my direction. We both quickly looked away.

"Okay." Liam sounded a little hurt. "I'll see you two after classes, then?"

"Sure," I said, trying to give him an encouraging smile even though James' odd behavior was setting my own nerves a little on edge. I will admit to a decent amount of curiosity about what James might want to discuss out of our friend's earshot, however.

"Yeah, we'll see you later," James agreed, his voice sounding a bit distracted, though he did pat Liam's tall shoulder as we gathered our plates and cups.

James and I were silent as we delivered our trays to the wash area. With his usual simple efficiency, he held the door for me as I exited. I thanked him with a generous smile which he returned nervously before falling into step with me.

We were quiet for much longer than we usually were around each other. The tension that had begun in the mess hall pressed in too thickly to speak, though we weren't holding hands or even brushing elbows the way we often did.

"So..." I started just as he cleared his throat. We both paused, then chuckled and each gestured for the other to start.

"Go ahead," I laughed with a shake of my head. "You're the one who just gave up his lunch to get me alone."

The blood rushed to James' face and I felt a touch guilty about being so blunt. "I really wasn't hungry," he muttered, cheeks burning red.

"Sorry." I put a hand to his arm and he glanced at me with those pale blue eyes. "Tell me what you were going to say. Please."

James cleared his throat again and shifted his weight from one foot to the other. "It's... well... it's no big deal. I just kind of wanted to say I'm sorry again. For what happened, you know, when the three of us went out. I feel like..." he paused, face still flushed but his eyes meeting mine a little more steadily. We'd paused on the path to the Fine Arts building and were standing in the shade of a large oak tree, facing each other. My arms had wrapped themselves nervously around my memory pad while James' slender fingers fidgeted at the edge of his belt. Finally he took a bigger breath and came out with it. "I guess the other day, when you asked me who else I was dating, it kind of hit a nerve for me. I realized that we haven't really had much alone time since you came to school. I like Liam, don't get me wrong, but you're... special."

I couldn't keep the grin from blooming across my face. I

felt giddier than any amount of alcohol had ever achieved. "No, we haven't seen much of each other just one-on-one," I agreed. "Not that I don't like spending time with you and Liam. But it is nice to have a conversation just the two of us."

"Yeah, it is," he agreed, the corners of his eyes relaxing a touch. "I guess I was hoping... well... kind of thinking that perhaps you'd like to have more than just a conversation or a quick research session. I was thinking more like dinner. At a place in town, not the mess hall. Just us. Sitting and eating and talking, just... us."

Looking into his rounded, hopeful, mortal face, I felt the flames in my chest push upwards until I was sure my whole body glowed.

"I'd love that," I said.

"Yeah? Really?" He sounded so surprised, as if he'd been sure I would reject him without the allure of Liam to entice me out the door. As if I hadn't been practically throwing myself at him back at Angelus Quietum, I thought with a mental eye-roll. I chided myself for being petty as I slipped my hand into his.

"Yeah, really," I echoed, and began walking towards the Arts building again. He allowed me to lead him along the path with a bemused smile on his face. I could feel the sweat on his palm and gave his hand a reassuring squeeze. "When do you want to set our little date? Tonight? Or is that too soon?"

"Tonight is perfect," James breathed, then his broad grin

faltered and he seemed to reconsider, "Or... maybe we should wait a day or two. I mean, we've already blown off Liam once today."

I wasn't as fond of my tall cousin as James clearly was, but I didn't really want to alienate him completely. He was a fun research partner, if nothing else. "Okay. Our next two day break is in a few days. Do you want to do dinner then?"

The strain around James' mouth finally faded away and he stepped closer to my side so that our bodies were brushing each other as we walked.

"Yes, that's just what I was thinking," he said. "There's that pretty little Hal-themed cafe in Landing Market. I don't have a hover car and without Liam, we can't teleport. But that place is close enough to walk."

"I think I'd enjoy a nice evening stroll," I replied. "It will burn off an extra helping of dessert, anyway." Then a thought hit me and I groaned. "No... wait. I promised Dad I'd visit him this break. And I really shouldn't cancel on him after the fight we just had, even if he is a pushy ass."

"Well, how about tomorrow night, then?" James suggested. "Classes are over by sixteen hundred hours for me. And you're out by seventeen hundred, right?"

"Yeah," I agreed with a relieved smile. "That should work!"

The Fine Arts building loomed ahead of us and, moving quickly so I wouldn't lose my nerve, I pulled James against the wall by the door. My back fetched up against the rough hewn stone, my hand pulling his arm around my waist even as my other palm found the slim curve of his spine. I was strong for a girl my size and James was not a large man. Suddenly, I found him pressed against me, one hand steadying himself against the rock wall while the planes of his chest put a tantalizing amount of pressure against my breasts. The smell of fresh, rain-soaked soil filled the air as the memory of our first kiss rushed over me. I reached up to brush the blond hair out of his eyes. It was feather-light silk under my fingertips.

"Gracie, I... I'm sorry we haven't..." he started but I shook my head at him.

"Shut up," I told him. "It doesn't matter."

I kissed him, my hands pulling his head down so that I didn't even have to stand on tip toe for my mouth to find his. He hesitated a heartbeat, then gave in to me, his mouth opening to mine as I explored him—no longer a timid or childish exercise but something intensely intimate and familiar.

When he pulled away from me, we were both out of breath and I, for one, found my body ready to do a lot more than just kiss.

"You should probably get to the studio," James said softly, his forehead leaning against mine as his fingertips brushed the wavy strands away from where they clung to my cheek.

"Yeah," I agreed, but I didn't move. We stood there enjoying each other, my arms wrapped around his waist while his fingers continued to play in my hair. "You know," I murmured after a long pause. "I can always work on this project after class. If you wanted to come back to my room..."

James chuckled and laid a kiss on my forehead. "Save something to look forward to on our date, hmmm?" To soften the blow, he caught my mouth with another kiss that I felt all the way down my spine before pulling away to stand just outside the shelter of my arms. "I shouldn't distract you from your studies. I'll see you at dinner tonight, though, right?"

"Of course," I said, giving his lingering hands a squeeze with mine.

With one last love-sick grin, the two of us went our separate ways.

Chapter 16

James (and Liam)

The next day I showed up for my first Overwatch class.

Mornings were dedicated to physical training. Vanessa met me at the entrance to the compound, taking a moment to introduce me to the security staff and instruct Stella to give me access to their trainee level clearance. Stella's core was housed in an underground bunker elsewhere on the property, so she was fully integrated into the Overwatch systems.

After security, we went to the training gallery. There were over a dozen Family members using the odd gym equipment. Jillian came up to us almost immediately, interrupting my survey of the other inhabitants.

"I'm so glad you joined!" she said, giving me a hug and handing me a small package. "Go ahead, open it."

Startled by the present, I pulled open the little bag. Inside was a lapel pin with the OW insignia, just like the one that was on Jillian's shirt now. Like me, she was wearing the Overwatch workout uniform. Vanessa sent one to me last night and it consisted of a simple blue, loose shirt and skin-tight pants that moved with me easily. It wasn't high fashion, but at least it was comfortable. With a smile, I put the pin on my collar as well.

"Thank you," I said to Jillian.

"I'm excited to train with you," she said. "I've never had another pyro to work with one-on-one."

"I can't wait for you to show me all of your tricks," I told her. Jillian's enthusiasm was contagious. "Especially the flying one!"

"Maybe we'll get to that today!" She winked. "First, though, I think we should introduce you to your class. Or rather, your classmate. We usually only take on one trainee at a time, but you're not a teleporter and we don't have any older 'porters free to partner you. So, Vanessa decided to make an exception. I believe you may have already met your new partner." Jillian gestured behind me.

I turned and my jaw dropped. "Liam?"

"I couldn't let you have all the fun," he said with a twitch of one dark eyebrow. The training outfit somehow sat more flatteringly on his tall frame than it did mine. I scowled up at him.

"I want someone else," I said, turning to Vanessa.

She shifted her weight and exchanged a glance with Liam. "I thought you said the two of you were friends? What's the problem?"

I flashed him a wicked grin. "He can't teleport for shit."

Liam's face, which had frozen in horror at my statement, relaxed into a sheepish grin. "Hey, I get where I'm going."

I rolled my eyes. "And occasionally you manage to bring my stomach along with us."

Vanessa cleared her throat. "I have been assured that he is in fact a moderate strength three-T, despite being over a tenth generation."

"He is," I said. "I'm just teasing. Mostly."

"Camphor evaluated him. You know he wouldn't exaggerate. Gracie's probably just used to teleporting with elder children," Jillian said with a twinkle in her eyes.

"If you mean with people who don't make you feel like you're about to turn inside out, then yes," I agreed.

"You'll get used to it," Vanessa said, turning from me to Jillian. "Can you handle things from here?"

"Of course," Jillian replied. "Come on, you two. You're mine for the next few weeks."

While we didn't get into the flying thing the first day, she did let Liam and I show her our skills on the wrestling mat.

Liam scoffed initially at the idea of grappling with me. However, it seemed that my city-raised cousin never had the benefit of martial arts training. It had been a few months since Dad's drills but the muscle memory hadn't left me. When I flipped him twice without letting him put a hand on me, Liam agreed that perhaps he could use a little instruction.

"This would be different if I could use telekinesis," he grumbled, picking himself back up for a third time.

"Bring it on, big boy," I said, pulling some flames up to

dance around my hands. "Just watch yourself. If you get psi, so do I."

"Hmmm... well, when you put it that way..."

"Settle down, you two. Okay, Liam. Here's what she's doing when she throws you like that," Jillian said, stepping in. She had me go slowly through the motion so that he could see exactly how I was shifting my weight to take the advantage of his superior strength and height and turn it against him.

"I think I'm going to have a lot to learn," he sighed, rubbing a shoulder.

***

The rest of that day flew in an anticipatory blur. Once I got over the shock of Liam joining me at the OW, the only thing on my mind all day was James.

Class lasted an eternity as I stared at the time on my memory pad, willing the minutes to go faster. Finally, the professor wound up her lecture and I nearly bowled over two mortal classmates on my way out the door. They gave me a glare as I called my apologies over one shoulder.

I'd rinsed off after OW practice that morning, but I dashed through the shower again anyway. Remembering that I would be taking a pretty long walk before and after the restaurant, I decided to forgo a dress and instead selected a fashionable set of pants, boots, and a top that Grandma Gloria had given me as a gift when I turned sixteen. It was a little more frilly and revealing than what I usually wore to class, but its pale blue color would bring out the deep sapphire of my eyes. Remembering James' remark before our outing to Amourie's, I did use a bit of kohl this time.

"Gracie?" James' voice said my name through my implant.

Nerves set my stomach into buzzing knots and I suddenly wondered if I would be able to eat at all on this date. I scattered a last dusting of tint across my cheeks and regarded myself in the mirror. I made an expression of disgust at my still-visible freckles, then took a steadying breath and tapped my implant to answer James.

"I'm ready to go!" I told him in what I hoped was a cheerful voice. "Do you want me to meet you at your room?"

"I'm already outside. Why don't you just come down and we'll walk from here?" There was something in his tone that sounded tired or hesitant. Though I told myself it was just my imagination, it made my nerves go up another level.

"Sure," I said. "I'll see you in a minute!"

I took the stairs breathlessly, and opened the door at the base of them so fast I all but fell into James' arms. Fortunately, the young Terran diplomat was braced against the wall next to the door so I didn't drag both of us to the ground.

"Sorry!" I gasped, catching myself with one hand on the stone wall and the other on James' arm.

"You okay?" James asked, blond hair falling into his face as he steadied me with both hands. I suddenly found myself exactly where I wanted to be—in James' arms, looking up into his gently concerned eyes.

"What? Oh, I'm fine. Sorry. I didn't mean to run into you." Despite the apology, I didn't move away from him. Instead, I leaned into his slim chest and tried to let the desire my head blind status hid from his telepathy shine through my eyes.

James cleared his throat and set me more firmly on my feet before awkwardly sidling away. That was definitely not the response I was looking for. I frowned after him. He gave me an almost sad smile over his shoulder, nervously smoothing back his hair and offering me his arm. Trying not to feel rejected, I collected myself and accepted his consolation prize with something approaching dignity.

"Maybe I'm the one who should be asking you if everything is okay," I said slowly, narrowing my eyes at him as we walked leisurely towards town. It really had been a while since I went anywhere socially without Liam, because being unable to teleport felt very unnatural. I forcefully put the other side of our little love triangle out of my head and refocused on James and his distant expression. "You look stressed."

A ghost of his usual smile flickered around the edges of his face. Then that gentle affection I recognized as just for me showed up in his eyes. Relief warred with caution in my chest as I took in the stress lines around his mouth.

"How do you read people so well without any psychic empathy? I swear, you're better than a telepath half the time." James shook his head at me, the familiar backhanded compliment buying him time to weasel out of answering me. Trust me, I knew when someone was dodging my questions.

"Dad gave me some good practice," I told him quickly before honing in on my line of inquiry with the usual dogged determination. "Now, be honest. Why are you upset? This date was your idea."

"What?" he shot me a look of confusion before giving me an apologetic sigh. "Oh! No, no, I'm not upset with you, Gracie. I'm just..." he trailed off, still looking distressed. Then, before I could nudge him again, he cleared his throat and went on. "Sorry. It's work related. Not you at all, I promise."

"Work related?" I repeated back, a frown on my face. We were approaching the edge of campus now, the trees thinning and the path widening ahead of us to accommodate the market square of downtown Landing. The alloy, stone, and timber store fronts lined the cobblestone square with the same fusion of colonial era architecture and more modern Cybele-based materials that also marked the older side of the University.

James took a deeper breath and stretched a bit, as if his shoulders and back were too tense to be comfortable. "I talked with Eva earlier and—" he paused before shaking his head. "Let's wait until we're sitting down and can really talk about it. Why don't you tell me about your day? How was the OW?"

I made a face at being put off, which reminded me of another reason for my expression of annoyance. "So far so good. I really like my trainer, Jillian. She's a firebird like me and super nice. Though, actually I had a bit of a surprise. It turns out Liam joined up, too. Did you know about his plans? Because he didn't say a word to me."

"He actually did it?" James gave a little laugh and shook his head. I couldn't decide if his forced smile hid sadness, anxiety, or jealousy but I had a feeling his real emotions weren't incredibly positive about our friend joining the OW. "He threatened to when he heard about you signing with Vanessa, but I wasn't sure if he was serious."

I frowned a touch myself at that statement. "Why would he mention it to you but not to me? And you could have warned me. I about had a heart attack in front of Vanessa when he showed up."

"Like I said, I wasn't sure if he was serious," James paused to open the door of the restaurant for me. I flashed him a grateful smile that I hoped held a little more heat than our usual friendly playfulness. Somehow our whole conversation ended up revolving around Liam. How had that happened, after I was trying so hard not to even think about our "third?"

"A table for two please," I requested at the front. The whole room was festooned with huge pink and purple blooms in giant ceramic flower pots amid a painted backdrop of palm trees. *Haltopia* was written in curved letters above the front counter. The plain, dark-haired mortal girl working as the hostess nodded at me with a polite smile and signaled for James and me to follow her.

"This is perfect, thank you," James said politely to the hostess as she seated us near a window facing out towards a wooded courtyard.

"Enjoy your meal," she said, using a small hand lighter to kindle the candle in the center of the table before leaving us to look over the menu which had popped up on our memory pads. I could have lit the candle with much less effort, but for the sake of not complicating things, I said nothing and kept my eyes on my pad.

James cleared his throat after a long moment of silence and I glanced up at him. His expression was cautious and a little sad.

"He only did it for you, you know," he said softly over the edge of his memory pad.

"What?" I asked, confused.

"Liam," he clarified. "He seemed nervous that you might get hurt. Kept talking about someone needing to watch your back. That's why he joined the Overwatch."

I swallowed hard, a sudden rush of affection for our missing third painting my cheeks pink. Remembering my earlier determination not to dwell on Liam on this date, I resettled myself with what I hoped was a bit more dignity in the high-backed, wooden chair.

"I'm a third-gen and he's a seventeenth. If anyone is more likely to get hurt in the OW, it's him, not me," I said a bit more sharply than I meant to. "He got lucky there weren't any older 'porters to pair me with, otherwise he wouldn't have even made the cut."

"That's what I told him." James looked genuinely worried as he set his memory pad down on the table. Suddenly, I was reminded of how soft his expression had been at lunch after Amourie's when the topic had come around to Liam. James met my eye and his mortal features were set in a very serious expression. "You'll look after him, right? If they're partnering the two of you, that means you'll be around to handle things if they get too dangerous, won't you?"

"Where was this concern when I signed up?" I asked with a hurt laugh.

James gestured dismissively with one hand. "I've seen you at practice. When it comes to pyrokinesis, you can keep up with your father, for Fate's sake. As long as you're paired with a three-T of any variety, you'll be fine. Like you just said, Liam is a younger child. He doesn't have the same brute force to fall back on. Trust me. I've seen his psychic strength hit a wall once or twice and he's pretty useless afterwards."

I frowned thoughtfully at that bit of information before inclining my head. "Yeah, of course I'll watch out for him. He's one of my boys. I wouldn't let him get hurt."

"Your boys?" James echoed, raising a blond eyebrow in amusement. Just then, a waitress showed up with two glasses of water and a broad smile on her face.

"What can I get for the two of you?" she asked, tapping her implant to set it to record.

"I'll have the pineapple glazed ham," I said. "With the mixed rice side."

"Very good choice!" The waitress beamed at me before turning to James. "For you?"

"The chef's salad," he said. "With no chicken and extra cheese, please."

"Coming up!" she replied brightly and swirled away in a cloud of exotic flower petals and dark curls.

Once she had gone, James took a sip of water and gave me a pointed look. "Well?"

My cheeks flushed as red as my hair and I quickly ducked his gaze. "Well, what?"

"Liam is one of your boys? Do I get included in this exclusive club, I hope?"

I mirrored his sip of water to buy myself some time. Suddenly, the wicker table under its glass top seemed incredibly interesting. "Well, it's a membership of two, so I'm not sure I'd call it a club," I muttered. "It's just something I started calling you and Liam in my head a while back."

The little smile on James' face told me he did not mind the nickname. "Gracie's boys, huh? I'll take it," he said, the teasing in his expression finally erasing the stress from his eyes for the first time all day. I found myself smiling back despite myself.

"Sorry. It's silly, I know."

James' hand covered mine and suddenly I was blushing for a new reason. "Nah, it's kind of cute," he reassured me. "And I..." He hesitated and the expression on his face was a bit pained. "I do want you to have a good relationship with Liam. Especially if it means you keep each other safe at the Overwatch."

"Liam is a good friend," I allowed. "But he's not..." I trailed off, my eyes searching James' face. He's not you, I wanted to say. Not the gentle, ethical, beautifully-flawed mortal man I'd been dreaming of since I was sixteen. But those faded blue eyes wouldn't meet my own and, despite the fact that he'd asked me on this date, I didn't have the confidence to put my heart out where he could shatter it so easily. "He's not what I came here to talk about," I recovered with a small amount of grace.

"No," James agreed, taking his hand from atop mine and rubbing his neck uncomfortably. "I suppose he isn't."

"It's okay," I reassured him. He looked so awkward. "Why don't you tell me about that work thing you were upset about earlier?"

"Oh, right." His expression closed down and I really thought he was going to cry. Then he gathered himself and cleared his throat. "Yeah... that's... well..." He groaned and rubbed his face. "My internship has been moved up. It wasn't supposed to happen until next year but I guess some things have been happening and they want me at the embassy by next week."

"Next week?" I felt completely blindsided. "What about classes? I mean, we have three more weeks to the semester after that. What are you going to tell your professors?"

"I don't know." The worry in his voice made me regret my immediate response. "Beg for mercy, I guess. Or hope they're willing to put their lectures on the net so that I can finish up the courses that way. Otherwise I'll have to retake the whole semester."

"Oh, I hope not. That sounds miserable," I said, swallowing hard.

"Yeah," he agreed.

"Here you are!" Our dismal musings were interrupted by the waitress delivering our food. The ham smelled amazing; sweet and savory on its steaming platter. I glanced up at the server and she flashed me a knowing smile. Just how obvious was it that this date was struggling? "Can I get you anything else? Extra dressing?" she paused, tilting her head at James.

"This is fine," he said, offering the woman a smile that lit up the kindness in his eyes. "Thank you."

"Everything looks good?" she asked, returning his smile in genuine kind.

"Yes, perfect," I said, picking up my fork.

Once she left, we bent to our meals silently. My mind raced, trying to find some way of looking at the situation that didn't leave a hollow, sucking hole in my chest. I just got him back, my heart whimpered, he can't leave me again now. I thought about our kiss and the beautiful promise I'd felt in my chest for the rest of the day. Now the thought made me want to cry.

I must have looked as dejected as I felt, because James' fingers brushed mine. I glanced up. He'd put down his fork to reach across the table. His light blue eyes were so incredibly gentle.

"I'll be back," he said, tilting his head at me. "After all, I can't graduate without at least another six courses. And I certainly don't think my government would allow an uneducated ambassador as the face of their most important negotiations."

I faked a smile. "I know. And I'll be stupid busy with OW training on top of classes, now. Still, I was hoping we could start doing this kind of thing a little more regularly."

He sighed and looked down at his salad. "Yeah, me too." We ate quietly for a while. Then he glanced up at me again. "Last year I thought being apart would change the way I felt about you, but—"he shook his head, his eyes soft "—the moment I saw you again it was like I was right back at Angelus Quietum. You're still the kindest and most beautiful girl I've ever met."

My face heated up and I quickly swallowed my bite of ham, wiping my mouth so that I could answer him. Before I managed to collect my thoughts, however, he went on.

"I'm not asking you to wait on me. That wouldn't be fair," he said.

"James—" I tried to cut in but he waved my comment

away.

"No, just... let me finish," he said. Obediently, I closed my mouth and watched him take a steadying breath. When he looked back up at me, his expression was nervous and vulnerable. Hope beat her frantic wings against the inside of my chest. "I've been training for this post my whole life. All I've ever wanted was to be a diplomat — to see the world and make a positive difference in it."

"You're so good with people. I'm sure you'll be a wonderful diplomat."

"Thanks." He offered me a more genuine smile. "But what I'm trying to say is that I didn't plan on meeting someone like you. You make every one of my rational, logical goals and charts go right out the window. When you're around, all I can think about is..." He flushed and swallowed hard, eyes darting away as if he were afraid of completing that sentence.

I probably shouldn't have laughed, but I couldn't help it. He looked up with a terrified expression on his face and I quickly squeezed his hand. "It's okay. I feel the same way."

We looked at each other helplessly. His fingers laced between mine, warm and alive.

"Well, at least we have tonight," I murmured.

His expression softened and his shoulders relaxed. "Yeah, we do."

I glanced down at my plate. "I think I'm done eating."

He was less than halfway done with his salad, but he

shrugged at it with a bemused smile. "Me, too."

We quickly paid for our meals and spent the walk back to campus with our arms wrapped tightly around each others' waists. Usually James and I talked easily about almost any topic we could bring to mind, but that evening we were silent as the sun set over the kyoss trees and the dormitory's dark silhouette loomed into view. By the time we shut his door behind us, the oddly somber mood had crystallized around us, holding back any words we might have spoken. Instead, his hands came up to my face and I pulled his hips tight against mine. Our lips met and we let our bodies say what we never could quite manage with words.

My fingertips climbed up his back whispering, "I need you. Don't go."

His lips on my neck answered, "I'd rather stay here with you."

My hands roughly pulled off his shirt and begged him to follow his heart.

His beautiful blue eyes, dark in the lamp light, begged my forgiveness as he laid his head on my bare stomach.

We didn't have sex. It wasn't for lack of interest on either side, but let's just say young men can get a little bit over excited. He was horribly embarrassed afterwards. I confess to some mild disappointment, but mostly I was content spending the evening in each others' arms. If there weren't any deep confessions of love or vows of chastity while we were apart, we made up for it by gently exploring every square centimeter of each other. Malcolm had been handsome, but he wasn't someone I'd been in love with for years. The feeling of James' lithe body pressed to mine as we kissed and ran our fingers through each others' hair was exponentially more satisfying than any casual one night stand could ever hope to be.

"Should I go back to my room?" I asked him when it had gotten late but neither of us showed any sign of moving. We were still naked to the waist, his heavy comforter pulled up over us to keep out the chill. My head was pillowed against his shoulder as his fingers slowly traced the curve of my neck.

"It's cold out there," he muttered, tucking the blankets more tightly around us and pulling me close again. His arms wrapped around me and his cheek pressed against my forehead. I sighed and snuggled closer.

We'd just begun to doze off when James startled awake. His body tensed in my arms and I looked up at him with sleepy concern.

"Liam just got that new Sorrow holo and wants to bring it over." James tilted an encouraging eyebrow at me. "I know you wanted to see that story when it came out."

"It's a big budget fantasy thing," I said with a shrug, burying my face more deeply in James' slim chest. "It won't have a shred of credible information we haven't already found ourselves in Stella's database."

"Probably not," he agreed. "But we've blown Liam off all evening. And I didn't mention this date to him unless you did."

"No," I admitted. "I didn't say anything."

James breathed in the scent of my hair and closed his eyes. "Which means Liam has no idea why we weren't at dinner or around the dorms this evening. And while I could lie here like this all night, I think in the interest of not pissing off our best friend, we might want to let him come hang out."

Most of my brain didn't give a shit what Liam thought, but I knew James was right about him getting pretty angry with us if we completely ignored him with no explanation. And, since I was going to be seeing him an awful lot at OW pretty soon, it seemed like a good idea to keep on my partner's better side.

"Okay, let me find my shirt," I grumbled.

I'd hardly had the time to get decent before Liam showed up in a spiral of blue psi. He was holding the holo disk with an expression of triumph on his face.

"You have no idea how much I paid for this thing!" he announced, brandishing the tiny disc case. "It's supposed to have interactive citations that sync with your memory pad, so you can see the original net posts about the historical events in the holo."

My interest perked up as I rubbed an eye and flopped back down next to James on the bed. He'd pulled on a shirt and a pair of exercise shorts but he didn't seem ashamed to climb right back into the warm nest of blankets and pillows we'd been curled up in moments ago. With a sigh, he rested his head against my shoulder and wrapped an arm around my waist.

Liam didn't so much as comment on our casually intimate body language. Once he'd popped the little chip into the comm and selected 'holo' mode, he surprised me by wedging his sizable frame onto the sliver of mattress on my other side.

"I've only heard good things in the reviews," our dark-haired friend said, slipping a long arm behind my shoulders and nudging my hip with his. James and I obediently shifted over to allow him more room. Before I knew what had happened, he'd kicked off his shoes and tucked the two of us under the blanket with James.

As it turns out, I was right about the holo. It didn't have any more information about Dad's colorful past than our research already managed to piece together. In fact, I hardly remember anything about it except for my disappointment with the lead actor. He looked nothing like Gabriel in my opinion.

What I do remember about that evening was the gentle warmth of being wrapped up in my boys' arms. I should have been angry with Liam for sticking his nose into my date with James, but I wasn't. In fact, with James falling asleep on my right shoulder and the safe vibration of Liam's voice in his long torso on my left as he kept up a witty commentary, I was as content as I'd ever been.

Chapter 17

Flying

"It's just force," Jillian explained. "Simple physics. For every action there is an equal and opposite reaction. All you have to do is set off a controlled explosion in the opposite direction of your desired trajectory."

"Uh huh." I tried to wrap my brain around it. The concept was simple enough, but the idea of having that amount of control sounded challenging.

"Just watch me," she said and pulled out her spark. That's what she called the little alloy device she used to start her flames. Within moments, the torrent of orange blossomed up below her and with a rush of wind she was airborne. We were standing outside for this exercise because, according to Jillian, the grass was softer than concrete.

"She does make it look easy," Liam commented, shading his eyes with one hand as he watched her make a circuit of the clearing and come back. She landed lightly in front of us.

"See? Simple as breathing," she said with a smile. "Once you get the trick of it you'll wonder why you never thought of it yourself."

"If you say so," I said doubtfully.

"Give it a try," Liam encouraged me.

"Okay." I stretched and gestured for them to give me some space. "Might want to stand back."

Obligingly, he and Jillian took a few steps away.

Carefully centering myself, I opened the fist on my flames and envisioned where I wanted them to go. I imagined them as a great force propelling me upwards and soaring over the treetops.

With an extremely loud roar, the power I kept so tightly locked away came blazing to life. I barely had time to scream before I was thrown violently upwards. With a gasp, I shut off the torrent of flame, but it was too late—I was well over twenty feet in the air. I shrieked again as I immediately began to free fall.

"Gracie!" I heard Liam shout my name, but I was too focused on my own predicament to glance in his direction. Almost more on instinct than anything else, I called on the flames again. This time, I moderated the thrust of their energy and, rather than sending me flying, they stopped my descent and let me balance precariously in midair.

"Ha!" I found myself laughing a bit hysterically. I glanced at Liam and Jillian. She had a restraining hand on his chest while his expression was a little wild around the edges. I'd given him a good fright, apparently. Fair enough, since I'd done the same to myself.

After that rough start, however, I figured out the art of flying by fire rapidly. Within a few weeks, I could circle the clearing and land almost as smoothly as Jillian. Liam could already fly using telekinesis, but my stamina with the flames was much greater than his. Thus, despite my less typical gift, it was becoming clear that being a third-gen gave me advantages the lower gens couldn't aspire to. Though he took it more calmly than I would have, Liam was beginning to understand he would always struggle to keep up with me.

This feeling culminated at the end of our training. It was a month before James was supposed to come back from his internship. Liam and I had been getting along remarkably well both in and out of the Overwatch compound. Training had been forcing us to interact in close physical quarters and, while I never felt as giddy around Liam as I had with James, I did look forward to the moments we had the opportunity to touch. And, though I would never have admitted it, I got an extra thrill from laying him out on the practice mat.

We had begun physical training with psi-enhancement a week before. This meant Liam finally had the telekinetic advantage he'd been longing for. Since I obviously couldn't use deadly force, he managed to pin me neatly a few times.

"There's got to be a way to get through that shield of yours," I muttered, rubbing my chin after he'd put it forcefully into the mat. "If I'd been able to connect, your stance would have been broken three moves back."

"You're never going to get that kind of force without telekinesis," Liam said with a self-satisfied smile and a commiserating pat on the shoulder. "Don't feel bad. You'd probably roast me in half a heartbeat if this weren't just practice."

"We've actually never pitted your fire against his shields," Jillian said thoughtfully. "It might be an interesting exercise."

"I wouldn't want to hurt him," I frowned up at Liam. He was so much taller than me that I barely reached the center of his chest. Even so, our flying practice had repeatedly brought home how easily exhausted his psi-power was, at least in comparison to my third-gen stamina. He didn't have any pyrokinesis to compare pure force with, though I could now routinely overpower Jillian's fire regardless of how hard she tried to shield from me. Vanessa hadn't been lying when she said I was scary-strong in comparison to the other Usuriels. I saw the way the other Overwatch members eyed me when they thought my back was turned.

"Let's have one more bout," Jillian said. "And see if you can push his shields just a little. I'd like you to at least feel what it's like to shield psi-fire, Liam."

He nodded, toweling off some sweat before stepping back onto the mat.

With a friendly bow, we squared off. My years of training made it easy to deflect most of his clumsy blows. Though he'd improved in the last few months, he still telegraphed every movement to my experienced eye.

Now he'd gotten the hang of my own rhythm. He knew that once I deflected a blow, I would usually strike back. The first time he teleported out of the way. I was familiar with that trick and didn't stagger. Instead, I swung a roundhouse kick in the other direction and was rewarded with a decent connection to his hip.

Unfortunately for my petite size, his sheer mass reinforced by his telekinesis made kicking him like slamming my foot against an alloy wall. I recovered quickly, but not before he'd managed to move inside my guard.

For a few quick blows, I was on the defensive; just narrowly keeping his fists from connecting with my already-bruised jaw. I knew it was only a matter of time before his enhanced speed got the best of me, so I grabbed one of his arms and used his momentum to force him onto his knees, twisting his arm neatly behind his back.

Without psi, this would have been the end of the fight. I wasn't large, but I was strong for my size. Once I got his feet out from under him there were a dozen ways I could pin him and we both knew it. However, it only took a short blast of telekinetic power to toss me from atop him. I caught myself with a small blast of flame which I quickly extended in his direction once I'd regained my feet. It wasn't much in the way of my pyrokinetic strength, but he was forced to put up a shield.

This time Liam startled me when he teleported behind me. He didn't usually use that trick more than once in a match, if only because it took a lot of energy that he preferred to conserve for telekinesis. He connected with the side of my head hard enough that pain and bright light exploded across my vision. I went down heavily to my knees, skidding across the mat in a half-daze.

Liam followed up on his advantage, knowing I wouldn't be down long. I saw him coming, a blur of dark hair and pale skin. A high-pitched ringing sang in my ears and a very detached part of my brain saw his careless opening. He thought I was too injured to see it, probably. Foolish, I thought. That's going to get him killed.

I launched myself up and into his midriff. Now his greater height was a disadvantage as it gave me an easier target. My fist came up and encountered the psi-shield he had the foresight to put up. Anger sparked that deep flame in my chest as I realized that he was about to overpower me out of brute psychic strength rather than skill for a third time in a row. With a defiant shout, my fire caught and suddenly my fist rocketed forward, propelled by a miniature explosion of psi-fire directly behind my elbow.

If I'd been sparring with my father, it wouldn't have mattered. But Liam was a younger child and his shield shattered under my fist like a glass bubble. I connected with his gut a lot more forcefully than I'd intended to. The blow spun him around and actually threw him across the mat. When he landed, he stayed down.

"Whoa, take it easy!" Jillian jumped onto the mat before I could even wrap my head around what happened. I stood where I'd come to my feet, breathing hard and staring at Liam's crumpled figure while my head swam back from the sea of adrenaline that had momentarily overwhelmed it.

"Shit," I breathed as things came back into focus. "Liam! Are you okay?"

By the time I made it over to him, Liam had rolled to his

knees but his head was still pressed to the mat and he seemed to be having trouble getting air into his lungs.

"What was that last move?" Jillian asked, glancing up at me. She'd dropped to kneel beside my injured partner, one arm around his back while the other rested on his shoulder. "Take it easy, Liam. Coriana can mend it if she's cracked a rib."

"I... think she just... knocked the air out of me," he said, pushing up to all fours before settling back on his heels. Jillian stood and gave him a little space. "I'll be alright. But that was... some punch, Gracie. How did you do that without telekinesis?"

"About the same way I can fly, I think," I said, looking down at my hand. Now that my heart rate was coming back down, I could think through what I'd done to break Liam's shield. "I just used the fire to increase the force behind my fist."

"Of course," Jillian looked dumbfounded. "Why haven't I ever thought of trying that?"

"Because it would be really hard to do if I needed a spark," I replied, walking towards Liam. "Sorry about that, man. I didn't mean to connect that hard."

With his usual rueful grin, Liam accepted my hand and pulled himself to his feet. He staggered a touch and put a hand to his side where I'd landed the blow. "Well, I'll be feeling it for a while, but I don't think there's any permanent damage. Sorry if I knocked any wires loose earlier, too."

I rubbed the side of my head where I felt a bruise

beginning to spread above my ear. "We'll both need to take it a little easier tomorrow, if I don't miss my guess," I chuckled.

"Well, there went my winning streak," he sighed. "For good, if I'm not mistaken, too. Now that you can break my shield, there's no way I'm getting the better of you for a while."

"Sorry," my smug smile undermined the apology.

"No, you're not," he muttered, dusting himself off. "But it's okay. I should know better than to pit myself against a third-gen. Honestly, I don't know what Vanessa was thinking when she partnered us."

"Just because you can't best her on the mat doesn't mean your skills aren't valuable to the partnership," Jillian tutted, patting his back. "If it makes you feel better, I'm usually the weaker one in my pair, too. Honestly, even though it's frustrating in the Tourney, it's kind of reassuring in the field. At least you know she can take care of you if things get ugly out there."

The two of them looked at me and I flushed. "Dad or Grandma Gloria would send me packing," I felt compelled to point out.

"I don't know about that," Liam said, slowly rubbing his side. "You're not just strong, you're a telepathic null. If they didn't see you coming, I bet you have enough juice to light either one of them up before they could shield."

I swallowed hard at that statement, my stomach suddenly

knotting. The idea of going after Dad or my grandparents made me feel physically ill.

Jillian nodded thoughtfully. "That might be true," she agreed. "It is a very real possibility that you are one of the strongest Usuriels on Cybele right now."

"Certainly she is one of the most frightening," Vanessa agreed, walking towards us. I hadn't even noticed her in the training gallery until now. "Which is why we're going to show you off at tourney this year. When the rest of the Family sees that little flame-punch you just threw, we won't have an incident for six months. Even the vampires will be keeping their heads down."

***

As promised, I went to visit Dad at Angelus Quietum on the two-day break after my date with James. We did a few larger chores around the farm that he'd been putting off. That took the whole first day and I, for one, fell into bed thoroughly exhausted. The next day we went for a long, leisurely ride on Aubrie and Charcoal. We talked about my grandparents and all of my classes except history and the Overwatch.

I found my father strangely easy to confide in about James and Liam. Once I got past the initial awkwardness of admitting that I did have an attraction to both of them, Dad managed to put me at ease by recounting a few of his own early relationships. It was a surprisingly candid conversation from my secretive parent, even if Olivia and Lauria didn't get mentioned. Then, he proved to be a good listener as I confessed how conflicted I felt about my boys.

"They're so different," I sighed. "And I definitely think I'd rather end up with James, personality wise. He's very ethical and honest... well, you remember. But, that's what I like about him, I think. He keeps me accountable. It's kind of a pain, but in a good way. I'm not sure I'm describing this well. He just makes me feel so comfortable and awkward at the same time."

"Oh, I think you explained it well enough," Gabriel said with a laugh. "I'm pretty sure that about sums up most of the romantic relationships I've had."

"Ugh, I can see why you haven't dated anyone in a while," I grumbled.

He chuckled as he pulled Aubrie's head away from a particularly interesting tuft of grass. It might have been my imagination, but his hands weren't quite as steady as I remembered them. "What about Liam?" he asked. "He was the dark-haired boy you worked with after the flood, right? The tall one?"

"Yeah," I agreed with his description of Liam. "That's him. I don't know. He's... Family. Which is kind of weird. But it makes seeing a future with him easier in some ways. I mean, I don't think he has a lot of ambition aside from Overwatch, which means we're kind of heading in the same direction."

"Mmmm," was my father's only response to that.

"Yeah, yeah, I know your opinion of OW. But still, it would be easier to date someone who isn't going to be stuck in a diplomatic embassy for sixty hours a week."

"True," Dad allowed, "but how do you feel about him?"

"He's... safe. Strong, compared to most younger children at least, and he has a wicked sense of humor. I feel relaxed around him," I said. "But I'm not sure it's a mutual attraction. There was one moment... but then... I don't know. He's more interested in James than me, I'm pretty sure."

"That makes things complicated," Dad agreed. With a subtle shift in weight, he guided Aubrie back the way we came. "Come on, let's go back to the house. There's something I want to give you."

We rubbed down the horses and got them settled in the barn before wandering back inside. Then, after taking showers and changing into comfortable night clothes, Dad told me to sit on the couch and close my eyes.

"It's a surprise," he said with an almost shy smile. The light inside cast his face in unflattering shadows. Had he dropped weight again?

"Okay," I replied cautiously, but I did as I was told. The wind of his teleportation tossed my hair about my shoulders.

"You can open them now," he said.

When I opened my eyes, he was holding a lovely dark blue dress in the very latest style. Its draping shoulders and cinched waist were all the fashion in Skykyle these days. I had a feeling that if I checked the tag it would be a designer Liam would recognize.

"Oh, Daddy, it's beautiful," I breathed, sliding to my feet. I took the fabric in my hands and caught my breath. It was feather-light. "This must have cost you a good chunk of the harvest!"

He shrugged and smiled at my reaction. "I was an ass earlier this week. It's the least I can do to say I'm sorry. Besides, it matches your eyes."

"Thank you!" I said, giving him a hug. His strong arms held me in such a familiar way it almost brought tears to my eyes. Strange, the things we don't appreciate until we leave home.

"I also have this," he said, summoning a small envelope from the thin air to his left. He handed it to me as I settled myself back on the couch.

"What is it?" I asked with a frown. I could count the number of letters I'd ever received on one hand. Most of them had been from him.

"It's from your grandmother," he said, leaning against the back of the sofa and draping my new dress across the cushion beside himself.

"Grandma Gloria?" I said questioningly, though clearly she was my only grandmother so it had to be from her.

I pulled the creamy card from its smooth, satin envelope and discovered golden lettering proclaiming: "You're Invited!" On the inside, it said, "We request the privilege of your presence at the Skykyle Sky Lounge on Landing Day at twenty hundred hours for a Family Celebration. Dress is formal. Please confirm your planned attendance to Gloria or D'nay Usuriel within a fortnight."

"Landing Day?" I murmured, glancing up at Dad. "That's at the end of next semester. Don't you usually just have them over and set off a few fireworks over the lake? I mean, one year they had a few cousins over at the Homestead, but I've never heard of them doing anything fancier than that. What's going on?"

Dad shrugged. "I'm not sure, but at least you'll have a reason to wear your new dress."

"Aren't you invited?"

"Got mine yesterday," he said with a smile, summoning his own little card with a flourish of fingertips. "I guess I'm shopping for a new dress tunic, next."

To my pleasant surprise, there wasn't a liquor bottle to be seen the whole visit. In fact, we managed to avoid the topic of his addictions altogether. That definitely made the visit go more smoothly.

I couldn't help but notice that his appetite wasn't what it usually was the second day and I would be lying if I said he looked like the picture of health. But I appreciated his effort to put the alcohol down for my visit too much to say a word about shaking hands or a few missing pounds. Instead, I gave him an extra hug on my way out the door and hoped that the next time we talked would be just as pleasant as this visit.

***

When I told Liam about the invitation he was incredibly jealous. Two days later his cream-colored envelope showed up and he had to parade it in front of me at the Overwatch compound.

"We should go together," he said as we walked towards the locker rooms to change out of our sweaty practice clothes.

"Together?" I raised an eyebrow at him.

He shrugged, color creeping into his cheeks. "Well, I mean, we are OW partners. We should... you know..."

"Go together," I finished for him, my face carefully composed in what I hoped was a thoughtful expression. "Not, like, a date or anything. Just professional partners."

"Right," he said, rubbing his face on the towel across his shoulders. "Unless, you know, you wanted it to be a date."

I glanced at him carefully. We'd been steering clear of anything remotely romantic since that disastrous trip to Amourie's. I found myself nervous about the idea of a date with Liam that didn't involve James.

"Is that what you want?" I asked cautiously.

He shrugged and tried to look cavalier. "I'm not sure," he

admitted. "I usually don't date women. But you're a little different. I don't think I'd mind trying it out."

I considered that. "Okay," I said. "We'll try it. Just this once."

"Just this once," he agreed, and went into the locker room.

Chapter 18

The Tourney

The morning of the Tourney dawned bright and clear, golden sunlight slanting through the high windows of the OW practice room. Between this event and D'nay and Gloria's party in a few days, the excitement among my fellow OW officers was at a fever pitch.

"You'll do fine," Jillian reassured us as she, Liam, and I walked into the room. "It's no different than the sparring we've done in class."

"Except everyone gets to watch her kick my ass," Liam muttered.

I followed his gaze to the huge chart projected on the back wall. My heart sank. Our first bout was against each other. I'd been hoping someone else would be the one to knock Liam out of the running. Failing that, a win or two before he got destroyed by an earlier generation would have done wonders for my partner's self-esteem.

"And then you get to watch her kick everyone else's," Jillian said, patting his shoulder. "Trust me, no one will be laughing at you by the end."

If there were any disparaging comments towards Liam after I pinned him in ten moves, they changed to respectful murmurs when I took my next three opponents in half that.

Liam himself also took a few rounds to forgive the thrashing. "Did you really have to kick me in the ribs that hard?" he whined, pulling his shirt up to reveal a bruise already purpling his fair skin.

"If I wanted you to stay down, yes," I replied, slamming down my water bottle on the bench beside him.

"You're not helping her focus," Jillian told him, tossing me a towel. "I thought you were a team. When one part of a team wins, you both do."

Liam rubbed his side and muttered.

I opened my mouth, but Jillian shook her head. "Let him get over himself. You have a job to do."

I nodded and turned back to the ring. Amber, a tenth gen 'porter and 'path, was warming up on the opposite side. Her short, dark hair fell into brilliant green eyes as she folded her neat figure in two. Like Liam, I could see the mortality in her round face, though her fair skin was clear and unblemished.

"It isn't fair to pit me against her," I murmured to Jill. "She's not even a telekinetic."

"Neither are you," Jillian replied cooly, "and out in the real world, we never know what powers we'll run into on a call. That's why this is such good practice. That's the point, remember?"

"Right." I did a few stretches myself, then vaulted the fabric barrier to stand in my place on the mat.

Amber joined me, her intelligent Family eyes sizing me up. She was taller than me, but not by much, and she took after our grandmother's side with the compact, lean torso. Her center of gravity would be low, I judged, since her curves were in the buttocks and thighs. Hard to destabilize but not a lot of brute force to counter—the opposite of what I was used to with Liam or Dad.

I was so busy analyzing the situation I almost got blindsided by the first blow. She aimed it efficiently at my jaw, closing so quickly it was hard to believe she wasn't a three-T. I broke the impact with a forearm, but she already had the advantage, stepping into my guard and forcing me to react rather than attack.

I was too practiced to panic. After parrying three or four punches, I grabbed her arm and used her momentum to land her ass on the mat. I came down on top, straddling her narrow waist with my knees while I pinned both arms above her head. She gave me wide, startled eyes for the count of two, then in a flash of green-tinged air she was behind me.

I ducked her blow, knowing she'd count on the surprise of her 'port. It was a stunt Liam liked to pull on the regular. Like he often did, she overextended the limb and I caught it. Using the coiled potential of my legs to add my weight to the blow, along with a little burst of fire for good measure, I plowed my fist into her chest.

She fell backwards, stunned. I released her, igniting another spark behind my elbow as I prepared a second blow to finish the match. She landed and turned towards me, raising an arm not to block but to cower. Her body curled, nearly fetal on the mat as she struggled to draw breath.

"Stop! Please! I tap!"

The fear in her face pulled me up short. I let go of the flames. Somewhere to my left the countdown went past three and the match called in my favor. It didn't matter. All I could see was the terror in Amber's Family-green eyes.

"Will she be alright?" I asked the medic who rushed in moments after the countdown.

He bent to Amber's chest, lighting it up with a gentle golden glow. Afterwards, she coughed but stood on her own power.

"She's fine," the healer reassured me with a pat on the shoulder.

"Good match," Amber called over her shoulder as she limped away. She didn't meet my eye.

"Nice work, Gracie! That was a clean take down," Liam congratulated me as I climbed back over the fabric edge of the ring.

"Thanks," I muttered, my fingers and toes tingling and distant.

Liam frowned. "You okay?"

"What? Yeah… just a little rattled. She got in my face pretty good at the beginning."

Jillian handed me a towel. "Shake it off. The next round will be up soon."

Through the next two matches, I couldn't shake the image of Amber's terror. Fortunately, I was able to win them both handily without pulling on my fire. My spirits were only moderately lifted by Liam's improved attitude. It was nice to hear him cheer for me instead of the icy glowering.

"Who's up next?" I asked him as I sank into the bench after pinning a massive ninth gen. I gratefully accepted the water bottle and took a long swallow.

"Eddie. He's that young seventh-gen who partners Opal." Liam draped the towel over my shoulders. I mopped the creases of my neck with one corner.

"The one on Dax's line?" I glanced over at the other side of the ring. A burly man with red hair and flawless, deep brown skin sat on the opposite bench. I recognized Opal next to him by her long, shining black hair pulled up into its usual ponytail.

Liam nodded. "I've heard his telekinesis is the match of an elder child."

"Great." I rubbed at my face with the towel. "How many more before I can say I won this thing?"

Liam patted my shoulder. "Pin him and you're in the final match."

"So two more," I muttered, pulling my hair out of its bun and recapturing the flyaway strands before tying it back up.

"Two more." Liam agreed.

I took one more swig of water, then stood and began shaking the stiffness out of my limbs. "Okay, let's get this over with. I'm ready for a hot shower."

Liam snorted. "Don't pretend you're not enjoying this." He softened his criticism with a wink. "Go show 'em how it's done."

I allowed a shadow of my usual cocky grin to spread across my face. My limbs were heavy and my skin tight with drying sweat, but I stepped into the ring with renewed energy.

Opal slapped her partner's shoulder. He spared her a crooked smile before taking his side of the ring.

The crowd of OW officers cheered when the bell rang. Eddie and I circled each other. I caught a glimpse of black and white streaked hair in the front row. I suspected it was Vanessa, but I didn't take my eyes from my opponent long enough to be sure.

Eddie favored his left leg. Each step was a little shorter on that side. I observed him for another circuit, watching the way he distributed the weight. He placed his foot at a telltale angle, signaling a bad knee.

I feinted to his right, attempting to goad him into extending the weak limb. He didn't take the bait. With a forearm block, he retreated to a more stable position.

A little lick of fire from his left forced him to take his eyes off of me. While he was distracted by putting up a psi shield, I landed a pair of blows to his core. I considered adding some flame strength to them, but decided to hold off on the bigger moves. The punches landed solidly but he didn't stagger. Instead, his left fist took advantage of my opening and connected savagely with my shoulder. The force spun me around and, before I could collect myself, his arms were around my neck.

A blast of psi-fire hurled us toward the wall. His telekinesis really was impressive, however. With mental reflexes so fast and strong I couldn't counter him, Eddie redirected the force of my acceleration, twisting us down back at the mat. With a thud that knocked the air from my lungs, he slammed me into the ground. My face impacted with the mat, sending searing pain through my skull. His substantial weight landed directly on top of me, pinning me neatly.

"One...two...three!"

My head spun as the countdown rang through the room. Cheers and cat calls rose from all sides but I couldn't focus enough to react. My limbs were leaden, trapped against the floor by Eddie's powerful mind. Tiny dots flickered in front of my eyes, obscuring the world.

"Winner! Eddie takes it!"

I recognized Jillian's voice calling the match. Then Eddie's weight left my back and I managed a clean breath. My head cleared and I pushed myself up on one elbow.

"You okay?" Jillian's voice was calm as she knelt at my side. I nodded.

"Gracie!" Liam's worried face appeared over Jill's shoulder. I waved off my trainer's hand and stood on my own, brushing off the dirt from my practice uniform.

"I'm fine, I'm fine," I reassured them. My face was burning, though I couldn't tell if it was from that last impact with the mat or humiliation.

Liam's large, warm hands tilted my face up towards his. His eyebrows pulled together in a scowl. "Well, that will leave a mark."

I shrugged him off and stepped out of the ring. "More on my pride than my face," I grumbled, rubbing the back of my sweaty neck.

"Well, at least you get that shower now," Liam retorted, following me to the bench where I picked up my towel and water bottle.

"Yeah," I agreed, my head off balance.

"Come on." Jillian wrapped an arm around my shoulders, steering me in the direction of the locker rooms. The crowd behind us roared its approval as Eddie and his opponent stepped into the ring for the last match. "After you get cleaned up, we'll go to Haltopia. I love their chicken wings."

I glanced over my shoulder at the ring one more time. Vanessa's single ice-blue eye met mine from the front row. A bitter, burning wave of disappointment rose in the back of my throat and I allowed Jillian to lead me into the locker rooms.

***

Eating and drinking with Liam and Jillian at Haltopia was just what I needed to steady myself after such an unexpected defeat. Despite our standing date, Liam and I hadn't really pushed the boundaries of friendship and this, like all our other meals, was completely platonic. Liam seemed to take the defeat as a slight against our partnership and got a little more drunk than I would have cared for. He managed to teleport us back to campus without turning anyone inside out, however, so no harm was done.

The next evening, Vanessa suggested that we have a little sparring match just the two of us.

"No psi," she said, "Just physical."

"Okay," I agreed.

It turned out my cousin was extremely skilled in martial arts. The way she moved reminded me of Dad and Adora—pure economy of motion, no energy wasted. Thankfully I'd been training with Dad for years, and managed to hold my own until the very end.

I had just gotten Vanessa into a pretty decent hold when suddenly I felt the wind of her psi-power pick up and with a quick telekinetic twist she turned the technique around on me. Before I knew what had happened, I was flat on my back.

"Hey, I thought you said no psi!" I complained as I accepted her hand back up to my feet.

"I watched your last match yesterday," Vanessa said calmly. "I've seen you take a punching bag off of its chain with that fire-punch technique you've come up with. Why didn't you use your best move from the start? You could have knocked him out in the first three blows. I think you would have won the Tourney, too."

I shrugged. The image of Amber's terror swam in front of my eyes.

"Out in the field," Vanessa warned, "you can't be timid. If someone is coming after you or your partner, you can't hesitate. Even if you think the person isn't strong enough to hurt you, it's always better to err on the side of safety. That means, incapacitate first, ask questions later."

"That seems a little harsh."

"You're a big gun." Vanessa's good eye held my gaze. "We'll let you start with some quieter things, but pretty soon you won't be going out unless there's someone really dangerous. You won't be mucking about with addicts and domestic disturbance. You're who we'll call for the really scary ones. That means you always have to go into a situation assuming the offender is dangerous and trying to kill you."

"You're really making me glad I joined," I muttered before I could censor myself.

Vanessa's mouth twisted in a grim smile. "People got to see you in action yesterday. I don't think we'll need you in for a big job for a long while. Even so, before I start sending you out, I need to know that you've gotten this concept through your head. You can't soften a blow because you're afraid of hurting someone. It could cost you your life. Or Liam's."

I frowned at her for a moment. "Okay, let's spar one more time," I said. "This time psi is an option."

Vanessa inclined her head at me and we squared off.

Let me just say, for the record, that I held my own for a few minutes. Between the muscle memory of a lifetime of martial arts training and knowing that Vanessa's shield was strong enough to deal with my flames, I discovered it was actually easier to throw everything I had at her. I'd never let loose at someone the way I did with Vanessa on that mat. We moved together in something that might almost be called a dance if it hadn't been so adversarial. My fire-enhanced punches rained down on her shields while her telekinesis tossed me from one end of the mat to the other. If I hadn't learned to catch myself mid-air with the fire, I probably would have slammed into the wall hard enough to break bones.

In the end, though, Vanessa's abilities were just more versatile than mine. She teleported into just the right place at just the right moment and that was the end of the match. With an elbow to my solar plexus, she slammed me to the ground and then her mind held me there.

"Okay, okay, I tap!" I said, panting.

With a smug smile, she glided to her feet and offered me a hand. "That was a good bout, Gracie. It was nice to see you really put your all into it."

"Thanks." I took her hand and, with the grace that only we Usuriels can manage, I used her own strength to enhance the blow I aimed directly at her jaw. Since I'm impossible to read, even for a high-level telepath like Vanessa, she was completely blindsided. She stumbled back, falling to one knee as the impact of my fist nearly knocked her off of her feet.

"Don't pull punches and don't let down your guard. Lesson learned," I said, breathing heavily as I stood over her.

There was a calculating expression on her face as Vanessa looked up at me, her ice-blue eye wide with some kind of emotion. I wasn't exactly sure what it was, but I'd definitely surprised her. Then a smile spread across her face and she raised a hand. I obligingly gave her a hand up, careful to watch her shoulders for any indication that she might return my blow. She didn't.

"Well, I'd say you're ready to start some junior officer work," she said, patting my back. Then she turned and walked away in the direction of her office, leaving me alone in the training gallery.

I remember standing there, breathing hard and soaked in sweat, watching her back fade away from me into the darkened background of the immense gallery. I wondered if I liked the lesson I'd just learned. It reminded me too forcefully of my father's warnings. Gabriel would never have approved of my last little move on Vanessa. Too late now. I wouldn't forget it.

Chapter 19

Landing Day

My grandparents' Landing Day party was probably the fanciest event I'd ever attended, including the post-flood ball. Which meant, of course, I had half a dozen livid bruises across my neck and face from the Tourney earlier that week.

"You can't go to the party looking like that," Liam said as he teleported us from the OW compound to our dormitory. Since I'd been the only bout he'd had, the only injuries he was sporting were to the midriff and back. I was so much shorter than he was that his most frequent training injury was cracked ribs. I envied him the ability to easily cover them with a tunic.

"What am I supposed to do about it?" I grumbled, fingering my cheekbone which wasn't swollen anymore thanks to my third-gen metabolism, but still looked bright purple.

"It's called makeup, beautiful," Liam said, cutting a sharp look at me. "Tell me you own some."

"I have a little lipstick and kohl," I said, running my hand through my hair. "I don't really get blemishes, so I've never used coverup."

Liam tisked at me, then tilted his head. "Well, Leesil has pretty much the same coloring and I bet she does get blemishes."

"I've always thought she looked so pretty!" I protested.

"Because she knows how to use coverup," Liam explained. "Come on, we'll comm her from your room."

Sure enough, Leesil was happy to lend me some coverup for the evening. "You guys are going to the Family party?" she exclaimed, eyes alight. "Jax and I are going, too! Do you just want to come over and get ready with us?"

I glanced at Liam who shrugged amiably. "Sure. Thanks, Lee," I said.

"Of course! Always happy to help out a cousin!" she replied with a laugh. "See you around eighteen hundred hours?"

"We'll see you then," Liam said and turned off the comm.

This is how I ended up sitting on a bed in Leesil's parents' house having my makeup done by two very enthusiastic Family members. Liam, it turned out, had a decided passion for the art, and Lessil appeared extremely adept in her own right. Together, they spent over an hour on my hair and face, fussing and making adjustments until they both sat back and nodded.

"Okay, you can look now," Leesil said, moving the door of her bedroom so that I reflected in its mirrored back.

"Oh..." I breathed, more than a little shocked at my reflection. I looked older; in my mid-to-late twenties at least.

My hair had been twisted up and back, away from my face in a style that reminded me of what I'd seen in the colonist-era holos James, Liam, and I had been digging through so much. My eyes glowed from the expertly applied kohl and my lips were bright red cherries ready to be plucked. There was no sign of the bruises that I knew still marred my neck and face. "You guys are good," I said, turning my head to look at the effect. "I wouldn't even be able to tell I was in the Tourney at all."

"I told you I would take care of it!" Leesil said with a laugh. "Okay, time for us to get dressed. Out with you!" She shooed Liam out the door. "You and Jax have to get presentable anyway."

"I somehow don't think anyone is going to pay attention to me with her on my arm," Liam said, giving me a flirtatious wink. I flushed, remembering our agreement to make this an actual date. I wondered if the pink even showed under the layers of makeup.

"You haven't shown me your dress yet, Gracie," Leesil said, pulling a sleek, pink frock from her closet. Leesil's room was decorated in soft shades of purple and yellow. Tastefully done, though clearly for a girl much younger than my twenty-seven-year-old cousin.

"Yours is lovely," I said, admiring the soft shade of pink that pulled the blush into Lee's cheeks. "Put it on! I'll get mine out of its bag."

"Can you help me with the clasp?" Leesil asked after a few minutes of the two of us getting situated. I obediently did the two clasps behind her shoulders that held the draping fabric of the neckline in place. "Well?" she asked, turning. "How do I look?"

"Beautiful," I replied, and I meant it. Her skin glowed with youth and that extra Usuriel something.

"Oh my... Is that an Ambria? How did you ever afford an Ambria dress?!" Leesil sounded as openly amazed as Liam had the first time I'd shown him my wardrobe.

"It was a present from my dad," I said quickly. Fortunately, the buttons on this dress were cleverly concealed in the front and I didn't need help getting in or out of it. I'd selected some more sensible shoes than on my trip to Amourie's as well. I really did learn from my mistakes, unlike certain Family members I could name. "Believe me, I could never afford something like this myself, not even on an Overwatch salary."

"I can't on T-gate pay," Leesil agreed. "It's perfect for you, though. It matches your eyes."

"That's what Dad said." I spread the flowing skirt and looked down at my figure. It wasn't as revealing as my cousin's dress, but it clung to just the right areas to make it equally sensual. I unexpectedly hoped Liam would find it attractive.

"Can we come in yet?" Jax asked. He was Leesil's mortal boyfriend and I thought he was rather plain with dusky brown eyes and sandy blond hair. His smile lit up when he caught sight of Leesil, however, and the expression on his face left no room to doubt his feelings for her. An ache in my chest hoped someone would look at me that way someday. Then I glanced over at Liam and another rush of heat warmed my face.

"Do you like it?" I asked Liam, swishing the material of the skirt a little. Leesil and Jax seemed determined to get all of her makeup onto his face before we left for the party, so we didn't need to worry about them interrupting our conversation for a while.

"You are..." he swallowed hard and seemed to realize he'd let his feelings for me write themselves across his face. He tried to put up a better shield but the damage was done. We were in trouble. What were we going to tell James when he got back? One thing at a time. "You're gorgeous, sweetie," he said finally, holding out a hand to me.

I slipped my hand into his and it disappeared in his huge palm. The cut of his tunic was handsome and just happened to be a similar shade of blue to my own dress. I suppose when you've inherited the same color eyes, it helps with matching outfits. I shoved my ambivalent feelings about dating Family aside and reminded myself that I was giving Liam a genuine try tonight. However we felt about it in the morning, we'd get to the complicated parts then. Tonight I was going to enjoy myself.

"Are we ready to go?" Leesil asked. She'd touched up her makeup and was now holding Jax's hand.

"We'll be right behind you," Liam said, pulling me closer to his side. The elder children only needed physical contact to teleport, but I knew he found it easier the closer I was. I leaned against him, my head resting comfortably on the swell of his chest. I might be able to get used to this, I thought, wrapping an arm around his waist. We hadn't even arrived at the party and we were already being more physically intimate than we had been in months; certainly more than we'd ever been without James.

His arm settled over my back as the breath of his power rose around us. It turned out, teleporting with Liam was much smoother when we had this much physical contact. I filed that away for future use.

I'd never been to the Skykyle Sky Lounge. "Upscale" might be too mild a term for the sparkling décor and expensive menu. Even the air smelled like money as Liam alighted us on its doorstep. Jax and Leesil, a few meters ahead of us, craned their necks up at the impressive crystal chandeliers in the entryway.

However, the beauty of the place paled in comparison to the people thronging among the mahogany tables and gold-plated salad bar. I was used to seeing Family scattered in the sea of mortals at University or in their workout attire at the OW compound. Here, over half the faces rang with the high cheekbones and fierce profile of our shared lineage. Fire and ice sang from every pair of blazing eyes and hair color was more saturated, more alive. In dress clothes, their slim, powerful figures glided with effortless grace.

The energy of the room felt electric as well. Everywhere,

little ripples of power pooled and tested each others' edges. Head-blind as I am, I kept stumbling into little eddies that raised the hair along my body like a mild current.

"Gracie!" Grandpa D'nay called, and I went to him for a hug. He looked amazing in a fitted white tunic with blue accents that matched both of our eyes. It seemed Gabriellan blue was the theme for the night. He gave my shoulders a tight squeeze. "You look beautiful. Here with our very own Liam, I see." He acknowledged my date with a forearm clasp.

"You look well, Grandfather," Liam said more formally. I nodded in agreement.

"Have you seen Dad?" I asked, trying to sound casual. In all honesty, seeing my grandfather looking fresh and young as the day he died only made the memory of my father's deterioration more painfully apparent.

"It's an open bar," D'nay sighed, gesturing through an arched doorway. "If I had to guess..."

"Whose brilliant idea was that?" I hissed, giving Grandpa a good glare.

He arched an elegant eyebrow at me. "Well, it is customary at such occasions. And it seemed unfair to punish everyone just because my son can't handle himself around liquor."

"That sounds like a perfectly sensible reason to skip an open bar to me," I snapped and started for the arched doorway.

Liam's hand caught my elbow before I could march away.

"Just take a breath, Grace," he said gently. "We're here to have a good time, not babysit your father. Remember?"

"Yes, but—" I started to protest.

Liam cut me off. "Besides, I see him over there by Jessie and he doesn't look drunk to me. I don't even think he has a drink in his hand."

"Oh," I muttered, feeling stupid.

Grandpa D'nay chuckled. "All that height has to be good for something," he said. "How have you two been? I feel like I never see you anymore, Gracie. How is school?"

"Actually, it's really good," I said, relaxing a bit. "I feel like I'm learning so much more than I ever did with Stella at Angelus Quietum."

Our ancestor eyed the two of us. "And I see you're cutting a path through the gentlemen, as well," he teased with a friendly smile.

"Ah... well... I don't know about a path..."

Liam chuckled. "She's the talk of the school. First third-gen in over a century and strong enough she should have won the Tourney this year."

I flushed. "I was eliminated by a seventh-gen."

"Yeah, because you pulled your punches," Liam insisted, loyally defending my honor. He tilted his head at Grandpa. "Do you and Gloria ever work with the Overwatch?"

D'nay gave a bark of laughter. "Over her dead body, I think. I don't object to it the way Gloria does, but she'd have my skin if I ever even considered working with the OW."

"She doesn't like the Overwatch, either?" I asked. "I knew Dad had a problem with me joining, but I didn't know Grandma would be upset."

"Oh, she doesn't care what you do, sweetie. She won't be angry with you. I just suggest staying off the topic, if you can. She never liked the idea from the moment the kids came up with it," he said, looking a bit weary as if the topic made him feel old. "I guess she spends so much time keeping everyone in one piece, she doesn't like the idea of being forced into hurting someone instead."

"The kids came up with it?" Liam pushed. His researcher's curiosity flashed in his midnight-blue eyes. "Which kids are you talking about?"

"Gabe and Adora, of course." D'nay waved a hand. "My kids. They were always trouble when they got together, those two. Not that they weren't trouble by themselves, too. Maybe checking on your father isn't such a bad idea, when I think of it that way..."

The fact that he'd mentioned Adora, let alone so casually, was nothing short of shocking. I exchanged a glance with Liam as we followed Grandfather through the crowd towards Gabriel. D'nay seemed in such a rare mood I almost wondered if he'd found the open bar already. Not that I was sure what effect alcohol would have on a re-animated vampire, nor had I ever known my grandfather to indulge in any mind-altering substances besides my grandmother.

Several people pulled D'nay aside as we walked through the glittering throng, laughing and talking about trivial things. As I watched him work through the gathering, I realized how different my grandfather's temperament was from his son's. Gabriel was someone you either loved or hated. There really wasn't much wiggle room. D'nay, on the other hand, clearly had a firmer grip on the art of diplomacy. No one ducked or whispered as he went by; instead they smiled and shook hands or gave him a quick hug before telling him about the latest generation's antics. Children ran up to him and he went down to one knee to talk to them before moving on. Despite how much he looked like my father, their personalities were worlds apart.

"Liam!" A blonde woman of about forty with huge, blue eyes turned to us as we approached the edge of the crowd. "There you are, sweetie! Oh my, what illustrious company you're keeping!"

"Hi, Mom," Liam said, ducking down to kiss the top of her head before turning back to me. "Gracie, this is my mother, Lorie Usuriel. Mom, Gracie is my OW partner. You remember, I told you about her."

"Of course! My son, partnered with a third-gen! And such a beautiful one at that." Liam's mother gave me a radiant smile. Aside from the eye color, Liam's mother really didn't resemble him much. I thought I saw a touch of her mouth, which was generously curved and very sensual—if also very mortal—in his face. However, his height and long features clearly came from somewhere else. "It really is a pleasure to meet you."

"Likewise," I replied, unable to resist her friendly enthusiasm.

"Where's Dad?" Liam asked, glancing around.

"Oh, he's off introducing your siblings to Lillian. I think he wants them to get jobs at the ranch this summer," Lorie said breezily. "They certainly don't seem interested in boutique work."

"Mom works in upper-end retail," Liam said to me as if this explained anything.

Lorie ignored her son's commentary and turned to D'nay. "And Grandfather, thank you so much for hosting this reunion. It really is wonderful to see everyone in one place like this."

D'nay smiled, gave her a hug, and a quick peck on the cheek. "We really should do these things more often, Lorie," D'nay agreed. "I can't believe we're into the eighteenth generation now! Did you see Jaria's little girl?" He indicated a few groups back where the infant was being shown off much to the delight of several older women.

"Oh, I can't resist a baby!" Lorie laughed, giving Liam's arm a squeeze and moving in the direction D'nay had pointed. "Have a good time!" she called over her shoulder to us as we moved on.

Finally, we arrived at the edge of the room where Gabriel, Jessie, and Carol had claimed a little table. My father was still thinner than I liked, but he'd put some effort into his appearance. I've described the way Dad cleans up before, so I'll save you the sonnet. Let's just say he looked good despite the missing kilo or two. The ladies at his table were nibbling on finger-food from the salad bar and Gabriel had his chin resting on one hand while he listened to their chatter. I could tell from his distant expression that he found their conversation benign and mostly boring.

"Ah, Dad! Nice party," Gabriel said, seeing D'nay approach. He flowed to his feet and gave his father a one-armed hug. Then he caught sight of Liam and I. "Oh, Gracie, that dress is perfect on you!" He gave me a winning smile and I went to his side for a kiss on the cheek.

"Thank you," I said, gliding back to allow Liam to greet my father. The two men shook hands while Jessie and Carol made their way around the table.

"Carol, you look... amazing," I said when she came to give me a hug. "I don't think I've ever seen you in a dress."

Her plump, weathered, farmer's face split in the familiar grin I'd known since I was small. However, that was the only part of her that was recognizable. Her hair—which was usually windblown or squashed under her hat—gleamed with metallic highlights, a true silver that matched her sparkling eyes. Her figure, I realized, was actually quite generous and it fit neatly in the silver-blue dress. The strong lines of muscle from tending her cattle were clear in her exposed shoulders and arms. I knew she was over a century, but if she'd been mortal I would have guessed closer to sixty.

"Why, thank you, Gracie," she said and put an arm around my father's waist. It took every ounce of control not to let my jaw drop through the floor when he smiled down at her and settled his hand on her shoulder. "I don't have occasion to wear one much, but your father insisted this time."

"It's a special occasion," he said, inclining his head to D'nay. "It wouldn't do to show up to a Family function in work boots."

"Says you," she muttered, giving him a good-natured smile.

Jessie cleared her throat and came over to give me a hug. "It's good to see you, sweetie, but I think one of my daughters just showed up. I'm sure I'll run into you again in a bit."

I lingered on the hug longer than I had to, regaining my composure. It wasn't that I begrudged my father the prerogative of bringing a date. It was just that he'd never expressed the least interest in doing so for the dozen or so years I'd known him; at least not to me. And the idea that his choice of date for such a fancy get-together was our neighbor Carol seemed downright ridiculous. I would never be able to wrap my brain around my father. Every time I started to feel like I had a clue what was going through his head, he threw me a complete and utter curve.

Almost the instant Jessie left, a mortal gentleman in the uniform of the Lounge staff came up and murmured something to my grandfather. D'nay nodded, then glanced at Gabriel.

"Mind getting everyone's attention?" he said with a

slightly mischievous smile.

"Sure," Dad replied, complete mischief in his expression. "Hey! Shut up and look over here!"

I'd known Dad could be loud. I'd also known he was the strongest telepath in the room, besides Grandma Gloria. Though, now that I thought about it, I hadn't seen her yet. Anyway, I assumed Dad used both his voice and his mind to make his message abundantly clear because, suddenly, all eyes were in our direction.

Gabriel cleared his throat. "Dad wanted to say something." He gestured for D'nay to take the floor.

"Thanks, Gabe," D'nay said with a genuine smile. "And thank you all for coming to this holiday celebration. It has been two hundred and ninety years since we landed on this rich and beautiful world. When I look across the faces here tonight, I couldn't be more grateful for what we've accomplished in that time. And what a gathering we have! This may be the most Family we've gotten together in one place in... several generations, I think."

A murmur of agreement went through the room. I didn't have Liam's height but even from there I could tell this was a large restaurant and our party filled it to bursting. There had to be well over one hundred Family members, their spouses, and children staring at us right now. My eyes darted through the crowd, catching familiar OW faces as well as many I didn't know.

"And now, I'm sure, many of you are asking yourselves

why we decided to host such an extravagant evening. I'm not one for suspense, so without further ado, let me introduce my lovely wife who has an announcement that I'm sure all of you will be quite excited about."

I quickly refocused my gaze on Dad and Grandfather D'nay. Dad hadn't changed his posture from earlier, his arm casually resting around Carol's shoulder. However, his Usuriel blank face had slammed down solidly and I had a feeling he hadn't been expecting this either.

Grandpa D'nay, on the other hand, looked as if he'd swallowed the moon itself. His broad grin fairly glowed with happiness and excitement.

The door to the balcony behind Dad opened and Gloria walked out with a smile on her face. She was dressed in a flowing gown and she'd let her hair grow to her waist where it had been curled into large ringlets. There was something different about her, and I couldn't put my finger on it. Then I realized that she looked heavier; her face and shoulders were plump and rounded as if she were carrying more weight than I was used to. It might have been me, but her bust seemed larger as well. I'd never seen Gloria's weight fluctuate so much as an ounce in the decade and a half I'd known her. I frowned, feeling as if there was something I was missing.

She walked serenely to her husband's side, sliding a hand through his arm. He smiled down at her before catching her lips in a quick kiss. Then, she looked out at the crowd and that wonderful golden wind picked up around her, tossing back her hair and flowing sleeves. Blue eyes blazed from her white face and, for a heartbeat, I understood why the Divinetas called us gods. Then she smoothed her hand over the draped fabric at her waist and the gentle curve of her ripe figure became incredibly clear.

Shock is not the word for what rippled through that room. Everyone took one look at her and knew. For the first time in over three hundred years, there would be a new member of the second generation.

I was so stunned that I missed the first part of what D'nay and Gloria were saying. When I refocused on their words, they were already announcing the gender.

"We've decided to call her Ileesia," Gloria said, beaming up at her husband.

D'nay returned her radiant look and leaned down to close the considerable gap in their heights. Their kiss was sweet and heartfelt; half a millennium together and still stupid in love. I suddenly found myself wishing James was there.

Quite a number of the older women rushed forward to make their congratulations to the expectant parents. Despite being relatively close to the center of the crowd, I felt like an outsider as the other mothers fawned and exclaimed over the idea of a new baby.

My father also hadn't moved to congratulate his parents. In fact, the look on his face was as perfectly blank as it was possible to be. Our eyes met for just the briefest of moments and I thought I saw something cross that calm mask. Was it fear? Regret? Anguish? I couldn't be sure, but it clearly wasn't a positive emotion. Then, just as quickly, Gabriel looked elsewhere and the expression disappeared.

Liam cleared his throat and nudged my elbow. A little receiving line had formed beside us to allow everyone to take a turn embracing the Matriarch and her consort.

Obediently I fell in line and stumbled through the process of offering congratulations to my grandparents.

"You'll have to babysit for us, Gracie," Grandma said with a mischievous glint in her sky-blue eyes.

"Of... of course," I stammered. "When I'm not busy with my studies..."

"Babies aren't that hard," Grandfather D'nay said with a smile. "It's toddlers you really have to watch out for. Especially Aware ones! But don't worry, you'll figure it out quickly if you come around often enough."

I had no idea what to do with anyone under the age of ten, so I doubted the truth of his words. However, I just nodded and gave Grandma another hug before moving on and letting the next Family member have their chance at a conversation with the couple of the hour.

Once everyone got their turn to offer their best wishes, D'nay announced that dinner was served. Large curtains were drawn away from immense glass doors, which were thrown open and the glittering throng spilled into an echoing hall with gleaming hardwood floors. The space was split between a dance floor with a string quartet and long, linen-covered tables. Places were set with exquisite china and tiny, handwritten notes bearing each guest's name indicating where they should sit.

Though we hadn't mentioned our date to anyone, Liam's place was set directly next to mine at the head table. Since he was quite a ways down the Family tree, I had a feeling D'nay had alerted his wife to the change in seating arrangements before they opened the doors. I shook my head at the attention to detail my grandparents had put into this evening as Liam and I settled ourselves across from Dad and Carol.

"A new second-gen. My goodness, I would have bet my best milker against that one," Carol laughed as she settled into her seat. My father didn't crack a smile at her joke. He'd looked positively shell-shocked since Grandma Gloria walked in. How could he not have known? He was close with his parents. Had they really not visited in the last four months? Or was my father honestly that willfully blind that he'd ignored his mother's condition up until now? He might have been able to overlook it for the first few months, but a psychic of his level should have known weeks ago.

"No one would have blamed you," Vanessa said, settling into the chair next to me. She was clearly replying to Carol's statement, though she flashed Liam and me a smile as she sat down. "It hasn't happened in anyone's lifetimes... except yours, of course," she said with a nod towards Dad.

"Thank you," he said. "I needed the reminder of my antiquity."

"That's true, though." Carol tilted her head at him. I could tell she was trying to keep the mood light. Judging by the expression on Dad's face, I wished her luck. "What was it like when Adora was born? You're the only one who remembers, besides your parents."

"Loud," he replied, a grim expression on his face. He idly

fingered the empty wine glass in front of him. "And painful. So we have that to look forward to."

"We have shielded birthing rooms now," a blond gentleman said. There were two empty chairs between him and my father, presumably reserved for my grandparents, though I couldn't read the name tags from my side of the table. I frowned at him, trying to figure out who he was. I hadn't seen him at the OW, though his sharp features said he was an elder child. A mousy mortal woman and two young teenagers with the Family cheekbones sat on the other side of him. Dax, I thought, imagining him in a green medical uniform rather than the tailored gray dress tunic he currently wore. "I'm sure it was much harder to shield in the confines of the *Inspiration*, but we shouldn't have that trouble this time around."

"Uh huh." My father looked unconvinced. He glanced over his shoulder as his parents came over to take the two empty seats beside him. Gabriel gestured to his mother. "Strongest psi on the planet. I'm not sure you understand what that means. The only one who won't feel it is her." He pointed at me.

"My labor with you hardly held a candle to Adora," Gloria said, patting her son on the shoulder as she sat down. "And I can already tell you that this pregnancy has been much easier than hers. More like yours, really."

"May she be a junkie rather than a sociopath," my father said, raising his empty wine glass.

"Gabriel!" Gloria gave him a horrified look.

"What? Everyone's thinking it. As usual, I'm just the only one willing to say it." He leaned back in his chair and set down the glass. "Which is why half the room hates me. Sweet Fate, Mother, what are you thinking?"

She frowned at him while the rest of the table held its breath. There was a long pause, then a low chuckle from the other side of Dax. I caught sight of Lillian as she said, "That third time is the charm?"

"Stop it!" Gloria was glowing again and this time I didn't think it was with pride or happiness. She pinned everyone at the table with a dangerous glare. "We are Family at this table and we will treat each other with the kindness and respect that such a title deserves." She paused to give Dad a particularly murderous look. "Do I make myself clear?"

He looked at her with a tight jaw and an arched brow. Then he glanced at me and his mouth softened. "I'm sorry, Mom," he murmured. "If this is what you want, I am happy for you."

"There, that wasn't so hard, was it?" she said, patting his hand and giving him a genuine smile.

Thankfully, before my father could answer, the wait staff brought out rich, steaming bowls of soup. My father said a quiet word to the waiter before he could leave and another server quickly brought two bottles of wine for him to choose from. Gabriel frowned a while at both of them before sending them back with more specific instructions. I watched all of this over the rim of my soup bowl, trying not to feel like this whole evening was spinning rapidly out of control.

The main course arrived and Carol gave me a smile as she confided that the steak was fresh from her farm. The seasoning was absolutely perfect and the meat as tender as anything I'd ever put in my mouth. Apparently this restaurant wasn't just expensive for its décor.

Finally, a waiter came back with Dad's requested vintage and he offered to pour Gabriel a glass. Dad waved him away, telling him to simply leave the bottle. Carol and I exchanged an unhappy glance as the server did as instructed.

"I'll have a glass of that, Gabriel," Liam said. It was the first time he'd spoken except to quietly compliment the food.

Dad glanced up at my date as he finished filling his own glass. "Sure," he said with a shrug, holding out his hand for Liam's glass.

"Well, now I have to try what Gabriel Usuriel thinks is worthy of celebrating such a momentous occasion," Vanessa said, sliding her own glass in his direction.

"Me, too," I chimed in.

Suddenly, my father was pouring out wine for the entire table, a small smile on his face while he shook his head. I wondered if he realized that, at least for me, more than half the motivation was simply to keep the entire bottle from disappearing down his throat. Glancing at the faces around the table, I suspected I wasn't the only one who had this thought. I'm not the only one who cares about him, I realized. I felt a warm rush of affection for the Family members at the table. Even Lilly handed down her glass to be filled. In the end, I think Gloria was the only one who didn't have a full glass by her plate.

I cleared my throat and raised my wine once everyone was served. "To the second generation," I said. I met my father's eye when I added, "All of it—old and new."

There was a murmur of agreement around the table and everyone drank. The look on my father's face was surprised at first, then a slow smile spread across his face and he inclined his head to me. I returned his affectionate nod, before looking over at my grandparents. D'nay was beaming at me and Gloria looked as if she might cry.

I loved them all so much, I thought as I sipped the horribly acrid wine. I'd never developed a taste for the stuff and apparently this was one thing the price tag of the bottle didn't help. I watched as Gloria made some comment that finally caught Gabriel enough off guard to make him laugh. In that moment they weren't mysterious immortals; they were simply the beautiful, loving people who raised me. For my father, I thought, I would drink this whole damn glass.

***

After dinner, there was dancing. What Usuriel function was complete without dancing? Liam seemed determined to win back some of my attention, which admittedly had been pretty thoroughly stolen by Dad and my grandparents for the first half of the evening.

I've mentioned the fact that the older generations were adept on the dance floor. Liam followed in their footsteps, at least in this area. I hardly had to think about where I was going; his arms simply steered me smoothly from one end of the floor to the other as naturally as breathing. Since I didn't have to focus on where I was going, I found myself free to enjoy the way his arm wrapped around my waist and the muscular swell of his shoulder under my palm.

Though I kept an eye out for him, Dad never made an appearance on the dance floor. Amourie and Jillian, however, showed off some moves that made me positively blush. I'd never seen anyone make courtly dancing into a sensual act, but if anyone could manage it, Amourie was certainly the one. Jillian was a bit of a surprise, but really she shouldn't have been. After seeing how well-toned and limber her body was from training at the OW, I should have guessed she'd be an excellent dancer. She kept up with Amourie far better than I would have, anyway.

"I can't believe James ever compared me to her," I muttered mostly to myself as we swept past the two women. Amourie was pulling Jillian out of an achingly beautiful dip so slowly I could watch each muscle in their torsos uncoil. It must have taken an incredible amount of strength and control to move that smoothly in such a gravity-defying pose.

"She's a pale reflection of you, tonight." Liam's voice startled me and I glanced up at him. I hadn't expected him to hear my little comment, let alone respond. I opened my mouth to protest his flattery, but then I caught sight of the unguarded look on his face. He meant what he'd said. Affection isn't quite the word for the surprising emotion that bloomed in my chest. Gratitude, perhaps? I'm not sure, but it was enough to make me press a little closer to him.

After a few more dances we were both flushed and thirsty. Liam left to fetch us some water before leading me outside to the balcony for some fresh air.

The view outside was incredible. The lights of Skykyle spread out below us; twinkling stars of humanity flickering in the night. Lake Cormorant reflected back the silhouettes of the tallest buildings, its surface softly rippling and distorting their incandescent glow.

"Well, I'm not sure I was expecting our first date to be such a historic occasion," Liam commented as we leaned against the railing, "but I'm still having a good time. What about you?"

I thought about it, then nodded. "Yes, I am," I agreed finally. "A new second-gen is... wow... crazy. But, now that it's sinking in, I think I'm actually happy about it. I mean, D'nay and Gloria obviously want another child. And there are a lot of Family members who are perfectly sane, productive members of society. Even Dad and Adora spent more time being stable than not. Chances are Ileesia will be fine."

"Probably true, from the big picture," Liam agreed, "but I'm tired of talking about Family royal lines."

"Okay, what do you want to talk about?"

"I could start with how amazing you look in that dress," he said, leaning back to admire me.

I was glad the pale light reaching us from the balcony doors wasn't enough for him to see how much pink he put into my cheeks. "Thanks," I replied. I let my eyes travel over his strong shoulders and the long, clean lines of his torso. "You fill a tunic awfully well yourself."

"I can't hold a candle to half of that crowd." He gestured to the ballroom. "Including you."

"If you could, we'd be too close to date," I pointed out sensibly. "As it is, I still find it a bit weird."

"Really?" He sounded surprised. He took a step closer to me, fingers coming up to my cheek. We'd been sparring partners for months and I'd never had the adrenaline rush of desire when we touched except that one incident before Amourie's. But this time, the tender look on his face made something in my chest kindle. When our skin brushed I felt that rush of warmth I'd only ever had with James. "You aren't looking at me like a sister right now," he said, voice low and deep.

"No," I agreed. "I'm not."

He leaned closer until there were only centimeters between us. The warmth of his body contrasted with the chill evening air. Then his hand on my cheek guided my lips

up to his; at first just a brush of lips to lips, then ever so
gently he flickered his tongue against mine. I gasped as a
tiny ripple of his psi slid down my spine, raising the tiny
hairs and making things deep in my body clench. How had I
ever thought I wasn't attracted to him?

A deafening explosion pulled us away from each other, heads snapping up to brilliant lights shimmering over the lake. It seemed the fireworks had begun.

There was a commotion inside and people spilled out of the hall onto the balcony with us. It also seemed our private moment was over.

Liam didn't groan or complain. Rather, he wrapped an arm around my waist and pulled me against the comfortable solidity of his chest. I leaned my head back. It didn't even rise above his shoulder. It made him ideal for resting against; warm and strong. We stood there, watching the colorful spectacle as the rest of the Family oohed and aahed around us, their beautiful faces washed in flickering rainbow hues. Jessie was in the cluster of people just to my left and beyond them, Gloria and D'nay stood in a very similar pose to Liam's and mine. Their height difference was less and their hands rested, fingers interlaced, against the swell of her belly, but I saw the same contentment in the way she leaned back against his shoulder.

After all this time, they're taking a chance on another child, I mused as the fireworks hissed and popped over the lake. With as much as Dad and Adora had struggled over the years, it stretched the limit of my imagination that my grandparents could take the leap of faith that was bringing another child into the world. Yet, as I rested against Liam's warm strength, I wondered what having a newborn second-gen in the Family would be like. I hadn't known Dad when I was that little, but he'd been so much happier when I was growing up. Maybe having a new little sister would help him have a renewed sense of purpose, just like he had with me. Perhaps that's what my grandparents were looking for, as well, either for Gabriel or for themselves.

"Gracie?"

I leaned my head around Liam's shoulder and saw Carol standing behind us. "Hey, where's Dad?" I asked. My stomach sank at the expression on her face.

"What's wrong?" Liam asked as I pulled away from his arms.

"I'm sorry to bother you." Carol looked like she wanted to be doing anything but having this conversation. "But I don't think his mother needs to deal with this right now."

"What did he do?" I groaned. Carol didn't answer. Instead she sighed and started walking back into the hall. I was grateful to feel Liam's hand on my back as the two of us followed her into the restaurant.

"Well, I've heard you wonder aloud if he could still actually get falling down drunk," Liam commented when we arrived at the farthest table at the back of the room. "I'd say the answer is yes."

"For fuck's sake, Dad," I muttered under my breath. The wait staff here was highly paid and professional. They'd cleared away most of the empty bottles. However, there wasn't much they could do about the passed out Usuriel draped across the bench seat.

"Do you think one of the healers should look at him?"

Liam suggested. I glared up at him and he shrugged helplessly. I'm not sure what he saw on my face but I could tell he was being cautious.

"He'll be fine in the morning," Carol said reasonably, folding her arms across her broad chest.

"I didn't know you were a healer," I grumbled.

"I'm not. I've just known your dad a long time," she replied as calmly as if we were discussing planting turnips. "I'm not a 'porter, or I'd have put him to bed myself."

I looked down at my unconscious father. There were no words for the anger and disgust rising up my throat. They filled my mouth with an acrid tang. "Come on, Liam," I croaked. "Do you mind taking us back to Angelus Quietum? Sorry about cutting our date short."

"Not a problem," Liam replied, stepping forward and sliding a hand under my father's chest. "He's heavier than he looks," Liam complained, hauling Gabriel off of the bench seat and into his arms. He made the movement smooth and natural, however. My father lay pale and helpless in Liam's big arms. I hated everything about it. I looked anywhere else.

"I'm guessing you need a ride back, too?" I asked Carol.

"If you don't mind," she said.

"I've never been to Angelus Quietum so you'll have to give me a reference image, anyway," Liam told her. "Gracie can't and I don't think it's polite to go through Gabriel's memories when he's passed out."

I put a hand on Liam's back and motioned for Carol to do the same. "Stay close. He's not as strong as Dad."

Carol nodded and stepped close enough that our shoulders brushed. She must have given Liam the reference image because my partner's mind picked up around us and, with a stomach dropping twist and fold, the four of us were in the living room of Angelus Quietum.

Chapter 20

Night Lights

Carol and Liam settled Dad in bed while I went in search of his liquor bottles. Without me around to keep him in check, he'd stashed them all over the house. I dug up a decent-sized crate in the barn and loaded all of the evil things I could find into it. Once I filled that crate, I went and got another. By the time Liam and Carol came out of the bedroom, I'd already filled both boxes and had a couple extra bottles on the step next to me. I'd carried all of it out to the back porch and was sitting with a full container of Skykyle's finest in one hand.

"Gracie?" Liam called. The wooden deck creaked as he and Carol stepped outside. "What are you doing?"

"Do you think this stuff is flammable?" I asked, not turning around.

"I'm pretty sure it is."

I hefted the bottle in one hand, tossing it gently to myself to test the weight of it. With one savage movement, I tossed it into the air. It arched over my head in blissful silence. When it hit the peak of its trajectory, I took aim with one finger. The bottle shattered into a plume of orange flames and dark shards of glass.

"Gracie?" Carol said my name gently.

"Did you lay him on his side?" I asked, still not turning to face them.

"Yes," Carol replied. "I can stay here tonight if you want to go back to the University. I'll make sure he's okay in the morning."

While she spoke, I rifled through the bottles to find

another mostly-full container. Once I'd selected my next victim, I repeated the performance. This time, a flicker of green from whatever poisons were in the liquor flirted with my orange flames when I sent it up.

"No, your services won't be required tonight," I told her, acid in my tone. "You can go home."

"What is that supposed to mean?" Carol asked, a touch sharply.

"I mean he won't be needing casual sex," I replied evenly, pulling out another bottle and tossing it into the air. "And since the only other reason I can think of that he might have brought you on this date is to keep himself from getting black-out drunk, I'd say either way you were a pretty miserable failure." The bottle exploded in a gout of sparks and flame.

"Gracie!" Liam's voice sounded shocked.

"It's okay, Liam," Carol said. Being very careful not to look in their direction, I reached blindly for another bottle. "It's been an unsettling night for everyone. I'll see myself home."

"I'm sure she doesn't mean it," Liam clucked like a mother hen. "She knows it's her father she's pissed at, not you."

"Oh, she knows where I live. I imagine she'll apologize herself when she figures that all out."

There was a moment of silence in which I said nothing.

"Okay." My date sounded tired. "I hope the rest of your

night is better."

The door opened again. Carol would let herself out the front. It was closer to her house and didn't currently have a pissed off firebird lighting up liquor bottles from the step.

I tossed another bottle and the explosion this time was satisfyingly loud. In the barn, Charcoal and Aubrie reacted in distress to the unusual noise. They'd been in loose boxes when I went in to get the crates. I knew they'd be fine, if a little spooked. My fingers found the smooth glass rim of another explosion-in-waiting.

"He'll just buy more, you know." The step behind me groaned under Liam's weight.

"Hmmmm." I gave him my father's very own favorite non-answer. I threw the bottle extra hard this time. It wasn't very full, and the liquor went up with more of a whimper than a bang. I frowned and tried to find one with a little more satisfying weight to it. "He might get some kind of message out of it," I muttered, more to myself than to Liam, as I found what I was looking for. "Besides, I'm hoping some of this stuff is expensive."

"Well," Liam sighed and sorted through a few of the bottles, "yeah... this one is. Oh wow, and this one, too. I think the Riland is older than I am. You at least have to let me try it before you send it up, Gracie."

I rounded on him, the fury I'd been channeling into those little explosions riding my whole body like an electric charge. Flames licked up and around my shoulders as I met his gaze. "If you ever want to kiss me again, I suggest you keep that poison away from your lips."

Liam regarded me with an expression that bordered a little closer to fear than I was comfortable with. Before I could shy away from him, however, he slowly handed me both bottles. His eyebrow quirked up with a touch of mischief. "Think you can do two at once?"

I hefted them, a grim smile tugging at the corner of my lips. "Absolutely."

It was immensely satisfying to hurl them rapid fire into the ink-black sky before letting that bitter rage loose in the form of pure, cleansing flame. The kyoss trees lit up with the light of the blasts and far off to my right I could see their reflection in Lake Angelus.

I'm not sure how long we sat out there. Over an hour, at least. Liam watched as I made my way through the whole collection. It had to be well past midnight by the time I'd finally sent up the last of my father's alcohol.

We sat in silence, listening to the small sounds of the night. A cool breeze lifted my hair and I glanced at Liam. He'd propped himself against the railing and found a stick to peel the bark from absently, watching me with large, dark eyes.

"Well, this has been a pretty awful first date," I sighed. "I'm sorry. You don't have to stay. Dad will probably be his usual self in the morning and he can send me back to school. And even if he's not feeling up to it, I can fly now. I'll make it back one way or another."

"Do you *want* me to go?" Liam asked, still fiddling with the stick.

I thought about it. "No," I replied slowly. "But I don't want you to feel like you don't have a choice."

"I don't mind sleeping on a couch now and then. Especially when they're as plush as the one in there," he said with a jerk of his chin. "Besides, I like keeping you company. Hell, it's probably better if someone is there when you see Gabriel in the morning. I wouldn't want Vanessa sending me after you for murdering your father."

I snorted and tossed one of the crates off the step. The stars winked down, reassuring in their familiarity.

"You know," Liam said slowly, "we didn't get to finish our conversation earlier."

I groaned and rubbed an eye. "I don't know if now is such a good time, Liam. I'm not thinking straight."

"I understand." His voice was gentle, but his hand crept to the back of my neck.

Before I could think about it, I'd wrapped my arms around his waist and laid my head against his chest. His reassuring heart beat under my cheek. It was incredibly intimate in a way that our kiss hadn't been. Tears hovered on the edge of my vision. I tried to stifle a sniff as one of them broke free and rolled down my cheek.

"Hey." His voice sounded even deeper through the wall of his chest. "It's okay. Your dad will be back to himself in the morning."

"No," I whispered, "he won't be. He'll be a ruined wreck

like he has been for years. Sweet Fate, Liam, he's going to kill himself with this stuff and there isn't a thing I or anyone else can do about it."

My friend and partner looked down at me with a gentle expression on his face. "Oh Gracie," he murmured and hugged me tight. "If I ever have kids, I hope they love me half as much as you love Gabe."

I gave a little laugh and wiped my face. "Ugh, well if they do, I hope you never ruin their dates by making horrible, embarrassing scenes."

Liam watched me lean back from him, a thoughtful look on his face. "It could have been worse. You've seen his temper when he's sober. He could have made a real drunken scene instead of passing out quietly in the corner."

"I suppose that means he's earned the privilege of being checked on before I go to bed."

"You know," Liam said as we stood to go inside, "if your theories are right, the man was forced to kill his last sibling. Now his parents are going to give him another little sister almost a century after the fact? I think I might get black-out drunk if I were in his position, too."

"Stop it," I grumbled. "Now you're actually making me feel bad for him."

Liam shrugged as we stopped by the linen closet to get him some spare blankets and pillows. "I can see how he'd be tough to live with, but from what I've seen, he isn't the monster people make him out to be. I get why you care about him."

"Glad *someone* does." I stuck my head in my old room to make sure nothing had changed. It hadn't. "Because tonight, I have no idea."

"Are you going to do a last check on him?"

I sighed. "Yeah."

"Do you want me to come with you?"

"No." I shook my head and looked up at him, feeling very tired. "I'll take care of Gabriel."

"Okay." Liam seemed awkward, standing in the door to the hallway. "Well, I'll see you in the morning then."

"Night."

I turned to go, but Liam grabbed my arm. I frowned up at him. His eyes searched my face, as if he were trying to put something into words. The serious set of his brow said it was way too intense for what I could handle right now. "Gracie... I..."

"Not tonight, Liam," I breathed. I closed the distance between us and placed a quick kiss on his lips. The flush in his cheeks as I pulled away spoke for him. "Thank you for getting us home. And staying with me tonight. You've been a really good friend when I needed one. I appreciate it."

He nodded quickly, hugging the pillow to his chest. "I'm your partner, remember? Whatever else we are, or aren't, you can always count on me to have your back."

"Thank you," I said again. I turned away and walked towards my father's dark room. "Goodnight, Liam."

"Gracie..."

"Go to bed."

"You looked beautiful tonight."

I paused in the doorway to my father's room. I seriously considered going back to Liam and letting him comfort me in a much more physical way. I was pretty sure he would be willing to oblige, but I still hadn't made up my mind on how I felt about him. If I ever did decide I was serious about him, I didn't want this night to be the one I thought of every time I saw him naked. I owed it to Liam not to use him that way.

"Thank you," I called back to him. "You're a lovely dancer."

There was another long pause and I wondered what was going through his head.

"Goodnight, Gracie," he said finally.

The hall light went out. I summoned a small flame in one hand and went into my father's room.

***

Gabriel was many things. My father. At one point, probably my best friend. He was a frustrating mystery and an intriguing puzzle; a long-casting shadow and a ready-made reputation. In some ways I hated him for how much he dominated my life. In other ways, I loved him for rescuing me from the darkest place I'd ever been and never allowing anyone else to take me away from him. He was a protector and a blind spot; an asset and a liability. For so many years he had been my entire world and every time I thought I had him pinned down and defined in my head, he flipped everything completely around on me. All these years and I still didn't know who Gabriel Usuriel really was.

At that particular moment I watched him, wondering if I was going to check on him or strangle him in his sleep. He was so still and silent I had to watch closely to see his chest rise and fall.

As I stepped closer to where Liam and Carol had left him, pale and too thin, on the bed, a flickering light caught my eye. My head shot up just in time to see Olivia glide into the hallway. I barely caught a glimpse of her but, for the first time ever, I thought there was something in her arms. Though I couldn't make out what it was in that split second, it was unusual enough that I paused to frown at the doorway. When she didn't reappear, I turned back to Gabriel's still figure.

I'd never seen my father laid low, not because of injury or physical illness, but because of his addiction. Well, Stella had shown me in the holo suite, but this was living, breathing real life. Sometimes that's what it took to bring things home.

"Dad," I said quietly, gesturing with two fingers to send my small burning globe hovering above the bed. The control I had with the flames these days was surprising even to me; I could hold that nightlight almost indefinitely. I wondered if Dad would be proud of me if he knew how much I was impressing the OW trainers. I knew he didn't approve of my membership, but somehow I thought he might like to know that his training hadn't been wasted or unnoticed. Well, I doubted we'd be able to discuss it civilly any time soon. Chances were, we'd have a nice blow up after this evening's escapades.

Pushing away yet another spark of irritation with my father, I leaned down and shook his shoulder. "Dad," I tried again. "I'm sleeping in my old room. Liam's on the couch. Call for us if you need anything, okay?"

Pathetic. That was honestly the word that came to mind when he didn't rouse even enough to flicker an eyelash in my direction. My lip curling in disgust, I turned away.

Olivia walked into the room carrying a sleeping child. I stopped cold, my hand still on my father's shoulder. She carried the red-headed little girl into the room without acknowledging me or my unconscious father. She sat down on the other side of the bed and looked up at the door. I followed her gaze.

My heart froze.

Gabriel walked smoothly into the room, his dark hair pulled back into its functional ponytail. He tucked an errant lock behind one ear and went to where Olivia was sitting on the bed. My chest felt encased in alloy as I saw the dark shape of the bathroom door right through his slightly-glowing shoulders. Yet I couldn't tear my eyes away as he leaned down to Olivia and kissed her gently before taking the sleeping child from her arms. With the utmost tenderness, he carried the still-sleeping little girl out of the room. With an inaudible sigh, Olivia laid down on the bed and faded away into sparkling motes.

Once again alone in the dark with my father, I suddenly found fear shouting down the anger I'd been clinging to. Flashbacks of a particularly disturbing dream flooded me: a glass slipping from pale fingers; my father's lips turning blue as I scrambled to keep his heart beating and his airway open.

"Dad," I said again, looking down at Gabriel with more urgency. His dark hair spread out behind him on the pillow, and he was terribly pale. Carol or Liam had undone the top button of his dress tunic so he could breathe more easily. The sharp edge of his collar bone flashed from its folds. When he still didn't rouse at my voice or touch, I slid my hand into the open fabric and laid it against his chest. His mechanical heart beat steadily against my palm.

He moaned softly and I snatched my hand back. My lips reformed into a thin line as his brow creased and his eyes flickered under bruised lids. He was dreaming, I realized when he didn't wake. If he was dreaming, he wasn't passed out anymore—he was asleep. Well, he wasn't about to be a ghost just yet. Comforted by that knowledge, I once again felt safe enough to be pissed at him. With a scowl, I folded my arms across my chest and stood back from the bed.

"Goodnight, Dad," I said and walked out the door, snuffing my nightlight on the way out.

Chapter 21

Breakfast

I woke the next morning to warm sun slanting across my white coverlet. I groaned and rolled over, deciding to push my luck in the hopes that Stella would forget to wake me in time for my morning chores.

I must have fallen back to sleep, because when I woke again the smell of a home-cooked breakfast and the sound of deep voices in the kitchen made me sit up and tap my implant for the time. It was almost mid-morning.

Why had Stella let me sleep so late? Who was in the kitchen with Dad? Was it James?

Then the last clouds of sleep cleared from my brain and last night came rushing back. The anger that had been flaming hot yesterday felt like a cold lump of lead in my stomach this morning. With a groan, I tossed the covers off and headed for the shower.

Clean, clothed, and halfway ready to deal with my delinquent father, I stalked out to the kitchen. I rounded the corner from the living room and walked into a scene of perfect domestic bliss. Liam saw me first, glancing up from where he sat at the table, showered and dressed, nursing a cup of steaming tea.

"Hi, Gracie," he said, offering me a cautious smile.

Dad looked over his shoulder from where he was making

sausage, bacon, toast, and eggs over the stove. "Good morning, sweetheart," he said, as if his entire collection of liquor bottles weren't smashed on the lawn out back. "You're just in time for a late breakfast."

Feeling like I'd send the whole house up in flames if I so much as blinked, I slowly moved to Liam's side. "We need to go."

"Why don't you sit down?" Liam suggested, an encouraging look on his face. I could tell he wanted me to relax and play nice, but I couldn't do it. Sitting down at my father's table for breakfast as if everything were perfectly fine was beyond me right now.

"I'm going to be late for class," I growled, running my fingers through my still-wet red curls. "Come on. We don't have time for this."

"At least have a cup of tea," my father said, bringing over several loaded plates. The smell was amazing. My stomach growled traitorously. "Besides, I don't think they'll expel you for missing a class or two. Family has to come first sometimes, right?"

I envisioned wringing his neck so vividly my gaze actually washed red. "Family comes first, huh, Dad?"

Liam's eyes widened as his gaze darted between Gabriel and me. He opened his mouth like he wanted to say something to stop the firestorm that was coming, but promptly closed it. Probably wise. The tiny sliver of my brain that wasn't about to fly off the rails in Gabriel's direction actually felt a little bad for him.

Dad noticed my expression and paused setting the table to regard me with dark, careful eyes. "I realize it wasn't... planned. But I am glad you and Liam are here to visit. Can we make this into a happy accident instead of another fight, please?"

I was going to kill him. The next headline Reporter Joe

was going to write for his celebrity-net would be "Gabriel Usuriel Dead: Third-Gen Firebird Murders Her Infamous Father Over Pancakes."

"No!" I all but shouted at him. "I'm not playing tea party after what you pulled. I had to check for a fucking pulse last night, Dad! You can't fix that with breakfast food!"

He scowled at me, a hint of his own temper finally catching in his eyes. Some odd part of my head felt satisfied that I'd managed to piss him off. Like misery, anger loves company. "People get drunk at parties. I didn't hurt anyone but myself so you can stop channeling your grandmother and act like a civilized person at my table."

"No one but yourself, huh? What about Carol? You left her without a way home, or did you even think about that?"

He did look slightly embarrassed about that one. "I figured Mom..." he started to mutter.

"Your pregnant mother, woman of the hour? Oh yes, like she needed to deal with your spore-bent antics last night!"

"Well maybe she could use a reminder of the less convenient parts of having children," he snapped, sounding for all the world like a petulant teenager.

"You are such an emotionally stunted ass!" I shouted. I was pretty sure there were flames crawling through my hair but try as I might I couldn't quite keep my fist closed on them. It took all of my considerable control to keep them from sending up the entire house. "You're over four hundred years old, Dad! Act like you've learned something since you were fifteen!"

"Gracie? Liam?"

The voice from my implant was completely unexpected. I blinked, thrown by Vanessa's even tone in the middle of my rant.

"Listen, I don't want to fight with you, Gracie," Dad said slowly, unaware that our argument had been interrupted. "For what it's worth, I appreciate you and Liam bringing Carol and me home last night. I'm sorry if it cut short your evening plans. That was not my intention."

I shot him a deadly glare as I tapped my implant. "Yes, Vanessa?"

"We have a situation. I'd like you and Liam to go meet up with Evan Kylar."

I glanced at Liam. He hastily popped a sausage in his mouth, downed the rest of his tea, and stood.

"Sorry, Gabe, but I think we've been summoned to duty," he said apologetically to my father. They must have had a decent conversation before I woke because I'd never heard Liam address Gabriel so casually.

"Overwatch calls, I suppose." It was my father's turn to shoot the two of us a displeased expression. "At least take something with you. Those calls can get awfully long."

"Don't think it means this fight is over," I snapped, though the empty cavern of my stomach finally prevailed enough that I snatched up a sausage as I stepped closer to Liam.

A tiny smile hovered on the very corner of my father's

mouth as I took a bite. "Be careful, you two."

"Humph," I sniffed. Then the wind of Liam's power rose around me and Angelus Quietum bled away in streams of color.

Chapter 22

Ryland

When the world stopped lurching and spinning around me, we were in an unfamiliar city. The red brick of the buildings seemed strange after the alloy and glass of Skykyle or the weathered stone of Landing. We were standing on a long, wooden platform above softly waving grass. Several hover cars were parked along the railings of the raised walkways. Roughly two dozen people walked in and out of the dingy storefronts with their heads down, tattered cloaks pulled tightly against the wind.

"Where are we?" I asked Liam. The air was chilly, and I was glad for the warmth of the sausage as I ate it in quick, fierce bites. The area didn't feel especially well-maintained; I spotted scattered patches of graffiti, and exposed beams gaped from wounds in the patchy roofs.

"Riland City, I think. I just took Vanessa's guide image. She didn't tell me where we were going," Liam said, glancing around. "But yeah, we're in Riland. Look, you can see some of the smoke damage from the massacre." He pointed to the base of one decrepit structure. Black streaks of heat damage dragged ghostly fingers across the rusty brick.

"That was over fifty years ago." I shook my head in wonder. "I can't believe you can still see the smoke stains." I fell into step behind Liam as he headed down the curve of the wooden walkway.

"Those fires burned long and hot," he said. "Besides, it doesn't look like this side of the city has had a whole lot of attention since then."

A group of men clustered near a building on our right. The building itself looked even worse than the rundown businesses around it. The windows were boarded up or dark and gaping like missing teeth. The black smoke damage streaking its walls marked it as older than half a century. It looked to me like the roof might possibly be original. I doubted the tenement got any power from the faded solar shingles.

The men who gathered near it were all dressed in thick, brown leathers. Their outfits were sleek and clean, clearly denoting some kind of uniform. It wasn't a huge stretch to think they were the police we were supposed to be meeting with.

A pock-marked, mid-thirties man with dark hair was complaining to his comrades as we walked up. "How long does it take? I mean, honestly, they can blazing teleport."

Liam cleared his throat and the man looked up, a sneer of annoyance on his rugged face.

"Get lost, youngling," he snapped. "This is watch business."

Liam lifted an eyebrow and glanced at me. I shrugged and put a hand into my pants pocket. I caught Liam reaching into the air by his left shoulder as we both pulled out our OW badges.

"Oh no," our mortal host groaned, hiding his dark eyes with one hand before letting it slide down to distort his thin-lipped mouth. "I call for Overwatch back up and they send me a couple of University students."

"We can leave if you prefer," Liam suggested, gesturing with one thumb, "but I doubt Vanessa will send anyone else..."

"Ugh, no. Fine. We have a vamp report and I'm not waiting until nightfall to clear this spore-hole."

I glanced up at the building in question. The door was slightly off of its hinges and the smell was apparent even from here. Someone had used it as a toilet in the not too distant past. I wasn't thrilled with the idea of going in there.

"What's your name?" Liam asked the whiny watchman.

"Evan Kylar. Why?"

"Of course," I sighed, and started walking towards the rundown structure.

"What's that supposed to mean?" Evan sounded even more pissed.

"Vanessa said to meet up with you," I said over my shoulder. "So I'm taking it the complaint just said there were vamps in there?"

"It's a spore-hole of all sorts," Evan explained, sounding a touch more civil. "But yeah, there have been at least two ex-spore addicts who say a vamp has been living on the top floor and feeding off the junkies. You can see the top floor is completely boarded up. I'd say there's a decent possibility they're telling the truth."

"They're using Angel's Foot in there?" Liam looked extremely unhappy about that idea.

I frowned. "That stuff's dangerous. Even one exposure can cause lung rot."

"Here." Evan pulled a small inhaler out of the pouch at his waist. "Watch's eye. Hits like a three-T, but it's better than coughing yourself to death in a few months."

I accepted the aerosol medication and inspected it before uncapping the mouthpiece and taking a dose. The vapor stung the inside of my mouth and lungs but I held my breath while the protective coating soaked in. Blinking away involuntary tears, I handed the applicator to Liam. He looked even more unhappy as he took a hit of the preventative himself.

"Oh that stuff is vile," Liam coughed, when he was done holding the requisite ten-count. Then he squared his shoulders at the spore-hole, as Evan had called it. "Well, this should be fun."

We were just taking the first stair when a car door slammed and we turned to see Jillian climbing out of her hover car a few yards away.

"Sorry I'm late!" she called to us. "My partner pulled a Gabe last night at the Family party, so I had to drive. What did I miss?"

My face went very still. I wondered if I'd mastered the Usuriel blank face or if any of the insane rage that boiled up at the mention of my father's humiliating antics showed through the mask. It must have worked because Jillian didn't seem to realize anything was amiss until she looked up at Liam.

"What?" she frowned at him for a moment, then her

brown eyes went wide. "Oh! Shit! I... it's a figure of speech! I'm sorry, Gracie, I shouldn't have said that."

"Can we just do our jobs, please?" I asked through clenched teeth. To my credit, I didn't leak any flames this time.

"Yeah, sure," Jillian said, swallowing visibly. She turned to Evan. "Please send the complaint reports to my memory pad when you have a moment. In the meantime, explain to me exactly what we're dealing with."

Evan nodded, apparently much relieved that someone who knew what they were doing had arrived. "Two hospitalized addicts reported exchanging blood for spores with a female vampire at this location as recently as sixty hours ago."

"Any indication she might be awake at this hour?" Jillian asked, glancing up at the decrepit tenement.

"No, but I'm not sending men in to clear the place until I'm sure she's been neutralized. We have good information there are at least a dozen addicts currently living here."

Liam rubbed the back of his neck. "Fantastic. So she has hostages if she's smart about it."

"Hopefully she's still dead to the world at the moment," Jillian pointed out, "and you should be able to take on a lone vamp by yourself, Liam. This isn't a bad introduction to field work, honestly."

Liam eyed the building doubtfully. "If you say so."

I wasn't much more enthusiastic about entering the spore-hole than he was, but I didn't voice my objections. Jillian took her dose of watch's eye and led the way towards the ruined building. Reluctantly, Liam and I fell in behind her.

The smell assaulted me first. I put a hand over my mouth and nose. It didn't help much as I stepped around the door. My eyes slowly adjusted to the dim light inside and I swallowed a wave of nausea; the filth was at a level I'd never experienced before. Despite the stills of blighted Skykyle we'd looked up on the net—not to mention my own mother's humble attempts at housekeeping in my youth—I was completely unprepared for what we walked into that day.

Broken memory pads, empty food containers, and dirty clothes were piled in layers around the moldering remnants of furniture. Stalks of the long grasses that grew in the alleyways outside tangled in the corners of the room. There was some kind of brown liquid seeping down the walls from the ceiling in several places, while in others it appeared to be sprayed from a standing height. I had a feeling this was the main source of the smell. Even more disturbing, small mushroom caps grew in several patches of damp on the floor. You didn't live on Cybele long without a healthy fear of fungus spores.

Something rustled near one of the pieces of furniture. I jumped back, grabbing Liam's sleeve in reflex. I sucked in a breath and immediately regretted it. Fortunately, Liam was steady under my hand.

"There are three in this room," he said, sounding as if he

were being careful not to breathe through his nose. He pointed to three bundles that I'd originally taken to just be piles of old cloth. Now that I looked closer, I saw filthy skin and hair peeking from beneath the debris.

"How can anyone live in this?" I asked, more to myself than anyone in particular.

"I'm not sure this is living," Jillian replied evenly. She didn't seem particularly thrown by our horrifying surroundings.

"Should we send for a medic or—I don't know—check on them?" I'd thought my father looked pathetic last night… I shoved that thought away, knowing it would take me to a place that made my chest hollow and sick.

"The mortal watch will take them to the hospital once we've dealt with the supernatural stuff upstairs," Jillian said sensibly, turning to the stairs. "Lung rot is treatable if it's caught early enough, though it may be too late for a few of them. I doubt the owner of the building will prosecute for trespassing, so they're not in danger of being locked up."

"I don't know," Liam observed. "We're in Riland. From what I've heard, they're kind of primitive around here. Didn't their Senate want to make addiction an actual crime?"

"That hasn't been a law since Earth," I protested, following him as he made his way towards the stairs. "It will never go over with the Family."

"Not so many Usuriels in this area," Jillian called from halfway up the stairs. "Come on, they said the vampire was supposed to be upstairs. That's our job. Leave the addicts for the mortal watch."

Liam took the first stair and froze. I all but ran into him as he blocked the entire doorway. "You okay?" I asked, trying to peer around his shoulder.

"Oh sweet Fate," he whispered. "Gracie..."

"What?" I demanded, frowning up at him.

With a surprisingly graceful shift in weight for a man his size, Liam set one foot off the step so I could squeeze around him. He put both hands onto my shoulders as I climbed the two steps to the first landing and got a good view of the stairway.

Sorrow. He surrounded me as I took the first step. Psi-blue flame, midnight-blue eyes, and pale feathers completely covered the crumbling walls. His name scrawled in elaborate script along the side of the stairs, blue fire painted to wrap around each letter. At the top of the stair, where Jillian had just disappeared through the top doorway, a surprisingly skillful rendering of my father gazed down at us. The painting raised one hand as if offering a blessing. Whoever painted this hallway had taken a ridiculous amount of time to detail the elaborate curls and whirls of dark hair and psi power as they rose from Sorrow's shoulders and spilled down the stairs. Even the feathers of his pale blue wings fell in elegant, looping curves. It was strangely beautiful in this vile place.

My chest was glass and it had just been shattered. I took the steps mechanically, my body distant and numb as if I'd been dunked in ice water.

"Sorrow watch me as with the spores I sleep," Liam read the script as he followed me.

"Sweet Fate," was all I could manage as I came to the top landing and found myself face to face with the painting. This Gabriel was slightly larger than life size, I realized standing next to it.

"You two coming?" Jillian called over her shoulder from the upper floor. I swallowed hard and tore myself away from the mural. I was going to have to process this later.

"Yeah, we're right here," Liam called to her as we stepped through the doorway and into what once might have been an upstairs hall. Now, the brick and timber construction of the building was completely exposed as almost all the walls had been torn down to rubble. I spotted several more unconscious addicts tucked against supports or on items of ruined furniture.

"This place would burn to ash in two breaths," I murmured to Liam, "and none of them would make it out. It's too dangerous for me to use my fire here. If we have to deal with this vamp, it's going to have to be all you."

"I don't think that's going to be an issue," Jillian said as he caught up with her. She stood over a particularly pale woman. The vampire wasn't especially pretty or ugly; in fact she looked completely ordinary except for the porcelain cast of her skin. Unlike most of the others, she wasn't covered in rags or huddled against the chill air. Rather, she sprawled long, lean limbs across the bare mattress she'd pushed against the wall. The same refuse didn't clutter around her, either, though a very thin couple were curled together just out of her arm's reach. They lay insensible, limbs tangled together. They bore fang marks on both of their wrists.

Liam snorted and made a face as if he regretted taking in that much of the noxious air. "They brought us all the way out here to deal with a dead vamp?"

"She won't be dead when the moon rises." Jillian pushed a black braid behind one ear. "And be glad they didn't call us after that. This makes life a lot simpler. We just transport her to holding and let the Council figure it out."

"Hey!"

All three of us turned as one of the lumps at the far corner of the room unfolded itself into a lumbering, unshaven figure. The clothes he wore must once have been the brown leather I'd seen on other Riland citizens. Now they were stained and tattered beyond any kind of recognizable style. His face looked gaunt and too thin for his bone structure, but he clearly hadn't been a small man to begin with. His broad shoulders made the slimmer Family build look ephemeral.

"Leave 'er alone!" The shambler bellowed at us.

"We're Overwatch." Liam flashed his badge again. "Our business isn't with you."

The addict didn't look like he understood what Liam was telling him. Wide-eyed aggression swept across his face and I caught a glimpse of a hefty piece of wood concealed in the man's thread-bare cloak.

"Liam, look out!" I called out.

I shouldn't have worried. Liam might not be an elder child, but he was a pretty solid three-T and he'd been training with Jillian for months. It took less than a cough for Liam to teleport the makeshift club into his own hand. Meanwhile, I'd moved in on the vagabond. I dodged his first clumsy swing. With a few rapid movements—more reflex than thought—I had him face down on the floor. Jillian came over with her restraints, secured his hands behind his back, and helped me haul him to his feet.

"Neatly done," Jillian said with an approving nod to the two of us. "Gracie, you and I will take this one downstairs and tell Evan the building is safe for them to enter. Liam, you teleport our spore-queen here back to the OW compound. Tell the guard in holding that you need a flatliner. He'll know you mean a cell for a vamp. Gracie and I will drive my vehicle back to the OW and meet you there."

Liam nodded and lifted the female vampire into his arms with ease. "See you two back at the compound," he said. Then he and the vampire disappeared in a rush of psi-wind.

"Okay, let's get this guy down to Evan," she said. The addict in question muttered to himself incoherently and I felt a little bad for him as Jillian led him down the stairs by one arm. None of the other inhabitants of the spore-hole stirred as we left.

"Everything balanced out?" Evan asked as Jillian handed off the restrained addict to one of the other members of the mortal watch.

"No big surprises," Jillian said, wiping her hands on her blue uniform pants as if she wanted to get the filth of the junkie off of her palms. "There was only one undead and I don't think she was over a decade turned. Pretty brave to start up a den of her own. How many is that this month in Riland City alone?"

"Four dens," Evan growled, looking unhappy. "It was a spore-queen then?"

Jillian nodded. "Most likely. She's been here at least a few months from the look of it."

Evan cursed under his breath and fingered his scruffy beard. "I've always said it was only a matter of time before the vamps got bold again. There's no way you could do a few block sweep to check for any more?"

Jillian and I exchanged a look. "I'm sorry," she said, spreading her hands. "But our three-T has already gone ahead with the vampire. We're not telepaths, and even if he were here Liam isn't a high level 'path. Which means we'd have to clear each building the way we did this one: go in and look around. I'm sorry, but we just don't have the time or numbers to do that kind of a sweep. Vanessa has told you this before. It would take Gracie and I the rest of the day just to finish up here and we both have other commitments."

Evan scowled. "This is how we ended up with a massacre! I don't know if you remember, or care, but the vamps were the ones who riled things up in the first place! They've laid low for a few generations, but I'm telling you, they are pushing back hard lately. Mark me, they aren't going to stop at addicts and prostitutes this time! But I guess the lot of you don't give a damn how many mortals get bled as long as your precious Family members stay safe!"

"We lost a second-gen in that massacre, in case you don't remember!" Jillian snapped. I'd never seen her get mad before. I knew she couldn't summon a flame without her spark, but the look in her eyes was blazing. "The Overwatch comes out whenever you have a legitimate call. We're just not willing to hang around and do your beat for you. There are only twenty-five of us. We can't patrol all of Cybele. We'd never sleep."

"I'm not asking you to patrol all of Cybele. I'm asking you to patrol Riland City, where we have the highest vamp demographic and a demonstrated history of violence," Evan argued.

"By that logic, we'd have to patrol Skykyle and Landing, too," Jillian retorted. "They have the highest Usuriel density and we've seen our fair share of incidents on that side of the continent as well. And we would love to, but we can't. We just don't have the people to do it. We can't cover Riland the way you're suggesting, let alone all three areas."

"Those 'incidents' didn't hold a candle to the massacre, and you know it."

"Second-gen, remember?" Jillian shot back. "Unless Gabe or Gloria lose their brains sometime soon, I don't think you're going to get that kind of an incident again. And I just saw them both at the party last night. They seemed perfectly sane to me. So stop fear-mongering and do your damn job!" She gestured sharply at the spore-hole before turning on her heel and marching off towards her hover car. I quickly followed her lead, feeling very unqualified for this argument. All I knew about the Riland massacre had been learned in Professor Joan's class last term.

"Don't get me started on Gabriel! That fucking addict is going to pull something one of these days!" Evan shouted after us. "Mark me, he'll go the way of his sister! If Vanessa has any sense in her head at all, she'll at least patrol Skykyle!"

I almost turned around, but Jillian's hand grabbed my wrist. "Just leave it," she muttered, and all but threw me into the passenger seat of her vehicle. The automatic straps wrapped around my shoulders, hugging me tightly and making the echoing chamber of my chest claustrophobic.

Jillian slammed into the driver's seat beside me and sucked in a breath between her teeth as the straps embraced her. She rested her palms on the control panel and closed her eyes. Then she straightened her shoulders and tapped in a few commands. The hovercraft immediately began a smooth ascent into the skyline to our left.

"I'm sorry you had to hear that," Jillian said softly once the buildings of Riland City fell away and the scenery turned to terraced rice fields.

I sat, staring out the window for a moment before answering her. If I'd been upset about my father's behavior last night, the incident had been savagely put into context by the dose of reality I'd just received. Between the abject desperation of the spore addicts, their almost mocking mural, and Evan's words, I felt as if my father's true nature was suddenly a lot clearer and far darker than even my worst imaginings.

"How much of Riland hates my dad as much as Evan?" I asked softly.

"Hard to say," Jillian sighed. "But he's head of their watch, so I can't imagine his views are completely radical. I know he's been wearing Vanessa down about patrols for years. We tried it once. It was completely worthless. We were stretched so thin that we were too exhausted to even deal with the few dens we did find."

Head of their watch. The head of Riland watch thought my father was going to lose his mind and burn down half of Skykyle. I let that fact soak in while the kilometers melted away below us. For a while we rode in silence. Then, I glanced at Jillian.

"Do you think Gabriel is dangerous?" I said it so quietly it's a wonder she heard me.

She was quiet for a minute before responding. "Your dad? No. Not really." I nodded and looked ahead, satisfied with the answer. My chest tightened when she continued talking. "He's strong enough to hurt people if he wanted to, but as far as I know, outside of defense or OW order, he's only ever deliberately injured himself."

"He does seem good at that part."

She glanced at me, a kind expression on her plump face. "Self-destruction? Occasionally. But four hundred years is a pretty good track record, despite the substance abuse. Hell, he managed to get blitzed on a generation ship full of mortals without ever flying off and injuring someone. If you remember, Orville happened when he was completely sober. If you ask me, that alone has to be a statement about his true temperament."

I rubbed my arm, trying to get the disgusting miasma of the spore-hole off of my palm. "Yet everyone talks about him like he's a villain."

"Some people do," Jillian admitted. "But those people don't usually know him. What do *you* think?"

I stared out the window at tiered rice paddies and twisting kyoss trees. "I don't know anymore."

"I find that hard to believe." When I didn't answer, Jillian rolled her eyes. "Forget the reputation. In my experience, Gabriel is lots of sarcastic wit and very little violent temper. It would take a truly exceptional situation to make him lose it." She glanced at me again. "If I had to guess, I'd say as long as you're safe and sound, he'll be just fine."

I considered that as the landscape melted into the more familiar wheat and cattle farms that surrounded Skykyle and, farther south, Landing.

"I'm sorry about my careless comment earlier, too," Jillian said as we came in sight of the Galloway Mountains. She cleared her throat, as if she were genuinely embarrassed by the gaff.

"It's okay," I said with a wave of one hand. "He is what he is. And as long as he's safely at Angelus Quietum instead of some spore-hole like that... well... I think I can live with it."

Jillian nodded. "That's probably a sensible way to think about it."

Chapter 23

Ariel's Solution

By the time we met up with Liam, he'd already settled the vampire in holding. She was to await a council hearing on charges of coercive feeding. It was an executable offense, but I didn't feel bad about delivering her for judgment. The condition of those addicts, and the way she took advantage of their illness, made me nauseous.

Liam and I got back to University too late for our classes, so we took quick showers before getting a meal together. I told him about Evan's parting words and he was sympathetic. He offered to walk me back to my room, but I declined, instead heading over to see my professors and ask for make-up work. I was up late in the library and, by the time I dragged myself back to the dormitory, the stars were out. I stretched as I put my hand to the door pad, ready for a solid twelve hours in my own bed.

I walked into my room and immediately froze. A familiar golden glow flooded the tiny room and I nearly collided with Ariel's beaming figure as she all but bounced on my bed.

Ariel's young, fresh face beamed exuberantly at me. Her green eyes sparkled as she waved her journal in my face, all but tugging on my shirt sleeve until I found my copy and opened it up.

"I'm tired, Ariel. This had better be important," I sighed as I cracked open the faded volume.

"I've done it! I've done the impossible! Even the Anori scholars said it was beyond our reach, but I figured it out! And you're the key, you beautiful child!"

I'd never seen Ariel's script so joyous, slanting and looping as if she couldn't contain her enthusiasm.

"Slow down. I don't know what you're talking about," I said. "What have you figured out?"

"Exactly what I promised! I've found the answer to the Gabriel conundrum!" I frowned up at her and she shook her head violently, red curls tumbling into her tired-yet-excited green eyes. "Come with me to my lab. I can explain more thoroughly there."

Without waiting for me to agree, she lunged into me. Her skin poured over mine like a scalding wave and I knew this would become extremely uncomfortable if I didn't go along with it. Biting back the feeling that everyone else seemed in control of my life lately, I obediently opened my mind to the flames as Ariel pulled up the image of her laboratory in the research center. Unlike our other trips, this wasn't a large step geographically and clearly it also wasn't as long time-wise either. It took barely a thought and I was standing in the center of a dimly lit, quiet, and organized lab.

"Gracie!" Ariel's voice sounded thin and worn, like the pages of her journal. I startled when I saw her. This Ariel's green eyes hid in the tiny webs of crow's feet and her coppery curls were shot with streaks of silver. She stood by a table full of tubes and microscopes, an array of slides and sample dishes set about in the clutter of controlled chaos. She gestured to a small group of them in front of her. "These are your samples, aren't they?"

I frowned and walked forward to see several small vials of blood labeled "Gr. Usuriel—3rd Gen."

"Must be," I agreed. "You took a sample almost a year ago. Don't you remember?"

She shook her head at me and gave a small smile. "I do remember a rather wild party when we were sixteen, but that's the only time we've met... in my current time-line anyway. When this sample showed up in the lab I knew it had to be yours, though."

"In this time-line," I muttered, trying to wrap my brain around the problems of time travel and ghost communications.

"I was hoping you'd show up soon, though. No, I take that back. I knew you would. You were born for this." Ariel's eyes held something I'd never seen before. It was strange and unnerving, as if she wasn't seeing me as Gracie but as something far more magnificent and fateful than a nineteen-year-old girl. I quickly looked anywhere besides the rapturous expression on her face.

"I don't know what you mean," I said. "I was the product of a fling between two drug addicts, from what I've been able to tell. No one meant for me to be born."

She touched my shoulder. "Gabriel may not have realized what he was doing at the time, but Fate knew. She put the key in your very DNA. The chances of that happening are... incredibly small. It has never happened before in recorded Anori history, at least not that I can find. They've been around for millennia and never, not once, has their line produced the perfect combination. Not, at least, until now."

"Wait, you're looking through Anori records?" I asked, my brows drawing together. "I thought we weren't in contact with Grandma Gloria's side of the family. That was the whole point of the Cybele colony in the first place, wasn't it?"

"We're not in contact. But I do have access to Gloria's personal database." She gestured to a large, leather-bound book that sat open on the holo table. I took a step forward to see it more closely but Ariel cut me off, her hand reaching out and tapping the table's power button. Instantly, the book flickered and faded to nothing. "I'm sorry, Gracie, but when I got access to those files, I promised I wouldn't share them. Not even with the Family. Some of the knowledge in them would be... dangerous in the wrong hands."

The furrows in my brow deepened. "Okay... so this mysterious database says I'm somehow rare? I'm not even a three-T, Ariel. I'm not anything special by Family standards."

"Says the woman currently talking to her sister almost a century before her own birth." Ariel gave me a half-lidded smirk.

She had a point. "So this is about the time travel thing?"

"I think it's tied together somehow, yes," Ariel agreed, stepping back to her table and picking up a familiar-looking vial with twine wrapped around its neck. "It has to do with the way your body deals with telomeres. You do know what telomeres are, don't you?"

I looked at her blankly. "We didn't talk about them in Awareness Theory."

"Everyone has telomeres, not just individuals of Awareness. They're repeating segments of code at the end of a cell's DNA. Over time, with many duplications, this code shortens and becomes distorted. This is what we observe as aging in mortals. I'm not going to get into all the technical jargon, but essentially the way Usuriels' bodies deal with telomeres is different from mortals. That's why we age more slowly or, in some cases, not at all."

"Okay," I nodded, finally starting to follow along.

"You are a special case. Your cells' telomeres are protected with low-active telomerase, just like the other immortal members of the Usuriel family."

"Wait... are you telling me I'm immortal? Like, Dad immortal?" I broke in.

"All Usuriels seem to have low-level active telomerase. For some of us, the activity level is just so low that its effectiveness can't keep up with the aging process over time," Ariel explained, gesturing to her own graying hair. "But yours is on the same level of activity as Vanessa and Dad, so most likely, yes. You're not going to age."

I took a deep breath and put a hand to my chest. My heart thudded solidly against the cage of my ribs. The few hundred years I'd hoped for had suddenly become an unending horizon. Forever. Not just forever, but forever at age twenty-five. It was an intimidating thought. I hoped I would handle it with more grace than my father.

"I need to sit down," I murmured. Ariel pulled up a stool and I perched on it while the lab swam with tiny dots of color.

"Do you need a glass of water?" Ariel asked, leaning over me in a maternal way.

I pulled another breath in through my nose and out through my mouth. The floating sensation faded and I shook my head. "No, I'm okay. Finish what you were trying to explain to me. Why is my blood any different than Dad's or Vanessa's?"

"Because of the RNA subunits your body uses in the telomerase." I looked at her blankly as she tried to explain. "Essentially, most Usuriel's use a type of RNA that isn't compatible with mortal RNA. The proteins merge well enough in reproductive processes, most of the time anyway, but in gene therapy the mortal RNA is too dominant."

She'd promised not to get technical but I was having a hard time following her anyway. "Can you simplify this a little?"

She scowled then tried again. "Your blood uses human proteins to do a process that only immortal proteins have done in the past. You are the link between mortal and immortal DNA." She gave me a significant look as if I should understand what this meant.

"I'm a half-mortal, half-immortal hybrid. So are you. We've known that for years. What's the revelation?"

"Ah, yes, for yourself." Her grin widened and she picked up the vial from the table. Its label read TT126-G. "But unlike me and every other Usuriel on the planet, when put through the right processes, your blood can be turned into this."

"Which is?"

"Usuriel in a bottle," she whispered, face alight. "The fountain of youth. The philosopher's stone. The elixir of life. This, Gracie, is immortality boiled down to its very essence. Any human man, or woman, could drink this and never age another day. In fact, if my theories are right, it would most likely return them to an adult-prime state. Say... somewhere around age twenty-five. Quite rapidly, as well. From my research, that process would heal any number of ills; even life-threatening cancers or wounds."

"Sweet Fate," I breathed, staring at the bottle. "Would it work on you, too? I mean, a less age-defying Usuriel?"

"It's hard to say. I haven't tested it on anyone but mortals. It should in theory. Though, I'm not sure it's something I'd want to play around with."

"What are you talking about? You could be young again," I pointed out. "Isn't that why you worked on this?"

"For me?" She gave a barking laugh that echoed strangely in the large room full of glass and liquid. "Fates, no! I made it for Dad, of course. Poor thing. I'm sure he's only gotten worse with time. I'd ask if he's climbed into a bottle or, Fates save us, a syringe again. But I can see from the look on your face that I don't really want the answer."

I tried and failed miserably at the Usuriel blank face. After the day I'd just had with Dad and his reputation, I couldn't hide my dismay at Ariel's accurate instincts. "He's not using anything stronger than alcohol at the moment, at least not that I can tell."

"Well, that's actually somewhat comforting," Ariel said with a small smile.

"But how can this help Dad? I mean, his problem is that he's too long-lived, not the other way around. If anything, he'd probably prefer to become more mortal."

"Dad's problem isn't his immortality," Ariel explained, giving me a kindly look. "It's his partner's lack thereof. You weren't alive to see it, but I was. I know what it was that broke him. It didn't happen quickly or dramatically. Hell, he knew how to heal from trauma; he's seen enough of it. This was something harder to recover from, something that left permanent scars. I saw his eyes as he watched my mother age and die."

I swallowed hard, wanting to shy away from the bleak

truth of her words. But, like Professor Joan's revelation of his addictions, this rang too true for me to ignore. When my silence lengthened, my sister went on.

"He's never been the same after that. Not even with Lauria. He's tried to be what she wanted, but his heart just isn't in it. It died a long time before Lauria was even born."

"Olivia," I whispered her name, one of the many that was outlawed in my father's home. Yet of all the painful memories Gabriel carried with him, it was her ghost that haunted Angelus Quietum.

"Exactly." Ariel held the little bottle up to the light. "Which is why I say you were born for this. I'm not sure, but I think something about your blood's unique mortal-immortal mix is what gives you this connection with time. Not only are you the key ingredient, you're the only possible vehicle. With your gift, you should be able to go back and give this to Olivia before she died."

"Wait." I held up a hand. "You want me to... what?"

"Go back to the time when I was sixteen," Ariel said steadily, holding out the little bottle. It gleamed green in the soft light of her working lamp. "We know you can jump that far and the bottle should fit in your pocket. If you can take clothes with you, you can take this vial. It shouldn't even tax your strength."

"Hold on," I protested. "Let's think this through a little. First off, do the people who take this stuff get powers like ours? I mean, we're not just immortal. We're psychics."

"Since it technically alters parts of their DNA, most likely yes." Ariel shrugged. "Some of the volunteers I tried it on gained low-level telepathy and telekinesis. But that can only be a benefit for Mother. After my sixteenth birthday, we encountered the Cat-Mantis controlled space. We could have used another psi-pilot back then."

My head finally sorted through the implications of her suggestion and I didn't like it much. "I hate to point it out, but isn't this a paradox? I mean, if Olivia is alive and well, I somehow don't think my father is going to end up having a one night stand with a random drug addict. I'd unmake myself. Which means we wouldn't have the elixir or a way to get it back to Olivia. Which means... now we're back where we started."

"No, no, I have a few theories about that," Ariel said, shaking her head. She walked over to another desk and pulled out a traditional book—the kind made of paper and a binding. She placed it on the table next to me, setting the stiff cover a little ajar so that it stood on its end. "Let me explain a few things I've learned about our multi-verse since I've been reading the Anori database."

I gestured with one hand for her to continue. She cleared her throat.

"Imagine that everything you know, everything on our planet and on Earth and all the universe in between, was all contained on one of these pages. Imagine that each letter is a life and that there is infinite room on this page for all the lives this universe contains."

"Imagining," I confirmed.

"Good. Now imagine that every page has the potential to spawn new pages when the possibilities contained within it no longer fit inside the linear framework. Like this." She folded a page and, pulling out a small knife from thin air, cut it along the fold. This created a second page that was tucked next to the first one. "Only, each one would be just the same size and moving in the same direction. That is, forward in linear time."

Now she was making my head hurt. "Okay. So, everyone is a letter on that page. They really can't interact with a different page."

"Not unless they go to the binding. Earth is close to the 'binding,' what the Anori call the dimension maze. That's why Grandma and Grandpa Usuriel left; it was too easy for members of other realities to show up uninvited."

"To get to another reality, we'd have to go back to Earth?"

Ariel nodded. "Most likely, yes."

"And you're saying that if I change time by giving Olivia the vial, I'm what, spawning a new reality?"

"That's my theory," Ariel confirmed. "And since you're critical to the events that would form it, I'd imagine you'd be pulled into the new reality rather than left in the old one. You wouldn't change but the world around you would."

I tried to envision what this would mean from my perspective. "So how would I go back to my time? I mean, after Olivia drinks the elixir, she alters the entire course of my history. I wouldn't be able to envision a real place as a guide image anymore, not in that new reality anyway. Would I be trapped in the past? Stuck on the *Inspiration* with no explanation to anyone of how I got there?"

Ariel held up the vial to the light. The opaque, green glass didn't give a hint of its contents' color. "In that case, Olivia and probably myself would remember what happened. I suppose that is a possible scenario. And there are worse places to end up than the *Inspiration*, if I may say so myself. However, I think it's more likely you'd be able to shift forward, just to a slightly altered future."

"A future in which I wouldn't ever have existed. No one would remember me, not even my own father or boyfriends." I categorized both James and Liam as significant others. That was a tangled mess for another moment altogether. But even so, I couldn't just abandon them. "No, at best I'd have to reintroduce myself to everyone that I know. At worst, I'd just up and disappear into thin air as if I never existed! I want to help Dad, don't get me wrong, but this crazy scheme isn't worth risking literally everything I know and love. Hell, if he even knew we were considering it he'd probably knock both of our heads together."

Ariel's mouth twisted in a wry smile. "That last is probably true," she admitted. "And I understand your reservations. It's a radical idea from your perspective, I know. Just think about it. I'd be happy to give you a reference image if you change your mind."

"I doubt it," I muttered.

"Even if you don't use the elixir on Olivia, at least keep it safe and away from mortals. It's a dangerous thing to have lying around. Maybe you or Dad could use it the next time you find someone you'd like to keep around a little longer," Ariel said gently.

I waved the vial away. "I have the elixir already. It's in the back of my closet back at Dad's."

"Where did you find it?" Ariel asked, her green eyes darkening.

"It was in the refrigerated storage over there," I indicated the large, heavy door I could see from here. It was so massive I didn't have to crane my neck despite being all the way across the room.

"That's where I'll put it now, then. It doesn't technically have to be cooled. The processes I've used on it should keep it preserved as long as it stays in a liquid state. It should be fine at Angelus Quietum."

I gave her shoulder a squeeze. "It's really amazing what you managed to do. You must miss your mother very much, to have made her such a beautiful gift."

"You have no idea," Ariel said softly, her face suddenly so old and sad I couldn't help but wrap my arms around her neck. Her slim hands came up to my back and we were silent, holding on to each other. I found myself feeling incredibly connected to Ariel. Here was another person who really knew and understood my father, perhaps more than I did, and she still managed to love him fiercely. It gave me hope for my relationship with Gabriel.

"Mom was really something special," Ariel murmured into my hair. "I know why Dad is so heartbroken. She never loved anyone halfway. It was all or nothing with Mom. If you were hers, she'd walk through the gates of hell itself for you. I don't think anyone will ever love Dad half as much as she did."

"Except maybe you," I replied with a smile, leaning back from our hug. Tears hovered on the edge of her soft, green eyes and I felt another rush of affection for my sister.

"Perhaps," she agreed with a sad smile. "Perhaps."

Chapter 24

Politics

When I got back, I had a hard time sleeping. I kept having visions of my father in that horrid spore-hole down in Riland. When I finally managed to fall asleep, good old-fashioned nightmares woke me twice. There wasn't anything clear or informative about these dreams; just a sense of helplessness and fear that made me wake in a cold sweat. After the second one, I gave up trying to sleep and took a nice, hot shower.

Feeling as if I'd finally managed to shake off some of the filth from my Riland run, I settled down at the desk in my room to do some school work. It was mostly Awareness Theory stuff, which wasn't all that comforting since Ariel wrote half the textbook. Still, it let me think about something other than Evan's parting remarks. They still rang in my ears when my mind wasn't focused on other things.

The sun was just rising when a knock came at my door. I scowled up at it, wondering who on Cybele could be up this early.

"James!" I exclaimed, a surprised smile breaking across my face at his familiar presence at my doorway. With as crazy as the last sixty hours had been, it was all I could do not to throw myself into his arms. "We weren't expecting you for another week at least!"

"We need to go see Liam," James said, his face deadly serious. My grin crumbled.

"What's wrong? We only went on one date, but that's about it. Nothing happened," I reassured him quickly, thinking that someone had been exaggerating what happened between Liam and I at the Family party.

"What? No, this has nothing to do with our dating... confusion." James waved a hand as if to dismiss romance as a secondary issue. It was a fair way to sum up the situation between the three of us, however. Confusion was certainly the word I would use for my emotions towards James and Liam most days. "Come on, I've got to talk to both of you and I don't feel like going over this twice."

"Okay," I agreed, shrugging a cloak on against the dawn chill. "I doubt he'll be awake at this hour, though."

"Then we get to wake him up," James growled, charging down the hall towards Liam's room. Fortunately, as another Usuriel, Liam's dormitory wasn't all that far from mine. It took us less than five minutes to be standing outside his door. "Come on, man, let us in!" James fairly shouted as he pounded on the door.

"Fucking Fate, do you know what time it is?" Liam complained from the bed as he opened the door with a telekinetic thought.

"No idea, but this is too important to wait," James said, striding into the cluttered dorm and perching on a tiny scrap of clear desk space. There wasn't anywhere else to sit, so I joined Liam on the edge of the bed. James raised an eyebrow at us, his expression suddenly a lot less thunderous. "Gracie said you two went on a date?"

Liam and I exchanged a startled look at his sudden change in tone. "Just the one," I re-emphasized. "And my dad ruined it like he does everything else, so you don't have to worry about it. We didn't do anything the three of us haven't already done together." That wasn't one hundred percent true, but close enough. Liam and I had been extremely close to kissing at Amourie's; I'd just round up and say we did.

"Hmmm." James fixed us each with a stare but then he shook his head. "It doesn't matter right now. We'll figure this—" he indicated the three of us with a rotating forefinger "—out later. Right now, I need to tell you about what I've learned at the Senate."

"Okay," Liam said, rubbing one eye and tugging a few blankets out from under me so that he could wrap himself a little more completely while sitting on the edge of the bed. "What's so urgent that you couldn't wait until after the ass-crack of dawn?"

James' brow knitted together, his faded-blue eyes dark in the yellow light of the sunrise outside. "What do you know about Garret Stafford?"

The name sounded vaguely familiar but I didn't pay

much attention to current events. I could vote, but Usuriels couldn't hold Senate office, nor could we run a Province as viceroy. Since Stella had explained that to me as a teenager, I'd had a hard time caring so much about who ran for office. The Family was complicated enough without worrying about power-hungry mortals.

"He's that parasite over in Riland," Liam grumbled, continuing to scrub at his face in an attempt to bring himself to wakefulness. "What about him?"

James' scowl deepened. "He's the junior Senator from Riland and he's certainly a mortal, not a vamp. In fact, I suspect he'd seriously object to that particular characterization. Near as I can tell, he'd burn every vampire in his Province and not lose a moment's sleep. He's stirring up some really nasty things behind the scenes of the Capital. Dangerous things. Especially for people like us."

"What kind of things?" I asked, narrowing my eyes at him.

James shook his head. "Some of it I can't talk about. But I will say this. The anti-Awareness and anti-Terran sentiment is growing. We weren't welcome in most meetings and the few I did manage to get into, the tone was very hostile. Doubly so if the Riland people were anywhere nearby. I'm not the only one who noticed, either. The Usuriel delegation nearly came to blows with Senator Stafford while I was in the room."

"Who is on the Usuriel delegation?" I glanced over at

Liam who shrugged his ignorance.

"Two twelfth-gens and a tenth-gen: Cora, Damien, and Daravan. They're all older and usually steady as kyoss. Even so, Stafford got to Damien so bad he actually lit up and got right in the Senator's face. For a moment, I thought he was going to pull a Gabe and snap his neck like a twig."

Why was my father synonymous with every bad behavior an Usuriel could display? I bit back a groan and decided to just ignore James' poor choice of words.

"What set him off so bad?" Liam asked, lifting one eyebrow. "I mean, they've been in politics a long time, right? Probably longer than most mortals. What did the Stafford guy say that got an older Usuriel that spore bent?"

James spread his hands. "They've been demanding more Overwatch coverage for Riland. That's their main demand that the Usuriels seem upset about. It wouldn't be so explosive, I don't think, except that Senator Stafford seems convinced that the Usuriels can hunt down any vampire or mortal that has a criminal thought in their head. He keeps accusing the Overwatch of ignoring the plight of mortals while only stepping in when there's a possibility that Family members might get hurt. Last I heard, he was pushing for a new law that would allow the Riland watch to hire telepaths to track down mortal criminals."

"I got to hear about that from the head of Riland watch yesterday," I muttered. "I was kind of hoping he was a crazy fringe, but I guess it's a common thought over there. It will never go anywhere, though. Sending psychics after mortals is against the charter."

"Riland's head of watch seems to think Gracie's old man is a danger to Skykyle City, too," Liam said, glancing at me with an apologetic expression. "Sorry to bring it up, but he should know."

I patted his hand to dismiss the apology. Ariel's steadying presence had restored a measure of my faith in my father. "It's okay," I said. "Dad's reputation is what it is. I can't change it. But I also don't have to agree with it. He might be annoying and self-destructive, but I don't think he's actually dangerous. At least, not to anyone but himself."

"Glad to hear you've finally figured out some of your issues with Gabriel." James gave me an encouraging smile.

"It's either that or let him keep running my life. And I'm pretty much as done with that as I possibly can be."

"So that's why you woke me up in the middle of a good dream? To tell me Riland is full of a bunch of spore-addled assholes? I could have told you that yesterday," Liam said, burrowing his head into my shoulder and wrapping his arms around my waist. Surprised at his forwardness, especially in front of James, I steadied his large weight against my side with one arm while resisting the urge to pull him closer. Something had definitely changed between us in the last two days.

James had a particularly cautious expression on his face. It reminded me of the way he'd looked at me in the parking lot of Amourie's when I'd left with Malcolm. It twisted something in my chest and I found myself offering him my other hand without really thinking about it.

I'm not sure if he wanted to make sure Liam didn't claim me for his own, or if he just needed reassurance after the way our friend had dismissed his anxieties. Either way, James took my hand and settled beside me on the bed. Its frame groaned as his solid weight added to its already heavy burden. However, he didn't wrap himself around me the way Liam had. Rather, he sat holding my hand in both of his as if it were something incredibly precious.

"Like I said." His voice was soft when he finally spoke again. "I'm not allowed to discuss all of it. But I'm trying to warn you. This could go very badly. I mean... I think there might be a war."

"A war?" Liam picked his head up off of my shoulder and scowled at James. "There has never been a war on Cybele. We're past that kind of savagery. Besides, the elder children would put down any kind of violence between mortal factions in less than thirty hours. One day and it would be done."

James shook his head, his face extremely bleak. I felt the first stirrings of real fear in my guts. "The Overwatch is the closest Cybele has seen to a standing army for hundreds of years. Because all of them are Aware and therefore excluded from government, the mortals have put up with it. Adora very nearly upset that balance sixty-odd years ago, but fortunately she was stopped. The massacre may have been what saved peace in the Provinces."

I glanced at Liam. I'd never heard this interpretation of the Riland massacre before. "What do you mean?"

"Just before the massacre, some old vamps had taken control of the Riland Senate. They'd managed to argue successfully in the courts that vampirism isn't the same as psi which meant the anti-Usuriel legislation that barred them from holding office didn't apply. Once it was legal to elect them, the vampires stoked the fires of paranoia over a Terran invasion. They billed themselves as the only people who could protect the mortal population from a technologically superior force. They won overwhelmingly. No one really remembers that part outside of Riland unless you really look into the politics behind the massacre."

"Professor Joan did mention something about it in passing," I agreed.

Liam twirled a finger. "I don't remember anything about vampires in the Senate, but what does it have to do with our current political situation?"

"Everything!" James snapped. "The massacre killed most of the vampires who were in government at the time. After the massacre, Riland reacted with a huge wave of anti-Awareness sentiment. Most of the individuals of Awareness in Riland are vampires, which means their population bore the brunt of it. There was violence on a Province-wide level. Over a hundred vampire families were burned along with their mortal consorts."

"Yes, now that we did discuss," Liam confirmed.

"The twenty days of fire," I murmured. "Professor Joan speculated that more people died in that wave of violence than the original incident in Riland City."

"Good, you've learned something at University," James squeezed my hand. I'm pretty sure it was more for his comfort than mine. "So, what I'm trying to tell you is that the vampires don't trust the Overwatch anymore. Ever since they failed to protect them from the twenty days of fire, there's been bad blood. The only thing saving them from coming into open conflict with the OW is the protection pact Vanessa signed when she took over."

"With vampires, how can there not be some bad blood?" Liam rolled his eyes.

"I'm not joking!" James hissed, eyes furious. "This isn't the moment for bad puns! People could die!"

"So people die," Liam replied evenly, his blue eyes remarkably calm as he rested his chin on my shoulder again. "They die every day. From old age, accidents, drugs, crime, disease. If I couldn't find the humor in it, I'd be a wreck."

James tilted his head at our friend, a slightly more thoughtful look on his face. "I'm not talking about random strangers, Liam," he said softly. "I'm talking about you and Gracie. I'm talking about me and my family. I'm talking about everyone who means anything to me. We are about to be on the front lines of a conflict that makes the Riland massacre look tame."

Well, he had my attention. "Take a deep breath and tell us what you know," I said, a note of command creeping into my voice. "Liam and I won't interrupt you again." I gave our tall friend a sharp look.

"Go ahead," Liam agreed, sounding slightly rattled.

"Thank you," James sighed, and rubbed at one eye. His eyes were sunken into dark folds and his mouth carved a painful line across his features. "Like I said, I can't talk about all of it. But what I can say is this. There's still a lot of fear in Riland over the idea of a Terran invasion. I don't know where they get this idea from, other than the fear mongering the vampires did decades ago, but they seem convinced we're insecure enough about food production that we'd actually try to come and take over."

I raised an eyebrow but I didn't interrupt. James saw my questioning look, however, and responded. "There's no truth to it, of course. We still utilize the hydroponics technology from the *Inspiration* to grow crops underground in case of shortages. It's cheaper to trade with the Provinces, of course, so that's our preference, but there's no reason to ever actually come to violence over supplies."

"But Riland doesn't believe you when this is explained to them?" Liam asked. "Sorry, I wasn't supposed to interrupt."

"It's okay." James waved a hand. "You're right. They're not listening to any kind of reason. The vampire population is finally starting to rebound and the mortals are scared. They're looking for a reason to arm themselves against any kind of Awareness. Terrans are a convenient 'enemy' to point to so that the vampires don't close ranks against the mortal government. Like I said... I can't talk about all of it but..." His voice dropped and his eyes darted around the room at the comm interfaces. They were all dark, as were the power lights on Stella's holo-cameras. "I think they're developing anti-Awareness tech that could take on even an elder child."

"The Terrans have that kind of tech," Liam pointed out. "But it's never been a problem."

"I'm not talking about avatars that can fly and probably land a punch as hard as a telekinetic. I've seen schematics for bullets that can pierce psi-shields. I've heard rumors of biological weapons, too—strains of things that will only go after immortal DNA. And I know for a fact that they're raising an army. I've seen the provision reports from their budgeting department. There's absolutely no other reason to purchase that much alloy and foodstuffs when they have surpluses in their own stores."

I exchanged a look with Liam. His face was no longer resigned. Instead, a thread of fear lurked in his Gabriellan-blue eyes.

"Those things don't seem aimed at vampires," Liam observed. "They'd be more effective against Usuriels."

"Exactly," James breathed. "Which is why I'm telling you, they're bracing for war. They know if the vampires feel threatened again, they're going to call on the Overwatch for protection. After their failure during the twenty days of fire, Vanessa won't have a choice. Unless she wants the vampires to actively defy the Overwatch, she'll have to honor their protection agreement. The government of Riland can't go after the vamps without also dealing with the Family."

"Unless we sit back and let the mortals purge all the vamps." Liam's voice sounded thoughtful.

"There's a word for that," James said bleakly. "Back on Earth they called it genocide. I can't imagine the OW just letting that happen. Even if Vanessa doesn't honor the protection agreement, I imagine there will be factions of Family members who try to help. Hell, there are enough mixed couples that there would be a few not-so-mortal consorts who would object to their significant other's detention. If they go after the vamps, the Riland watch will have to go up against Usuriels at some point."

"So they're arming themselves to do just that," I muttered, ice forming in the pit of my stomach.

"When this all dissolves, you and Liam are going to be on the front lines," James said, looking miserable. "I've even overheard your name in a few quiet conversations, Gracie. They're aiming for you in particular."

Of course they were. I was the new, flashy, big gun in Vanessa's arsenal. It would have been odd if they hadn't been doing research on me. Still, hearing him say it poured ice water into my veins.

"I don't care what they're planning," Liam said after a long silence. "You can't convince me Gloria and Gabriel will sit around quietly while mortals slaughter their descendants. And I will bet on the Usuriel Matriarch against any kind of human tech every time."

The deep freeze in my guts thawed slightly at Liam's words. "Dad may be drinking again, but I still wouldn't want to face him in a fight. And if he really thought I was in danger, I don't think he'd just put his feet up. He'd show the Riland mortals their place without breaking a sweat, I'm sure."

James shook his head slowly. "I know you two are Family and you're used to relying on the strength of the first few generations to be invulnerable. But there's a reason D'nay and Gloria ran all the way to Cybele. They're not the strongest immortals that ever lived. If Senator Stafford has his way, he'll find their weaknesses and he will exploit them. And afterwards, I don't think the Family will ever be the same."

Despite the golden light pouring in the window, I shivered and found James' arms joining Liam's around my waist. Both boys leaned into me, their heads tucking against my shoulders as my arms wrapped around their backs and pulled them tightly against me.

I was the strongest, I realized as we silently huddled on Liam's bed. Out of the three of us, I was the only one who might be a genuine threat to Riland's mortal force. It made me a target. It also meant that if I was smart about it, I might have the strength to protect James and Liam from Evan and his ilk. For the first time, being a third-gen wasn't a novelty or an annoyance. It sat like a heavy weight on my shoulders, a mantle of responsibility I'd never asked for.

"Don't worry," I whispered to my boys. "I won't let them hurt you. If things get bad, just stick close. I won't let anything happen to you. I promise."

Chapter 25

I'm Not Your Olivia

Despite James' urgency when he arrived on campus, nothing came of his warnings for a long while. As all but the most bone-deep scares do, our fear of a conflict breaking out in the Provinces slowly faded.

Even if there had been signs of political unrest at that point, I'm not sure the three of us would have had the time or energy to worry about it. Life, it seemed, had decided to catch up with us. The end of my second term hit with a vengeance and my schedule was so packed with studying, classes, training, and junior officer work that I hardly got to see James. For several weeks, it was as if he weren't even back at all. We managed to meet up for a quick meal here and there, but hardly had the time to sit and talk. We couldn't get to anything of consequence, let alone sort through the tangled web of relationship issues that were hanging above us.

Liam, on the other hand, was a constant presence at the Overwatch. As I'd surmised during James' early morning meeting, things had changed between us. What had been a low-simmering fire now turned to an explosive force ready to erupt every time we brushed against each other. On the practice mat, the sexual tension was thick enough to cut with a knife.

In the three weeks after the Family party, I ended up with a concussion and a black eye. Two days after my head was cleared for contact training again, I slammed Liam into a wall hard enough to snap his collar bone. Coriana, the OW healer who supervised at the compound, fused it back in place, but Liam's whole shoulder was a rainbow of dark colors for almost two weeks.

Jillian shook her head at us as we straggled into practice. Despite kicking the spore-dust out of each other for over a month, Liam and I still lit up with psi the instant the other one got within arm's reach.

"Honestly, the two of you need to pick one of your rooms and get it over with," Jillian said when we got close enough.

I glanced up at Liam and found him studiously looking anywhere else. "I don't know what you mean," he said, blushing furiously.

"Oh, come now." Jillian leaned on one hip as her full cheeks swelled into a suggestive grin. "You wouldn't be the first set of OW partners to end up venting some tension in the bedroom. This is stressful and time-consuming work. Sometimes the only person I see all day is my partner. No one would judge you. Just use protection and be safe about it."

"Isn't that the same thing?" I muttered, hiding the heat in my own cheeks by adjusting the straps on my workout boots.

Jillian shook her head, her expression sliding from teasing to serious. "No, actually, not for Aware individuals. Sometimes we have to remember that even though our partner can take a lot of punishment in the ring, that doesn't mean they can handle it in the bedroom. Shields are down and passions are up. Quite a few people have gotten hurt during 'extracurricular' activities."

Liam frowned. "I've never had any problem with my mortal lovers."

"You're not the one I'm worried about." Jillian gave me a significant look.

"Who, me?" I gestured to my chest. "I've never lost control of my fire, not even when I'm angry. I can't imagine I'd have a problem... in that situation."

"Have you ever climaxed with a partner?" Jillian asked, raising an eyebrow in my direction.

I thought I couldn't turn any more red. I was wrong. Liam and I were not looking at each other so hard we actually had our backs to each other.

"I didn't think so," Jillian said after a long, awkward silence. "Just watch yourself. You don't need a spark to light up a room and orgasm doesn't lend itself to control."

"Fuck, why does that thought do it for me?" Liam muttered, sounding halfway between turned on and embarrassed. I empathized.

"Because you're a Gabriellan male, and your sense of self-preservation is completely off," Jillian replied smoothly. "Call it a design flaw, but you're all that way. One way or another, you're drawn to the exact things that most sane people know are hazardous to their health."

Jillian's horribly accurate comparison between Liam and my father instantly had a cooling effect on my libido.

"Can we just do our workout and get out of here? I have homework for my other classes to get done." I sounded waspish, but I didn't care.

Jillian paused. "Are you sure you don't want to take the morning off and... solve your problem? I won't even make you do double bouts tomorrow. Sex is good exercise if you do it right."

"No!" I snapped, cutting off any reply Liam might have had. "You know what? The two of you take a bout. I'm going to work the bags and go home."

Without even a glance over my shoulder at them, I stalked off to vent my confused frustration on the punching bags.

Jillian wisely didn't bring up the issue again.

***

I usually met up with Liam for lunch in between my science and ceramics classes, but that day I skipped lunch and went straight to the studio. I told myself I was catching up with a project, but truthfully I didn't want to deal with my OW partner. By the time evening rolled around, my stomach growled angrily at my ribs. Instead of going to the mess hall, I found a snack in my room and tried to focus on chemical equations.

"Gracie?" Liam's voice sounded halfway between coaxing and frustrated.

"Leave me alone," I muttered, but I didn't double tap my implant to block him out.

"I know you're hungry. Stop hiding and come down to eat something." He sounded a bit like me when I scolded my father. I hunched my shoulders at the comparison in my own head. When I made no reply, I heard his sigh through the implant. "Come on, you'll have to deal with me at practice tomorrow, anyway. Do you want me to teleport up to your room or will you come have dinner like a civilized person?"

"Fine," I snapped and slammed my memory pad down so hard it's a minor miracle it didn't shatter. Fortunately, its plex glass was pretty thick and I'm not a telekinetic. I grabbed a jacket on my way out and stomped more than walked to the dining hall.

I had no idea what food I was picking up as I wound my way through the cafeteria. All I cared about was not looking at our usual table in the corner. When I finally had to sit down, I stared fixedly at the orange tree in its planter.

"I'm sorry Jillian upset you," Liam said quietly. His sleeve rustled as if he were still eating something. I took a bite of my food mechanically. It tasted as nondescript as I felt. "Do you want to talk about this?"

"No!" I snapped, and took another big bite. Once my mouth was clear, I groaned. "No. I know we have to talk about this, but I really don't want to."

"Gracie... let's just pretend for a moment that James doesn't exist."

"But he does!" I said, spinning in my chair to face him. "He does exist and he's someone that we both... really care about. If we do this without him, it's going to hurt him. You know that, don't you?"

I'd never had a hard time tuning out the Family features before, but lately everything about Liam sent my pulse rate through the stratosphere. It made me want to put a fist right through his pretty face.

"He's never around anymore, Gracie. I know we care about him, but he's going in a different direction. I mean, in the end James is a Terran and we're Usuriels. We belong to two completely different worlds."

I turned back to my meal, eating quickly as if I could vent some of my angst through the act of chewing.

"Gracie," Liam tried again but I hastily swallowed and shook my head at him.

"No," I breathed. "Don't say it."

"You're not a telepath. You don't know what I'm going to say."

"I don't have to be." I stared down at my plate. "I know you. You don't make a habit of dating girls, so whatever you think you feel for me, it must be pretty damn strong or you wouldn't be wasting your time." I ran my hand through my hair. "I get it. I'm not even going to say I don't feel some of it, too, because I think you know that I do. But I can't pair with you, Liam. Please don't ask me to. I just can't."

The look on his face was cautious, but I could see the fear in his eyes. I didn't want to watch it evolve into heartbreak and I was very much afraid that it might by the end of this conversation. I quickly looked anywhere else.

"Okay," he said slowly, "and that's because..." he left the end of the sentence open for me to fill in.

"Because," I repeated, "every time I start thinking I'm genuinely attracted to you for who you are, someone will do what Jillian did today. They'll compare you to Dad. Or you'll say something that reminds me of him. Or you'll just... look the wrong way. I don't know. But somehow or another, I keep realizing that the things I'm attracted to in you are the exact same ones that make me murderously furious with my father."

Liam raised an eyebrow. "You can't date me because I remind you of Gabriel?"

I spread my hands helplessly. "I know we're over a dozen generations apart. And hell, you're at least fifteen generations away from Dad. But it doesn't change the fact that the more I get to know you, the more I realize that you're a twenty-year-old version of my father. And I love him, but I've seen how that story ends. It's not pretty. I'm attracted to you, but I can't go on that ride again. It's bad enough being his daughter. I can't date his descendant, too."

"I'm not an addict or a drunk. I mean, I haven't touched alcohol since you asked me not to. So what exactly are these things that make me so Gabriel-esque?"

"Dad didn't use at your age either," I countered, "and it's only been a few weeks since the party. Even Dad can stay sober that long."

"I'll stay away from drinking as long as you want me to. And I'm not going to get four hundred years to get into trouble, Gracie." Liam sounded a touch gentle. "I'll be lucky to see two hundred. If anyone is going to have a few more years than they know what to do with, it's more likely to be you."

I swallowed hard. I hadn't told my boys about Ariel's revelation about my immortality, but it sat like a new weight that never completely left my shoulders. "Even more reason for me to avoid my father's footsteps," I muttered. Then I caught sight of Liam's expression and I felt as if a giant hand were closing around my chest. "Don't look at me like that. I know I'm a redhead, but I'm not your Olivia."

"I'm not so sure about that." I was staring at my plate again so I couldn't see if he was close to tears, but his voice sounded painful.

"I am," I lied.

"Well... if you change your mind..." Hope clings to any glimmer of indecision. I tried not to give him any.

"I won't." I picked up my tray and walked away, my heart like lead in my chest. I knew this was the right thing to do, but it felt like I'd just taken a knife and hollowed out the entire space inside my ribs. I hated romance. Just like sex, love was overrated.

***

The next morning Liam was late to practice. When he did show up, he wouldn't meet my eye. I headed over to the free weights to avoid his painful presence. The day after that, however, things felt a little more normal and Jillian managed to coax us into a bout. Some of the sexual tension had died down because neither of us landed in the medical wing this time.

By the time a week had passed, the two of us were back to having lunch together. If we didn't flirt quite as much as we used to, we still sat closer than strictly required. What can I say? My self-control was only so good.

Aside from the romantic issues, my involvement with the Overwatch was a pretty big success for those first few months. Liam was a steady and reliable partner, for all his flippant sense of humor. We rode along with Jillian for about a month and a half before Vanessa decided the two of us were competent enough in the field to be sent out alone. I think the fact that we were understaffed may have had a bearing on that decision, but she was right. With Liam as three-T and me as the big, scary firebird, we managed to deal with the low-key mischief of vampires and younger Usuriel generations just fine.

I remember one of the first calls we got where the vamps were actually awake enough to protest. Liam grabbed the pissed-off vampire and forced him to stand where he could take a good look at me.

"Do you know who that is, my undead friend?" Liam asked. The only indication that he was holding the vamp in place rather than merely putting an arm around his shoulder was the tension in his large hand. My partner was strong, physically and mentally, in short bursts. As long as you didn't ask him to hold it long, he could lift as much as the older three-T's these days.

The vampire didn't give Liam a response, glowering at me

with glittering, dark eyes. He was still pulling shadows to tremble about the edges of his figure and I could tell he was seriously considering trying to force his way past us. We'd interrupted a nasty domestic dispute with his mortal partner and I had a feeling he was hoping he'd get away without a strike on his record if he made nice with her later. Since her torso was every shade of black and blue I'd ever seen and the tell-tale pallor of over-feeding made her lips almost white, I was hoping she'd have the sense to put him out this time.

"Allow me to introduce Gracie Usuriel," my partner went on conversationally. "You may have heard of her. Firebird. Gabriel's youngest daughter. Considered one of the most powerful Family members born since the *Inspiration* landed."

The vamp's expression lost its angry reluctance in favor of caution. "She looks like an elder child," he hissed, "but I can't even feel her energy from here. If she's so strong, why can't I hear her?"

"She's head mute," Liam explained, "but what she lacks in telepathy she makes up for in fire. Lots and lots of fire. Gracie?"

I caught sight of the vamp's mortal partner watching us with large, brown eyes from the doorway. I'm not telepathic, but I could almost see her calculating the risk of trusting us. I can keep you safe, I thought, and tried to let that thought show in my face as I pulled a curtain of flame down around myself.

"Fucking Fate!" The vamp nearly jumped straight out of Liam's grasp. My partner braced for that reaction, however, and hardly even showed the effort of holding the wayward undead in place.

"You listen very carefully to me," Liam said evenly as I allowed the flames to flicker slowly around the edges of my vision. I knew better than to interrupt Liam when he was on a roll. He had a knack for knowing exactly what to say in situations like this. I, on the other hand, was good at being scary as fuck. We mostly stuck to those roles lately, and it seemed to work. "You are going to lay your hand on this memory pad and let me record this strike. I have a feeling that this is not your first. Am I right?"

The vamp's jaw worked as if he weren't happy with this question. Clearly the answer was yes. However, after a long pause, he put his palm to the memory pad and allowed Liam to record the incident in our database.

"Looks like this is strike two," Liam said, raising an eyebrow at me. Internally I breathed a little sigh of relief. I was dreading the day we had to take someone in with a third strike. That meant a council hearing and a decent chance of execution. I didn't like the idea of killing someone for something less than a truly heinous crime. It was one of the few things I didn't like about Awareness law.

"You got lucky," I glowered at the vampire, giving a good performance of being disappointed. It never did to let them know we were anything less than eager to enforce the law.

"Look at me, Jeremiah." Liam didn't have to glance at the memory pad to remember the vamp's name. Telepaths: it was nice to work with them sometimes. "If we have to come back here again, Gracie won't need to be gentle about things. She's an all-or-nothing weapon and I don't think she'd lose any sleep over using her power on you."

There was real fear in Jeremiah's paper-white face as he cut a glance at me. I tried to look as threatening as possible.

"Okay, I think you get the point," Liam said with a fluid shrug. He moved to my side. "Come on, Gracie. Let's go."

I leaned in to Jeremiah one last time. "Touch her the wrong way again and I'll scatter your ashes in the nearest river," I growled. His eyes got very wide and I knew I'd made an impression, at least for the moment. Such measures weren't even close to necessary, of course. None of the vamps on Cybele were older than a century or two. Taking out their heart was perfectly effective at preventing them from ever waking again. Even so, we did usually burn the bodies just to be sure. I found, however, that mentioning an understanding of the old Earth lore freaked out the vamps we'd met.

With a last parting glance at the mortal girl, I stepped to Liam's side. She didn't move from the doorway as Liam's power tilted and bled away the world around us.

"A nice last touch about the river. His expression was good enough to frame as a still," Liam chuckled as we walked to our rooms. "That was the shortest domestic we've handled so far. I'd say we're getting pretty good at this whole teamwork thing."

"We do seem to be getting into a good rhythm," I agreed,

giving his big frame a nudge with my shoulders.

He glanced down at me and for a moment his eyes lit up in the dark like incandescent blue gems. Then I watched him remember our conversation and look away. It tore at the inside of my chest, but I hunched my shoulders against it. I really needed to find a way to talk to James. I had a feeling Liam just wasn't going to be able to accept my rejection until I made things official with another man.

Usually the thought of finally pairing with James made me feel giddy. This time, though, all I could think about was the look in Liam's eyes when I told him about it the next day. It would crush him, I thought, and suddenly I found myself in one of those rare moments of total clarity.

It hurt just as much to think about telling James about getting together with Liam as it did for the reverse. Which could only mean one thing: I was in love with both of them. Not just flirting and having fun, these were my best friends. They were the people I ran to when I was upset or excited or simply bored. I loved them in a way I'd never really experienced before, not even with Dad or Grandma Gloria. If I dated one of them, it was very possible I might lose the other. Even so, it was obvious from the last few weeks that Liam was in pain from our current situation. I wasn't sure how long it would take, but eventually I'd lose them both if I kept us all in this haze of uncertainty.

"I'm not dating a baby Gabriel," I muttered to myself as we went up the stairs in near silence. "James it is."

Fortunately, Liam didn't seem to hear me.

Chapter 26

Born for This

Finding a way to approach James alone continued to be an extreme challenge. Almost a month went by without any opportunity to talk with him sans Liam. Diplomatic responsibilities took a toll on him and even when the three of us managed to meet for a meal or a cup of tea, he seemed so exhausted I had a hard time adding to his burden with emotional issues. We still hugged and held hands as easily as breathing, but having an official 'talk' just never materialized.

In the meantime, life was continuing regardless of my dating status. The last term ended and a new one began. Liam and I were acknowledged as full Overwatch members at a brief ceremony that none of my immediate family attended. Liam's parents waved and wiped tears from the sidelines as if it were the proudest moment they'd ever had. When they hugged me afterwards, I felt a stab of awkwardness for how pleased they seemed about our partnership. The way Liam's mother looked at me, I had a feeling she could just imagine red-headed grandchildren.

Then, I had one of those days where everything goes horribly wrong.

I was walking into the OW compound when an annoyingly familiar face came towards me from down the hall to the administration offices.

"Gracie! My goodness, you look grown these days." Reporter Joe looked almost exactly the way I remembered him from the flood: middle-aged, balding, and extremely obnoxious. "You must have fallen out with your father if you've joined the OW."

I gave him a perfect Usuriel blank face, but internally I wanted to grab him by the neck and demand his sources. How did this man always know the Family better than I did?

"Actually, I just visited him last week," I said truthfully. It hadn't been a long visit, but we'd had a meal with my grandparents in Chronourea Valley. Grandma Gloria was in her third trimester and took the whole 'glowing with pregnancy' thing to a new level. I'd been civil and Dad had been sober, so overall it was a pleasant evening.

"Well, he certainly can't be okay with this." Joe flicked a finger at my workout uniform.

I shrugged. "I'm grown," I said, before realizing I was confirming the reporter's assumptions. The triumphant gleam in Joe's eye told me I was right. I really hated that reporter. With a sigh, I shifted my weight to one hip and glared at him. "What are you doing here? I somehow don't think they're going to let you join OW."

Joe chuckled as if I'd made a decent joke. "No, no, just stopping by to see a few people. Vanessa knows better than to suppress the freedom of press."

I raised an eyebrow, but didn't comment. Instead, I gave him a twisted attempt at a smile and began moving down the hall again. "Well, don't trip on your way out."

"Ah, Gracie?" Joe sounded especially ingratiating. My stomach turned, but I glanced at him anyway. "You have a unique perspective on your father. I'm sure a lot of people would be interested in hearing about Gabriel Usuriel from his daughter's eyes."

I snorted and turned away. "I'm sure they would."

"I'm serious." Joe put a hand on my arm. Gooseflesh rose in disgust at his touch and I pulled back. The reporter seemed unfazed by my reaction. "If you ever think of anything that would make a decent story, come to me. I'll do the hard part. You just have to count the money. I'll make it worth your while, I promise."

"Get lost," I snarled and stalked off towards the training gallery.

"Just think about it!" Joe's voice was cut off by the door sliding shut behind me.

"Who was that?" Liam asked as I strode over to the mat where he was looking at a memory pad.

"No one important," I grumbled, tossing my towel over the bench beside the mat. Liam had a frown on his face and wasn't doing his warm ups even though he was wearing his workout uniform. "How's your mom? You were on the comm to her when I left the dorm earlier, weren't you? Not trying to snoop, but your door was open."

"Oh, she's fine. All worked up about this New Paradise place. Have you heard of it?" Liam asked, tilting the memory pad so I could see the pictures of palm trees and sunny beaches.

"No. What's New Paradise?"

"It's some Awareness-only settlement on the western continent. I guess it's just been terraformed with the latest techniques. Mom said a bunch of the Family in Skykyle are keen to visit over the next long break."

"An Awareness-only settlement?" I echoed, glancing over my shoulder at Vanessa's office window before doing a few half-hearted stretches. Figuring my excuse was secured, I moved a little closer to see the pad better. "That sounds interesting."

"Eh, something about it doesn't sit right to me," Liam muttered, his long face drawn in a scowl. "It reminds me of what James was talking about right after he got back from his internship. Something about the Riland mortals thinking individuals of Awareness were all in league together or conspiring or..." He shook his head and tapped through another set of screens. "I dunno. I guess that's why I figured I would try to log in to the Overwatch database and see what they had on it."

"Well?" I asked, watching him scroll through the net search. "Any classified entries?"

"Mostly it's the same information I found on the University's net. You know, building permits, advertisements for the Awareness community's new 'utopia,' a few articles in leisure review net sites. But there were a couple of references exclusively on the OW net. I tried to bring them up but they sent me a security code and it isn't taking my authorization. We're full members now, though, so we shouldn't be locked out of anything." He offered me the pad with a confused expression.

"Hmm," I murmured thoughtfully as I took the pad in my hands and studied the error message. The interface was requesting a user's bio-authorization. I tried placing my hand over the screen, but it denied my clearance just as thoroughly as Liam's. "Huh, that is odd. Well, Vanessa did say we'd have some probationary terms until we graduated University. The 'full member' status was just so we could start drawing a salary."

"Yeah, I know," Liam agreed. He'd been the one who petitioned Vanessa to let us in a little early. Unlike Dad and my grandparents, Liam's family couldn't afford to help him with much aside from a place to sleep over long school breaks. He hadn't explicitly said as much, but I was pretty sure he was sending a good chunk of his new salary home to his parents to help out with the bills. As a result, I felt a little guilty about flaunting my now-flush bank account. On the plus side, it kept my spending relatively modest and I was starting to gather a sizable nest egg for after graduation.

"But it doesn't make me feel any better about this 'New Paradise' idea."

I tapped through a few more entries, but he'd summed up the information pretty succinctly. Liam had always been adept at finding things on the net.

"Well, maybe we should mention it to James next time we see him," I suggested. "He spends enough time at the embassy now. If there are rumors in the political circles about this place, he'll know about them."

"Not a bad idea," Liam agreed.

I glanced over my shoulder. Jillian was chatting with another workout regular a few mats away. We were members now and it wasn't as if we had to answer to Jill anymore, I reminded myself. With a sly glance at Liam, I leaned in closer.

"You know, we've never put my father's name into this database since we became full members."

An eager grin spread across Liam's face and that answering gleam of passionate curiosity sparked to life in his deep blue eyes. There was a reason I liked spending time with Liam before we ever joined OW.

Just like that, Gabriel Usuriel's name got plugged into the memory pad. I don't even remember doing it. But I do recall playing around with the search parameters to select 'Overwatch database.'

The results were momentarily overwhelming. My father had indeed been an active member of the OW for a very long time. Hundreds of case files lit up the screen. I blinked at them, unsure where to start.

"Wow, I don't think we can go through all of this right now," I said slowly. I knew from history class that my father used to be in the highest levels of OW. Seeing the documentation in Overwatch's own database brought it home in a much more solid way, however.

Liam tilted his head at the pad, then reached over my shoulder and went back to the search parameters again with a few flicks of his large fingertip. "Well, we know that Adora asked him to be the head of enforcement almost immediately after it started. He ran this agency for the majority of its existence—up until Vanessa took over. This isn't new information."

I nodded in agreement and tried to ignore the warmth of my partner's arm resting on my shoulder. Of course, that meant it was the only thing I could focus on.

"Right. Of course he's all over their database. I'm not sure what I expected to find," I said as Liam rearranged the list. First he eliminated the general membership rosters and daily activity reports. Then he took out the incident reports that listed Gabriel as the arresting officer or on-duty supervisor. I don't know what prompted him to do it that way, but I guess it made sense. Eliminate the mundane and you'll leave the interesting stuff exposed.

"What's that?" Liam muttered, pointing to an execution order that hadn't disappeared with the rest of them. You always knew a death warrant for what it was because the system color coded it orange. This one was labeled with a random file number just like all the other execution orders, but its date was after my father had left the Overwatch.

"Open it," I said, frowning at the file. "You eliminated all the ones where he was a reporting officer. Maybe he's listed as an executioner? I mean, I could see them calling him in if someone got squeamish."

"Or perhaps as a witness?" Liam agreed, tapping the file. Immediately, another security clearance blocked the screen. My frown deepened as Liam laid his palm against the pad to no effect.

"Really?" I muttered in frustration, tapping the file again. When the security screen came up, I tried my own hand this time. I was expecting the same result, but instead the file flashed green and spilled its contents across the pad.

I didn't understand what I was looking at for a moment. I thought it must be a typo or some other kind of clerical error. Why would my father's name be on the top of the warrant? That was where the criminal's information went, not the officer's. Then I caught sight of the city code: 006— Skykyle slum district. My face burned and my stomach dropped sickeningly.

I'd just opened an order for my father's execution.

My eyes darted across the page, trying to take in all of the information at once. It blurred together, the words refusing to make their usual, logical sense. Finally my panicked gaze caught the top corner. The order's status was listed as "renewed—active."

I couldn't breathe. The walls of that giant room were closing in and there was no more air to suck into my lungs.

"Gracie? Liam?" Vanessa's voice made my panic spike to an even higher peak. My head shot up, my eyes wide and my body taught as a plucked string. My heart slammed in my chest as I stared at the head of Overwatch's advancing figure. "This isn't the University library. If you need to do research, there are better places than the middle of my practice gallery."

I opened my mouth, but nothing came out. What did I do? Vanessa knew about the order. She had to. The OW database was essentially hers. I'd seen her quote sections of it from memory without even tapping her implant. Hiding this document would do less than nothing to protect Gabriel. Yet, announcing my father's doom to the entire practice gallery seemed like a very bad idea. I froze.

Thankfully, as always, Liam knew just what to say in a difficult situation.

"Vanessa, I think we need to have a conversation in your office," he said, wrapping his arm more tightly around my shoulders.

Vanessa's good eye flickered between us, her expression serious. She gave a slow nod and Liam's mind joined hers in the shift up to her overlooking office.

My head still swam even after the room materialized around me. I stared at Vanessa's great, solid wooden desk as if it were a tiger ready to pounce on me.

"Let me see," Vanessa said, holding out a hand for the memory pad. I'd tucked it protectively against my chest, as if shielding the document might protect my father from what it meant. Feeling incredibly exposed, I slowly did as she asked and handed her the pad.

Vanessa looked down at the document and her face became grim.

"You shouldn't have access to this," she muttered, pressing her palm to the pad. "I'll have to have a talk with Stella."

"Really? That's what you have to say?" Liam sounded almost more offended than I was. I blinked between the two of them, a buzzing white haze of numbness taking grip of my head. It was leaking away the fear and panic, however, so I tried to relax into it.

Vanessa's expression was hard as she met my partner's furious glare. Then it softened as she turned in my direction.

"I'm sorry this is the way you had to find out, Gracie. I realize there's something harsh about seeing it on the official letterhead. But, come now. I've heard what avid researchers the two of you are. This can't come as a complete shock," she said evenly, laying the pad down on the top of her desk. It made a sharp *tap* as plastic hit wood. I flinched.

"We've been looking into the Family, yes," Liam agreed cautiously. "But we've never uncovered anything to warrant something like this."

I caught his expression of concern out of the corner of my eye. If I hadn't been somewhere between numb and panic, I think I would have felt gratitude for how well he was handling the situation. As it was, I felt trapped in the four walls of that office. I stared at her windowsill, running my eyes over the green vial and the little white raven figure with its feather tied about its neck with fraying twine. I wished I had the courage to fling myself through the glass of the window and fly far, far away from that damned memory pad and everything it represented.

Vanessa raised her good eyebrow at him. "Honestly? I've heard you speculate aloud that the Sorrow legend wasn't exactly so mythological." Her brow knit together in something almost sympathetic as she turned to me. "I know this is hard, Gracie. I'm fond of Gabriel, too. I had hopes he might be able to keep his sobriety this time. But, especially after the stunt he pulled at the Family party, you must know what your father is by now."

I sucked in a breath, the flames catching in the pit of my chest. The burning anger cleansed away the numbness, leaving something between fear and rage in its wake. It felt so much safer to be angry than afraid. I clung to the fire like a lifeline.

"What is it that you think he is, exactly?" I hissed between clenched teeth.

Vanessa planted her hands on her hips and looked unhappy about being forced into this conversation.

"Despite his good intentions, he's a terminal drug addict," she said slowly, meeting my gaze. "You've lived with the man. You know he can't control the drinking. And it's getting worse again, not better. It's only a matter of time before it goes past that and we all know it."

"Whoa, whoa, hold on. Are you actually suggesting the council has voted to execute him because he's a recovering addict?" Liam sounded appropriately outraged. Thank Fate, because if he hadn't expressed some of my anger verbally, I might have set Vanessa alight on the spot.

"Not just any drug addict," Vanessa countered, holding up a finger in Liam's direction. "A second-gen drug addict who has shown himself to be prone to violence. Gabriel is too strong to be as unstable as he is. He's dangerous. It's only a matter of time before he manages to hurt someone, either intentionally or by accident."

"Well, if we're going to assume the Sorrow thing is true, then he managed to use for over six decades without losing it and burning down half of Skykyle," I pointed out. "If you had such a problem with his instability, why didn't you do something about him back then?"

Vanessa tilted her head at me. "He's too strong to put in a cell and screwing up the determination to execute someone takes a bit more emotion than you might think. Even for high-level telepaths, shielding a strong emotion is one of the most difficult feats. Unless we happened to find him when he was completely passed out, there's no way any of the OW could shield strongly enough to hide our intentions from a psychic of his level. We'd never get close enough to hurt him, let alone finish an execution order."

Liam nodded slowly. "Okay. I guess that makes sense. But if you can't complete the order why keep it active?"

Vanessa moved around her desk and settled in the chair. "It's actually just recently been renewed. Mainly because the council thinks we now have someone who can complete it."

I felt more than saw Liam turn to look at me. Vanessa's one-eyed gaze was steady and unblinking. The last of the blood left my face.

"No," I whispered, shaking my head. Without Liam's hand on my back, I would have stumbled back a step.

"I'm sorry, Gracie. I wanted to wait a while longer before we renewed. See if Gabriel could make a better adjustment to losing you around the house. But with his very public reaction to Gloria's pregnancy, there are other members of the council who are getting nervous. And the truth is, we waited on Adora," Vanessa said, almost gently. I wondered what shades of green my face had turned. "Everyone knew she was dangerous, but she never actually worked her way up to intentionally hurting someone. Until the massacre, that is." Her good eye met mine and held it remorselessly. "Do we really want to wait for your father to overdose and take every person sleeping in the apartment building with him to the grave? His mind is strong enough to do such a thing."

"But he never has," I croaked, fighting to speak past the mortal dread in my chest. "Even as sick as he has been in the past, Dad's never actually intentionally hurt anyone but himself. We can't hunt him down and kill him over something he might possibly do in the future. You might as well execute me for being able to burn down a building. Just because I can doesn't mean I will!"

Her expression disapproved of that little logical jump. "You're not getting so intoxicated you can't stand, let alone control your pyrokinesis! It's nothing short of a miracle your father hasn't killed someone yet! You may not have lived through it before, but a lot of us have. This is how it starts with him. Admitted, Sorrow was a new and terrifying low. But all that proves is that he's unpredictable. We're seeing clear warning signs that he could have another break over Ileesia's birth. How long do we wait before we take action to protect the people around him?"

I stared at her, unable to speak as the fear and anger congealed into a solid lump of alloy in my chest. Finally, Liam broke the silence.

"The law sets out a pretty clear statute. We wait until he's demonstrated behavior that is an undeniable threat to others. Unless you know something I don't, Gabriel hasn't harmed anyone outside of the OW order since the *Inspiration* landed." The calm logic in my partner's deep voice was grounding. Even so, my hands still hadn't stopped shaking. "And let me get one thing straight," Liam went on, lifting a finger in Vanessa's direction. "The Council renewed the order, but Gracie is the only one who can complete it. Am I right? If so, that means you have to get her to sign off on this before you can take any kind of action."

Vanessa's mouth was a grim line as if she didn't like admitting this. After a long moment, however, she inclined her head. "As strong as we are, Lilly and I are third-gen three-T's. Gabriel would hear us coming in a heartbeat, and if he's not passed out, he'd be fully capable of killing either one of us. Possibly even both of us together, if he's having a good day. Gracie though... Gabriel and Stella both trust you and you're beyond head blind. You can get close enough to make it quick and relatively painless. Honestly, when I found out about your particular skill set, this was a big reason I wanted you with the OW. Just in case Gabriel or one of the other elder children started slipping. It's almost as if you were born for this."

Her words were an odd parody of Ariel's two months earlier. Much as it had in my sister's lab, Cybele began to lurch under my feet. Had Gabriel known there was an order out for his head? Was this the reason he didn't want me joining the OW? I was genuinely going to be sick.

"Born to be my father's assassin," I breathed, the room making slow circles around me. "Fucking Fate."

"I know this isn't what you had in mind when you signed up," Vanessa's voice was cautious, "but I've heard you say yourself that we have a responsibility to the mortals and the Family to keep the weak and vulnerable safe."

I gave her a wide-eyed expression of horror at my own words being used to justify this mockery of justice. When neither Liam nor I said anything, Vanessa went on in an even, almost cajoling tone.

"Be honest with yourself. How will you feel if he does snap and take out a city block? Will you be able to live with those innocents' blood on your hands?"

For just a moment I tried to envision Dad melting down to the point of complete combustion. What could possibly put him there? I thought back to our fight in the dormitory.

If I hadn't pushed every button the man had then, what was left?

"He wouldn't," I said finally. I could see the doubt on Vanessa's face, but I went on quickly before she could open her mouth again. "Like you said, I just spent the last ten years living with him. If anyone knows what he's capable of, it's me. And the man who raised me would never hurt anyone without a really good reason. All this talk of him being unstable and dangerous is just that—talk. Gabriel hasn't actually done anything that deserves a death sentence. Unless there's something you aren't telling me?"

Vanessa's mouth formed a thin line, but she shook her head. "Nothing you don't already know, I think. But his last episode was dark enough to get the council to sign off on his death warrant."

"He pulled himself out of that pit over a decade ago. I'm not killing him for mistakes he made when I was a toddler."

"There you have it," Liam said with great finality, making a gesture between the two of us. "You said Gracie is the only one who can fill the order. She's just told you she isn't willing to do it. So I'd say, unless something changes, that warrant isn't going to be completed any time soon."

She licked her lips and leaned forward. The head of Overwatch didn't look happy but she also didn't look surprised. "You're sure I can't change your mind?"

"Completely," I managed between clenched teeth. With a swirl of long, red strands, I turned and charged towards the door.

"Give us your word." Liam's voice was low and on the border of anger as I walked away. I paused at the door and glanced at him over my shoulder. He had a very serious expression on his face as he met Vanessa's good eye. "I want your word that you won't send anyone else after Gabriel."

I froze, waiting for her response.

"I told you, Gracie's the only one who could get close enough." Vanessa's back was very straight. "But I will give you my word as well, if it will make you feel better. The two of you are one of our best new teams. I'm not trying to alienate you. I'm just trying to be honest. And the truth is, Gracie, it's within the bylaws for you to refuse an execution. If we don't find another officer willing to attempt it—which we clearly don't have for your father—then the order will expire in a year. We would have to renew it again if we wanted to activate it. Without your action, Gabriel is safe enough. From us, that is. I can't promise the same from his own behavior."

I conceded to drop my hand from the door plate, but I crossed my arms angrily across my chest and didn't take a step back into the room.

"However, if you warn him about the situation, use some care. If you mention there's an order out for him, you'd be breaking your confidentiality oath. That's a dismissible offense," Vanessa warned, her voice sternly controlled.

I ground my teeth and said nothing.

"Not to mention you might goad him into doing something foolish out of a sense of self-preservation," Liam said carefully. "You wouldn't want to give anyone an added incentive to go after him, right?"

I shook my head unhappily at Liam's argument. I knew Vanessa was right—even the strongest of the OW would never stand a chance against my father if he decided to defend himself. Short of him melting down in public, Vanessa would have a hard time convincing anyone to even attempt bearding Gabriel in his own element.

"Okay," I said, rubbing an eye with the heel of one hand. "Fine. I won't say anything."

Vanessa nodded as if satisfied. Then an empty look came across her face and she tapped the side of her neck.

"Yes?" She was clearly replying to someone via her implant. Liam took a step in my direction as if he were going to follow me out the door and give her some privacy to finish her call. Vanessa held up one finger, catching our eyes in a signal to wait before we could exit. "I see. Yes, I understand. Okay, I'll send a team right away. Yes. Alright. Yes, I understand it's serious. I'll send someone strong enough to deal with it, don't worry."

Liam met my worried glance as Vanessa tapped out of the conversation and turned to us.

"Can I consider this matter closed?" she asked, arching her unblemished eyebrow in my direction.

A piece of me wanted to tell Vanessa to take every order in the database and shove them up her ass. But I'd worked hard to become one of the youngest members of the Overwatch and, as ironic as it was, I did still believe in what the agency stood for. I was fairly certain Liam and I had been making a positive difference the last few weeks and going to bed satisfied with a day's work wasn't something I wanted to give up.

I glanced at Liam and saw the naked fear on his face. This was his career on the line, I realized. If I quit, they'd never keep him on. He'd be superfluous at best with any other partner; a liability at worst. I met his deep blue gaze and knew I couldn't take away the one chance he had of pulling himself out of the hole of poverty his family was trapped in.

"Yeah," I murmured, "it's closed."

"Good, because we need an elder child in upper Riland. Do you feel up to going or shall I call Camphor and go myself?" Vanessa glanced between the two of us, her expression serious but not angry.

"It's up to you," Liam said, gesturing to me with one hand.

I took a deep breath to settle my nerves. It didn't work completely, but I had a feeling staying busy was a better idea than sitting around obsessing about my father's execution order.

"I'm fine," I said, taking a step back into the room and holding out a hand to Liam. "Give Liam the reference. We'll go."

Vanessa nodded in approval. Liam took my hand, profound relief on his face. I couldn't even fake a smile, so I just squeezed his hand. Obediently, he pulled on his psi and the world bled away into swirls of blue.

Chapter 27

The Ryland Farm

I was completely unprepared for the situation we materialized into. Training could only do so much. Eventually, experience had to be the teacher. I'd thought I was a full-fledged OW member. I'd thought I'd experienced emotional trauma in the form of my father's ever-present and heartbreaking issues.

I was wrong.

We were by the ocean. That was my first impression as Liam's psi-wind died down and a salt breeze rose to lift my hair instead. From the top of the hill we'd teleported to, I could see rolling farms stretching out to the shore and off into the horizon's distance on every side. A picturesque two-story house stood overlooking the lovely landscape—a barn and several storage buildings sharing the same fenced-in bit of pasture. I was strongly reminded of Angelus Quietum and I had another surge of longing for the safe innocence of my childhood.

"Fate save us." I'd never heard that tone from Liam before. I followed his gaze and broke out in a cold sweat.

The middle-aged mortal was dead. The angle of his head

and neck were unnatural and the smear of blood congealing on the barn wall behind him was large enough that I knew he'd bled out in moments. He'd been thrown by something and landed on a protruding prong used to hang farm tools on the outside of the structure. It must have been with a decent amount of force, too, because the metal had ripped through his entire chest wall and sprayed blood everywhere. The wind shifted directions and I had to cover my mouth for fear I'd be sick from the smell.

"It's broad daylight," I said, eyes darting around the serene pasture. Nothing but cattle grazing calmly down the slope of the hill. "A vamp couldn't have done this. It had to be a Family member."

Liam didn't dispute my logic. "Come on," he said and led the way around the building. "I'm getting some fear in this direction."

As if timed with his observation, a guttural cry sounded from ahead. Liam and I broke into a run as we rounded the side of the house.

There were two—somethings—in the center of the tidy chicken yard. A young woman with a long-handled hoe was backed up to the side of the house, her eyes wild as she swung the garden tool in a threatening arc. The two strange figures in front of her seemed unperturbed by this and stood staring at her as if waiting for something.

When I say strange figures, I mean it. There was something off about their proportions, but I couldn't put a finger on it. They struck me as neither male nor female, though their clothing was fitted so neatly it must have been tailored. Their skin was flawlessly smooth and their hair so saturated in hue that it almost seemed metallic in the mid-day sun.

I'd never seen such perfection outside of an elder child, but their features weren't Usuriel. I'd know a Family member from across the room and even a glance told me these individuals weren't kin. It was something about the cheekbones and the angle of the nose, I thought. Not that their features were any less pleasing; it simply wasn't Usuriel beauty I was looking at.

"What's going on here?" I called as we approached the

stand-off. Liam wasn't beside me, and I glanced over my shoulder to see that he'd hesitated a few strides around the building. The look of confusion on his face made me pause and take stock as well.

"Get away from me!" The woman shrieked, brandishing the hoe with renewed vigor. Terrified tears rolled down her cheeks.

"Take it easy, we're Overwatch," I said, pulling my badge out of my pocket and holding out my other hand to show her that I meant no harm. "Can you tell me what happened to the gentleman in the front?"

A ragged sob burst from the woman's chest but she didn't lower her makeshift weapon. "They killed my Da!" She gave a savage thrust with the hoe towards the unusual individuals standing in front of her. "And now they're after me!"

"Gracie, I think we need to back up," Liam said slowly, suiting action to word and taking a careful step backwards. I frowned at him while trying not to take my attention away from the pair menacing the woman.

"What has you so spooked?" I hissed, trying to keep my voice low. Sometimes my lack of telepathy was a serious liability.

"I can't hear them." Liam sounded genuinely afraid. "They're as head mute as you are."

I blinked, startled by this information. Then, one of the figures moved.

I've mentioned before that animals have a certain kind of motion—something that relies upon bone and muscle working in tandem. Whatever these individuals were, they didn't move like that. One moment they were still, the next they were a blur that defied even the most powerful of Usuriels. It wasn't what I would call graceful. In fact, there was a wrongness to the suddenness of it, as if there were a flipped switch rather than an intentional thought.

A fist connected with my shoulder. Pain shot down my arm and broke through my caution. The training I'd done all those years, from my father's instruction at the edge of Lake Angelus to the ring with Jillian and Liam, kicked in without a conscious thought. My body pivoted to absorb the blow even as my fire flashed out, sending a controlled burst between myself and my attacker. It wasn't a huge blast, nor as hot as I could summon, but it sent the strange figure tumbling in the opposite direction while propelling me back towards Liam's safe, telekinetic presence.

"What the..." Liam seemed as stunned as I was that I'd been attacked unprovoked. His face was serious, if a little wide-eyed, as I landed on my feet next to him. "Are you okay?"

I flexed my arm and nodded. "It'll bruise, but I'll be fine. Damn, it hit me as hard as your telekinesis, though."

The individual that had advanced on me was now in a semi-crouch about a meter away from where it made contact with my shoulder. My flames caught it in the chest and I could see where the cloth had burned away from its pale, perfect shoulders. It looked up at me and tilted its head in a too-smooth motion. Getting a better look at its eyes sent the hair down my spine on end. My breath caught. Electric orange swirled in its iris while tiny rivers of blue energy flowed under its pale skin.

"Don't pull your punches," I gasped at Liam. "They aren't human. Sweet Fate, they aren't even alive."

"What do you mean?" Liam hissed, his eyes darting from the now-sobbing young mortal to the two menacing figures several meters apart in front of us.

"I mean they're Terran avatars!" If I hadn't been so worried about having my hands free to defend myself, I would have clung to Liam in terror. But my training held and instead I took a firmer mental grip on my flames.

That was about all the time we had for discussion. Without a single word, the two avatars moved with simultaneous, deadly speed. I braced myself, ready to let loose a torrent of flame, when I realized the mortal girl was directly in the path of destruction. If I sent fire at the avatars from this angle, I'd roast her alive.

In the split second I hesitated, Liam acted. With one hand, he grabbed my shoulder. The world spun sickeningly before solidifying us directly next to the young woman with her death grip on the hoe. She looked at us with a stunned expression.

I steadied myself and took note of the Terran's new positions. They'd charged for where Liam and I had been standing but caught themselves before they slammed into each other. Their heads swiveled about as if confused about where we'd gone. Then they caught sight of us and gathered themselves smoothly into perfectly erect postures before gliding in our direction.

"What are those things?" the girl whimpered, shrinking back against us as the avatars advanced.

I took a step forward, putting myself between the Terrans and the more vulnerable two individuals I was responsible for.

"Liam, get her out of here," I said, calling down a wave of fire to dance around my body. It felt strangely reassuring to roll the flames along my skin. It was partly a warm up and partly to prevent my OW partner from trying to teleport me along with him. I spared a glance in his direction and saw the heartsick expression on his face as he realized I meant to take the Terrans on by myself.

"Gracie... if they are Terrans, they're each as strong as a full grown three-T. They'll kill you."

I shook my head, red curls tossing in the wind of my own flames. "I'm not pulling punches. Which means I can't have you and the girl in the way. Take her to safety, then come back with reinforcements. I'll hold their attention until you get back."

For the first time, I saw the Usuriel blank face overcome Liam's expressive features. He knew this was our job. This was what we'd been trained to do. If he couldn't get past the heartbreak of letting me put myself in danger, there was no way we could stay OW partners. For the sake of our working relationship, he swallowed the emotional pain and disappeared with the mortal in a shower of blue sparks.

I turned back to the avatars just in time to see them blur into that mind-boggling speed. Now, however, there was no mortal or partner for me to be careful of. I planted myself firmly before opening myself to the fire. I let it roar outwards in a scalding wave that sent them flying away from me.

All I could see was roiling flame. I'd never called down such a complete maelstrom, but even so, I didn't feel as if my strength were taxed. My abilities had grown, some calm part of my brain observed.

Though I could have sustained the flames longer, I allowed the initial wave to burn itself out. The avatars had been sent back a dozen meters this time, their feet leaving torn grooves in the now-smoldering grass. The neatly tailored clothes had mostly burned to ash along with the majority of their hair. Ribbons of hotter flame had melted long lines in the pale flesh of their chests and arms, leaving those brilliant rivers of blue energy to gleam strangely through the gaps in their skin. The material on their faces must have been different because they were untouched. They looked up at me with those oddly-spinning eyes as if I were merely an annoyance. Then they rushed me again.

Instead of pushing them away, I sprang upwards. Summoning a quick blast of fire, I soared into the air before alighting neatly on the roof of the farm house. I took care with how I planted my feet on the slippery solar shingles. I looked down at them and wondered what their next move would be.

It was with another one of those too-fast movements that they mimicked my actions and leaped into the air. Of course they could fly, I groaned inwardly. Well, that made things tougher.

This time I didn't wait for them to get close. Instead, I pulled on the Usuriel strength and speed that made me such a challenge for Liam on the practice mat and leaped back into the air.

With another controlled blast of fire, I grabbed the first avatar by the ankles and spun it mid-air. Using its own momentum and another calculated burst of psi-flame, I slammed it head-first into the ground. Seconds before I followed it, I slapped a hand to the warm soil and used the flames to rebound upwards. A last blast of psi-fire exploded over its crumpled form as I landed neatly back on the roof.

A bit out of breath, I stood looking down at the fallen Terran. I scanned the area for the other avatar but saw nothing in the immediate vicinity. The one I'd thrown into the ground seemed pretty well broken. In any case, it didn't move from the twisted position it had landed in. After a few minutes, I still didn't see the other avatar, but that made me more nervous than anything. Putting my hands on my hips, I paced along the edge of the roof, my head turning in all directions as I tried to bring my heart rate back down.

A scream from the other side of the building snapped my

head in the direction that Liam and I had originally arrived. In a few quick strides, I was peering over the peak of the roof and down into the red ruin that was the front barnyard.

A woman with gray hair had dropped the load of groceries she was carrying into the house and stood in abject horror in front of the corpse. I could hear her sobbing breaths from the roof. My heart broke for her, but she was advertising her presence to the second avatar. I swept the area with a critical gaze, looking for the Terran I knew was lurking.

Sure as trouble followed my father, I caught sight of the darting motion of the avatar as it rounded the corner of the barn. With less than a thought, I launched myself at the android, twisting myself in mid-air to land a solid kick to its torso. The impact actually flipped me backwards and I had to use another bit of flame to keep from landing on my head. Instead, I executed another nice mid-air turn and caught myself in a crouch that slammed one knee painfully into the ground.

The Terran flew into one of the storage buildings so hard the whole structure collapsed on top of it. The mortal woman's shrieks gained a new level of urgency, but I knew better than to let her distract me. I didn't think I'd hit the avatar with enough force to disable it. If I didn't finish it quickly, the mortal and I would both be in trouble. I stood slowly, my shoulder and knee throbbing. If these were the only injuries I came away with today, I was pretty lucky.

As I'd expected, the wreckage of the storage building shuddered as I walked towards it. Old crates and splintered boxes of foodstuffs tumbled apart to reveal a battered-looking avatar. One arm had been wrenched out of its socket by my last blow, and I could distinctly see an indentation in its side where my kick had connected. It seemed to be having difficulty getting back to its feet, and it wasn't moving as smoothly as earlier. It looked up sharply as I approached, orange eyes whirling.

"Tell whoever sent you that the Overwatch won't allow this kind of attack," I said, meeting the thing's spinning gaze. Then, I let all of the anger and fear of the encounter solidify in my chest and I summoned the flames. For the very first time, I didn't temper them whatsoever. All the heat and blazing force my mind could bring to bear blasted down on the avatar with merciless efficiency. The thing shrieked once, its frame twisting in the inferno's incandescence. Then it was still.

The sound of the safety coming off of a shotgun next to my ear made me freeze in place. Slowly, I put my hands up and turned as carefully as I could towards the sound. The mortal woman's gray hair fell in her face as her shaking hands held the gun to my head.

"What the hell did do you do to my husband? Where is my step-daughter?" she gasped, brown eyes blazing in swollen, red folds of skin.

I swallowed and tried very hard not to send the flames in her direction. There was every chance she could blow my head off before I managed to kill or maim her. And besides, she really wasn't the villain here. I didn't want to hurt her. Even so, I saw my death reflected in her terrified gaze. A single false move and she'd likely shoot me on the spot. I internally cursed my lack of three-T status for the millionth time.

"Madam, I am Overwatch. My partner teleported the young woman we found near the house to safety. From what I could tell, she wasn't hurt, just scared." I tried to keep my voice as even and calm as I could, despite being slightly out of breath from my last little show of pyrokinetics.

The woman was breathing harder than I was and I'd just sent up the biggest explosion of my career. I could see that she was hanging on to her nerves by a bare thread. I blinked slowly at her and tried to look as gentle and innocent as possible.

"How do I know you're telling the truth?" Her voice shook as badly as the gun and I was afraid she might squeeze the trigger purely by accident.

"You just watched my one and only psychic power. I'm a firebird. If I had the strength to do that—"I gestured carefully towards the barn a few meters away from us "—wouldn't I have bent that gun barrel in half by now? Please, madam, I'm not here to harm you. Put the gun down and let's talk about what needs to happen next in a calm and civilized manner."

Abruptly, the gun disappeared from its position pointed

at my nose. Startled, I realized the woman hadn't lowered the weapon but rather that her hands were now simply empty. I looked up and breathed a sigh of relief to see Liam striding towards us with the gun in his hand. Jillian, Vanessa, and Evan were on his heels, faces grim as they took in the messy scene.

"Are you alright, Gracie?" Vanessa asked as Liam walked quickly to my side.

I acknowledged my partner's presence with a quick squeeze of one arm, but I leaned away from him so he knew I didn't want to be comforted; if I let him hold me, I'd lose it again, and that wasn't what I needed right now. So, rather than embrace me as I think he would have preferred, Liam settled at my shoulder and stood glowering at the mortal woman as if he would have liked to point the gun in her direction.

"I'm fine, thanks," I said, proud of how well I kept my voice under control. "But you're not going to believe me when I tell you what just happened."

Vanessa glanced over at the still-smoldering remains of the second Terran avatar. The smell of burning plastic and oil made the air acrid. She scowled, her good eye calculating. "Is that what I think it is?" she asked, picking up a piece of wreckage and poking at the Terran's remains.

"You people think we're crazy!" Evan's voice grated on my last nerve but I clenched my jaw and forced myself to meet his dark eye. "But this is proof. The Terrans are mounting an assault force. Mark me, they've had Riland's bread basket in their sites for decades."

"This isn't an invasion force. It just looks like a few rogue individuals." Vanessa sounded grim as she addressed the head of Riland watch.

"Well, if we'd had an Aware patrol up here, we could have stopped this before someone got killed," Evan snapped.

"Is it really a Terran avatar?" Jillian leaned closer to Vanessa, her face concerned.

"It seems so." Vanessa didn't sound any happier about this fact than I felt.

"What happened to the other one?" Liam asked, looking around a little nervously.

I gestured to the other side of the house with a thumb. "I took care of that one first. It's in the backyard."

"Document this," Vanessa said sharply, handing Jillian a memory pad from the air to her left. Our trainer began using the built-in holo-camera to scan the entirety of the scene. "While she's doing that, come show me the other Terran," Vanessa beckoned to me and Liam as she stalked to the back of the house.

"Wait! What just happened? Where is Angelica?"

The mortal woman sounded shrill, but I didn't blame her for being upset. Evan put an arm around her shoulders and led her towards the door of the house.

"The young woman Liam teleported to the OW compound is just fine, I assure you. Come, sit down and tell me exactly what happened." Evan did apparently know how to speak nicely to someone. Even if it wasn't me, I found myself hating him a little less. Or maybe I was just numb from all the shocks I'd had today. Either way, I was glad he and the gray-haired mortal were occupying each others' attention, because I didn't have the energy to deal with either of them at the moment.

Liam's hand on my shoulder made me jump as we followed Vanessa to the back. The ringing, white noise of numbness I'd had after my previous conversation with Vanessa that morning was back. I clenched my hands into fists, which were shaking again. Strong emotions simmered under the adrenaline buzz I was currently riding. Hopefully I could hang on to the blankness long enough to make my report. I really didn't want to sob my way through it.

"You just took down two Terran avatars all by yourself." There was awe in Liam's voice as we approached the smoking remnants of the first avatar. "Sweet Fate, Gracie."

Vanessa nodded as if to agree with my partner's impressed assessment of the situation. Pulling another holo-camera from thin air, she quickly scanned the remains into our database. Then, with a sharp gesture, she telekinetically lifted the crumpled figure from its smoldering crater and laid it out in a more natural position before scanning it again.

"This is good work, Gracie," Vanessa said with a nod. "As clean and efficient as Lilly or I could have done."

"You wouldn't have ended up at the end of a mortal's

shotgun, though," I grumbled, managing to feel a pang of embarrassment over that debacle despite my post-adrenaline haze.

Vanessa gave a fluid shrug. "Everyone's set of skills has strengths and weaknesses. The fact that you're too strong to deal gently with mortals is why Liam's a good partner for you. And he was back in time to defuse the situation, which is how your team is supposed to work."

I ran a shaking hand through my hair and nodded at her calm logic. I felt a touch steadier under her praise.

"So, can I address the real issue here and ask why the fuck Terran avatars are tearing up cattle farms in Riland?" Liam's question made my heart rate shoot up again. Echoes of that early morning conversation with James floated through my head. "I thought they needed relays to connect to their bodies back in Terra Nova. How were these two able to function in the Provinces? And even if they have found a way to extend their range, why go after peaceful farmers?"

Vanessa shook her head slowly, a solemn look on her Family features. "I'm not sure, but it's trouble we don't need right now." I felt as if I was seeing under her carefully controlled mask as she rubbed next to her bad eye. "This is going to give Garret Stafford more ammunition, that's for certain." She then swore much more thoroughly than I'd suspected she was capable of. "We're running out of time," she muttered under her breath at the end of the long list of expletives.

"What do we do now?" I think I was wondering aloud more than asking my superior for direction. However, Vanessa shook herself and got that calculating gleam back in her eye.

"First, record your reports," she said, voice once again in control and commanding. "Then, take the rest of the day off. It's only noon and it's already been a real winner." Her gaze flicked up to my face. "And make sure you eat something, Gracie. You just fought the equivalent of twenty men. You're on your feet now because your body isn't sure if you're safe or not yet. Once it realizes the threat is over, you'll crash hard if you don't refuel. Trust me, I know."

I found it strange to hear the exact advice my father would have given echoed from the person who'd asked me to kill him earlier in the morning. For a split second I wondered if Gabriel had been the one to train Vanessa. How hard had it been for her to discuss that execution order this morning?

Liam pulled his official memory pad from thin air and distracted me with the reporting process. We uploaded the data from our implants that recorded heart rate and psi activity as well as other key stats. Then we walked through the incident with the holo recorder going. It was hard to go back and record the tragedy in the front barnyard, but I managed not to throw up as we recorded the body so I counted it as a win. By the time Liam and I were done with our report, my hands were shaking as much out of hunger as spent nerves.

"Come on," my partner said as I sat down heavily on the back step of the farmhouse and put my pounding head in one hand. "Let's go get some food before you pass out on me."

I didn't have the strength to argue with him, so I just nodded and let him pull me tight against his body for the teleport. I appreciated how much smoother his jump was when we were in closer contact, even if it undermined my determination not to be intimate with my OW partner.

Manners dictated that teleporting inside a building that wasn't your personal domicile, or the home of one of your passengers, was rude. The only exceptions were genuine emergencies. I guess Liam decided today counted as a crisis, because the next thing I knew we were standing next to our usual table in the mess hall. With one hand, Liam pulled out a chair and with the other he very firmly but gently pushed me into it.

"I'll get you something to eat. Just sit here a minute," he said, his voice holding that note of quiet command he was starting to perfect on our OW runs. I was pretty sure he'd have to catch me if I tried to get up, so I simply nodded again and let him gather two trays for us.

I'm not even sure what Liam set in front of me, but I fell upon it like I hadn't eaten in days. I couldn't remember ever feeling so ravenous. The food was gone before I really even had a chance to taste it. Even so, I felt much steadier afterwards. With a sigh, I leaned back and sipped at the large glass of water Liam had put next to my plate.

"Feel better?" he asked, tilting his head at me. He was still eating his meal at a more civilized pace.

I started to nod, then thought better of it. "I'm not about to faint anymore," I allowed. "Thanks."

Liam grinned, revealing a touch of the flirtatious boy I'd met almost three years ago. Had it really been that long since the flood? So much had changed since then. It felt like so much longer.

"What are partners for?" he asked with a wink.

Once, I would have blushed at his humor; now, it made my chest tighten. Staring at my empty plate, I tried not to think about everything that had happened that morning. Of course, my brain instantly started obsessing over every detail.

"Hey." Liam put a hand on my knee and I glanced up at him. I'm not sure what kind of pain was in my eyes but, I saw the look of concern on his face as he met my gaze. "Why don't you go take a nap or read a book for a while? Something nice and brainless. You've had a few good shocks today and I think you need a bit of a rest."

I tapped my implant for the time. "My Ceramics class is in fifteen minutes. I always feel better in the studio," I said, pushing my hair back from my face. "If you don't mind giving me a ride back to my room, I even have enough time to get changed into something that isn't covered in sweat and ash."

"Class isn't exactly how I like to unwind, but you do seem

more grounded after mucking about in the mud," he admitted. Then his voice turned soft. "And you never have to ask for a ride, you know. Just tell me where you want to go and I'll get you there."

I glanced up at him at that last statement, expecting to see a bit of leftover hope for our romantic involvement. Instead, I saw something raw and painfully close to what I'd seen in my father's face too many times. In my determination not to date Gabriel's descendant, what had I done to the free-spirited young man James and I had found so charming? I ducked away from his wounded gaze and picked up my empty tray.

"Don't worry about it," I muttered. "I'll walk."

To my surprise, Liam let me go without protest.

Chapter 28

A Diplomat's Choice

Despite taking the time to walk back to my dormitory and change, I made it to class on time. Even so, the clay didn't soothe me the way it usually did. I couldn't help going over what happened that morning.

"Gabriel's too strong to be as unstable as he is."

Vanessa's voice rang in my head. I pushed that thought away only to be confronted with the bloody wreck the Terrans made of that innocent farmer in Riland. I heard the step-daughter's strangled cries; smelled the burn of human flesh. The smoking remains of the avatars I'd destroyed flashed vividly in my mind. Every time I got lost in the clay, I found myself muttering little phrases to myself that pulled me back into the swirling pit of anxiety and fear.

"I'm talking about you and Gracie and everyone I care about." I found myself repeating James' words as I walked out of the studio feeling as exhausted and lost as I'd gone in. "If there's a war, you'll be on the front lines."

There was my real kernel of anxiety. My feet pulled me towards the mess hall feeling once again like I was half-starved, but my mind continued its swirling panic. For once, my biggest problem wasn't Gabriel. So the OW didn't care for my father. That almost wasn't news. Lillian was on the council and I'd known my sister's view on our father for years. And, although the execution order had been initially shocking, I trusted Vanessa enough to take her word. As long as I wasn't willing to complete the order, my father was safe from the Overwatch. As Liam had said, all I had to do was nothing.

The Terrans, on the other hand, had come out of the clear, blue sky. What were they doing in the Provinces? I knew for a fact that James wouldn't have given up his avatar if he'd had another choice. So was this a recent political development or some kind of leap forward in tech? What would that mean for Riland and their anti-Awareness campaign? Had I just witnessed the first steps towards a war between the Terrans and the Provinces?

All of my tangled thoughts congealed into a sick knot in my stomach. What if the reason James was staying away wasn't that he was trying to salvage the diplomatic situation at all. Maybe he was too afraid that Liam would pick up on the plans he'd been briefed on. Perhaps that was why he hadn't been able to talk about everything during our early morning meeting. He could tell us about Riland's threatening behavior, but he would have been honor-bound to keep any Terran plots away from the Usuriels. My throat felt like it was going to close as I changed directions and ran to James' door.

"James Galling! I need to talk to you!" I tapped my implant and all but shouted his name as I rounded the corner to his hall.

"Gracie?" James' even voice was normally so reassuring through my implant. This time however, my whole body tensed at the sound. "What's wrong?"

"Are you in your room?" I asked, not waiting for an answer before pounding on the door.

"Take it easy, you'll take the thing off its track," James said as he palmed the door open from the inside. When he caught sight of my face, the irritation melted away into concern. "What happened? Is Liam okay?"

"What? Oh, yeah he's fine." Aside from the fact that I've been crushing his heart into shards of glass, I thought, but I wasn't there about dating issues. "Listen, I really need to talk to you, but I don't think the hallway is a good place to have this discussion. Can I come in?"

"I'm kind of busy," he started, a tired look coming over his face as he glanced over his shoulder at the cluttered dormitory. Observing my expression again, his eyes softened. "But for you I can take a short break. Come on in."

"Thanks," I breathed and walked into the little space I'd occupied with Liam and James so many times. It had been months since I set foot in it, though, and the room felt both alien and familiar at once. I cast about for a place to sit, but stacks of notes, holo programs, and memory pads were everywhere. Even the bed looked completely covered. I wondered when he'd slept last because I had no idea where he'd find a place to lie down.

"What has you so upset?" James asked, turning to face me as the door hissed shut behind him.

I rubbed at my face and tried to get my thoughts in order. It had seemed so clear while walking outside in the fresh air. Now that I was here—facing the object of both my deepest affections and now my most terrifying fears—I found myself unable to formulate the words to explain anything coherently.

"Can I use your comm to hook up to the net for a moment?" I asked after a long pause. "I think it might be easier if I just show you."

"Uh, yeah, sure." James' brow wrinkled as he tapped his implant and said a command to bring the screen online.

Once he'd activated it, I took over the comm link and logged into the OW database. I knew I was in some murky territory with the Overwatch regulations, but I was too upset to care. I somehow doubted Vanessa would dismiss me for showing James a single still. With a few quick commands, I pulled up the picture I was looking for.

I turned just in time to watch all the color drain from James' face as the smoldering avatar filled the comm screen.

"What is that?" James asked, his eyes wide and his skin white as Angel's Foot spores. For a moment I thought he might be sick. I knew the feeling.

"You tell me." The level of anger in my own voice surprised me.

"I don't know," he said. Despite lacking any kind of telepathic ability, I was pretty sure he was telling the truth. "I promise, Gracie, I've never seen anything like this before."

"It looks an awful lot like an avatar to me," I said evenly, though the venom had died down at his bewildered response.

"I know it does," James agreed, stepping closer to the screen. "But that's not the way they're wired. Look, here and... here." He pointed to several severed connections that were exposed through the android's burned skin. "I've never seen an avatar put together like that. Those are where the safety releases are in the torso. If something overloads an avatar's circuits, that's where the breakers are that keep the feedback from getting to the flesh. I don't see any safeties on this thing. No Terran in their right mind would link up to an avatar without safeties."

"Sweet Fate," I breathed. "Do you mean to tell me that whoever was hooked up to this thing had no way to sever the connection when I blew it apart?"

"Not unless there's a different type of safety I don't see." James turned to stare at me, white showing around the edges of his faded-blue eyes. "Wait, you mean to tell me you did this? You're the reason it's torched to hell?"

"Yeah, that's all me." I wasn't sure how I felt about taking credit for this particular feat. The look on James' face was bordering horror and I suddenly couldn't meet his eye. I'd seen James look at me with a multitude of emotions; until now however, I'd never seen genuine fear. That look twisted something inside me and I found a touch of anger rising to cover the pain in my voice. "Listen, they weren't just minding their own business. You should have seen the mess they made of the poor Riland farmer they attacked."

"They?"

"There were two of them," I admitted. Maybe this had been a mistake. I was already sharing more information with James than I'd intended to. Even so, I needed to know exactly what I was dealing with. If these weren't Terran avatars, Fate knew what they were.

"Gracie, I know you're in some gray area in the Overwatch bylaws for bringing this to me," James said slowly. His beloved, familiar mortal face was extremely serious as he gripped my arm. "But I want you to know that you've done the right thing. If we can head off a diplomatic incident over this, we might still avert all-out war. Even so, I can't help unless you tell me everything."

There were deep shadows under his eyes and he looked a shade on the thin side for his frame. James always put off eating when he was stressed. Despite this, his blue gaze was as honest and earnest as it had always been. I'd been truthful when I told my father that James was the most ethical person I knew. He might omit some things if he'd promised not to tell, but he wouldn't outright lie to me. At the very least, I was pretty sure he wouldn't be able to meet my eye while he did it.

"James," I said slowly. "You know I care about you. A lot. And in most things, I trust you completely. But for this, I need your word. I have to hear you promise me that you knew nothing about these... things." I gestured with disgust at the figure on the screen. "And that, to your knowledge, the Terrans aren't trying to invade Riland. Or any of the other Provinces for that matter."

He met my gaze steadily. "I swear to you I have never seen one of those creations before. And allow me to completely reassure you that the last time I talked with Eva and the other Council members, they were as terrified of the concept of war as I am. By that I mean we are completely and utterly committed to a diplomatic relationship with the Provinces. War is the last thing any of us wants."

"Okay," I said slowly, searching his face for any sign of duplicity or deception. There was none. "I believe you. I'll tell you what I know."

James cleared off a space for the two of us to sit on his bed. I perched on the edge of the mattress beside him and let everything spill out into the quiet of his dorm room. It said something about how much the strange androids in Riland had upset me that I completely skipped over Vanessa's revelation about my father that morning. Instead, I jumped right into the OW assignment and described what had happened once Liam and I teleported in. I watched as James' face went from concerned to grim as I explained the farmer, his terrified wife and daughter, my handling of the two threatening androids, and the reactions of my superiors.

"Sweet Fate," James breathed when I was done. I'd thought he was pale earlier, but now he was downright green. "This is an extremely dangerous situation. I have to go to Eva with this."

My chest froze. If he talked to his people about the situation, Vanessa would undoubtedly find out I'd warned them. That sounded like a dismissible offense to me. My body tensed in fear at the thought of being fired from the OW. Then, in the wake of that thought came another. If it averted a war, wasn't that worth losing my place at Overwatch? What was one job to thousands of lives? I took a deep breath and nodded.

"I think I'd better tell Vanessa I had this conversation with you," I said slowly. "But I do understand. You need to do what you can to keep the peace."

"Thank you, Gracie," James said, his face beginning to get a little color back. "You have no idea how grateful I am that you trust me enough to tell me this. Honestly, you may have just saved all of Terra Nova."

"As long as it saves you, I'll be content."

The words came out before I could really think about them. James blinked at me, mortal-blue eyes slightly startled at my honesty. After the day I'd had, though, there wasn't much filter left to screen out what I really thought. It wasn't a good time to bring my feelings out into the open, but then, it never seemed to be a good time for James and me.

"Oh, Gracie," James breathed, taking my jaw in his hands and tilting my face up to his. "You wild, beautiful angel. What I wouldn't give to make things different. If it wouldn't start a Cybele-wide war, I'd run away with you and never look back."

I frowned, watching the longing and regret slide over his face with a growing sense of anxiety. This time, however, my fear had nothing to do with global politics.

"What are you talking about?" I asked. "Why do we have to run anywhere? We can be together right here. I know we're both busy at the moment, but it won't last forever. Things have to slow down eventually, right?"

James closed his eyes and leaned his forehead against mine. It was warm and safe and sent that little catch of desire trembling in my chest. Even so, I felt his resignation and had a dreadful feeling I wasn't going to like the way this conversation ended.

"I'm a diplomat, Gracie. I represent the Terran government here. Everything about me has to reflect their interests. Do you understand what that means?"

My stomach sank. "What, you aren't allowed to choose your own pairing? That's... that's downright Earth-level backwards."

He leaned back a little bit from me, fingers sliding down my arms to pull my hands into his. "I get some say in it, of course," he explained, "but you're not just anyone. You're an Usuriel; Gabriel's daughter. Marrying you would only add fuel to Riland's claim that the Terrans and Usuriels are dangerous and plotting together to take over. I love you. I hope you know that by now. But my own happiness isn't worth the destruction of everything we care about."

I closed my eyes and suddenly felt a surge of self-recrimination for what I'd been doing to Liam for weeks. Knowing that James felt the same way I did, but couldn't bring himself to be with me was... well, the word devastating comes to mind. Though, honestly, I'm not sure it does that all-encompassing, hollow-chested, body-numbing emotion justice.

"When exactly were you planning to tell me this?" I asked, thinking back on all the times he'd slipped his arm around my waist while we were walking from the mess hall to the dormitory. Dozens of held hands, smoldering glances, and brushed shoulders rose up like a protest in my chest. All those little touches and insinuations that added to the wonderful buoyancy of hope I'd carried around for him so long; they each felt like a betrayal and a lie.

"I had no idea how serious the political situation was until my internship," he said, sounding as miserable as I felt. I glanced up at him, feeling some small relief that our initial flirtations at Angelus Quietum hadn't been completely and utterly doomed from the start. "And even after that, I kept hoping the Riland crisis would blow over and we'd be able to pick things up where we left off." He shook his head, his features looking drawn and much older than the two decades I knew he laid claim to. "But it's only gotten worse, not better. After what you just showed me, it will take an honest miracle to keep the peace. Even if we can manage it, I'm not going to have time for a relationship in the foreseeable future. Your illustrious parentage aside, I couldn't ask you to wait on me while I sort this out. It could be a lifetime's work."

"If you asked me to, I would," I muttered, fighting like hell not to let James see me cry.

"No, dear heart, I couldn't." His eyes were dry but still incredibly sad. He touched my cheek. "A third-gen Usuriel willing to wait on me. Sweet Fate, you are so beautiful. I don't know what I did to deserve your affection, but it truly is the greatest honor anyone's ever given me."

"Then let's do it," I whispered. "Let's run away. Terra Nova, the Provinces, and the Family will figure things out on their own. I don't care about any of them anymore. Just take me far, far away from here. I'll be perfectly happy as long as I'm with you."

Heartbreak filled his gaze as he shook his head.

"I'm so sorry, Gracie." He said my name as if invoking it might keep me a little closer. I closed my eyes, pulling away from the only man I'd never been conflicted about loving. It killed something inside me to do it, but I couldn't let him comfort me after he'd just broken my heart.

"You have to tell your people about the Riland attack," I said quickly, standing and brushing away tears that stubbornly refused to stay in my eyes.

"Yes, I should probably do that as quickly as possible," he agreed, coming to his feet and looking at me as if he'd give just about anything to take me in his arms. Instead, he clenched his fists by his side and watched me with tortured eyes.

I tapped the comm screen to log myself out of the Overwatch database. Vanessa might forgive my good intentions in telling James about this incident, but she most certainly wouldn't understand if I left the whole database open for him to rifle through.

"Honestly, I do wish things were different," James sounded nearly as heartbroken as I felt.

"Don't," I hissed at him, feeling another wave of tears ready to flood up. "Just... don't."

"Gracie... please. Don't leave like this." He reached out to me. "Just because we can't be together doesn't mean I don't care about you. I want us to stay friends. You're an incredibly important person to me."

"As an informant on the Family?" I snapped, eyes blazing. A breath of fire crackled around my shoulders and I clamped down on them hard. It wouldn't do to send the whole building up in flames over a bad break up. "Oh yes, I'm incredibly important to you, Mister Diplomat."

It wasn't a fair or kind thing to say. He'd just admitted that he loved me and I could see my own torment reflected in his face. Still, he'd just hurt me in a way I'd never experienced before and that wonderful Usuriel temper wanted desperately to hurt him back. His expression said I'd succeeded. Then his face closed down and I saw what the Riland delegation must see when he walked into the negotiation room. Pleasant, guarded, and extremely blank, James gave me a mortal equivalent that I would pit against the Usuriel blank face any day.

"I really should make that call," he said.

"Don't let me get in the way." I walked out the door.

Chapter 29

Grayson

I should have run to Liam. I should have gone to the strong, steady partner who loved me and had always been there when I needed someone to lean on. After all, he couldn't control the color of his hair and eyes any more than I could control the political climate in Riland.

Or, failing that, I should have run to Gabriel—the other man who, despite all our recent anguish, had always taken care of me when the rest of the world turned its back. For all his failings, I loved my dad and, as long as it wasn't with a knife in my hand, I knew I was always welcome at Angelus Quietum.

If my men weren't the ones I wanted to confide in, it wasn't as if I didn't have other options. Grandma Gloria or Leesil would have happily talked about relationship issues, even if I might not have been able to confide every part of my bad day to them. Hell, even Jillian would have lent a friendly and willing ear if I'd called upon her. Oh my, how I wish I had.

But after my excruciating conversation with James, I was

exceptionally aware of how poorly I'd used Liam. I couldn't go back to him right after James' rejection as if he were a consolation prize. All of my other objections to our relationship were still perfectly valid, I reminded myself. But, without James as a siphon for my affections, I knew it was only a matter of time before my OW partner wore me down. I'd been fighting a losing battle against our mutual attraction for weeks now, and I suddenly had a lot less reason to continue objecting. Besides, the longer we worked together, the more I saw Liam as himself and not some pale echo of my father's genome. Even so, I'd been talking myself out of his arms with such determination that it felt wrong to go searching for comfort in them now.

As for my father, Vanessa's deadly request sat between my shoulder blades like a wound I couldn't reach to staunch. How could I look him in the eye without seeing her monocular gaze and the orange tab of his execution order? He might not be able to read my mind, but Gabriel would know something was wrong. I'd lied to him by omission before, of course, but I somehow thought this might be different than my time travel. After all, even in my dreams, I'd only ever tried to save my father. Just thinking about what Vanessa wanted me to do made me feel so dirty I wanted to peel my skin off and burn it.

I suppose I should blame my solitary upbringing in Angelus Quietum for the fact that the women didn't even cross my mind. With James, Liam, and Gabriel crossed off my go-to list, I felt completely and utterly alone. Perhaps it was that the only person I'd had to rely upon for so long was my father, and the idea of running to another woman when I needed support just wasn't a natural one for me. Or perhaps I simply wasn't thinking straight and I let my heart overwhelm my sense. It wouldn't be the first or last time that happened.

So, instead of tapping my implant and asking for a shoulder to cry on, I wandered outside the dormitory feeling empty and extremely lost. I didn't even pick a direction, I just started walking. The air was cool enough to make my cheeks burn as I meandered between the towering pines on the outskirts of Landing University. I passed through Landing proper, the market still open and lit with rows of tiny lights while professors and their spouses wandered the stalls picking up fresh produce. I walked through the housing district, past the still-boarded up house on Cambria Street where I'd saved those two vamps from the house fire. It felt like that incident happened a lifetime ago to someone I hardly even knew anymore.

When I got past the edge of town, I looked up at the setting sun. It painted the woods in purples, pinks, and golds. With less than a thought, I pulled on my flames and rose above the treetops to get a better view. Outstretched before me was the slope of verdant forest surrounding Landing. Off to the west, the great peaks of snow-covered mountains tops reflected pink into the tiny glimmer that was Lake Angelus. Without giving it too much thought, I pulled on my power again and let the flames propel me towards the safety of home. Maybe, if I was lucky, Gabriel would be asleep when I got there.

Before I'd gone too far, however, my skipped dinner caught up with me. If I hadn't just had the most stressful day on the face of Cybele, it probably wouldn't have mattered. But I'd fought the equivalent of twenty men before noon. I was physically and mentally exhausted. Since I was way too keyed up to even consider sleep, my body decided that its other source of energy needed replenishment. Hunger slammed into my gut so hard my stomach actually cramped in on itself.

It was that moment when the great mushroom top of Amourie's loomed into view. Its tiny lights sparkled in the twilight, and a few hover cars came over the horizon to land nearby. They had to serve more than just alcohol, I reasoned, as my empty gut sent me another pang.

I landed on the edge of the clearing and paused to look over my outfit. I hadn't changed since the ceramics studio, so despite the fashionable cut of my clothing, I had a few splashes of clay across my pants and boots. With a sigh, I ran my fingers through my hair and decided that I was there for the food, not casual sex. It shouldn't really matter how disheveled I looked. In a moment of vanity I glanced around at the mortals in their revealing outfits and thought that my third-gen features probably looked better in my studio clothes than they did in their clubbing best anyway.

Amourie wasn't at the door tonight, but a plain mortal

girl gave me a smile and a greeting as I walked up.

"Do you have a food menu?" I asked her, trying not to look completely desperate. "I mean, something other than mixed drinks?"

Her smile deepened and she nodded. "Of course. It isn't extensive, but we have a few things for people who want to enjoy dinner before dancing."

"Wonderful. Where do I put in an order?"

A few minutes later I was seated at one of the little tables eating a very belated evening meal. Fortunately, I'd been too busy to spend much of my new Overwatch salary, so I put my hand on the payment pad and let the tab ring up to whatever it liked.

As I ate, I watched the dancing crowd go from a few scattered individuals and couples to a roiling mass of people that undulated under the lights. I lost myself in their movements and interactions, making up little stories about them as they courted and drank. I remembered the last time I was here and how happy I'd been dancing with James and Liam for that first little while. I wondered if I'd ever be that optimistic and carefree again.

When the server came by, I ordered water and continued to sit, utterly lost in thought.

"Are you sure you don't want something stronger than this?"

The voice at my elbow was velvet and my OW instincts flashed to life, identifying the speaker as someone Aware. I pinpointed its source as a neatly dressed man in his mid-twenties. His blond hair was as clean and well-maintained as his outfit. He wasn't Family—that much was clear—but I still found the regular planes of his features pleasing. If I hadn't just had one of the worst days of my life, I probably would have been happy to make his acquaintance on a dance floor. He was holding the glass of water I'd ordered in one graceful hand. He settled the drink by my empty plates.

"I don't really care for alcohol," I said, a sour smile twisting my lips into something that wasn't happy. "But thank you just the same."

He nodded and shifted his weight to one hip, his hand coming to rest on one of the empty chairs behind me. His gaze drifted to the dance floor I'd been contemplating so solemnly. I narrowed my eyes at him and nodded to myself when I caught the tell-tale iridescent reflection of the lights in his eyes. I'd thought him a bit pale, and it only made sense; if he was Aware and not Family, he must be a vamp. Having successfully identified his nature, I lost interest and turned back to watching the crowd.

It probably said something about how confident I'd become in my own fire that I was willing to turn my back on a vampire while in a club alone. But after those avatar-like things this morning, I couldn't summon up the energy to be afraid of someone who didn't intend me immediate harm. In fact, as he stood and I sat, watching the dancers and lights flicker like the ephemeral mortals that they were, I found his company strangely comfortable. Just two immortal passengers on this strange ride.

"You look sad," he said after a long while.

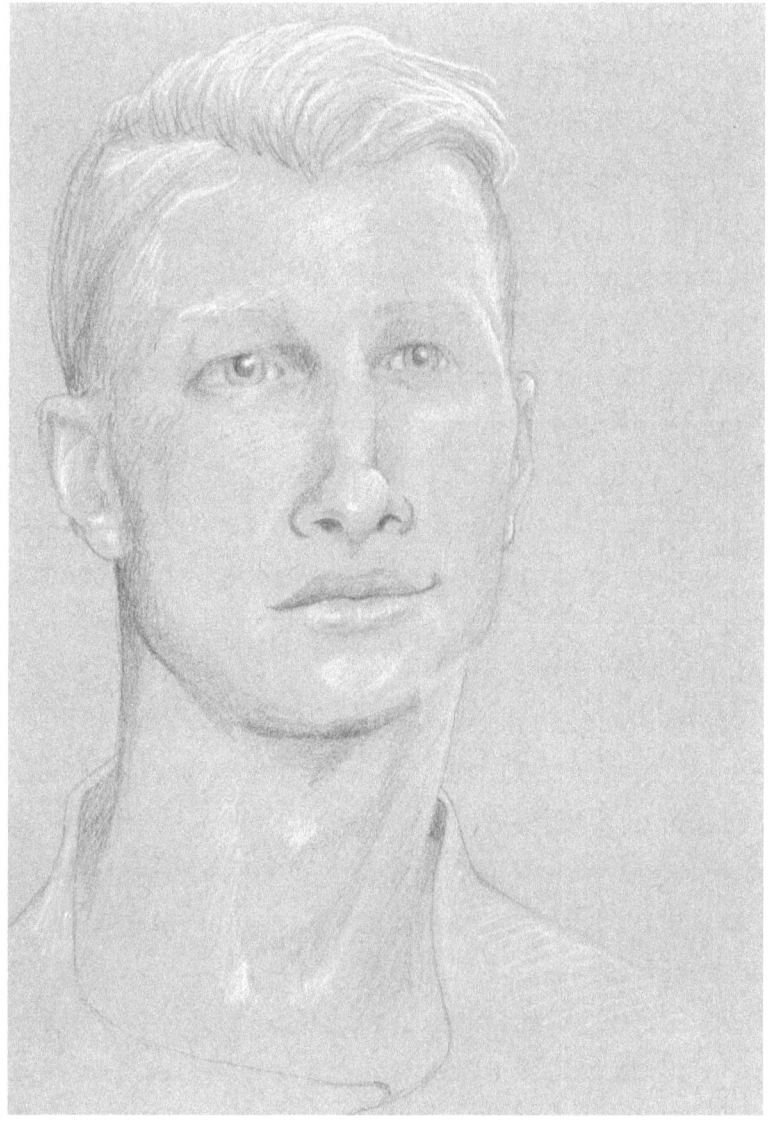

"Hmmmm," I replied, sipping my water. I didn't look up.

"Boy trouble?"

"Among other things," I admitted, still not turning to face him.

"I've had a bit of girl trouble lately, so I can relate. My name's Grayson. Mind if I join you?"

To my own surprise, I gestured at one of the empty chairs to my left. "Do what you want. I'm not much company right now."

He moved with animal grace to lounge more than sit in the chair next to me. From this angle, his eyes were more blue-green than gray. He pondered me intelligently.

"You're an elder child, aren't you." It was more of a statement than a question.

"Could be," I allowed, sipping my water again.

A small smile curled the edge of his lips. "I bet I could see a sunrise with you." His voice sounded somewhere between cautious and sensual.

"Well, you cut right to the chase, don't you?"

His shrug was not as fluid as my father's, but it was a fair approximation. "I like to be honest about my intentions. If you're not interested, just say so now. I won't be upset. It's not as if you even know me. But when I saw you sitting here, I had to at least ask."

I considered him thoughtfully. All day, I'd felt as if things were spinning out of my control. No one seemed to care about my thoughts or opinions. Starting with Vanessa and ending with James, I'd been bullied, attacked, guilted, and dismissed. Even Liam, my perfect partner, wanted more from me than I felt able to give. Now, this complete stranger wanted something from me, too. I should have been furious and on the verge of torching him on the spot.

Yet, I wasn't. Rather, I found his polite and tacit request intriguing. What he wanted required nothing but a few ounces of blood and, if we felt like it later, a little casual sex. It was blissfully unemotional and completely uncomplicated. Finally, something I could do that would satisfy those raging hormones Liam had been stoking all month while avoiding the emotional fallout. Better yet, I'd actually make someone happy doing it. It felt like it had been quite a while since someone seemed genuinely pleased about who and what I was. What sealed it though, was how undemanding he was about it. For the first time that day, I felt like I had a real choice and that my decision would be respected.

"I'm untasted," I warned him. "There's always a risk you'd have a bad reaction."

His smile deepened and I saw a flash of sharper teeth. "Oh, I've dated a few Usuriels. I've never met one that didn't agree with me."

I gave an assessing thought to my own physical state. I was much more solid after my meal. It shouldn't be a problem to donate a few swallows of blood. For a high-level Usuriel, that was usually all it took to induce the change for a vampire, at least according to my Awareness Theory book. "Okay. So... I don't think you want to do this here."

"No," he agreed and glided to his feet. I admired the sleek way his torso was put together. He had some very clean, strong lines under that tunic. I was looking forward to getting him out of it. The lack of emotional complexity to that desire was utterly freeing. I slipped my hand into his cool one and let him pull me to my feet.

"Oh," I added conversationally, "before we go anywhere secluded you should probably know I'm a third-gen firebird. If you try anything... unwelcome... I promise you won't see a sunrise again." I summoned a little line of flame to curl around my shoulders to illustrate my point.

"Sweet Fate, you are magnificent," Grayson breathed, eyes alight as he looked down at me.

Despite myself, a genuine grin spread across my face. "You know, you might be just what I needed tonight."

His cold fingers found my jaw and I clenched down on my flames to keep another lick of fire from catching in my hair. My eyes must have been incandescent because the look he gave me was pure hunger.

"Amourie has a few rooms in the back," he managed, clearly having a hard time speaking past his own desire.

Grayson wasn't all that tall. I didn't even have to stand on tip-toe to catch his mouth with my own. His lips were strangely cool, yet pleasingly soft. He seemed too startled to respond for a moment; then his hands cupped my face as he parted my lips with his tongue. My heart didn't skip a beat the way it had with Liam or James, but my body certainly didn't mind Grayson's touch.

"Come on," he gasped, pulling away from me and grabbing my hand before charging off towards the right-hand side of the crowd. I let him pull me in his wake, my body relaxed and ever so slightly numb. For the first time that day, I didn't feel as if I were fighting with the fear and anxiety inside my head. It was such an unexpected and welcome relief. I didn't question it. I just let Grayson lead me to a small, cozy little alcove full of plush couches and was grateful that I no longer felt conflicted or alone.

The tiny room off the main mushroom dome was so low-ceilinged it was a good thing neither of us were very tall. The inside was strung with tiny blue lights that washed out Grayson's pale hair and eyes into something ethereal. He looked quite beautiful as he glanced back at me shyly. Now that we'd reached the privacy of the alcove, he seemed afraid I might be less inclined to go through with things.

He shouldn't have worried. After the emotional and sexual confusion of James and Liam for over a year, my body was screaming at me for denying its needs. Now that I'd decided Grayson was a safe outlet for those desires, I wasn't going anywhere until I'd satisfied both of our hungers.

I advanced on the vampire with single-minded intensity, sliding one hand into the opening of his shirt while I pulled his head down for another kiss with the other. I wondered if he was unused to his 'prey' being so predatory. Then again, Usuriels weren't known for playing coy. If he'd dated a few of us, he probably knew we weren't too shy.

"You haven't even told me your name," he gasped as I undid the buttons of his tunic and pulled it over his pale shoulders. They were as muscular and strong as I'd hoped under the fabric. I explored them with my mouth. Though the heat of the club had me sweating, Grayson remained cool to the touch. Despite the number of unpleasant encounters I'd had with vamps through the OW recently, I wasn't bothered by his nature. I was as Family as it was possible to be. Who was I to judge another individual of Awareness?

"It's Gracie," I told him, putting a hand to his chest and pushing him onto the overstuffed couch. He raised an eyebrow at me, as if he were surprised at my strength, but he obediently lay back into the pillows adorning the plush surface. I allowed myself a smug smile as I admired the fine angles of his chest and stomach stretched out across the cushions like an invitation. Then my gaze made its way up to his face. There was something beyond sexual desire in his eyes.

I'd known, of course, that vampires got sex and food kind of mixed up. Because all of their primal needs blended into one, they could be easily overwhelmed by its intensity. Or at least, so said the Awareness Theory textbook and OW manuals. I'd never experienced the real thing until now.

Need. For him this wasn't a relaxed, optional exercise. This was a life and death physical requirement. I saw it in the way his eyes flashed and his shoulders tensed, as if he were restraining himself from overpowering me and taking what his body was begging for. Maybe there was a little of my father's lack of self-preservation in my head, too, because that look nearly undid me.

With a quick, easy movement I tossed my loose studio shirt onto the floor, leaving me in a form-fitting camisole that exposed my neck and arms. My body flowed onto the edge of the couch where I leaned over Grayson's waist and let my hair tumble away from my long, unblemished neck.

Between my hip and my hand, tension vibrated through his body as he looked up at me. He was breathing hard as if he were having a really difficult time focusing on anything but the pulse under my skin. His tongue crept out and wet his pale lips.

"Well," I prompted, running a hand through my hair to get it fully out of the way. My wavy strands liked to cling to everything, but I managed to get most of them onto one side so the other one would be clear for his convenience. "Isn't this what you wanted?"

He nodded quickly, eyes on the verge of wild, but still clearly holding himself in check. "You are going to be a very heady drink," he whispered, his voice obviously not completely under control. "I'm going to be pretty helpless for a while afterward."

I raised an eyebrow, startled to realize he was concerned about his own safety rather than mine. It made sense, though. I knew Usuriel blood was more of a drug than a meal to a vampire, especially an Usuriel of my generation.

However, I hadn't thought about the fact that he might be in an altered enough state to be vulnerable after the bite.

"You're the one who's done this before," I said with a shrug. "What are you expecting?"

"With Amourie, I'm usually only out for a half-hour or so. But she's a ninth-gen. If you're a third... well, I might be unconscious for quite a while."

I considered that somberly. "It makes sense that my blood would be stronger than hers."

"You don't have to stay if you don't want to," he said, his gaze flickering up to my neck as if he couldn't quite help himself. Even so, his voice was steadier. "But... I'd rather if you didn't leave me completely alone. The staff here knows me. If you're uncomfortable staying or need anything, just let them know, okay?"

I frowned at him. "I thought you asked me to watch a sunrise with you. Isn't that how this all started?"

A tiny smile cracked the mask of hard control his face had fallen into. "Even if that means babysitting me until morning?"

"I accepted your offer, sir. One sunrise. No more, no less," I said matter-of-factly. "Though if you felt like entertaining a lonely and extremely sex-starved third-gen for a few hours somewhere in there, I wouldn't object."

His smile was genuine as he reached out to caress my cheek with his fingertips. I let my eyes roll shut and shivered under the chill of his touch. "And you said *I* was what *you* needed tonight," he murmured. "You have no idea how much I need this right now."

"Let's do it then," I breathed, leaning into his hand.

Grayson didn't need another invitation. With the grace of his kind, his body rolled upwards into a sitting position, both hands coming up to cup my face. I leaned back as he came forward until the two of us were eye-to-eye. The lights bled his skin blue and white as his intense gaze drank in the planes of my face. Then, with a movement too fast to see, he tilted my head to the right and sank fang deep into the bend of my neck.

There was a shock of pain, then a blossom of pleasure that ran down my body more effectively than any kiss. I hadn't expected that part, though I suppose I should have. I gave a small, involuntary sound, my fingers digging into his bare chest as he took a long swallow. I suddenly understood why someone would keep coming back for this.

Grayson shattered the moment, recoiling away from me as if he'd been burned. Breath hissed through his teeth as his head bowed and his hands clutched at my shoulders.

My body still rang with the pleasure of his bite, but with a blink or two my head cleared and my desire became concern.

"Hey, you alright?" I asked, giving his shoulder a gentler squeeze.

His skin, which had been so cool moments before, was now burning hot to the touch. For a few heartbeats, I don't think he had the strength to lift his head to look at me. When he finally did, the fear and agony in his face etched themselves into my brain much the same way that dead farmer's had earlier in the morning.

He only held my gaze for a few brief seconds before his neck bowed and his whole body tensed. The cry he gave voice to is something I've heard over and over again in so many nightmares—high, breathless, and helpless. His fingers would leave bruises on my shoulders, I was certain, but I didn't twist away from his grasp. Instead, I tried to steady him as best I could, my hands moving gently against his sides to draw his attention away from the pain and back to me.

"Breathe through it," I told him, knowing enough from my Overwatch training to realize he'd pass out if he didn't stop hyperventilating. Well, a mortal or Usuriel would. I wasn't so sure about a vamp. The scalding fever he'd developed made me think his body might be working more like a mortal's at the moment. "Is this something that's happened before? Or is something wrong?"

His reply was to double and bring up the blood he'd just swallowed as a black splash across the pillows beside me. I did appreciate the fact that he'd turned his head so it didn't hit me. I rolled to his side so I'd be out of the way if he managed to bring anything else up, but I don't think he'd fed recently enough to do so. He spent a decent amount of time attempting to find something else to purge from his stomach, but only succeeded in bringing up empty air. When he could finally draw a decent breath again, he was shaking so badly his teeth were chattering. I'd slid an arm around his waist and I'm pretty sure that by the end of that first bout, it was the only thing keeping him upright.

"I'm going to go get Amourie," I told him, trying to ease away from the death grip he had on my shoulder. "I don't think this is how it's supposed to work."

"No, no, I... think it's passing..." he didn't sound much better to me and his fingers on my shoulder were still bruising. I glanced at his face. His once-porcelain skin was now so flushed he looked nearly purple in the blue lights. Even so, he did seem to be catching his breath. Perhaps things were starting to settle down for him, I decided when the shaking subsided. In any case, he was able to shift his weight away from me and lay down across the half of the pillows that weren't sprayed with my blood.

"Is there anything I can do?" I asked, leaning back into the empty space beside him, my body curling protectively between him and the open doorway. Call me paranoid, but after the day I'd had it felt safer to be between Grayson and anyone that could possibly disturb us, especially with him in such a helpless state. I was starting to understand why he hadn't wanted to be left alone.

He shook his head, eyes closed tight and body tensing with pain again. "I've never had a ride where it didn't knock me out for the change," he ground out, teeth clenching as his hand found my arm and began to squeeze. "I'm sure that's why it hurts... so damn much. I've heard of such a thing but never thought... I'd experience it. Bloody hell, it's almost worse than coming down."

"Sorry," I said contritely, though I did feel better about the situation now that he'd explained it. I knew reverting back to a vampire state was painful, but I'd always read that the transition into a more mortal condition was actually euphoric. Most texts had described it as the equivalent of an extremely powerful high, though the type and intensity of it varied greatly depending upon the individuals involved. "I guess my blood doesn't have mind-altering effects," I said, putting a hand over his on my arm. "That's a warning I'll have to give next time."

He glanced up at me with eyes so dilated they looked black. His breathing was getting faster again and his other hand had crept up to press against the slim taper of his waist. Clearly his stomach was bothering him again.

He opened his mouth as if to say something but at that precise moment something changed because his body twisted violently and I felt his fingertips lengthen into the deadly claws his kind could summon. They dug into my flesh as whatever new torture my blood had visited upon him rode through his body unmercifully. His eyes were shut tight, his face a mask of pure agony, and I knew he hadn't meant to hurt me. His instincts just didn't know how to deal with this kind of threat and lashed out in the only way they could. Still, I knew my forearm would be bloody when I got it back from his grip.

"Are you sure this is just a reversion?" I asked as he

curled around the hand on his gut, the entirety of his body a quivering knot. He'd rolled towards me, letting go of my arm in favor of the front of my shirt. I appreciated the reprieve from his claws, but from this close his skin was so hot it almost burned my hand. I pushed his hair back to peer into his face. When it became clear he couldn't answer me, I frowned and tapped my implant.

"Amourie Usuriel?" I called. "It's Gracie Usuriel. You remember, Gabriel's youngest? Can you spare a moment?"

"Gracie?" Amourie purred through the implant, her voice velvet even through the technology. "I am a touch busy."

I sighed. "Are you at your club?"

"Yes," she sounded a bit put out. Great. I was about to make her mood even better.

"Well, so am I," I said, "and I think you'd better come to the back. Second alcove on the left. One of your regulars isn't doing so well."

"I see," her voice seemed less pissed and a little more thoughtful. There was a long pause, as if she were sending a spare thought in my direction. "Sweet Fate, Gracie, what's going on down there?"

"I think you might want to come and see for yourself," I replied, looking down at Grayson's whimpering form. "I think you may know this vampire... personally. Calls himself Grayson?"

She swore at that one, but as I'd suspected, she materialized in the room within moments.

My great-grandniece was as ethereally beautiful as I remembered her. The blue light in the room washed out her skin to a pure white while darkening her lips and eyes into shapely suggestions of sensuality. The look of pure fury on her face when she saw the vampire curled up in my arms was enough to convince me that they'd been more than casual lovers. Fucking Fate, I thought this day couldn't get any worse.

"What have you done?" she gasped, sounding more angry than concerned as she strode over and put a hand on Grayson's shoulder.

He flashed pain-dark eyes in her direction and managed to whisper what I thought was an apology. It was cut off by another wave of pain that made him curl more tightly around the hand clutching at his waist.

"Fate's bloody balls." Amourie could apparently swear quite creatively. "Untasted third-gens? Are you actually insane? This isn't exactly the way to win me back, you idiot. This is how vamps get hurt!"

I groaned inwardly. Perhaps calling Amourie hadn't been the smartest course of action. I somehow doubted her yelling and emotional warfare would be helpful at the moment. If I'd been a telepath and able to summon her without speaking aloud, I would have called for Grandma Gloria then and there.

"Gonna be sick again." Grayson's voice was so quiet I almost didn't hear him. When I figured out what he'd said, I quickly climbed to my knees and helped him struggle back to a kneeling position. Amourie glared at us darkly, but she did wrap an arm around his waist to help steady him.

I'd expected him to simply dry heave again or perhaps bring up some bile. I was completely unprepared for the huge wave of blood that poured out over the entire couch. When I say wave, I mean it. I'd never seen so much blood in my life; not even on the farm in Riland that morning. And it didn't stop at one heave, either. Grayson clung to me and Amourie as he brought up fountains of black, viscous fluid that soaked the cushions under my knees and spilled onto the floor. Every time I thought it was over, he'd tense again and bring up more. How he possibly had that much blood in his body, let alone in his stomach, was beyond me.

I met Amourie's eye above Grayson's trembling back. Things were officially out of the realm of explainably bad. This wasn't just an odd reaction, this was wrong. If we didn't get him help fast, I was pretty sure Grayson was in real trouble.

"How much did he take?" Amourie asked, her expression no longer angry or jealous. Instead, her eyes were wide and her mouth grimly flat.

"Not that much," I said with a shake of my head. "Not even close."

"I didn't think so," she murmured, rubbing his shoulder absently. "Alright, love, I'm calling Gloria. You just try to take a deep breath for me, okay?"

Grayson nodded weakly, resting his head against

Amourie's shoulder while he took advantage of a slight respite.

I suspect Amourie conveyed the urgency of the situation to our ancestress because it wasn't long before a golden glow lit the room and a very pregnant Matriarch materialized with a rush of psi wind.

I, for one, was very glad she'd responded quickly, because Grayson was going downhill fast. He'd stopped bringing up blood, but now he'd begun to writhe and make strangled cries in Amourie's arms. She held him looking distraught herself, her slim hands splattered in dark droplets of blood as she struggled to keep the convulsing vampire in her arms.

"What happened?" Gloria said, taking control of the situation instantly. She raised an eyebrow at the pale blue room and turned to me. "Some better lighting, if you please, Gracie."

I nodded quickly, relieved to have something useful to do. With less than a thought, I summoned a small globe of fire to hover in the far corner.

Instantly, color blossomed across the room and the amount of red was truly disturbing. Gloria's eyes got very wide as she took in the scene, one hand rising protectively to the round curve of her unborn child. I could almost see her putting things together as her gaze flicked from the bite on my neck, to the cascade of bloodstains across the furniture and floor, before finally coming to rest on Grayson's struggling form.

"I... didn't mean for this to happen," I breathed and found

tears very close to the surface. I fought them down, knowing this was not a useful response to the situation. There would be plenty of time for me to have a complete and total meltdown later, I promised myself, but right now Grayson had to take precedence over my emotional needs.

"No, of course you didn't, sweetheart." Gloria's face softened and she put a hand on my shoulder. "But I need to know exactly what you did so that I can help your friend. Okay?"

I blinked rapidly to forestall any more tears. "I don't think we did anything unusual. Just some kissing and—" I indicated my neck. "Really, he barely took more than a swallow. Certainly not—" I gestured to the floor and the vast amount of blood that covered it.

"So it was just you, not you and Amourie?" Gloria asked, glancing over at the ninth-gen.

The club owner looked like she was fighting down tears as well, her big brown eyes luminous in the firelight. She shook her head, red curls tumbling about her shoulders as she looked down at the man in her arms. He'd clearly gone past coherence, because he'd sunk claws deeply into her upper arm in his attempt to twist away from the pain. She didn't seem to care.

"Grayson's never had this kind of reaction to my blood," she said, velvet voice nearly drowned out by his involuntary cries.

"Let me see him," Gloria said, gliding to their side.

Amourie glanced up as she came, eyes dark with fear. I think she knew, even then, what the end of this was going to be.

Gloria's left hand found Grayson's jaw while her right settled on his chest. To my surprise, he was lucid enough to focus on her face as she leaned over him.

"Please." His voice shook and strained with agony, but even so I could hear it from where I still knelt on the other side of the couch. "Just... make it... stop..."

Slowly, Gloria nodded and gently pulled up one sleeve. "If you want the pain to stop, child, I need you to drink. I promise, afterwards you won't feel anything."

Amourie took a gasping breath, tears now rolling unashamedly down her face; those beautiful features twisted into a mask of grief. My chest clenched hard and I shifted closer, hoping I was misunderstanding exactly what was going on.

Grayson's eyes flickered between Gloria and Amourie. Then his back arched in another spasm and this time his scream was ear-shattering. Amourie's sob was a heartbreaking counterpoint. She held his twisting body with a strength that only an Usuriel could have hidden in that petite figure.

Finally, after what felt like a very long time, the vampire calmed again. He was breathing hard and his lips were as pale as his white skin.

"Drink, child," Gloria said again. She'd made a small cut on her wrist, extending it to Grayson. "We won't leave you alone. We'll be right here."

"Amourie?" Grayson's voice sounded like a lost child, and I closed my eyes against the emotional pain in it. It was somehow worse than the physical pain he'd been in all night.

She nodded quickly, brushing away her tears on her shoulder since her hands were full with him. "It's okay, love," she said, voice thick with crying. "I'll be right here when you wake up."

He didn't need to be told again. The smell of blood had to be the deepest instinct his brain had. Even so incredibly sick, he latched on to Gloria's wrist with swift efficiency.

Like my blood, it only took one swallow before his body reacted. With a gasp, he went rigid again, body convulsing helplessly. This time, however, his eyes rolled back and his hand fell limply from Amourie's arm. It was quickly clear that he was unconscious.

"Will it work?" Amourie asked quietly, glancing up at the Matriarch. A tiny flame of hope burned in her eyes as she scanned my grandmother's face.

"We'll know in a moment," Grandma replied, laying her hand on Grayson's blood-speckled chest again. "My blood is stronger than Gracie's, but it may only add to the effects. I don't know if it can cancel them out."

"Come on, Gray," Amourie breathed. "Fight for me."

The three of us watched Grayson closely. He'd quieted a bit but those awful, spine-bending convulsions hadn't stopped, it just seemed he no longer felt them. I found my gaze darting between the desperately ill vampire and my grandmother's watchful presence. After a while, Gloria's hand on his chest lit up with a touch of psi again and her expression went distant. I knew she was monitoring the effects of our blood on Grayson's struggling body. When she finally looked up, her eyes were grim.

"I'm so sorry, Amourie," Gloria said softly, shaking her head. Then she put a hand on my great-grand niece's arm and lit it up with a little golden psi. The claw marks faded to naught. "He won't feel the rest of it, though. His suffering is over."

"Sweet Fate, what was he thinking?" Amourie sobbed quietly, holding Grayson close and pressing her cheek to his forehead. His body still seemed caught up in the effects of Gloria's blood; muscles twitching and convulsing in strange, unconscious patterns. However, his face was calm and his eyes were closed even as his spine arched in another of those dreadful shocks. Gloria lent a hand in keeping him in Amourie's arms, supporting his shoulders and neck with one arm. Her other hand found and squeezed the club owner's hand.

"I've never seen anything like it, Amourie. He and Gracie couldn't have known. We've always warned the vampires that Usuriel blood is unpredictable, but up until this point it's never been fatal. There was no reason for them to think this would happen," Gloria said gently. Her bright blue eyes flashed in my direction again and I swallowed hard.

"I'm sorry," I said before I could think too hard about it, "but did you just say this is fatal? You mean, he's going to die from this... from me? There's nothing else you can do for him?"

Grandmother and Amourie looked up at me with so much pain and regret. Gloria looked like she wished more than anything she didn't have to tell me the truth. Amourie's gaze held loathing on top of the heartbreak. I felt as if someone had just sucked all the air out of the room.

"Gracie," Gloria said softly, "this isn't your fault. We've known for a while your gifts are extremely unique, but there's never been an indication that it might cause this kind of reaction. There was no way of knowing without... well... this..." She indicated Grayson's helpless form.

I watched in horror, as the vampire's convulsions got worse. Amourie and Grandma Gloria were having a harder time holding on to him. And now strange, black streaks formed around his mouth and bled down along the veins in his jaw and neck. They moved just slowly enough that I couldn't quite see them move, but when I looked away and looked back they were suddenly several centimeters longer.

"No," I hissed through clenched teeth, backing against the wall and pressing myself to its oddly-textured surface. The room was too small and too hot and I was genuinely about to follow Grayson's lead and be violently sick. "This... can't be happening!" I shook my head and closed my eyes, pressing my hands to my face to further block out what I didn't want to be true. When I opened them again, however, the black lines had found their way down to Grayson's chest and were heading rapidly for his heart. "Fuck. Fuck fuck fuck fuckfuckfuckfuckfuck...."

"Gracie, take a breath." Gloria sounded concerned as she reached out to me. "Come here, child. It's all right. You didn't mean to do this. Do you want me to send you home?"

I shook my head, knowing that I couldn't leave until everything was over. I couldn't bring myself to say "until Grayson died" even in my own head. Even so, I knew that if I'd caused it I couldn't live with myself if I just walked away. Trying not to think too much about it, I edged closer to my grandmother. She laid a hand on my forearm and, with a single pulse of warmth, the scratches Grayson had left across it disappeared.

"Amourie," I whispered, "I... am so sorry..."

"Don't!" she hissed, dark eyes bright with anger and tears. "Apologize to him if you want. Maybe he'll forgive you in the afterlife. But I don't think I ever will!"

If it hadn't been for Gloria's gentle hand on my back, I think I would have turned and run despite the guilt.

"If it means anything to either of you." Gloria's voice was so soft and melodious. She almost sang the words. "This could very easily have happened to me almost five hundred years ago."

Amourie and I glanced at each other, and then back at the Matriarch. Seeing that she had our attention, Gloria nodded and continued. "It's true. The first time D'nay took my blood, I was convinced I'd killed him. Truthfully, I'd given no thought to the fact that my blood might be a bit stronger than a mortal's. I didn't even warn him about my nature. I just flashed some pretty blue eyes and let him do what came naturally. It was absolute blind chance that the combination of our chemistry happened to work out in his favor. Almost four hundred and fifty years of marriage and eighteen generations of Usuriels, all because when I took the chance Gracie did tonight, Fate smiled instead of turning Her back."

I swallowed hard and brushed away a few stray tears. I'd always wondered how D'nay and Gloria met. The idea that they'd simply seen each other at a bar seemed so mundane for such an incredibly historic and powerful couple.

"Were you just curious about what being with a vampire would be like?" I asked, my annoying curious streak coming out before I could censor it. "Or was he just so handsome you couldn't resist?"

Gloria gave a small sound that might have been a chuckle, though she hid it well. It wasn't exactly the moment for mirth. "That might have been part of it," she admitted. "But at the time, I told myself it was all about the money. My brother and I had a bet, you see."

"You met Grandfather because you let him bite you to satisfy a wager?" Amourie sounded as scandalized as I was.

"We were all young and stupid once." Gloria couldn't hide the little smirk that crept across her face this time. "Though I was older than Gabriel is now, so I suppose I really should have known better. It all worked out pretty well in the end, though... for the most part, anyway."

A ragged gasp from Grayson drew our attention back to the dying man. Gloria's face lost all of its gentle reminiscent glow and suddenly her blue eyes looked so much like my father's I had to look away.

"What I was trying to say, though—" Gloria's voice was still gentle by my ear "—is that you shouldn't hate yourself for this, Gracie. It's in your nature; in your very DNA—both the attraction to what might hurt you, and the ability to destroy it without intending to. You couldn't help what you are any more than Grayson could help being drawn to it."

I glanced at the Matriarch, her face solemn as she looked down at Grayson's pale form. Where the black streaks had blazed a trail, now a strange glow bled downwards from his lips, into his jaw and down his neck. The black lines clustered densely around his heart and had spread out, down his torso and across his shoulders to flood over his arms. His brow knit together again and he made a small sound as another violent spasm hit. I wondered if Gloria was overestimating the power of her blood to keep him under because it seemed as if he were starting to feel the painful deterioration again.

"Sweet Fate, Gray," Amourie sniffed, her eyes on Grayson's face as his body relaxed again. With one hand, she pushed the hair away from his face before running fingertips along the edge of his brow. "Why didn't you wait for me? I always came back. I thought you knew that."

Grandmother made a small, soothing noise and put a hand on her descendant's arm, but Amourie shook her head as if unable to accept the Matriarch's comfort.

"As if a fling with Jillian could take the place of what we had," my beautiful cousin hissed and I could hear her anger still simmering despite the lower tone of her voice. Who she was more furious with—herself or her ex-lover—was probably unclear even to her. "Well, I guess you showed me, you fucking idiot. Way to give me a taste of my own capricious medicine." She paused, looking down at him. A small whimper came from deep in his throat, and I thought I saw him turn his head just the slightest bit towards Amourie's reassuring touch. She leaned in even closer, her face almost brushing his as she murmured in his ear. If I hadn't been less than a meter away, I wouldn't have heard her next words. I still wish I hadn't. "Well it's working. I'm jealous and scared, okay? I get it. Please just come around and tell me this was some kind of nasty joke. I'll never stray again, I swear it. Just pull through this for me and I'm all yours."

Despite my best efforts, silent tears were streaking down my face as I watched Amourie press her lips to Grayson's forehead.

"We all make mistakes and hurt the people we love," Gloria said gently, "whether we intend to or not. It's the downside to being so close to someone. We take them for granted and think they'll always be there when we get back. Unfortunately, that's sometimes not the case."

I would have thought more on her words, but the strange light crawling down those vicious lines in Grayson's skin had begun to grow into something quite distracting. Whatever they were, they seemed to be causing the vampire a lot of pain, because he was fighting the effects of Gloria's blood; tossing his head and twisting his shoulders as if trying to escape the agony eating him from the inside out. The light grew and grew, bleeding from his skin until it was so blinding I could no longer look directly at him without making my eyes burn and water. I put up a hand to shield my face even as he began to make desperate, ragged cries. They tore at the same place in my chest that James and Liam seemed determined to abuse. I shut my eyes tighter.

"No! No, please! Gray, I'm so sorry, love. I'm so sorry!" Amourie sobbed even as his screams reached a fever pitch.

Chapter 30

Honesty

Blinding light.

It exploded across the room like an enormous release of psi power. It rippled down my skin and lifted my hair like the wind of a teleport. I gasped, turning my face away and putting up my hands to protect my head as the pressure grew, pushing down on me with a crushing weight. It was all I could do to force air into my lungs through the thick, syrupy air.

As abruptly as it had begun, the power faded away. Even from behind my closed lids I could tell the room was once again dark. Complete, ringing silence met my searching ears. Frowning, I cautiously opened my eyes and moved my hands away from my face.

The room was so dark I couldn't make out anything but the shape of the arched doorway. I was still in the same little back room of Amourie's, from what I could tell. However, instead of the plush cushions and couches, square edges of boxes and crates stacked haphazardly about the little space resolved in the faint blue light from the hall.

"Grandmother?" I called into the empty room. "Amourie?"

There was no response.

I felt dizzy and disoriented, as if I'd just been on a really rough shuttle ride. Staggering slightly, I got up from the kneeling position I'd been in. Instead of an overstuffed sofa, I was perched on the edge of one of the wooden storage boxes that littered the room. I clung to its rough surface, trying to get my head to stop spinning and my heart rate back down to something reasonable. Panic rose in my gut, not improving my equilibrium.

"Amourie?" I called again, walking towards the door. The movement fortunately helped the blood get back to my brain because the world stopped tilting around me as I made it to the hall. I leaned against the oddly textured wall, my hands still shaking and the now-familiar numbness of emotional shock setting in rapidly. I tried to breathe deeply. Curling up in a ball and crying my eyes out wasn't going to solve anything.

The brassy beat of the club's main dance floor became much clearer in the hallway. Over it, I heard Amourie's characteristic croon. My mind spun even faster and the fear I'd been pushing down leaped wildly at the inside of my ribs. Sucking in air through my teeth, I focused on figuring out what was going on.

Had I passed out from the impact of whatever psi had gone off in the room earlier? That didn't make sense, since I'd still been kneeling when things came back into focus. Nor could I imagine my grandmother leaving me unconscious in the back of a club for any length of time—certainly not long enough to clean up the room and for Amourie to be willing to get back on stage.

Had I unintentionally traveled in time? Besides my little flame light, I hadn't called on my fire at all. However, Grayson's fatal overdose, or whatever I was going to call what happened to the unfortunate vampire, had been caused by my blood. Could it have somehow triggered a time-related event? I tapped my implant for the date and time. According to its internal software, a little over two hours had passed since I'd walked into the club.

"Confirm date and time with net sources," I told the chip with a frown. A little green light flickered in the corner of my left eye before displaying the word 'confirmed.'

By the time my brain had spun up to this point, I'd reached the main dome of the nightclub. The usual drinking and dancing crowd buzzed with an energy that set my already fried nerves to a jittery edge. I tried to keep the logical train of my thoughts on track, but I was quickly overwhelmed by the emotional toll of possibly the absolute worst day I'd ever had. By the time I'd made it over to the edge of the stage, my entire body was shaking.

Fortunately, Amourie's set must have been over because with a riot of sound and lights, her song ended. The crowd surged forward, swallowing me up with enthusiastic mortal bodies. Too numb to care, I let them jostle me this way and that. It only lasted a few moments before the crowd dispersed towards the bar and left me trembling next to the stage as Amourie leaped down.

I must have looked as bad as I felt, because my niece did a double-take when she glanced at my face. "Gracie? Is that you?" she asked, her expressive face pulled into a frown of concern. "What happened? Are you okay?"

"Where's Grayson?" I asked, trying to hide the tremor of my voice by glancing around. Maybe I'd just imagined the whole thing. The thought of going the way of Adora terrified me more than almost anything, but at least if I was crazy then it was possible I hadn't just unintentionally killed someone. Sweet Fate, how bad was it when I was rooting against my own mental stability?

"Who?" Amourie asked, a perfect eyebrow arching as her gaze flicked down my outfit. "Is that blood? Are you hurt? Should I call someone?"

"What?" I glanced down. I hadn't managed to stay out of Grayson's way as much as I'd thought. My hands and arms were covered in dark flecks of drying blood and my studio pants had ink-black stains on both knees. Now that I thought about it, I could feel the wet cloth clinging to my legs.

With a gasp, I wrapped both arms around my torso in an attempt to keep myself upright. It worked, though I couldn't stop the tears that rushed up.

"Hey now, little cousin, take a deep breath. Come on." Amourie took my shoulder gently but firmly and led me over to a quieter side of the room. There, she teleported a small glass filled with a clear liquid and wrapped my hand around it. "Here, this should take the edge off. One swallow."

I could smell the liquor and the only thing it reminded me of was throwing bottles off of a porch. I threw the glass violently away from myself, more than a thread of flame sliding along my shoulders. All that emotional energy wanted somewhere to go, and that tiny spark of anger was all it took to feel as if I was going to light up the entire club.

"I'm not my fucking father!" I hissed. "I don't need to be anesthetized! I need to figure out what the fuck is going on!"

Amourie looked startled, but she'd been running a club full of vampires and Usuriels long enough that her composure didn't break. "Okay, sweetie, relax. I meant no offense. Who were you asking about earlier?"

"Grayson," I said, forcing myself to close my fist on the flames. They relented under protest. However, my flair of temper left me a little more steady on my feet. I ran a hand through my hair and grimaced, realizing I'd probably just streaked it with blood. "The vampire. Your boyfriend... or ex-boyfriend maybe. You know, about your height, blond, nice shoulders."

"Never heard of him," Amourie said smoothly, a flirtatious smile sliding across her lips as she leaned into a sensual hip. "Though I might take an introduction if your description is accurate. I've always liked a man I could look in the eye. It makes things intimate."

"If this isn't his blood—" I looked down at my hands "— then whose is it?"

"Now you're starting to scare me," Amourie murmured. She got a distant look on her face, and I suspected she was mentally searching the club for anything out of place. I don't think she found anything because there was confusion in her eyes when she refocused them on me. "What happened to this Grayson vamp? Why is his blood all over you?"

"I... I'm not sure," I replied honestly, putting my face in my hands. My neck pulled a little painfully as I put my head down and I slid my fingers to the bend of my throat. Twin fang marks greeted me, and I swallowed hard. I'd been bitten tonight. That apparently hadn't been fantasy at the very least.

"Well, whatever happened, it doesn't seem to be in my club," Amourie said slowly, eyes narrowed at me. "So I don't think calling the watch is going to be helpful."

I nodded in agreement. I really didn't want to try explaining this to a mortal watch. I hadn't broken any laws, Awareness-based or otherwise, but I had a feeling they wouldn't be thrilled with my inability to explain how I'd become covered in blood.

"In that case, can I give you a ride somewhere? Angelus Quietum, maybe?"

In one way or another, I'd been wishing myself back to my father's house all day. Feeling as if I was holding myself together with gum and twine, I decided not to fight it.

At my nod, Amourie put her hand on my shoulder again.

She wasn't as rough a ride as Liam, but she wasn't an elder child. The transition made my already swimming head begin to ache.

The safety of Angelus Quietum's living room was so beloved and familiar I nearly broke down the instant we arrived. I managed to hang on to a sliver of that buzzing numbness while Amourie glanced around at the flickering shadows cast by the fireplace.

"Grandfather?" Amourie called, peering around the tall back of my father's armchair. It was currently facing the fire, its shadowy bulk blocking any view of its occupant.

"Hmmm?" Gabriel must have fallen asleep in the chair, because he rubbed an eye as he leaned over its arm to frown at my niece. "Amourie? What are you doing here in the middle of the night?"

"I think your daughter needs someone to watch her for a bit. Are you sober enough to deal with it?"

"Gracie?" My father's expression sharpened, and I was a bit surprised that he wasn't too drunk to glide gracefully to his feet. It was the only piece of good luck I'd had all day. I bit down on a sob and both of them glanced at me with concern. "Yes, yes, of course. I have her. Thank you for bringing her home."

"Any time," Amourie replied before stepping away from my side and melting into golden sparks.

"Gracie?" Dad ducked his head to peer into my face, one hand coming up to touch the shoulder Amourie had just abandoned. "Are you hurt, sweetheart? What happened?"

"I... don't know," I whimpered, tears rolling down my cheeks. Looking up into the sharp, Usuriel features of his face, lit so gently by the flickering light of the fireplace, the weight of this dreadful day came slamming down on my head. I hugged myself tightly, knowing that if I let him comfort me I'd never hold it together. Even so, a little sob escaped my throat before I could help it.

"Oh, sweetie." He pulled me against his chest and wrapped his strong, safe, familiar arms around my shoulders. "It's okay. I'm right here."

That was all it took.

The floodgates opened and that was the absolute end of my control. I sobbed and shook as if I'd been dunked in ice water, my hands clinging to the back of his shirt like a drowning child. All the pent-up fear, anger, heartbreak, and guilt came rushing out, and suddenly I found it choking me. My chest was tight and I couldn't breathe, my face hot and sticky as I fought with my overtaxed body to suck air into my lungs.

"Easy does it," Dad said calmly. "In through your nose, out through your mouth. Think about your breathing and nothing else. In and out."

I tried to do as he said. I'd done it a thousand times if I'd done it once. Tonight I was just too far past any kind of rational thought. My brain kept spinning and my chest kept tightening, and even though I knew I'd pass out if I didn't calm down, no shred of my usual control answered my call.

"Okay," Gabriel sighed. With as little effort as I might a small child, he swung me up into his arms. The sudden movement startled me enough to suck in a deeper, gasping breath. "Come on, let's sit down."

As easily as if I weighed nothing at all, my father carried me over to the couch. He sat down and set me gently into the seat beside him, shifting his own weight so that we were facing each other. I clung to his arms, fighting to breathe. Every muscle I had was so tense my joints were actually starting to ache from the strain, but for the life of me I just couldn't relax.

"How many pictures are in this room?" Dad asked.

A little confused by the question, I glanced at him. With a gesture of his head, he indicated the painting above the mantle.

"Tell me how many pictures there are in the living room," he repeated.

"Ummm..." My voice shook, but I looked at the oil painting of the *Inspiration* that hung over the fireplace. "Well... there's that one... it's been there forever."

"What is it of?"

I sucked in a deeper breath and realized he was trying to distract me from my panic. Oddly enough, it seemed to be working. I tried not to fight it.

"It's the *Inspiration* and its shuttle fleet orbiting Cybele," I said, my voice the slightest bit steadier, though still embarrassingly out of breath.

"Good," Dad nodded. "Are there any others?"

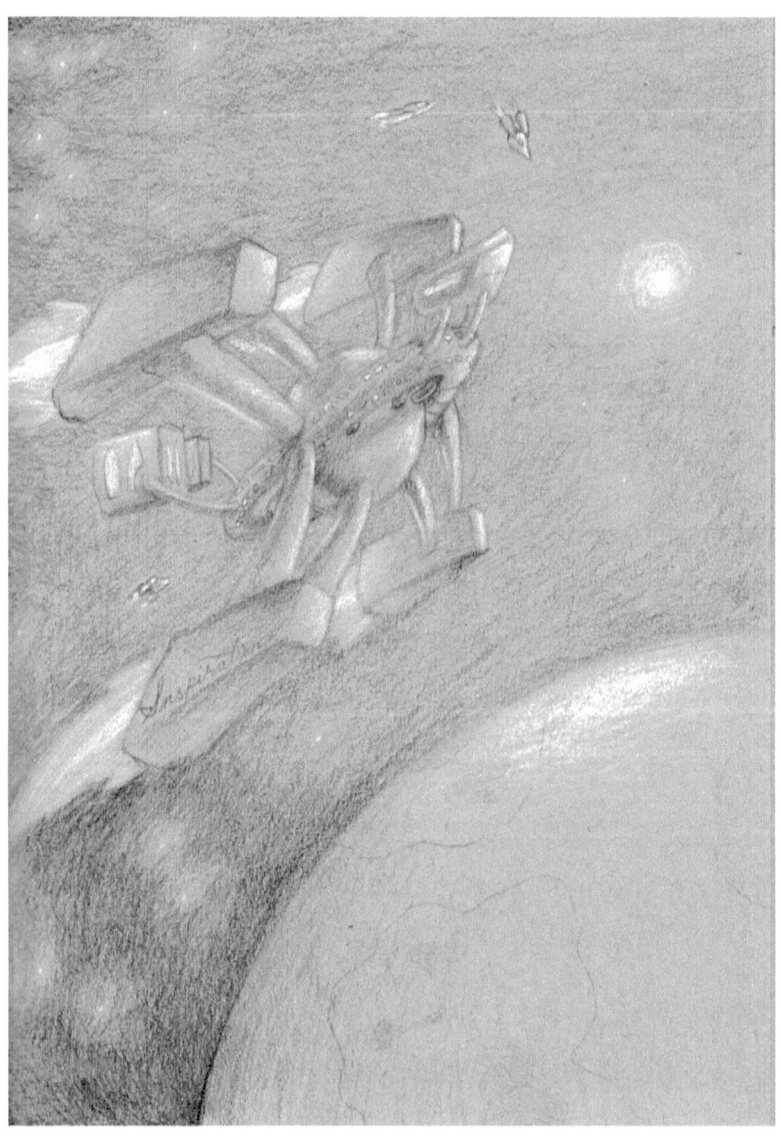

I scanned the room, trying to remember what he'd had displayed before I left for school. "There's the still of you, me, Grandma, and Grandpa on our vacation to Hal," I said, seeing the dark outline of its frame by the front door. I couldn't see our smiling faces from here, but it was a pleasant enough memory. Even so, thinking about Grandma Gloria made the muscles in my back give another terrified spasm. This time, though, I was able to breathe through it and force my shoulders to relax just a touch.

"That is one of my favorites," Dad said with a smile. Then his eyes flicked over by the hall. "Keep going."

"Oh right, the still life," I said, turning in that direction. To my surprise, however, there was no longer a little painted arrangement of fruit and wine by the hall door. Instead, a nicely framed still of me in my Overwatch uniform hung in its place. "Is that my OW portrait?" I asked. "I thought you still didn't approve of me joining."

He shrugged, leaning back from me with an indulgent smile. His hands slid from my shoulders to my hands and gave them a quick squeeze before he folded them in his own lap. "It's a good picture of you," he said. "And besides, as you pointed out to me quite forcefully, you're grown now. If this is the career you want and you're doing well in it, then I'm proud of you."

I sighed and realized that he'd successfully calmed me enough to stop shaking. In fact, looking at the genuinely proud expression on his face, I had a moment where I thought that perhaps my life wasn't completely falling down around my ears. Then I remembered the conversation I'd had with Vanessa that morning and suddenly I couldn't meet my father's eyes.

"Do you feel a little calmer?" Dad asked.

I nodded, still deliberately looking at my hands which had ended up spread on my own thighs.

"Good. Now, do you want to tell me what has you so upset?"

A thousand things, I wanted to scream, every dreadful part of the day rushing up and over me again. Vanessa wants me to kill you and the Terrans might go to war with Riland, I thought. James and Liam and Grayson and... fucking Fate, Grayson. My head spun.

"I..." the tears rushed up again, pushing against my throat until I had to gasp the last of the sentence out in a sob. "I think I'm losing my mind, Daddy. Not like the usual Family crazy. More like..." I stopped myself before I said her name, but I think we both knew who I was thinking of.

"Oh, sweetheart, no. No, take it from someone who has seen a lot of crazy over the years. You are absolutely one of the sanest members the Usuriel Family has managed to produce. That I can honestly swear to," he said quickly, putting his hand on my knee.

I shook my head, sniffling.

"Well, what makes you think you're going mad?" Dad asked. "I've never heard this concern from you before. What happened tonight to make you suddenly doubt your sanity?"

"I... I'm not sure," I whimpered, panic turning the inside of my mouth sour. "I don't know what happened and... fucking Fate, Dad, I don't even know if I can explain it."

"Start at the beginning," he said sensibly. "How did you end up at Amourie's?"

"James and I had a fight," I admitted, the embarrassment of discussing my love life with my father momentarily helping me rein in my anxiety.

"Do I need to knock those two boys' heads together for you?" Dad asked, narrowing his eyes. "Say the word and I'll have both their hides on my wall by tomorrow night."

"No," I sniffed, shaking my head quickly. The sudden movement didn't help my developing headache. "I was upset, but it's not really his fault. He can't help who and what he is any more than I can."

My father's eyes were extremely sad. "I'm sorry, sweetheart."

"It's okay," I said, even though it wasn't. Not even close to okay. Not really.

"So you broke up with James and decided to go have a drink?" Dad asked gently.

I shook my head again, a little more gently this time. "No. After our fight I just sort of started wandering. I ended up at Amourie's by mistake more than anything. But I was hungry, so I went in."

"Makes sense," Gabriel said, putting an arm on the back

of the couch and settling back to listen to my story.

With my father's gentle, accepting audience, the whole evening flooded out. Meeting Grayson, a rather edited version of our flirtatious conversation, the bite and its aftermath. I told him about Amourie's reaction, Grandmother's attempt to override my blood with her own, and then the strange flash of light that seemed to erase any sign of the entire encounter.

"Wait a minute," Dad said, leaning forward with a sharp look on his face. "If you weren't bitten by Grayson, whose blood is all over your arms?"

I rubbed at a larger smudge of dried blood on my wrist. "No idea. Same goes for the bite mark."

"Let me see." My father tilted my neck to the firelight and examined the fang marks with a frown. "That's a vamp bite and no mistake," he muttered, "but there isn't a vampire on Cybele old enough to roll an Usuriel—let alone hard enough to produce hallucinations. Except maybe Dad, of course, but," he waved a hand to dismiss such a ridiculous notion. "And that's assuming anyone can breach those iron shields of yours."

"So it wasn't a mind trick?" I asked, sick dread beginning to replace the panic in my guts. I wasn't sure it was any better—just calmer.

"No, I don't think it was a mind trick." Dad frowned at me thoughtfully. I was a little surprised—if grateful—at how calmly he was taking the whole thing. Of course, he'd lived through some pretty insane situations over the years. I supposed four hundred years would give anything some perspective. "You said Amourie didn't remember who Grayson was?"

"No, she'd never even heard of him," I said, "and you should have seen the way she was crying over him just minutes earlier. I mean, all-out heartbreak. They might not have been exclusive at the moment, but some part of her was really in love with him."

"Not just the event, then," Dad murmured, "but everything about him..." His scowl deepened and he tilted his head at me. "I've heard of this before. Where, though? I know I have." With one finger he tapped his chin as if he were chasing down an elusive memory. "Wait! I know it! Stella!"

"Yes, Gabriel?" Stella's form bled from the darkness like a silver ghost.

"Access my mother's personal database," Dad said quickly. His eyes were bright but serious. "Mortis... or... Temp something... Come on, Stella, hurry up!"

The AI frowned at him, her silver eyes shifting to where I sat on the couch. I'd never seen her so much as pause for my father before. But clearly, she was hesitant to access the database in front of me. Finally, she seemed to decide that my father wasn't going to just forget or change his mind because she lifted her hands and the large book I'd seen in Ariel's lab appeared in her palms.

"Oh for the love of... you look through the damn thing.

I'm not sober enough to squint at all that fine print," Dad complained.

Stella gave him a look that said she was about as thrilled with his drinking as I was. Even so, she flipped the book open and said, "Do you have a particular search in mind?"

"Time poison. It's temper-something," he pressed the heels of his palms into his eyes as if willing his brain to clear. Since I'd never seen Gabriel so much as stumble over even the most inane of details, it probably was the bottle of whatever liquor he'd emptied before I arrived that was preventing him from instantaneous recall. Even so, if that was the worst effect of his drinking tonight, I wasn't going to fight about it. We had more pressing issues.

"Temporal Mortis," Stella said, clearly reading from the book in her hands. "Also called Fate's Stillbirth, this poison is one of the three Immortal Deaths. Derived from the blood of a fate, it causes death to occur at every point in an individual's timeline. This results in an effective erasure of the individual; a complete unmaking from corporal and temporal existence."

I stared at Stella, feeling a bit like she'd just hit me in the head. "Complete erasure?" I echoed dumbly.

"I knew I'd heard of something like this," Dad said, nodding slowly. "Temporal Mortis. It was what started the first Great Immortal Conflict... I think anyway. It's been a really long time since I read the Anori histories."

"You are correct," Stella said, flipping to a new page of the gigantic tome. "The unmaking of Arch-Admiral Darthan

Elisriel started a chain of events that prompted the Anori to invade the Avalon Mortal Realm. Since that conflict, the use of Temporal Mortis has been banned on both sides of the Immortal Spectrum."

"That's how you know something's dangerous," Dad sighed. "If the demons won't even touch it. Thank you, Stella. That's what I needed to know. Good night."

"Demons?" My eyes were wide and I glanced between Dad and Stella like they'd both grown new heads. The AI gave a helpless shrug before she faded away into the dimness of the room. I turned to Dad, feeling as if there was a whole subject that had been missing from my education. I'd known there was a lot about my immortal ancestors that I didn't know, but this was a little more than I'd expected. For once my curiosity wasn't my primary concern, however. "No, wait, put this in reverse a second. You think somehow Grayson was poisoned by this Temporal Mortis? How is that possible? I mean, if it's an Anori poison, how could it be here on Cybele? We've come a very long way to avoid all of the dangerous immortal stuff."

Dad's expression was grim as he met my gaze. His eyes looked far, far older than twenty-five. "Yes, we've come a long way to avoid the darkest parts of our ancestors," he agreed, "but there are a few things that we brought with us."

I frowned at him. "Like what?" As far as I knew, the database itself was the only Anori artifact we had.

"Our DNA," he said gently, taking my hand. My stomach

clenched as I realized what he was implying. My fear must
have shown on my face because he gave me an extremely
sad smile. I think he meant it to be encouraging, but it just
tore at my chest even more. "The primary ingredient for
Temporal Mortis is the blood of a fate. Not uppercase Fate,
goddess of predestination, but lowercase fate. That is, a
mixed-breed immortal who has an affinity for time."

I felt as if he'd just knocked the wind out of me. "Sweet
Fate," I gasped, the room lurching into motion again. "I... I
just killed... no... unmade... fucking Fate, Dad..."

"Easy, sweetheart," Dad said, squeezing my hand and
putting his other hand on my arm to steady me. "You had no
warning that your blood might be poisonous. I mean, you
have an affinity for fire, not time. Not to mention this is
some pretty esoteric knowledge."

I gazed at him helplessly, knowing I didn't have the
emotional control to hide the guilt in my expression. His
steady response had calmed me enough to take a few even
breaths and allow Cybele to solidify around me again. Even
so, I could feel tears threatening in the back of my throat.
"Just because you have one gift," I whispered, "doesn't mean
you can't have another."

Dad's expression wasn't quite one of surprise. He stared
at me a moment, eyes a little too wide. Then his face went
grim and his eyes closed. "You've had other dreams, haven't
you," he said slowly, "besides the one with your mother."

"Yes." My voice was so soft, even I could hardly hear it.
The room no longer spun, but I felt empty and hollow. I'd

lost hope that what I'd done to Grayson was some kind of mistake or illusion. One way or another, I killed him. In fact, it seemed very possible I'd completely erased him from existence altogether. Did that count as killing him? I wasn't sure, but I had a feeling that if they weren't equivalent, then what I'd done was worse.

"The night before the flood." Gabriel's voice sounded painful. When he opened his eyes, I knew what was behind that tortured gaze. It had haunted me for three years. "James said you had a nightmare, but it wasn't just a dream, was it?"

I swallowed hard and shook my head. "No. I'm pretty sure it wasn't just a dream."

"Sweet Fate, Gracie," he murmured. "What did you see?"

What had I seen? Death and pain and despair. The reek of decay and filth clung to the memory like a slimy miasma. Before tonight, I'd held a certain amount of anger in my heart for my father's cruel actions in that dream. Now, however, on the other side of involuntary manslaughter, I had a little more compassion. What would my doomed tryst with Grayson look like to a disembodied spectator, chopped up and out of context?

"Adora," I whispered her name. "The night she died."

Gabriel looked like he'd just swallowed shards of glass. "Did you..." he almost brought the words out, then seemed to choke and had to start again. "Did you... see everything?"

I nodded and wondered if my face reflected back the pain

and horror of what he'd done. I suspect it did, because suddenly a liquor bottle was in his hand. It appeared as if he'd hardly even thought about it—like it had become second nature to drown out these memories before they overwhelmed him.

"No, Dad, don't." The words came out before I could stop them. All of the usual checks on my honesty were completely gone by that point. It was just me and Gabriel, more raw and unfiltered than we'd ever been with each other. I hoped to everything holy that we managed to both come out on the other side of this conversation mostly whole. "Please. We have to talk about this, and I know it's painful. Believe me, I haven't known how to do it any more than you have. But before we can, you have to put the alcohol down. Please. I'm begging you."

The look he gave me was extremely conflicted, as if some part of his brain knew he had a problem and should do what I'd said, but the emotional side of his nature just couldn't handle facing what he'd done to his sister all those years ago.

"Gracie..."

I put my hand over his on the neck of the bottle. "I'm not kidding, Dad," I said, trying to sound both firm and gentle at the same time. After the conversation I'd had with Vanessa that morning, his problems inspired more fear than fury. I'd already been responsible for one death tonight. If I had any chance of saving my father, I had to at least try. "I'm not just asking as the daughter who loves you. I'm telling you, as a member of the Overwatch, this is going to be the death of you. One way or another. Are you understanding me? Please, just give me the bottle."

"It should have been the death of me a long time ago." The pain in his voice was old and worn, but no less real. Even so, his fingers released their grip on the neck of the bottle and let me slide it out of his hand.

"Thank you," I breathed, setting the offending container on the floor slightly behind me where it would be out of his sight.

"Sweet Fate, Gracie," he whispered. "No wonder you ran off to University. How could you even look at me after that?"

I frowned at him and realized he was waiting for the rejection. He hated himself for this. I could see it in the way his body almost cringed away from me. I wondered just how much self-control it was taking for him to hold himself in that seat across from me; knowing that I knew his darkest secret and was about to pass judgment.

"I was a little shocked at the time," I admitted. "But I've read a lot about the Riland Massacre since then. The psi-fire was unpredictable and burning for almost a week. The response crews were having casualties daily. She was killing people, Dad. You didn't have a choice."

He sighed and ran a hand through his hair in that little stressed gesture we shared. "So Mom and Vanessa have always maintained," he said. "But they weren't there. They didn't see it." He shook his head as if the deed were so monstrous that anyone who witnessed it would never forgive him. Clearly, he hadn't forgiven himself.

"I did," I said softly. His blue eyes flashed up at me, catching and reflecting back the firelight. I had to prove it, I realized, and cringed inwardly at the horror I was about to bring out into the open. Maybe our relationship would be a little healthier for it, I hoped. "It was smart of you to drug the wine. Adora always enjoyed seeing you let down your inhibitions around her. She never could resist a drink with her brother."

"No, she never could." A small reminiscent smile played at the corners of his lips. Then he frowned. "But you never met Adora. How would you—" He wasn't that drunk, and I'd never heard anyone complain about his intellect. I watched him put it together as he scanned my face. "You've seen more than just that incident."

"A little," I admitted. "And James, Liam, and I dug through a lot of Stella's old holos from the *Inspiration*. Between my dreams and our research, I've gotten a chance to see Adora in action a handful of times. From what I could tell, she was unstable from the beginning, but she'd really lost it by the end."

"I always loved her, but yes. She was a little wild, even from the beginning. And at the end..." He faded off before turning those tortured eyes on me again. "You don't hate me? Even after..."

Instead of answering him verbally, I did what he'd done for me when I arrived that night and wrapped my arms around his shoulders. I hugged him tightly, feeling the comforting strength of him, and fleetingly wondered what it was about me that he found safe and familiar.

My embrace startled him, because he went rigid under my hands. Then, with a small sound, his hands came up to my back and he held me close. When I slid back from him, there were tears in his eyes. Mine felt cried out for the most part, but I still swallowed hard before I could speak.

"You're my dad," I said simply. "Whatever else you are, you're also the man who checked my closet for monsters when I was little. You're the one who accepted my gifts and taught me to control them. The part of that dream that always terrified me the most was the thought that I might lose you."

Gabriel reached out and touched my cheek gently. For the first time in what seemed like a very long time, his eyes didn't look quite as haunted to me. Then he let his hand fall back into his lap and he shook his head, a self-deprecating little smile on his face. "You come running home in search of a safe haven and end up staunching my emotional wounds. I'm not quite sure how that happened. But I am sure you are the best thing that's happened to me in several centuries."

"I love you, too, Dad. And honestly, our conversation was what I needed right now, too, I think," I sighed. "At least I'm pretty sure I'm not completely losing my mind anymore. Even if I did just…" I think I lost some color at that last sentence because Dad put a hand on mine.

"It was a mistake, sweetie. An accident. It could have happened to any Usuriel who has ever taken a vamp to bed," he said in that same firm but gentle tone I'd used with him earlier. "Learn from your old man's mistakes and don't torture yourself over it. Learn something, forgive yourself, and move on. Don't run from it, and don't try to punish yourself. Believe me, it just makes things worse in the end."

"That's what Grandma Gloria said," I muttered, demonstrating my own version of his hair smoothing gesture. We were a lot alike, my father and I. More so than I think I'd realized up until that point. I looked at him then, handsome and damaged, yet still here and sober enough to take care of his distraught daughter when she showed up unannounced. If he'd survived all the trauma and despair of the last four hundred years, I thought, perhaps I'd survive the fallout of this dreadful day as well. Maybe not unscathed, but not broken beyond repair either.

"I just wish there was some way to make things right," I said slowly. Then, I frowned. "Maybe... maybe there is..."

Gabriel raised an eyebrow at me. "Gracie?"

"You said I'm a fate, right?" My words were faster now, my voice more excited as I began to reason things out more clearly. "My time travel isn't a one or two time fluke or some kind of hallucination. This is real. This is a recognized psi ability and I'm not making it up. Grayson's reaction confirms it."

"Wait, this has gone beyond dreams?" My father's voice sounded cautious. "You've actually traveled in time before?

Physically?"

I nodded, my mind spinning with the possibilities. Before now, I'd never really thought about pushing the limits of what my time powers could do. Ariel had always been the catalyst—the one with the vision and the motivation—to my time exploration. But what if I was the one to initiate a shift? Why should it work any differently just because I wasn't traveling with a ghost? I pushed myself to my feet and started pacing, trying to think things through.

"If I go back a few hours and keep myself from going to Amourie's in the first place," I reasoned aloud as I strode back and forth in the empty space between the couch and the fireplace, "then Grayson would never have met me. It shouldn't be hard to talk myself out of going in a random direction. Just point myself back to the dining hall and maybe I'd end up taking my frustration out on Liam instead of..."

"No, Gracie, that's a seriously bad idea." Gabriel didn't rise from the couch but his posture was suddenly much more tense. "The database is full of parables warning about the danger of crossing a fate. Even full Anori knew better than to anger one. But, in almost every story, the fates who acted without guidance and attempted to use their powers to alter history for their own benefit all ended very badly. I can think of a whole handful that end with the fate unmaking themselves or a loved one."

I shook my head, waving off his objections. "It's not like

I'm trying to re-write things for myself. It would be for Grayson and Amourie. Besides, I'm only going back a few hours. What possible unintended consequence could come from preventing this tragic accident?"

Dad opened his mouth to continue arguing, but I'd already made up my mind. Holding the image of the hallway outside James' room in my mind, I pulled on the flames.

Nothing happened.

"Seriously, let's think this through," Gabriel said, completely unaware that I'd made the attempt. "If you go back in time and warn yourself about this, you'll have no reason to go back in the first place. I know that fates are a little more immune to paradox than the rest of us, but that just seems..."

I listened to him ramble while I scowled at my unexpected failure to shift in both time and space. Deciding to try again, I closed my eyes and concentrated all of my will on the jump. Just as before, it was about as effective as every attempt I'd ever made at telepathy.

"Ariel!" I shouted, cutting my father off mid-sentence. "Get your ghostly behind down here! I need to time jump and it's not working!"

Now Gabriel did gawk at me like I'd lost my mind. However, if it saved Grayson's life, I wasn't sure I cared what this timeline's Gabriel thought of me. Hopefully, I'd be erasing this conversation from history entirely by the end of the night. Even so, no characteristic glow made its appearance.

"Are you... talking to *my* Ariel?"

"What other Ariel would be hanging around here? She's the one who has always initiated the time jump before," I said with an impatient gesture. "Didn't you know you live in a haunted house?"

Dad stared at me for a moment, then his eyes darted around the room as if looking for some kind of specter. If he'd never seen them up until this point, however, I somehow doubted he'd ever be able to perceive the ghosts.

"Ariel never even lived here," he said slowly, "so why would she haunt Angelus Quietum?"

I'd been avoiding his gaze since I'd called for Ariel, but now I met his concerned eyes. "Why do you think?" I asked, putting my hands on my hips. "She's worried about you."

His eyebrows went up on that one. "Worried about me?"

I nodded, eyes darting around the room for her again. "Who do you think warned me when you had that heart attack when I was twelve? I should have been off doing chores for the next two hours. I would never have known anything was wrong. Stella probably would have called for help once your vitals dropped to critical, but I've always said you set her thresholds too low. Grandma Gloria could have easily arrived too late. Ariel saved your life that time."

It was Dad's turn to stare at me like I'd grown a new head. "It's been going on that long," he breathed. "Right under my nose. Why didn't you ever say anything?"

"I tried once," I felt the need to explain. "After Ariel's first attempt to send me back in time nearly landed me in shock at Grandma Gloria's house. But you didn't listen to me. After that, I guess I just figured you'd either dismiss me or think I was crazy if I tried to talk about it."

"Sweet Fate, that's what happened." Gabriel looked like I'd delivered a ringing blow to his head. "That makes so much sense. How didn't I see it? For Fate's sake, I'm such an old fool."

"You're not a fool, old or otherwise," I said, trying for gentle but a decent amount of my irritation with a particular specter coloring my tone. "You just conditioned me to keep secrets far too well."

"Ah, well," he sighed. "In that case, I suppose I am reaping what I sowed."

"Indeed," I agreed, still scowling at the empty shadows. "Where is she? Maybe I need her journal." Suiting action to word, I charged off in the direction of my old room.

When I got there, everything was just as I'd left it from my last visit. Even in the near-perfect dark I had no problem finding the small bookshelf under the window. Running my finger along the spines of my old sketchbooks, I quickly discovered the gap where Ariel's journal should be. I'd taken it to school, I remembered with a jolt of irritation. How could I have forgotten? I always packed it when I left for a visit, but this time I hadn't been expecting to spend the night anywhere else. I suddenly felt naked without it.

"Find what you're looking for?" Dad asked. "Stella, lights

at fifty percent."

I glared at the overhead light as it flared to life. "No, it's not here. I forgot I took it to school." With a groan, I sank dejectedly onto the bed.

"Is this some kind of artifact you've used to communicate?" Dad asked. Like I said, lack of intelligence has never been Dad's problem. He stood leaning in the doorway as if he wasn't quite sure what to do with himself.

"Yeah. Maybe that's why she's not showing up. I don't remember the last time I didn't have the journal in easy reach." I put my face in my hands. "Maybe I'll just wait and try tomorrow. I'm so tired I can barely see straight."

"Things will seem clearer from the other side of a good night's rest," Dad agreed. "Do you want me to take you back to your room at University or would you like to spend the night here?"

I glanced down at the familiar pile of pillows stacked at the top of the bed. "I'm already on the bed," I muttered, feeling as if my eyelids weighed metric tons. My head had passed from dull twinges to a steady ache and, even as smooth as my father made it, I didn't really want to teleport anywhere right now. "I think I'll just sleep here if you don't mind."

"This is still your home, Gracie. You're always welcome here." Gabriel's voice was gentle. For a moment, I thought he was going to leave. But rather than turn to go, he lingered looking almost shy in the doorway.

"What is it, Dad?" I asked when it became clear that he was just going to stand there like a nervous suitor.

"There aren't any... others... are there? Ghosts, I mean." Dad sounded almost hesitant about asking, but there was raw need in his face when he glanced back up at me.

I considered lying to him. What good would it do for him to know *she* was still around? In fact, since he couldn't touch or hold her, knowing she still hung about longing after him might just be a new level of mental torture. But the look in my father's eyes was so desperately hopeful that I knew I couldn't keep it from him.

"Just one," I said slowly.

I'd thought I'd seen pain in my father's eyes before. I'd been wrong. The look in them at my words proved Ariel's hypothesis about what had truly broken him. I hadn't even said her name, but he and I both knew who else was haunting Angel's Rest.

"She likes to travel with her daughter," I murmured. "Though, when you have a really bad day, she'll show up alone. I've never spoken with her though. I'm not even sure she knows I exist. She's only ever had eyes for you."

For the first time tonight, he completely shied away from me. Some grief is just too personal to share, I guess, even with the people who know and love us best. He took several, shaking breaths while he hid his face behind one hand. I wondered if I had made the right choice by telling him.

"Thank you," he said quietly after a long silence. His voice was low and I could tell he was having a hard time keeping it steady. "You honestly don't know what a gift you've just given me. But I thank you for it, just the same."

"Dad..."

"Good night, sweetheart," he said abruptly, cutting me off though his tone was still gentle. "Get some rest. You look exhausted. I'll be in my room if you need me."

I met his eyes and for the first time in almost three years, he looked a lot more like the man who raised me. Sad, yes, always; but also steady and strong. Despite the anguish of the evening, I found myself smiling up at him.

"Good night, Dad. Sleep well."

Epilogue

Gabriel's Gift

I woke up the next morning with Ariel's name on my lips. I lay in bed, staring at the safe, familiar ceiling of my childhood bedroom as the fog of sleep cleared. I felt as if there was an important idea simmering in the back of my mind, but I couldn't quite reach it.

"The elixir!" I sat straight up in bed, eyes wide as my brain finally put together the pieces it hadn't been able to in its exhausted stupor last night. With less than a thought, I tossed the covers off and ran completely naked to the back of my closet. I'd shed my bloody clothes last night but hadn't had the energy to bathe. Thus my arms were still splattered with the dried echoes of Grayson's bloody death as I pushed my clothes out of the way and began scanning the little shelves at the back of the closet. How hadn't I made this connection earlier? I pulled down the little vial. It was right where I'd left it—a little dusty, but no worse for sitting on a back shelf for a few years.

"Ariel?" I called, looking around the storage area and out the door into my room. The ghost still didn't appear at my request, but I somehow felt safer with the vial in my hand. It had to be the antidote, I thought. If it was made from my blood, could heal serious wounds, and keep a mortal from aging, this stuff had to be the opposite of whatever poison I'd unintentionally created by mixing my essence with Grayson's curse. Even if I heeded my father's warning and tried to minimize paradox by delivering the antidote to Gloria rather than warning myself last night, perhaps I could still save Grayson's life.

Well, no matter what course of action I decided to try, I needed a shower first. I looked down at my blood splattered skin and felt an unexpected pang of sorrow at the thought of washing it off. If I couldn't save him, I was erasing the last evidence that Grayson had ever existed. I pushed the thought away with a firm act of will, then forced myself to grab my robe and head towards the shower. I kept the little vial of elixir on the bathroom counter where I could easily see its green shape even from behind the semi-opaque shower wall.

As I soaped and shampooed, my fingers set off the dull ache that was his bite on my neck several times. I found it strangely reassuring that even after the shower water had stopped running pink, there was some kind of proof that last night had really happened.

I tapped for the time as I tossed on a comfortable old pair of work pants and a collared tunic very much like the ones my boys liked to wear when we went someplace a little fancier. It was cut shorter than theirs and sewn to accommodate a female bust line, but even so, it reminded me of good times with James and Liam. It made my chest tighten to think of how young and carefree we'd all been last year. All my other clothes were at school, however, so I gritted my teeth at the painful nostalgia and buttoned it up until it covered my chest with a reasonable amount of modesty. Then, clutching the little green vial of Ariel's elixir, I went out to the kitchen.

Unsurprisingly, my father was already making breakfast when I arrived. His hair was pulled back neatly and his work-a-day farm clothes looked clean and crisp. I sat in my usual seat at the kitchen table and watched him bustle about, getting rice and eggs cooked and ready. He moved with such a flowing efficiency of motion. It seemed to me that it had been a long time since Gabriel looked quite so put together, especially first thing in the morning with nothing to do that day but feed chickens.

He turned to get the juice out of the cooling unit and must have caught sight of me out of the corner of his eye because he jumped back a good meter. His face lost all its color and a hand went to his chest in surprise. Then he got a better look at me and took a deeper breath.

"Sweet Fate, Gracie, you nearly scared the life out of me," he said, leaning against the counter. "How did you come in here so quietly?"

I shrugged and tried to give him a smile. The trauma of yesterday still sat too heavily for it to be wholehearted, but I attempted it anyway. "Sorry, I didn't mean to scare you," I said honestly.

He waved away my apology with one graceful hand and went back to getting the juice. "You're on break today, aren't you?"

"Huh? Oh, yes. There's no school," I agreed.

"Good," he said with a nod. "Perhaps you'd like to help me around the farm a bit? Take your mind off of... unpleasant things?"

I fiddled with the vial in my hands. I'd meant to talk to him about the antidote, but I wasn't quite sure how to explain it. "I don't know, Dad. I'll stay for breakfast, but I'm pretty sure I need to go back to school after that."

Gabriel shook his head. "You're not still on about that whole 'fixing it' thing are you?"

"It was my fault." My voice sounded closer to tears than I'd expected. "I have to at least try to put things right. I owe it to Grayson and Amourie."

Dad walked over to the table with a large plate of eggs, rice, and toast. He set it in front of me.

"I've been thinking about that," he said, his voice sounding gentle yet resigned in a way that told me he had bad news to share. My stomach tightened as I watched him make his own plate and sit down. "I hate to point this out," he said slowly, glancing at my hands still clutching the vial in my lap, "but even if you go back in time, I'm not sure there is a way to fix this. If your blood worked the way the database says Temporal Mortis is supposed to work, then going back to yesterday won't save Grayson. He isn't there to save anymore. You erased everything about him, including your initial encounter. You can't stop something from happening if it was never going to happen in the first place."

I frowned, my brain trying to keep up with what he was saying. "So... what? My memories of him aren't real anymore? I can't get back to the time I remember because it doesn't exist anymore?"

"Or isn't in our reality." Dad took a bite of toast. "You've changed the timeline, sweetheart. Some things just can't be undone. Like scrambling an egg." He lifted his fork to demonstrate. "I have all the pieces, but no matter what I do with them, I can't make this egg back into what it was before I cracked and cooked it. I'm pretty sure that's what makes Temporal Mortis so fearsome, even to the most powerful immortals. Once it's done, even a fate can't undo it. There's nothing left to save."

I sat there and felt the reality of what he'd said settle into my chest. He was right. If I'd truly erased Grayson's entire timeline, then he wouldn't be at the club yesterday any more than he would be tonight. Unlike last night, the knowledge of the finality of my fatal mistake didn't inspire panic. Instead, sick dread and an overwhelming sense of loss came over me like a crushing weight. I took a deep breath and was a little surprised when my chest rose and fell. Was I still alive? It didn't feel like it.

"I'm sorry, Gracie," Dad said, putting a hand on mine. We sat in silence like that for a long moment. "You don't have to go straight back to school, you know. You can stay here for the whole two-day break if you want to. Or even longer if you like. Take the time you need to get your head right about this."

I swallowed hard and shut my eyes. "Thanks," I whispered.

There was another long pause and I considered trying to force myself to eat some of the breakfast my father had prepared. I'd been hungry moments ago. The very idea of food made my stomach turn, however, and I found myself simply sitting and staring into nothing.

"What's in your hand?" Dad asked, turning back to his meal and spreading butter on his toast.

I glanced down at the vial and wondered how much I should tell him. Well, I'd all but come out and told him about the execution order last night. With Adora, the time travel, ghosts, and dreams now out in the open, why bother keeping this last painful secret? Silently, I set the little green bottle on the table.

"Ariel gave it to me," I said. "She called it Usuriel in a bottle. It's not really mine, anyway, I don't think. She made it for you. You should probably have it."

He frowned at the little vial before picking it up and examining its label. "Usuriel in a bottle?" he asked, an eyebrow lifting in my direction. "I am an Usuriel. What would I do with such a thing?"

I shook my head. "I'm not sure you're understanding," I said slowly. "She didn't make it for you to use on yourself. She made it so you wouldn't have to be alone anymore."

Comprehension dawned on his face and was followed by a look of such utter grief that I couldn't look at him. I let my eyes close and felt the weight of his pain add to the lead in my chest. If this was how I felt at twenty, how much worse would things be when I was four hundred and twenty? It was as close as I'd ever come to understanding my father's desire to medicate the world away.

"Grace," he left the "e" sound off of my name that time, and for some reason it made it sound more sincere. Then he took my hand in his and pressed the little bottle into my palm. Startled, I looked up at him. I don't think I'd ever seen someone look so sad without tears. "I'm not as familiar with the database as my mother is or Ariel was. But I do know that if you're a fate, you're not going to age. You'll be like me, stuck at twenty-five for the rest of eternity."

Slowly, I nodded. "Yes. I already know. Ariel told me."

He gently closed my fingers around the vial. "Then you're going to need this in a few years," he said, giving me a gentle smile that surprisingly reached his midnight-blue eyes.

I looked down at the vial in confusion. "But with this you can find someone to be with again. Someone who won't age and die in your arms. Someone you can be happy with after all these years."

Dad smiled, eyes sliding shut as if he knew he couldn't keep the pain out of his gaze even if he could make his mouth lie. "There won't be another one for me, Gracie," he said and I could hear the honesty in his voice. "I never believed in Fate or Destiny, not really. Not until Liv, anyway." He sighed and there was a small pause before he continued. "But after four hundred years... I think there is a limit to how many times your heart can fall in love. Well, maybe not everyone's. Maybe just mine. I'm not sure. But I did try again after Olivia, and it didn't work. Lauria was everything I could have wanted in a woman and I went through the motions but... no." He shook his head, eyes open again but distant. "I won't be marrying again."

I felt the finality of that statement and had a sick feeling that I knew what he was trying to tell me. "Dad—"

"No." He shook his head again and squeezed my hand around the vial. "You have the chance to have a real happy ending. I can't rob you of that. Not when anything I'd find now would only be a consolation prize."

I put the vial to my breast and felt my throat tighten. "Where does that leave you?" I whispered.

He touched my cheek gently. "Playing with my grandchildren, hopefully," he said. And if the smile didn't quite reach his eyes this time, I decided I could let it be.

***

I did as my father suggested and stayed at Angelus Quietum that break. I needed some time and space to get my head back where it needed to be and the farm was such a safe haven after everything.

My father and I were on the best terms we had been since he picked up a bottle. We did chores and rode the horses together. In the evening, he actually got out his memory pad and read aloud to me like he had when I was a small child. It was a very satisfying replacement to his solitary watch by the fire.

Those were the last happy days I spent with him. Even if I regret the tragedy that landed me there, I am grateful I had that time at Angelus Quietum with Gabriel. Even in the dark hours that came later, I think the memory of those days were part of what kept my heart from completely closing against him.

At the time, I thought that my issues with my father might just be over. He seemed genuinely untempted by his usual vice and, if I had a few difficult moments while my head and heart wrapped themselves around the tragedy I'd caused, they were overshadowed by the sense of relief that Vanessa's dire predictions about my father's instability seemed to be overstated. If someone had asked me then, I would have told them nothing could ever make me doubt my father again.

I would have been wrong.

However, I won't taint the memory of that lovely little vacation from reality with the blood and suffering that came after. No, in my heart that is where I want to remember us— Dad and I—curled up on the couch at Angelus Quietum reading after a long day of riding. If there is an afterlife for people like me, I hope that's what it's like: safe, warm, and content next to someone who knows and loves you for exactly who you are.

Glossary

Angel's Foot - a drug made from the spores of specific mushrooms native to Cybele. Use and exposure can lead to lung rot, a degenerative respiratory disease that is fatal without prompt treatment.

Angelus Quietum - Gabriel's farm on the banks of Lake Angelus, in the foothills of the Galloway Mountains situated halfway between Skykyle and Landing.

Awareness - A slang term for any individual outside of the mortal norm, usually with some kind of psychic powers.

Cambria - a species of giant, house-sized mushrooms that populated Cybele before the terraforming.

Cybele - The colony world settled by the Usuriels and their moral crewmates approximately two hundred and seventy years before Gracie's birth.

Death's Head - a species of fungus that populated Cybele before the terraforming. Their spores can cause a range of respiratory issues, from shortness of breath to asphyxiation and death.

Divinitas - A group of religious extremists who believe the Usuriel Family are actually divine emissaries that have come to lead mankind in the correct direction.

Firebird - a slang term for a pyrokinetic, someone who can conjure or control fire.

Hal - a large, tropical island south of the main continent on Cybele. It was named for Gabriel's son, Harold, who died along with his husband, Sam, in a shuttle accident shortly after landing.

Heart Ship - the original psychic drive of the generation ship, *Inspiration*. The heart ship was designed to allow Gloria to merge with the four main engines and achieve faster-than-light travel. Gabriel's one and only attempt resulted in a near-fatal injury that later required his heart's replacement, while Adora eventually took over the majority of Gloria's shifts in the heart ship.

Holo - a three-dimensional projection of light that can move and be set to synchronized sound.

Inspiration - The generation ship that brought the colonists from Earth to Cybele around the year 100 AT (after takeoff).

Landing - Also known as Inspiration Landing. This is the original settlement where the colonists landed from the *In-*

spiration and began terraforming Cybele. This is also the location of Landing Hospital and University — the most advanced and only major such institutions on Cybele.

New Terra - a mostly-frozen northern continent of Cybele, inhabited by the Terran people.

Overwatch - the psychic police force run by the Family.

'Porter - an individual who can teleport.

Provinces (the) – a group of self-governing territories with a loose central government located on the main continent of Cybele. Skykyle, Landing, and Riland are all Provinces.

Psi - a shortening of 'psychic,' this refers to any power or ability wielded by an individual of awareness. It is often used to describe the energy generated by such powers as well. The amount of psi energy an individual has at their disposal is influenced by the individual's innate strength, their physical health, and their access to resources such as food, water, and sleep.

Psi-pilot - The term for a less-power-intensive psychic interface than the heart ship. The original psi-pilot replaced a damaged organic relay on the *Inspiration*'s main bridge. This allowed two telepathic and telekinetic individuals to merge with the engines at once, creating a solution that was actually better than the original. Later, smaller shuttles and the mining craft were also fitted with psi-piloting interfaces that allowed them to achieve faster-than-light speeds.

Pyrokinesis - the psychic ability to conjure or control fire. Shortenings include "pyro" and "firebird."

Riland - a province and city on the main continent of Cybele. It is home to the largest vampire population and was the location of the White Woman Massacre.

Skykyle - a province and city on the main continent of Cybele. It is the most densely populated city on Cybele and is the location of Gloria and D'nay's Landing Day party.

Spore-bent - slang for "angry" or "upset." Taken from Angel's Foot addicts who are looking for a fix.

Stella - The main AI of the generation ship, *Inspiration*. She was later fully integrated with several libraries and databases on Cybele, including the Landing University library, and Overwatch's mainframe.

Telekinesis - the psychic ability to move objects with one's mind.

Telepathy - the psychic ability to read thoughts. Almost all telepaths are also empathic, which is the ability to read emotions, with the notable exception of Adora Usuriel.

Teleportation - the psychic ability to transport objects and people from one place to another with one's mind. Also known as "'porting."

Terran - the Terrans were another space faring group from Earth. Originally a group of researchers, the radiation created by their vessels' faster-than-light drives proved to be disastrous to their health. This prompted advanced medical research, including the technology to replace organic organs with inorganic parts. Now settled in New Terra, Terrans use robotic "avatars" to interact with the world while keeping their flesh bodies safely cocooned in nutrient tanks. Avatar technology is outlawed in the Provinces on the mainland of Cybele, including Riland, Landing, and Skykyle, which forces Terran diplomats and visitors to abandon their avatars and interact "in the flesh."

Three-T - a psychic individual who has all three of the big "T" abilities - telepathy, telekinesis, and teleportation.

University - the largest institution of higher learning on Cybele. It is located at Inspiration Landing. Also known as Landing University.

Usuriel - the surname of most psychic individuals on Cybele, also known as the Family. The Usuriel Family consists of all individuals who are descended from the bloodline of D'nay and Gloria Usuriel. Once someone marries an Usuriel, they adopt that surname, regardless of gender. All blood descendants of D'nay and Gloria possess some amount of Awareness, though the type and strength of their psychic powers varies widely.

Vampire - an individual infected with a blood-borne curse, usually transmitted by drinking the blood of someone who is also infected. Blood to blood contact can also transmit the curse. Individuals with vampirism enter a dormant state during the day in which they are indistinguishable from a freshly-dead corpse. Exposure to sunlight will cause intense, painful burns and is often fatal if exposure is prolonged. Vampires can only gain nourishment by feeding on the blood of the uninfected. However, many of these traits and attributes are altered when a vampire consumes the blood of an Usuriel.

ABOUT THE AUTHOR

Abigail Silver grew up in Pennsylvania and currently lives near Charlotte, NC with her husband, son, and fur children. When she's not reading, writing, or drawing (which is rare), she enjoys blasting music with the windows down on long road trips.

ACKNOWLEDGMENTS

I can't begin to explain how impossible I once thought this would be. The idea that I would be publishing my own work, let alone two books in two years, was as fantastical as teleporting a spatula from thin air. Yet somehow, here I am, laying out my second book in as many summers. I know I couldn't make this journey alone, so without further ado, let me say some special thank yous.

First and always to my parents and brother, who have been so supportive of my new publishing efforts. I may have gotten misty when I was asked to sign copies of Child of Awareness for my mom and dad. I think that's the way it should be. I can think of no higher honor than having my novel sitting on their shelves. My brother has also done his part by leaving my book out where his friends could find it and become enthusiastic fans (Hi Kevin!)

Next, thank you to my husband and son who give me so much love and inspiration to draw from. Their faith in me never waivers and it's from that solid, loving base that all of my strength and creativity flows. Thank you for your patience and endless support.

After them must come my best friend and partner in fictional crime, Harlow Kelly. Her honest dialogue about all things in life and in our imaginary worlds is truly invaluable. I'm always incredibly grateful to call her a friend.

The other betas and critique partners on this journey are also important. Some of these listed have read only a part of the series, some are long-running critique partners, and still others are new writing friends. They include: J.A. Waters, Jordie Nichols, Jessica Ritchey, Jessica Blasko, Rachel Greene-Phillips, Theresa Gonzalez, Ann Darlington, George Beckman, Marisa S, Paula Braley, Rebecca Amiss, Ernie Fink, CD Storiz, Jesse Hindman, and so many others. For anyone who caught a typo, gave feedback on characters or plot, or simply gushed over Liam, James, and Gracie's love triangle with all points involved, thank you. You're the true reason I feel worthy of putting these books out into the world.

Thank you to the teachers who poured their knowledge, patience, and love into me so that I could pour it into my work. Thanks to you, I know the difference between verbs and nouns and maybe even how to string a few adjectives together.

I would also like to acknowledge the source imagery for some of my illustrations. I started with very specific visions of many of these characters and scenes, but every good artist needs reference material to help that vision stay true to life. So thank you Harlow Kelly for the crate of bottles reference and to the following photographers on UnSplash.com: Gabriel Silverio, Ravi Patel, Christopher Campbell, Steady Hand Co, Ioana Casapu, Evan Wise, Alexis Chloe, Geroge Gavasalia, Emiliano Vittoriosi, Riccardo Vicidomini Varotto, Xiaolong Wong, and Norbert Kundrak. Also a posthumous thank you to Dante Gabriel Rossetti, whose work inspired both the cover art of Book 1 and Book 3, and the title of Book 3 in this trilogy.

And as always, to you, dear reader—thank you for coming along with Gracie on this beautiful ride! I promised my first readers that this would not be a trilogy that took a decade to publish, even if it took that long to write and refine. So far I am living up to that promise. If it were not for you and your support, this story would have sat quietly alone on my hard drive. Thank you for sharing this vision and bringing Gracie to life each time you read a page!

With eternal gratitude,

Abigail Silver

www.ingramcontent.com/pod-product-compliance
Lightning Source LLC
Chambersburg PA
CBHW021834010726
47493CB00005B/1398